# A MOMENT IN TIME... a diary

## By Jan Howard
### Edited by Linda Bruder

### Acknowledgements

A huge thank you to Linda Bruder, my long-time friend and fellow journalist, for her fantastic editing skills and editorial suggestions that greatly enhanced this book.

Thanks also to family members and friends for their encouragement, and particularly my son, Vernon Howard, for his web design and technical skills that helped bring this book to publication.

## Prologue

She was a daughter, a sister, and a teacher in training. Her diary, presented to her by her father, tells the story over a one-year span about her relationships with her family and friends, and her experiences briefly as a teacher in training in Roxbury, Connecticut.

Eunice Nicholson could not tell what her future would be as she began that journal on January 1, 1880.

The diary reflects her love for her family and friends and they for her. It is a bittersweet story. Its beginning months reflect happiness, visits with her sister and friends, outings with her father and mother, and the days spent at school. But her life soon changed.

Her diary has come down to me, saved by her sister, my great-grandmother. Its ink is fading, her words are sometimes unintelligible as they wind around the page, mixing with another day's entry.

Literary license was taken by this writer with Eunice's daily entries in some cases due to illegible words or unclear emotions, where I added feelings and thoughts as to how her life might have been. Knowledge of our family's history also helped in adding more detail to the story of my grandmother's aunt.

The story that follows, based on that diary, hopefully does not deviate too far from what was true of her life in 1880.

## A Present From Father
### Eunice Nicholson
### Roxbury, Conn.

It is only a small diary but, to me, it is special. It was a Christmas gift from my beloved father to his youngest daughter.

Christmas was special this year. It's difficult to believe that it is New Year's Eve, and the year 1879 is almost history. I was 19 in November, no longer a schoolgirl but a teacher of those who are not much younger than I.

I remember sitting on the parlor floor in front of the fire early Christmas morning, admiring the tree and feeling truly blessed. The gifts I had received on Christmas Eve were things I needed. Mother had knitted me gloves, a scarf, and a matching hat to wear when I walk to school every day. She also made me a vest to wear over my blouse for extra warmth in the schoolhouse, which is drafty and never seems to get warm enough to keep out the chill. Sarah and Frank gave me oranges and candy.

I also received a ferule* that Grandfather made for me, with my initials EN engraved on it with some swirls and grooves as decoration. Last spring, Mrs. Baglin, my teacher, asked me to help her with the scholars, and I have been doing so since September. She had left teaching after she was married but returned after her husband died and her children were in school. Now I am again learning from her so I too can become a teacher. She is a wonderful role model, and I have learned so much already.

I doubt very much if I would ever use the ferule to discipline the girls in the school, but it is extra special because Grandfather made it especially for me.

Christmas morning was very busy. After we had investigated what was in our stockings, I had sat daydreaming in front of the tree. Mother was already at work in the kitchen preparing breakfast and some of the dishes that would be served for Christmas dinner. Sarah was busy with Normie, who is almost two years old. He is already a handful. She and Frank have been married for three years, but I still miss her being here every day to share my thoughts and dreams.

*Ferule: a flat stick or wooden ruler-like device, used for reprimanding mischievous young girls.

Christmas was especially wonderful because Sarah, Frank and Normie came to our party on Christmas Eve and stayed overnight. It felt good to have her in the room next door. I also enjoyed playing with Normie and his toy soldiers and trains.

Sarah had set the table for breakfast, and Frank was helping Father in the barn. Sarah came into the parlor to talk about the party. It had been very entertaining and festive, with the tree trimmed with apples, homemade cookies, quilted snowflakes and stars, candles, strands of cranberries and popcorn, and topped with our Christmas angel.

Most of our neighbors stopped in, as well as my friends and Sarah's, and there was food and hot cider, and Mother played the piano for caroling. We played some party games, such as charades. My friend George, who I have known since I was a little girl, is especially good at charades. He and I were partners during most of the games. We even bested Sarah and Frank with one phrase. After everyone had gone home, we exchanged our gifts, though I didn't receive the diary until Christmas Day.

Because we knew our gift giving that night would be too late for him, Sarah helped Normie open his gifts from us after supper on Christmas Eve. We greatly enjoyed watching his joy and listening to his squeals of pleasure over each of his gifts while listening as Sarah read A Christmas Carol. He would open his presents from Santa on Christmas morning. When I was a little girl, Santa was known as Father Christmas, but Santa Claus is a good name, too.

Of course, Normie enjoyed himself so much with his new toys and all the guests paying attention to him that he didn't want to be taken to bed, even though it was two hours after his usual bedtime and he was close to falling asleep on his grandma's lap.

Christmas morning, though we were reluctant to leave the peacefulness of the parlor, there was work needed to be done so Sarah and I helped Mother prepare breakfast and ready the ingredients for pies and bread that would be baked after we returned from services. When Frank and Father came in from the barn, we all gathered about the dining room table, bowing our heads as Father offered our thanks for what God had provided.

Later we all went up to the center of town to church. There were many more people than usual, and it was hard to find a place to tie up the horses. Everyone was smiling and greeting each other as we went into the service. The church was decorated with wreaths and swags of greenery with red bows, and Mr. Coad preached about the birth of Jesus. Then, after the closing hymn, we were in the buggy on the way home again to prepare for dinner.

Christmas dinner was festive. The table looked beautiful. The tablecloth was snowy white, and Sarah had made a centerpiece of greenery and red candles and berries. It was very pretty. We had baked turkey and venison and cooked lots of vegetables. Sarah and I had made apple and pumpkin pies and loaves of bread.

After we were unable to eat one bite more, we cleared the table, leaving the washing up for later. We dressed up warm and took a walk to the river and back. Then, we sat in the parlor and talked until Sarah, Frank and Normie had to leave to get home before dark.

It was when we stood at the door watching their buggy go up the road toward the schoolhouse that Father gave me the diary. It was such a surprise

Now it is December 31. Tomorrow starts a New Year, and I look at the words I have written on the inside cover of the diary and wonder what words I will write to mark the days to come.

Keep a diary, alas what shall I write. Sickness and pain is all that I have and go to bed and get up so the days and nights go on, till time is no more, and if we have not lived rightly here while on this sojourning land, oh sad will be our end when our lives are reckoned. If we have done right here, it will be well for us by and by."

### Thursday, January 1, 1880

There is very little space in the diary to tell about all the things that happen during the day. Because there are three days to a page, I must write small and only the most important things from my days. Any entry here will be only a small moment in time

I arose early today to the scent of bacon frying. Mother had let me sleep because there is no school today. I bathed and dressed, and when I went downstairs, the kitchen was cozy warm from the wood stove. Father had already eaten and gone out to the barn to do chores, and Mother and I enjoyed a quiet breakfast together.

It was a pleasant day. Since there was no school, I stayed home all day and started working on the quilt for my bed. I began making the blocks and will begin piecing them together once I have enough. My quilt will have a simple block pattern in shades of blue to match the curtains Mother made for my room. I found the pattern for it in one of the farm magazines that Mother receives and liked it.

I had purchased some yard goods the last time I was in Danbury to see Sarah, so I have enough material to work on my quilt for a while. I'm also going to include some of the leftover material from the curtains in it.

At night, Mother, Father, and I went up to the Rorrabacks for a get together. Many of our neighbors were there, and some were playing cards, such as whist\*, while others, such as the younger people, sat around and talked. My friend George was there. We had a very good time talking about when we were young and our school days together. I was sorry when we had to leave, but as it was we got home very late.

*\*Whist: a game played with 52 cards by two teams of two players each (origin unknown).*

## Friday, January 2

Today I was up early because it was a school day, and I didn't want to be late. It doesn't look very good if the students arrive before the teacher's helper, especially when she only lives a short way down the road from the schoolhouse. Mrs. Baglin is the teacher at the school, and I am in training so that I can be a teacher someday.

It is my responsibility to start the fire in the wood stove so the building is warm when Mrs. Baglin and the scholars arrive. I also get to ring the bell to begin class.

I washed and got dressed in a chemise, knee length drawers, corset and petticoat, and dark colored stockings over which I wore a black skirt, white shirtwaist, my new vest, and sturdy boots. Despite all these layers of clothing that must weigh about 30 pounds, though it was a clear day, I could already feel the cold. After putting on my wristwatch, I hurried to get to the kitchen where the heat of the wood stove would stave off the chills brought about by my cold bedroom.

Mother was busy making oatmeal at the stove. I kissed her good morning and helped myself to a cup of coffee while she dished me out some cereal. Father had been up for a while and was in the barn taking care of the animals before he would leave for the hat shop. Mother and I had time to talk about the previous night's party and to make plans for the day while she made me a lunch of some chicken and fruit.

School was uneventful today. The children were a little spirited after having a day off, but there was no need for the hickory stick or my new ferule, which Mrs. Baglin admired. We ate lunch grouped around the wood stove, and then spent a half hour outdoors playing hide and seek, tug of war, and leapfrog. Then it was back to lessons until four o'clock when we all went home.

Mother and I took tea with Great-Aunt Emeline after I got home. Mother had the buggy ready when I arrived, and after putting my books in the house, off we went. We were surprised to find that a neighbor, Mrs. Mallory, was also visiting. We had an enjoyable visit and then returned home to prepare the evening meal.

After dinner, I did some piecing on my bed quilt before going to bed.

## Saturday, January 3

It was a beautiful day today, cold, but clear. After breakfast, I was correcting some papers for school when Father came in and asked if I wanted to go up to the Center and to the Hollow with him. Of course, I did! It was a perfect day for a ride.

I bundled myself up in a warm cloak while Father hitched up Bess to the wagon and off we went with a blanket across our laps for extra warmth.

We went to the store and then to the post office, where Father received a letter from my cousin, Willie, who lives in New York. He read it, then gave it to me to read on the ride home. It was very newsy, and it was good to hear from him. I plan to write him a letter as soon as I have time.

When we arrived home, Father went to the barn to finish his chores. He chopped wood for the fireplaces and the wood stove and brought potatoes from the root cellar. While Mother and I peeled potatoes and finished making dinner, he started a fire in the parlor fireplace so it would be warm for us later.

After dinner, we read for a while and then played Whist before going up to bed.

### Sunday, January 4

We had eggs and ham for breakfast. The hens have been laying well, and we have even had some to sell to our neighbors. After breakfast, Mother, Father, and I went to church. The weather was cold, but clear in the morning, but it changed to freezing rain.

We were to attend a concert at the church at night, but it was cancelled because of the weather. I had seen George at church and looked forward to seeing him that evening, so I was disappointed it was canceled.

After lunch, we spent the day in the parlor before the fireplace, reading and talking, and I worked some on my quilt and wrote a letter to Aunt Fannie, who is Mother's sister and Willie's mother. Mother was busy sewing a new dress from a pattern she had bought at the store last week.

Father was out most of the afternoon taking care of chores in the barn and chopping more wood for the fireplaces and wood stove, which he piled on the side of the house.

During the evening, we played Whist, and Father read from the Bible before we went to bed.

### Monday, January 5

School was uneventful today. Everyone felt cold despite the wood we put in the stove. Two of the older boys brought some more wood from home and stacked it near the door. They also brought in water from the well.

The schoolhouse is located at the end of the road where I live. It is small, one of several one-room schools in our town. The scholars are of all ages, from the very smallest to the oldest, not much younger than I.

I help to teach all grades from first and on up. All the children come from the area, and I have known some of them all their lives. They and their parents often visit my parents and me, and we, in turn, pay calls to them.

Around the four walls of the school there are slab seats for the scholars, with two or three benches without backs for the younger children. There is a rough desk for two or three children when they are taking a writing lesson. There is a blackboard on the far wall.

In the center is the stove, which the older boys and I keep supplied with wood, but the room is rarely overly warm no matter how much we try.

It's difficult to teach so many different ages. Many of the older scholars have heard the same lessons over and over, but I like to think that by that time they really know them. For this, I get paid $10 a month as a trainee.

For calls of nature, there are two privies in the rear of the school, one for the boys and the other for the girls. There is also a small shed for the horses that some of the older children ride to school. Most of the children, though, walk across the fields and down the roads to get to school. They bring their lunches in buckets, and at noontime we all gather around the stove to eat.

We don't have many textbooks, and I must say the ones we have are well thumbed. We have Doball's arithmetic, and readers and spellers, a geography, and a general history. Sometimes someone will bring in a globe or a map that is of interest.

To study nature, we often go outside, to look at the trees, and in the spring and fall the wildflowers that grow in the fields around the school offer us another look at nature at its most beautiful. Sometimes we walk down the road and through the woods to the river to find what types of birds and wildlife we can see.

After school, I walked briskly home because of the cold. The sun was out bright, but some clouds on the horizon were a harbinger of a coming storm. After Mother, Father, and I had dinner, I pieced one block of my bed quilt.

Mother and Father were not home when I got home because they had gone to Southbury to the veterinarian with Willie's dog. Willie left him here during the summer, and we have gotten very attached to him. He loves the cows, especially chasing them, which does not please Father. He says it upsets their milk.

When Mother and Father came back, they said they had stopped at Emeline's, but she had gone to Danbury to see Sarah and Frank. She is expected to return Friday so we will have news of them at that time.

## Tuesday, January 6

The clouds yesterday brought with them a very stormy day for today. It snowed in the morning, and it was slippery trying to walk to school. Some of the children did not attend. Perhaps they are sick, or their parents felt it was too bad a day to come.

Of our 25 scholars, about 18 were in attendance. We did some artwork, drawing winter scenes, and had a spelling bee in addition to the usual reading and arithmetic.

I used our new sewing machine tonight. I'm making a new dress for church from a pattern I bought recently at the fabric shop in Danbury. I also did some repairs on my skirts and shirtwaists that I wear to school. I didn't have much time to work on my quilt, but I hope to finish it soon so I can feel warmer at night. It gets very cold in my room once the fire in the fireplace goes out. The cold always seems to make me cough.

I miss Sarah. It seems a long time since she was in the bedroom next to mine and we would go back and forth to see each other. Now it is more difficult to see Sarah because she lives in Danbury. Of course, we can use the train cars to go see her, Frank, and Normie, but it would be so much nicer if they lived here in Roxbury. They are talking about moving to New Milford where Frank works. It would be better for him, but it would still be far for us to go to see them.

## Wednesday, January 7

Mrs. Baglin had me teach the younger scholars today while she tested the older children in preparation for the school board visit. The members of the school board come to the schools to review tests, particularly for the older children, so it is important to test them often in preparation so we can be sure they are retaining the skills they have learned.

It was just a short time ago that I was being tested by Mrs. Baglin, and here I am now learning to be a teacher. Time goes by so fast. One day you are a student, the next a teacher. How I look forward to having children to teach on my own. That will come, I expect, I just need to be patient and learn as much as I can about how to be a teacher. Mrs. Baglin is a wonderful example.

Since it was a nice day I took the younger children outside for a while, and during recess we threw snowballs and made snow angels. Of course, everyone's outer clothing was thoroughly wet, and we had to hang the coats by the fire to dry during the afternoon.

After I arrived home this afternoon, I learned Father had brought home a letter for me from Sarah. I read it right away, but all was not good news. Sister is not feeling well, and she would like me to go to Danbury to see her. She knows I can't because of school, but I know that when she feels unwell she wants someone from her family with her. Frank, who is a plumber, is always working during the day. Someone always needs him. Also, Normie is a handful, particularly if you're not feeling up to the task of caring for him.

George came to visit and stayed for supper of ham, sweet potatoes, and canned beets. I went to school with him, and he is now working in the hat industry in Danbury as a bookkeeper. He told us many funny stories about his workday and people who work with him.

George is so much fun, though when we were in school, he sometimes teased me. I guess that's what boys do. Now he is a very serious young man, very intent on his work. He is also very handsome. I wonder if he has a girlfriend in Danbury. He doesn't seem interested in anyone here in town.

## Thursday, January 8

I usually enjoy school, but I was worried all day about Sarah. I want so much to go see her and comfort her, but it isn't possible this week because Mrs. Baglin really needs me because of the testing.

I feel so guilty that I am not able to be more helpful to Sarah, but as I was leaving for school this morning, Mother said having children is a full-time job, even when you are sick, and Sarah would manage without me. Mother said Sarah would just not do some of the household chores so she would have the energy to take care of Normie. I suppose that is true, but I still would like to be with her. There is so much work when you are both a housewife and mother.

After school I ran home, hoping to find another letter from Sarah but there was none. I was hoping to hear that she was feeling better. Instead, Father was at the kitchen table writing a letter to Sarah, offering her advice and giving her our warm wishes that she was now feeling better.

I asked him to tell her that I spoke with Mrs. Baglin about her letter, and that she said I could go to see Sarah next week after the testing of the older children was completed. Of course, I hope that Sarah is feeling better by that time, but, in any case, I can be of help to her so she gets some rest.

While Father was finishing his letter, I did some more sewing on the machine and then helped mother with dinner.

### Friday, January 9

Though it was cloudy today, it did not snow, and did not seem as cold. The older children finished testing today, so I will be able to go to Sarah's next week, which makes me very happy. I can't wait to see her and Normie, and Frank, of course. I miss Sarah so much. We were always together when we were children. Even after three years, it's strange to be apart.

Mother had done the washing today, and after I came home from school, I helped her take the clothes off the line. The linens smelled so good from hanging in the fresh air, but they also felt cold. We folded the laundry in the kitchen by the wood stove, chatting about my day at school and my upcoming visit to Sarah in Danbury.

Father had gone to New Milford and came home with a new pair of glasses, which he said helped him to see much better. He said he heard that the building of the canal across Panama began on January 1. It is thought, that once it is completed, it will shorten the time it takes to transport goods, plus lower the costs for the shipping companies.

I sewed in the evening, putting some finishing touches on my new dress. I haven't had the time to work on my quilt the last few days, but I should have my dress ready to take with me to Sarah's.

### Saturday, January 10

It was very nice today. The sun was out so the temperature seemed warmer, so much so that I decided to walk up to the center and back after lunch. It was invigorating, and I felt good being out in the air and active. I stopped in the store and bought some calico to piece into my quilt. I also saw some of our neighbors while walking, and, of course, had to be neighborly and stop to talk once in a while.

When I arrived back home, I helped Mother with the ironing. It's a lengthy process. I kept one flat iron heated on the top of the stove while using another. When it wasn't hot any longer, I would exchange it for the other, and so it goes, back and forth. It took some time but we soon had it done and all the linens and clothing stored away.

Father had a successful afternoon hunting rabbits. I imagine we will have stew for dinner one night. Father recently acquired a new dog for hunting and captured several foxes in three days.

### Sunday, January 11

I always love to go to church. It gives me such a peaceful feeling for the day. It was a nice day, and we rode to church in the buggy. I didn't feel the need for a blanket around my legs because my cloak is long, as well as my skirt so I was warm enough.

A piano concert took place in the afternoon following the service. Mother had prepared a chicken and an apple pie to take for the shared luncheon. The church provided coffee and tea.

Mr. Coad's sermon this morning urged us to give as we could afford to the missionary fund so we can spread the Christian word to others who don't know about Jesus. I thought it was a wonderful sermon. I like the idea of people spreading the word to others that have never heard it before. I wonder what it would be like to go to a strange place to preach the gospel. I would think it would be exciting, crossing the ocean to a far-off place, but also very frightening. I don't think I would ever want to be that far away from my family.

We all enjoyed the concert. First, everyone had gathered in the church parlor for luncheon, which was very enjoyable. George joined us at our table, and then we all went back into the church for the concert.

I love music so much. I always enjoy it when Mother plays the piano at home. I wish I had learned how to play. I suppose it's not too late and would probably be helpful once I am a teacher.

### Sunday, January 12

I was very busy today. Before going down to breakfast this morning, I put out some of the clothes I will be taking to Sarah's tomorrow, and my good cloak in case we go calling. I don't know how long I will be staying, so I want to make sure I have enough warm clothes.

When I finally went downstairs, Mother had my breakfast ready. We eat hearty, especially in the winter, it seems. This morning we had eggs with ham and fried potatoes, bread and butter, and coffee. I felt well fed when I headed up the road toward the schoolhouse.

The scholars were boisterous today—one boy had the hickory stick laid on him. Mrs. Baglin then sat him in the corner as an example for the others if they misbehaved. I think he will think twice before ever pulling a girl's braid and making her cry again.

Studies began as always with the salute to the flag. We then did some arithmetic, followed by reading and spelling. The older students are to memorize the poem, "Beautiful Snow," by next week. After lunch, we took a walk to the river. It was cloudy, but not storming, but certainly looked like it would, and it did, all night.

After dinner I worked some on piecing my quilt. Mother had done the wash today, so I helped with ironing, then put some of my clothing away and laid out what I wanted to take with me to Sarah's.

Aunt Emeline called in the evening. She had visited with some friends and then had gone to Sarah's for the day yesterday. She said Sister is still poorly, and Normie is wearing her out. I'm glad I'm going tomorrow. I'll be able to help keep him entertained while Sarah gets some needed rest. I'll miss being home, but Sarah needs me now.

### Tuesday, January 13

I didn't go to school today because I was preparing to leave for Sarah's. It snowed all morning, and I was afraid the cars* would be delayed, and I wouldn't be able to go. At lunchtime, Father came home from up town and brought the mail from the post office.

*railroad cars

I received a letter from Willie, which was very newsy. He always cheers me up. I miss him and Aunt Fannie. It seems so long between their visits.

I was overjoyed that the weather cleared in the afternoon. The cars would get through, and it would not be a snowy walk from the Danbury depot to Sarah's. Father, of course, is going with me to make sure I get there safe. He has some shopping to do and will stay over at Sarah's this evening and come back on the cars tomorrow.

Mother carried Father and me up to the Roxbury depot in the buggy. Father helped me with my baggage. There was more of it than I had thought, and I never would have been able to take it all without him. When I'm ready to come home, he will come for me.

We kissed Mother goodbye, and soon we were on the cars headed for Danbury. The cars are drafty and bumpy, especially in the winter, but I was so excited about seeing Sister, Frank, and Normie that I didn't mind. Father read the paper almost all the way, and I just sat looking out the window, watching the landscape go by.

The time went by quickly, with some stops in between, but soon the cars were pulling into the Danbury depot. It was still cloudy, but at least it was no longer snowing so we had a more pleasant walk to Sarah's because the sidewalks had been cleared in most places.

Sarah, of course, was very glad to see us. Father brought in my baggage, kissed Sarah, and said he would be back after shopping and making some calls. Sarah and I just hugged, we were so happy to see each other. It seemed so long since Christmas.

I could see she is still not feeling well, and I was glad I was able to come to help her. Normie was glad to see me and insisted that I play with him and look at a book. It was wonderful to be there.

Father came back a few hours later, and Frank came home from work in time for the supper that I had prepared. We had ham, boiled potatoes, squash, and fruit for dessert. I can't wait to do some baking. Sarah hasn't been able to do it, and we are out of bread.

## Wednesday, January 14

It was cold today but it was a good day to iron and bake. After breakfast, Frank left for work. I made an apple pie and had it in the oven while I ironed some of Frank's shirts and Sarah's skirts and shirtwaists. In the afternoon, after Father left for home, I went down to Main Street to get some boots. My shoes are good for indoors, but not for walking out in the snow. I've needed them for some time, so it was good to find a pair that would be serviceable for the cold, snowy months ahead.

How I long for spring. I'm anxious to put some flowers in the ground, and to smell the wonderful scents of spring. It may only be January, but I am already tired of the snow and cold. I never seem to be able to get warm.

After supper of leftover ham, vegetables, and the apple pie I made, I put Normie to bed and then we talked for a while, but Sarah tired easily so we all went to bed early.

## Thursday, January 15

I miss being at home, and the children at school, but Sarah needs my help. Frank goes to work every day, and Normie is full of energy. I played with him in the morning and read him a story before putting him down for a nap.

It was a cloudy, gloomy day. I finished the wash, and after lunch made bread, another pie, and some muffins. That should give us enough for a few days.

While Normie napped in the afternoon and Sarah rested, I worked on her quilt. She has not felt up to working on it, so I thought I would help put it together.

Her quilt is quite different from mine, with darker shades of blue and gray. It will match the curtains she has at the windows and the carpet in their bedroom. The spare room where I sleep when I come to visit is very small, but just right for one person. Normie's room is a little bigger, and he has plenty of room for his toys.

I was so lonely for Mother and Father that I wrote a letter home. I know I will see them very soon, but writing the letter made me feel closer to them.

## Friday, January 16

The morning started out cloudy, but by the afternoon it was snowing and the wind was blowing so hard it was causing the snow to drift everywhere. I had planned to go out to see some friends, but changed my mind with the change in the weather. The snow was too deep even for my new boots.

Instead, I worked some more on Sarah's quilt. It is coming along nicely, but I can only work on it when Normie is napping. He is so curious about everything that I must keep a close eye on him. He wants to go outside, but I told him the snow was too deep and the wind made it too cold. Instead we played with his toy trains, sitting on the floor in his room.

Frank did not come home from New Milford, probably because the cars could not get through. When that happens, he stays at a friend's house.

## Saturday, January 17

This was another cloudy day, but there was no snow. The men have been out clearing the sidewalks and the streets of the drifts so the buggies and sleighs can get through.

I finished the ironing and then baked some apple pies in case someone should come to visit, but no one came, probably because it is very cold.

Sarah is not feeling as well as she did yesterday and stayed in bed until noon. I fixed her a light lunch, but she didn't feel very much like eating. I try to keep Normie quiet so she can rest, but he's only two and doesn't understand that mama is not feeling well.

Frank was able to come home this morning. We had an early supper, and in the evening, after I put Normie to bed, I worked some more on Sarah's quilt.

## Sunday, January 18

Sarah had a bad night last night, and I was up with her and helped with Normie who woke up because of all the activity that was going on. We didn't get to bed until three in the morning. Frank was very tired today because of helping to minister to Sarah, but he didn't have to go to work so he can rest.

It seems strange to stay at home all day. If I was at home, we would have gone to church and either had visitors or would have gone visiting. I miss that.

It was cloudy again. I'd love to see the sun. It might cheer Sarah and make her feel better.

It was a quiet day, with no visitors and no place to go because we were all tired from last night with little sleep. I read for a while after lunch and played with Normie and read to him while Sarah and Frank rested. I'm hoping that Sarah will be better soon so I can go home. While I have friends here in Danbury, it's not the same as being home, and because of Sarah's condition and the weather, I have not been able to go visiting.

## Monday, January 19

At last some sun today, but still bitter cold. Sarah did not feel better, and finally agreed to have the doctor come. My new boots came to good use when I went to fetch the doctor, because there is still quite a lot of snow on the sidewalks. The doctor said Sarah needs to rest or he is afraid she will get pneumonia. He gave her a medicine for her cough. After the doctor left, I did the wash and cleaned the house. There was so much to do, and it had to be done around caring for Sarah and Normie. I just hope Normie doesn't get sick, too. If he does, I will need more help. Perhaps Mother could come if that happens.

Later in the afternoon our friend Katie came to visit and stayed to dinner. I fixed a roast of pork with some baked potatoes and, of course, pie.

I think Katie helped raise Sarah's spirits because she ate more supper than usual. After dinner, Katie and I played cards while Frank and Sarah talked.

Katie left about 8 o'clock, and we retired early. It had been a busy day.

## Tuesday, January 20

It rained today, but it did not freeze. The temperature is a bit warmer than it has been. Perhaps we are having a late January thaw. Some of the snow did wash off the sidewalks.

After breakfast, I baked some bread and biscuits and doughnuts for breakfast tomorrow and after lunch I did some more sewing on Sarah's quilt. It is almost done.

The doctor came in the afternoon to see how Sarah was doing. I hope I'm not getting the grippe. I had a bad headache today and my throat felt sore. I can't get sick because I have too much to do between the housework, meal preparation, and taking care of Normie. Sarah tries to help but tires quickly, and I send her back to bed. I try to keep Normie busy so he won't bother her, and when Frank is here he helps by taking care of him. Normie loves to spend time with Papa, and it's wonderful to watch them together.

## Wednesday, January 21

The sun was out bright today, but the temperature has gone cold again. This morning I ironed and then finished the quilt. It looks wonderful, and I took it right into Sarah and put it on the bed to help keep her warm.

Sarah couldn't thank me enough, but said she felt guilty that I had to finish the quilt for her. I told her it pleased me to do it, that I love to do things for my family.

She has also been working on Normie's new dress*, but when she became sick she had to stop because the close work hurt her eyes. I sewed on it for a while until it was time to prepare dinner.

After dinner, Frank, Sarah, and I talked for a while after Normie had been put to bed, and then retired early.

*Dress: Boys typically wore dresses until they were reliably toilet trained, about age 3 or 4

## Thursday, January 22

The sun has left us again. After being cloudy all day, the rain started at dinnertime and it became very stormy later.

During the day, I finished sewing Normie's dress and made some bread for dinner.

I really miss the scholars at school, but Sarah doesn't seem much better, so I don't know when I will be able to go home and return to help Mrs. Baglin.

I had a letter from Mother today. She said George came by to visit and asked for me. She thinks he has what she calls "intentions." I feel I'm much too young to think about that, and I'm not sure how I feel about George. He has been my friend all my life—it's difficult to think of him as a suitor. It's difficult to think I am now old enough to have a suitor.

I wonder if Mother is wrong. George is so handsome and could have any girl he wanted. Why would he choose me? I think I am rather plain and uninteresting.

I didn't tell Sarah because she would tease me. Some things from our childhood never change.

Late in the afternoon some of Sarah's friends stopped by to see how she was, and she felt well enough to visit with them for a while. I kept Normie occupied while they visited by reading to him and playing with his toy trucks and trains.

After dinner, Sarah, Frank, and I played cards for a while. The wind whistled at the windows, and you could almost feel the cold through the walls.

### Friday, January 23

What a wonderful day it was today. It was so warm that it felt like spring was in the air. I took a short walk out to enjoy the fresh air during the morning while Normie was napping, but I'm not feeling very well. I have been sneezing and coughing, and the headache is still with me. I must have a bit of what Sarah has had.

I found the dress that Sarah is in the process of making and made the buttonholes for it. After we had dinner, Frank and Sarah played cards while I read Mark Twain's "The Innocents Abroad" by the fire. How exciting it must be to travel to far off places, but I don't think I would want to be there without my family. I would miss them so much.

When I become a teacher, I wonder if I would be near to my family or would be working somewhere else in the state. I don't know if I would like that, but I do so much want to teach that I suppose I would eventually grow to like wherever I was. I have so many friends in Roxbury and surrounding towns that I have known for a long time that I don't know how I would be comfortable with strangers. But I suppose after a while they would not be strangers any more.

### Saturday, January 24

Sarah was feeling better today, and so was I so I decided to go down to Main Street and get the newspapers. I saw some people I know and enjoyed talking with them.

When I came back, I cleaned out the closets and did some of the week's baking. We needed bread and biscuits, and I made an apple pie.

After dinner, I pieced two blocks for my bed quilt. It feels good to be working on my own quilt now that Sarah's is finished.

It is very quiet here—no one came to call, and it was another early night for all of us.

I, however, could not sleep. I guess I just wasn't tired enough to go to bed so early. Instead, I kept thinking about my future and where I will be in a few years. Will I be married? Will I have children?

I know schools don't hire women as teachers if they are married. That doesn't seem fair. No one holds it against a man if he is married. Of course, if a man is married, his wife is at home caring for the children. If a woman's children are cared for, why should it matter, especially if she really wants to teach. Women should be able to do anything they want.

I think it must be very difficult for women to give up teaching if they marry and lose their position to a single woman or a man who is either married or not. I wonder if this will ever change. Perhaps by the time I am a teacher, it won't be an issue.

## Sunday, January 25

We did not go to church. Sarah is still not feeling well, and my cold and headache is worse so I did not feel well enough to go out.

During the afternoon, Frank and I took turns playing with Normie to keep him occupied. Frank took him outside for a while and helped him make a snowman in the back yard, complete with charcoal eyes and a carrot nose. They even put a hat on it. Normie was so happy when they came inside and insisted that I look out the window to see their work. I told him it was the handsomest snowman I had ever seen, and he just squealed with delight.

When Normie went down for a nap, I began to make dinner. I don't know how Sarah ever gets anything done when she and Normie are alone during the day. I can barely get things done, even with Frank's help with Normie.

After supper, a friend of our family, Charlie Kish, came to visit, and we talked and played cards. Then he went home, and we retired for the night.

This is what I miss. If I were at home, we would have had lots of company to while away these wintry afternoons and nights. We would play cards and games and talk about current events in town and the state. We do that here, too, but it's different because Sarah isn't feeling well and Frank and I are both tired from caring for her and keeping Normie entertained.

I can't wait to go home and see my friends, but I won't be able to go until Sarah is better, unless Mother comes to relieve me. Perhaps she will.

### Monday, January 26

Spring seemed to be in the air again today, but the snow is melting and making a mess of the roads, according to Frank. Mud everywhere, and wagons getting stuck. Frank said even the trains were slow today. He works in New Milford, so he has a long ride from Danbury. He and Sarah are planning to move to New Milford sometime soon. It will be easier for Frank to get to work, and Sarah won't have to worry about him getting home in bad weather. New Milford isn't any farther than Danbury, so it will not be like they will be moving far away.

I was very busy today with the wash and caring for Normie. Sarah is not much better, despite another visit from the doctor. I am very worried about her.

While Normie was napping, I read more of Mark Twain. After Frank came home, I made dinner. We retired early to our beds because Sarah was still not feeling well.

### Tuesday, January 27

The day was gray and cloudy and very disagreeable, and after dinner it started to rain. Today, I did the ironing, which took most of the morning, and then cleaned the floors. Housework is hard work, especially when you're trying to get it done with a little one about your feet all the time. Normie doesn't mean to be in the way, but he misses being with his mother, who is still not feeling well so I am the next best thing since his papa is working.

I don't know when I will be going home, though Mother wrote asking because Mrs. Baglin stopped in to inquire. She must be needing my help. Our scholars can be very boisterous during the winter, and she needs me to help keep them entertained and interested in learning. They would rather be out throwing snowballs and building snow forts, which I do with them during recess.

I do miss being there, and don't mind the work because I love it. I can't wait until I'm able to be a teacher somewhere, but it takes time and one must be patient.

I admit, Diary, that I once loved recess. It makes the scholars happy to be just children, I believe. All too soon they will be grown up and out in the world. Time goes by very fast once you are out of school and working, whether at home as a wife and mother or in any of the trades that men pursue.

I often wonder what the future holds for young women. Will they someday have jobs outside the home, other than as teacher or nurse?

### Wednesday, January 28

I had hoped to be going home today, but Sarah felt very sick so I knew I would not be able to leave. Sarah can't seem to throw off the grippe, and the doctor has been to see her three times. He gave her more medicine and said she was to stay quiet.

I cleaned the house today, and after dinner I was happy to see Father and Mother as well as Katie and Mrs. Murray. Father and Mother said they decided to come so they could help me with Sarah and Normie and the housework and cooking. I was so relieved because I'm still not feeling that well myself.

We had a nice visit with Katie and Mrs. Murray, but, if I am to tell the truth, I was relieved when they made their departure, and I could go to bed. Mother fussed over me, giving me some hot tea and tucking me into bed, making sure I was warm enough. It felt so good, just like when I was a little girl and she made me special foods when I didn't feel well. She would make me eggs on toast with warm milk on them so they would be soft and go down easily when I had a sore throat. Sometimes I wish I could be little again. With those thoughts, I quickly went to sleep.

### Thursday, January 29

I felt so much better with Mother and Father here to help. It gave me a very welcome respite from some of the responsibility I have been feeling. I love my sister, Frank, and Normie, but sometimes during the last few days when I have not been feeling well, either, I longed to be home. Mother and father being here was almost as good as being able to rest in my own bed at home. Wherever they are, it is like home.

Sarah felt somewhat better today, but is still weak, but Mother insisted that I take some time for myself. In the afternoon, I walked over to Katie's and spent the night at her house. We talked until very late and worked on our quilts.

I was glad to have some free time, and just be myself without having to worry about Sarah or Normie or what we would have to eat for dinner. Sarah, Frank, and Normie are in good hands with Mother and Father, and I am so glad they are here.

Of course, they came because of their concern for Sarah, to make sure she is getting better, but they were also concerned about me and to make sure I'm getting over whatever illness I have had. I felt better just getting out and being with Katie. She is such fun and has a wonderful sense of humor that makes you forget your worries and just enjoy her company.

### Friday, January 30

Because mother is here to help, I didn't have much to do today. I cleaned the floor for her, and then Katie came over and asked me to come to her house again. I spent the night there, and Mother and Frank came over after dinner to visit. They said Sarah is feeling better, and she and Normie were sleeping.

Father stayed at Sarah's in case she needed help with Normie if he woke up during the night. It sometimes takes a while to get him to go back to sleep. Then you rock him or sing to him. I've had to do that a few times. He is so sweet and lays on your lap and watches your mouth as you sing and rock. Sometimes he would touch my face with his hand. It's such a special moment. He hates to give in to sleep. I think he likes the company during the night.

It's times like that when I feel I would like to be married someday and have a family.

After Mother and Frank left for Sarah's, Katie and I worked some more on our quilts and then played cards until we went to bed where, of course, we didn't sleep. We talked and laughed until very late. I hope we didn't disturb her parents. It's always so much fun when we get together.

### Saturday, January 31

I came back to Sarah's after an early morning breakfast with Katie and her family. During the morning, Father went to town to do some shopping and see some people. It was raining but cleared off in the afternoon when Father and I left to get the cars back home.

Mother is going to stay with Sarah for a while to help with the work and to take care of Normie. She said Sarah is feeling about the same, and still needs help, but I need to get back to school because Mrs. Baglin has been inquiring about me. On the way from the cars we saw my friend Carrie near the Depot.

It seemed strange to be at home without Mother. I don't remember the last time she wasn't here. Usually we all go someplace together, so no one is ever missing from our family. I sometimes wonder how Sarah feels now that she is married and has moved away. Does she miss us? I've never really asked her. I know she loves Frank and Normie, but how does she feel without us nearby?

I wonder if I will ever feel so strongly about someone that I will leave my family as Sarah did, and so many other women have done. I suppose if you love someone you want to be with them, just as I love my family now, and want to be with them. I can't imagine not being here, but I suppose the day will come when I will want to be married and have children of my own. I must admit that I sometimes daydream about the man I would marry.

I love Normie, but I don't know if I'm ready to be a mother when I still feel like I am my parents' child. Does this seem strange? I'm only 19, but several of my friends have already been married. Perhaps I'm the one who is wrong. I just want to be a teacher.

I think if we didn't have Normie, I would not understand the younger children as much as I do, even though they are older than him. As to the older children, it wasn't that long ago I was one of the scholars being taught by Mrs. Baglin so I know how they can become bored, particularly when we are concentrating on lessons for the younger children that they have already learned. It is then up to them to study so they don't waste that time. It does take some discipline to study and not just sit there and daydream. I know, because in the past I have done the same thing.

## Sunday, February 1

It seemed strange not having Mother here. I made breakfast for Father and me and then we drove Bess up to the church for services. Mr. Coad preached on Deuteronomy Fourth and Fifth about laws to live by, particularly keeping the Sabbath day holy.

I spoke a short time with George following services, and visited with a few of our neighbors. We then came home for luncheon, after which Father went to the barn to take care of some chores.

It was a very quiet day. I finally answered Willie's letter during the evening and will post it tomorrow. I miss him. He spent last summer with us, along with his dog. We had some good times, playing cards, driving about town, and wading in the river. He's younger than I am, but he's so much fun.

Was I encouraging to George today? Do I want to be? Why does he seek me out? I don't see myself as a beauty. In fact, I think I am rather plain and not very exciting. On the other hand, I think George is quite handsome. He is tall, much taller than I, and has dark wavy hair and brown eyes. He always dresses very nice.

George and I have always been friends. Perhaps Mother is misreading his interest in me, and it is only friendship.

In the afternoon, Father began preparing mason jars for starting tobacco plants that will remain in the house until spring when they can be planted in the field next to the barn. Early in the spring, the tobacco field must be fertilized to ensure a good crop.

Father raises broad leaf tobacco that requires no shading and is grown without a cover. Broad leaf tobacco is used for cigar wrappers. It ripens at the same time and is harvested in September. While that is good, because it doesn't require picking every day during the summer, it is very labor intensive because it needs a great deal of maintenance.

Many of our neighbors also raise tobacco because it is very profitable. One of our neighbors paid off his farm's mortgage in five years with proceeds from his tobacco sales.

## Monday, February 2

It was cold walking to school this morning, but there was no sign of any storm. School was as usual. We spent recess in the yard, playing games such as leapfrog and blind man's bluff, to keep warm. My friends Carrie and Emma were at school today. They have both been sick since I last saw them.

Aunt Emeline's husband, John Kitcher, came to call and had supper with Father and me and spent the night. He will go home to Danbury on the cars tomorrow. I wrote a letter to Mother for him to deliver. He said Aunt Emeline is not feeling too well, either. It's that time of year. So many people are sick. I hope Sarah is better.

I did the wash after school and hung it out to dry. It smelled so fresh when I brought it in, but oh it was cold, so I folded the sheets and clothes by the wood stove. After washing the supper dishes and drying them, I hemmed the new tablecloths Mother had made.

I miss Mother. I'll be glad when Sarah is better, and Mother can come home. I think Father feels much the same, but at the same time he also knows Sarah needs help at certain times and one of us goes to help. I wonder if she will have other children. One child seems to take a great deal of time and worry. So many of my friends have several brothers and sisters. I wonder if Mother wanted more children after I was born, but I remember she was always busy with just Sarah and me to feed and clothe and to teach proper behavior.

## Tuesday, February 3

It was snowing very hard when I awoke this morning, and my room was very cold. I washed and dressed quickly and went down to the kitchen where Father already had a fire going in the stove. I put a kettle on for tea and began preparation for breakfast while Father was in the barn taking care of the animals. Slices of ham, eggs fresh from our chickens, and warm rolls would fortify us for the cold outside.

A glance outside the window told me the snow was getting deeper by what seemed like minutes. I knew Mrs. Baglin and the students would not be able to get to the school today, at least not until the storm stopped and the men cleared the roads. A long day with no school stretched ahead of me. I wondered if Father would be able to get to the cars to go to work. If he could, I would be alone for the day.

I heard stomping outside and watched as Father reached in the doorway for the broom to brush the snow off his boots. Snow whirled about the door as he entered, followed by a draft of very cold air, though he shut the door quickly behind him.

He gladly accepted a warm cup of tea after removing his wet outer garments near the door, and settled himself at the table to drink it while I finished making breakfast. He said Mr. Cooley, the missionary, would probably not receive his donations tonight because the event at the church would most likely be cancelled because of the storm.

Father said he would ride Bess to the cars, rather than take a chance on the wagon becoming stuck on the way. It was much too deep to attempt to walk, he said. He would leave her at the livery.

After Father left I was alone, which gave me the feeling of what it must be like to live by yourself. I have never in my 19 years been alone. Our house has always been filled with family and friends, something I would miss if I were alone all day, as Sarah is when Frank is at work. Of course, she has Normie, which I'm sure is some comfort during the long days. He also keeps her very busy so she probably doesn't have time to think about being lonely.

During the morning, I did some of the ironing and after lunch I spent some time working on my bed quilt. Despite my earlier feelings, the hours flew by, and soon Father was home again, and it was time to prepare dinner. Later, we read by the fire, Father the newspaper, and me a book by George Eliot, who is my favorite author.

### Wednesday, February 4

It was very cold today, but the sky was clear and there will be no more snow, at least for today. Because the roads were somewhat clear, I went to school, knowing most of our scholars would arrive. I started the fire in the wood stove and was ringing the school bell as Mrs. Baglin arrived.

The day was as usual, with reading, writing, and spelling exercises, plus recess where the children threw snowballs and made snowmen and snow angels. Following recess, they came back into class, wet from the snow and rosy cheeked from the cold. They, like me, were dressed in layers, including heavy stockings and boots.

After hanging their wet garments to dry, we gathered around the Franklin stove for a story session and to warm up, and soon it was time to go home. The classroom is always so poorly heated with only one stove. It takes many hours to have a good fire. Those of us lucky enough to be near the stove, which is in the middle of the room, often feel too warm while those not near the stove feel cold.

Connecticut was one of the first New England states to supply stoves to the schools so I guess we should be thankful that we don't feel any colder than we do. The classroom can also get very smoky since the building has only one door and very few windows.

The wind had picked up, and we found the snow had drifted in some places to high banks. I walked home quickly, pushed by the wind that whipped about my skirts. Once home, I removed my wet boots and started a fire in the wood stove and the fireplace to take the chill from the house. The kitchen was soon toasty warm.

George stopped by on his way home from work. A group of us from church had hoped to go sleighing tomorrow night, but the drifting would make that difficult if not impossible, we decided.

Since Father was not yet home, George did not stay, but headed for home. I was disappointed about sleighing, but again wondered about my feelings about George. He seems to be coming around more often, and I'm not sure how I feel about that. We often find his card when we return home from a visit. I wish Mother were here. I need to talk to her. Hopefully, Sarah will be well soon, and Mother will come home.

### Thursday, February 5

It was a very clear day, with a very blue sky, but also very cold. School was as usual with most of our scholars present because the roads were cleared. We had the usual lessons of mathematics, reading, and writing, and a spelling quiz. I put the mathematics problems on the blackboard for Mrs. Baglin and helped correct the papers. Most of our scholars did well on the spelling quiz but mathematics is still a challenge for many of them as it always was for me.

It is interesting to teach children of different ages. Some of the older children have heard these lessons time after time, and while I am teaching the younger children their letters and numbers, they read or do other work with Mrs. Baglin. I noticed that some of the older scholars were also paying some attention to my lessons. Perhaps they needed to refresh their memories.

After school, I found a letter for me from Aunt Fannie and enjoyed reading it over a cup of hot tea and a slice of bread and butter. She said Willie would be coming up to see us soon. That will be good because I haven't seen them since they attended our Christmas Eve party.

In the afternoon, Father went up to the town center to the Town Hall where they have an exhibit of new farm equipment. He's hoping that they will have information on a McCormick horse-drawn machine for corn. I stayed home and worked on my quilt for a spell before starting dinner.

The kitchen was warm from the wood stove when Father returned in time for dinner. I had brought more wood in from the pile outside the door. It was very cold outside, and I was glad to be inside again. I'll be glad when winter is over, so I can again plant my flowers and go berrying. These cold days seem to take my breath away and cause me to cough.

### Friday, February 6

It was another clear day today with some high clouds. I went to school early as usual, so I could get the wood stove started. The building was very cold from sitting all night without any fire. I was dressed in layers as usual to offset the cold, but it was bone chilling. The scholars and Mrs. Baglin arrived, and soon we were at work

That afternoon, my friend Carrie came to visit and spent the night in Sarah's room. Millie Voss also stopped by for a short time. After she left, Carrie and I talked while I pieced one block of my bed quilt.

While we were talking, Father read the newspaper by the parlor fire and went to bed before us. He misses Mother. I hope Sarah is soon well enough so Mother can come home.

I did not mention George to Carrie because I'm not at all sure of what his intentions, if any, may be. I don't think I'm ready to think about it, much less talk to someone, other than Mother, about what I should do if George were to approach Father about calling upon me as a suitor. If I talked to Sarah about it, she might tease me, but perhaps not.

I have a difficult time thinking about having a suitor. I don't feel old enough to have a suitor. Oh, Diary, I know that some of my friends are already married, but it doesn't seem the right time for me. I truly want to be a teacher someday. It doesn't seem fair that a woman must choose between marriage and teaching. Perhaps someday that will change.

## Saturday, February 7

It was a very rainy day and cold, but the rain did not freeze. Carrie and I were up early, our bedrooms being very cold, and after a hearty breakfast of eggs and bacon in the toasty kitchen, we spent some time talking before the fire in the parlor. Outside it was dreary, but inside we were warm and snug.

I finally told her about seeing more of George recently, and she playfully teased me that I had a beau. Is that true? He has said nothing to me to make me think that, but he is paying more attention to me lately. I know I blushed when she was teasing me, but I'm not sure how I feel about him. I think he would first speak to Father to make sure it was acceptable to call upon me. As it is now, we are just friends and do things with our other friends. I enjoy that and am not sure I would want anything more in my life now.

After a lunch of bread and ham, Carrie and I went up to town and went to see Mrs. Baglin and had a nice visit with her. When we came home later, we baked bread and a cake. Carrie and I talked more in the kitchen while I was ironing, a not too easy task because I had to keep alternating the two irons to get the heat required. After some time, I had ironed two of my skirts and shirtwaists that I wear to school and my dress for church.

## Sunday, February 8

It was a beautiful, clear day. After breakfast and chores, Carrie and I went to church with Father. The sermon was inspirational, but the church was cold even with all the people there. I saw George. He smiled at me, and Carrie nudged me in the ribs and giggled. Father gave her a look that meant it was inappropriate, even though the service had not yet begun. I didn't talk to George because he was talking to someone else when we were leaving the service.

After we arrived home and father had settled Bessie down in the barn, we had a lunch of cold chicken in the kitchen, then went outside for a walk. It was cold, and we were glad to come back to a warm fire in the parlor fireplace.

Father tended to chores in the barn for a while and then joined us. We talked about today's sermon and read for a while. Carrie and I took turns reading aloud from the Bible. Later, after dinner, Carrie went home because she and her family were expecting guests. I was very sad to see her go and felt very lonely without her and without Mother.

After dinner, Father and I read for a while in the parlor. He had put more wood on the fire and it was comfortable to sit and read. He went upstairs and replenished the wood in the fireplaces so our rooms would be warm when we went to bed.

Father and I went to bed early because tomorrow we are back to school and work. I dressed for bed quickly, snuffed out my light, and was soon under the covers for warmth.

## Monday, February 9

Today dawned clear but very cold. I washed and dressed quickly and went down to the kitchen to make breakfast. Father had already started the fire in the stove, and the kitchen was very warm compared to the upstairs. By the time he returned from the barn, I had oatmeal, eggs, and hot coffee ready. Soon after Father left to go to work, and I walked to school where it was a day like any other. Chores, lessons, and recess. Carrie arrived after school and walked home with me. She is going to go to the donation for the missions at the church tonight.

I decided not to go, though Father went. I was content to stay in the warmth after a cold day in the schoolhouse. I knew George would be there, but I'm still unsure about how I feel about his recent attention and what his intentions might be. Father doesn't seem to have noticed or he would be asking me questions that I am not ready, or even able, to answer. I wouldn't want him talking to George, asking him what his intentions are if they are only as friends, especially since he has not asked Father if he could call on me in a more formal way.

I understand in some cases that young women receive possible suitors through acceptance of calling cards and that courting couples call each other mister and miss, rather than by their given names, until they know each other better. I can't imagine that would be true of us, since we have known each other and our families our whole lives. We already attend outings, such as church suppers, country and county fairs, and lectures with our parents or young married friends. I don't think that would be any different than now.

### Tuesday, February 10

It was not as cold today as it has been, though it was cloudy. There was no sign of more snow at least for today. Because it was a bit warmer, the schoolhouse did not seem as cold, especially after I got the fire going in the stove.

Our scholars were more energetic, and it was difficult to keep them interested in lessons. We took a longer recess so they could run and play and be more attentive when we returned to class.

Before school, Carrie came and got some of her things she had left here the other day and went to school with me, which made the day pass a little more enjoyably.

When I got home from school, I found Willie had arrived as predicted by Aunt Fannie. He has a few days off from school. We spent the rest of the afternoon catching up on what has been happening in our lives, and then he kept me company in the kitchen while I made dinner. We talked and laughed, and it was so wonderful to have him here.

During dinner, Willie kept us laughing with his stories about his days at school and how he and his friends spend their time away from school. I'm beginning to realize that life is very different for boys and young men than it is for girls and young women. They do seem to have much more freedom.

During the evening, while he and father talked around the parlor fire, I pieced one block for my bed quilt. I have quite a few blocks completed, and it won't be long before my quilt is finished, and I will be warmer at night.

## Wednesday, February 11

Today was such a beautiful day for February. My friends Eliza and Minnie stopped by the school to say hello. It was good to see them.

Following the noon recess, I left school, so I could go to South Britain with Willie. We took Bess and the wagon and had a good time visiting friends there. We had a good talk going down and coming back. It wasn't so cold, so the ride was enjoyable, and we had blankets over us in addition to our layered clothing.

I wanted to talk to Willie about George but found I couldn't. He's younger than I am so I don't know if he has had the experience to help me. I was also uncomfortable talking with him about such things, even if he is my cousin. I was also afraid he would tease me, and I would feel embarrassed.

Willie helped with making supper and the cleanup after. We played cards for a while with Father, who seemed tired so we all went to bed early.

## Thursday, February 12

It was cloudy early this morning and rained later. School was as usual, except no outdoor recess because of the rain. We spent the time talking, telling stories, and reading.

When I got home from school, Father had been to the Post Office and brought back a letter from Frank and a valentine for me from George.

Father raised his eyebrows at me but didn't say anything. I imagine he's waiting for Mother to come home before raising the subject of George's increased interest.

How do I feel about the valentine? I admit to a blush as I opened it, which I'm sure did not go unnoticed by Father. It was only a card with a verse and his name, nothing more. It was very innocent, much like valentines I have received from him and other school chums in the past. It was nothing I should be concerned about. Or should I be?

Father took Willie to the cars to go home to New York. I miss him already. We had so much fun while he was here. I wish his stay could have been longer.

### Friday, February 13

Walked to school this morning in the rain, and it rained all day. It was another indoor recess day, one not as nice as yesterday. The scholars wanted to run and play outside, but it was raining too hard, and all that would be accomplished would be they would get very wet and probably muddy. Instead we played some indoor games, such as charades. We even had a spelling bee that they seemed to enjoy because it was just for fun.

After school, I went home and after dinner, over a cup of hot tea, wrote a letter to Sarah. I hope she is getting better and feeling stronger every day. I miss Mother as does Father.

I cooked a ham for dinner, with cabbage and boiled potatoes. It tasted very good, and Father said it was as good as Mother makes. That made me feel very good.

Before going to bed early, I sat in the parlor by the fire and pieced another block for my bed quilt. These winter evenings are perfect for such tasks. In no time at all, I believe the quilt will be finished. It will make my room so much prettier, plus keep me warmer during these cold nights so I won't cough as much and will be more rested the next day.

### Saturday, February 14

I arose this morning to another cold, rainy day, a good day to stay inside. Father and I had breakfast together before he went to New Milford on the cars for some shopping and to see friends. After taking him to the depot in the buggy, I was glad to come home to the warm kitchen. I got out the washtub to do some wash, and because it was raining, and I couldn't hang the wash outside, I hung the clothes and linens in the kitchen near the wood stove so they would dry.

Then after a cup of hot tea, I set about baking. We were out of bread, and I also baked two apple pies and an apple cake. This kept me busy for most of the day until I met Father at the depot. He had picked up the mail at the Post Office, and there was a letter from Mother. It made me homesick for her so Father said I should go to Danbury soon to see her and to help Sister pack for their move to New Milford. They are moving there to be closer to Frank's work.

Following dinner, we sat by the parlor fireplace, reading and talking until it was time to go to bed.

### Sunday, February 15

It was very cloudy when Father and I went to church this morning and looked like snow. I talked to George for a few moments before the service but did not see him after. When we came out from church, we found it had been snowing very hard for a while and we had a hard ride home in the buggy.

It felt very good to get inside once we were at home. Somehow the blankets were not enough to warm us on the ride home. Father brought in wood for the fire and for the kitchen stove, after which I made lunch of soup and sandwiches.

It kept snowing during the day but stopped in time for us to attend an organ concert in the Congregational Church in the evening. We took Bess with the sleigh because there was still enough snow on the roadway.

The music was beautiful. I loved it. There was a social hour after the concert, and we saw several of our neighbors who were brave enough to fight the snow and cold to attend. Everyone said they could not wait for spring. It has been a cold, wet, snowy winter.

On the ride home later, we kept tucked under the blankets because it was very cold. I wished Mother had been here. She loves music so much. I wonder if the Danbury churches have such events. Perhaps she has been able to attend some event there while Frank stayed home to care for Sarah.

### Monday, February 16

Compared to yesterday, today was a beautiful day. No clouds and full sun with blue sky. It was good to see the sun.

I, of course, went to school, but Father had told me to tell Mrs. Baglin that I would be at Sister's for a few days helping her pack up her household goods and clothing for the move to New Milford.

Mrs. Baglin understood the need for me to go since Sarah had been sick and the move would be too much for her to do alone.

Father went up town to the depot to meet Frank, who came up on the train today and stayed the night with us so he could accompany me to Danbury tomorrow. He took tomorrow off so he would be with us to do some of the heavier lifting.

During the evening, while he and Father talked and played cards, I did the ironing, making sure I had enough clothing to take with me and that Father had enough until the next washing.

I went to bed early because we would be leaving for Danbury the next day. I can't wait to see Mother, Sarah and Normie.

## Tuesday, February 17

I arose early to prepare for my visit to Danbury. It was a nice day, sunny but cold. Following a hearty breakfast, I packed my clothes and Father hitched up Bess to the wagon and drove Frank and me to the Depot.

After what seemed like a long ride, we arrived in Danbury and walked to Sarah and Frank's house. I was so glad to see Mother. I have missed her so. She was well, but Sarah seems to be about the same as she was when I was with her.

Though I was glad to see her, I was also glad that Mother could go home for a spell. She seemed very tired from taking care of Sarah, plus trying to keep up with Normie, who has an abundance of energy.

After lunch, Frank took up the carpets and took them outside to clean them while Mother and I started packing non-essential household items in boxes Frank had obtained from the grocery store. I could not believe the number of things they have collected since their marriage. When we filled a box, we tied it shut and put it with the others that Mother and Sarah had filled before we came.

While I helped Sarah, Mother prepared dinner. I know she is looking forward to going home tomorrow. She misses Father, plus there are tasks she needs to do that I did not have time to do because of being at school most of the day.

After sitting in the parlor talking for a while, we all went early to bed.

## Wednesday, February 18

It was another clear day today. After breakfast, Frank and Mother left for the train. He is to escort her home where Father will meet her at the depot and then was to go on to his work in New Milford.

After making lunch for Sarah and Normie, I went down on Main Street to do some shopping for groceries and other things Sarah needed.

During the evening after dinner we sat by the fire in the parlor. I pieced one block for my bed quilt while Sarah read to Normie. Then I helped her put him to bed. A little while later she said she was tired and went to bed. I soon followed. It was too lonely by myself. Now I miss Mother because she left for home, and I am here again.

## Thursday, February 19

It was a very pleasant day today. There were no storms. Frank, Sarah, Normie and I had breakfast together, and then Frank went on the cars to New Milford. He will be staying in their new house there while we are packing and preparing for the move.

While Sarah was resting, I did some work on her new dress.

After the dinner dishes were washed and dried and Normie put to bed, Sarah and I sat in the parlor and read for a while. I wanted to talk to her about George, but somehow could not put my thoughts into words. Perhaps it's because I don't know what I think of it myself so how can I explain it to someone else, even my sister? Anyway, there really isn't much to tell, just some additional attention from someone I've known all my life. I really shouldn't pay too much time thinking about it because George and I have always been close friends from when we were small.

I think I'm afraid that Sarah would laugh at my doubts that someone from my youth would be interested in me as an adult. Sometimes I don't even believe that I am now considered an adult. I feel like I have more in common with the older scholars in school than I do with those of my own age because some of them are now married or being called upon by suitors. One or two of my friends have been married since they were 18 and are already expecting.

I don't feel I'm ready for any of that though my friends seem happy enough being a couple rather than unmarried persons.

## Friday, February 20

It was a very clear, sunny day, but Sarah and I stayed home all day. She did not feel well enough to go out. Normie was good about taking his nap and while he was asleep we worked on Sarah's dress.

She still tires easily, so when Normie got up later I played with him while Sarah rested before dinner. I always look forward to my time with Normie. I really think I would like children of my own someday. Would I be a good mother? I feel so, though I don't think I'm quite ready for it.

While I was playing with Normie, George called. He did not stay long because he had to take the cars to Roxbury. Sarah and I had a cup of tea with him, and he remarked on the number of boxes we had filled to be taken to New Milford. It is a lot of work to take apart a household of belongings, but soon Sarah will be setting everything up in her new home, which must be very exciting for her. Then Normie will have a larger yard in which to play, and they will be close enough to the Green to walk down to the street or to go to see friends.

After George left, we had dinner and after washing up the dishes and putting them away, we spent some time reading to Normie before Sarah put him to bed. We played cards for a while, and then went early to bed because there is more work to do tomorrow.

## Saturday, February 21

When we arose this morning, it was snowing, and continued to snow until noon when it cleared off. We needed some things at the store so after lunch I put on my warm boots and went down to Main Street to do some shopping.

When I got back, Sarah and Normie were resting so I cleaned the kitchen floor and baked bread and a cake for supper. After Normie was asleep, we played cards for a while and then went to bed early because Sarah was feeling tired. I wasn't tired, so I read for a while in my room. I also admit to some daydreaming, thinking about my future and wondering what it will be like. Will I become a teacher as I so much desire? Will I marry? I know Mother and Father love Normie and would welcome more grandchildren.

I wonder if Sarah and Frank will have more children. I love Normie, but I would love to have nieces to spoil with dolls and tea sets and to read stories to, but I'm still not sure about being married and having children myself.

Also, there are the many tasks a housewife must complete every day in addition to caring for the children when they are not in school. I think it must be difficult to get all these chores completed. Just being here with Sarah has convinced me that a married woman with children cannot afford to be sick, especially if she is far away from family and friends and must fend for herself. Sarah is very lucky that Mother, Father, and I are available to help her when she is in need. No, I don't think I am ready to have a suitor or to even think about getting married.

## Sunday, February 22

Today was a nice change from what seems like continuous snow. Sarah and I stayed home but had some visitors.

My friend Katie came to call in the afternoon as well as Mrs. Wheeler. Uncle Beach also stopped in for a while. It was nice to see them and to hear their news.

After everyone went home, Sarah, Normie, and I had supper. While Sarah was getting Normie settled for the night, I wrote a letter to Mother and Father and one to Frank in New Milford. He has been up there all week working as well as preparing his family's new home.

Sarah seems to be bearing up well to the endless packing we have been doing. My back hurts from so much bending and reaching, and I am concerned about her doing too much after being ill.

It's no wonder that we go to bed almost as early as Normie because we are both exhausted. I do insist that Sarah take some time to rest in between chores but there is much to do before the move.

Having company today gave us both a break in between the work.

After dinner, we relaxed by the fire in the parlor, talking. Sarah is full of ideas for her new home and is excited to begin her tasks there. I hope she does not get sick again through all of this. When I think about it, I imagine Mother, Father, and I will be helping her and Frank settle into their new home. I just hope to have a few days to rest before it all starts again in New Milford.

## Monday, February 23

The day began cloudy but eventually became nice. In preparation for their move to New Milford, I took Sarah's front room carpet up and started to pack some of the household items she won't need here.

I also went down to Main Street to do some shopping. I enjoyed the walk even though it was cold. I wonder how Sister will like living in New Milford. Many of our friends are here in Danbury, but I suppose they will visit often, and we do have relatives and some friends in New Milford. It's so easy to take the cars to get from one town to another, and it takes less time than a horse and buggy or riding horseback as some of the men still do.

I like to ride but Mother doesn't think it is seemly that I prefer to ride astride rather than side saddle. She insists that if I'm going to ride to a neighbor's or friend's that I use the side saddle. Around our house, though, I prefer astride and do so whenever I can.

The packing took me almost all morning, and I gave the front room a good sweeping after I took the boxes I had packed and put them with the others. Father will have a lot of work loading the wagon for the trip to New Milford. I suppose he is already enlisting some of my uncles to help. Some of the larger items will be sent via the cars to New Milford, and he will need help in moving and transporting them to the depot.

It is much work to move from one house to another, especially when at any distance, and I think Sarah and Frank will have a lot to do before they feel like the New Milford house is truly home. I hope that this is their final move. I don't think Sarah could go through this again.

After dinner, Sarah and I were tired so we lounged by the fire in the parlor, but with some of the things that previously made it feel warm and cozy packed away, it already seemed like no one lives here.

### Tuesday, February 24

Today was another nice day, with sun and blue sky. We stayed at home, and I helped Sarah with the wash and then hung it on the outside line to dry. Everything was cold to the touch when I brought it in later. Sarah and I folded by the fire, and what would not be needed was set aside for packing later.

After lunch, I packed the extra linens and some other household items for the move while Sarah took care of Normie. Later, I took Normie for a short walk in his pram, but it was still too cold to stay outside very long. He was red-cheeked and sleepy when we returned, and Sarah put him down for a nap.

Looking around Sarah's house, I realized we have done a great deal of work. The place feels strange without the familiar items that have been moved into boxes for the trip to New Milford. Soon we will need to leave so the furniture and larger items can be taken to the depot or taken by wagon to the new house.

In the afternoon, some of Sarah's friends and their children called so we stopped packing to enjoy tea and cake with them. I love the tradition of people gathering for tea in the afternoon. It is a pleasant way to spend the time with friends or family.

Later, after they had left for home, Sarah and I made supper for the three of us, then she put Normie to bed. He was tired from playing with the children, so he went willingly without any fuss.

Before going to bed early ourselves, Sarah and I read the Bible and the newspaper.

### Wednesday, February 25

It was cloudy today, but there was no storm. We sprinkled the wash, and after warming the irons, I did some of the ironing while Sarah made lunch.

She said she was feeling better so after lunch she went down on Main Street to get some calico fabric to piece for Normie's bed quilt. She also brought me a hairpin that was very pretty.

While she was gone, I watched Normie, who was very good. He even took a nap, which gave me time to finish the ironing before Sarah returned. I don't know how any woman gets everything done every day, especially when they have children. If Normie had been awake, I would not have been able to finish the ironing because I would have had to take care of his needs.

It was an uneventful day, otherwise. No one called in the afternoon, so we had tea together with some cake. Later, we had a light supper, and after cleaning up the kitchen, we read some for a while. I also did some crocheting on a scarf for my dresser at home, which I think will be very pretty when I'm through. Then Sarah and I went to bed early because tomorrow will be another busy day.

## Thursday, February 26

It was another cloudy day, but there was no snow. Katie came over to visit and kept me company while I packed some things for Sarah. They will be moving everything soon, and Sarah and Normie will be staying with Mother, Father, and me until things are settled in New Milford.

During the evening, Katie watched Normie while Sarah and I went to visit Dr. Bennett, a friend of our parents. We had tea and cake with them and had an enjoyable time.

On the way home, it began to snow. It was very pretty at first but began to snow heavily by the time we arrived home. I was glad I had worn my new boots.

Sarah was feeling very tired so she checked on Normie, who was already asleep, and then excused herself to go early to bed.

Katie and I played cards for a while, and then she left for home, and I was left alone by the fire in the front room. It's not looking much like a home any more with so many things already packed for the move. I think Mother plans to help Sarah settle in once she is in New Milford, but it will be fun having Sister and Normie with us.

I miss the good times we had when we were younger. So much has changed in the three years since Sarah and Frank have been married. I wish we saw more of Sarah, but she has a great deal to do at her home and Normie takes up a lot of her time. It will be fun having Sarah with us, but it won't be like it once was when we shared secrets and had long conversations about our futures.

Sarah always wanted to be married and have a family, just as my goal was always to become a teacher. Every day I go to the school house to help Mrs. Baglin, I know this is what I am to do in the future.

### Friday, February 27

It was a beautiful sunny day today after last night's storm. The streets and yards looked so fresh and clean from the new snow. After doing morning chores, we dressed Normie warmly and went down on Main Street to shop and then went to Katie's where we spent the night. Great-Aunt Emeline was visiting, too.

During the evening, Katie and I went over to the house and packed some more household things. We now have several boxes ready for the move to New Milford. It's difficult to believe how much people can accumulate in just a few years.

Today was Father's 50th birthday. I would have liked to have been there, but he understands that Sarah needs my help. I had bought him a new cap that Mother was to give him today. I think she was going to give him a new shirt. She planned to make his favorite gingerbread cake for tonight's dinner. It is especially good with fresh whipped cream on it.

Helping is what our family does all the time. If you need help, everyone helps. This is one of the best things about being a member of a large family. It is never boring when everyone gets together.

Some of the uncles and cousins will be helping Frank move furniture into the new house once it arrives. Several wagons will be needed to transport everything. Mother, Sarah, and I will make food for Father to take to New Milford for all the helpers.

### Saturday, February 28

It was cloudy today, but at least it did not snow. We visited with Katie, her mother and Emeline very late last night. Great-Aunt Emeline did not stay the night but went home a little before 2 o'clock. After breakfast with Katie and her mother, Sarah, Normie, and I came home to Roxbury on the cars.

Mother was very glad to see us, especially Normie. After being with him for several days, she missed him. Now they will be staying with us until their new house is ready.

Father took the wagon to Danbury this afternoon to get Sarah's trunk, which would have been too heavy for us to bring with us. When he returned, we unpacked it and put away their clothing and personal items.

It's going to be like old times having them here. I would

imagine Frank will visit often, and we will have some family get-togethers when Mother's brothers and sisters will be here, at least those who don't live very far away.

I'm looking forward to card and board games and visits with friends. Everyone will want to see Sarah while she is here in Roxbury. Perhaps we will go sleighing, if drifts don't get too deep. It will be fun to have Normie to play with. He made sure his toys were in the trunk when we were unpacking so Sarah gave him a couple and he ran to show Grandpa and Grandma, no doubt to entice them to play with him.

### Sunday, February 29

Though it was sleeting and snowing early in the day, it cleared off nicely. Frank came from New Milford and stayed all night. Sarah was very glad to see him.

He said the work on the new house is almost done, and soon Sarah and Normie will be able to go home. Not too soon, I hope. I suppose it seems selfish of me to want to keep them here longer, but I'm so happy to have my sister for this time. We can talk and laugh the way we did when we were younger.

During the evening, we had visitors. David Evans and Wallace came to call on us. Mother, Frank, Sarah, and I entertained them. Father had gone to the meeting at the schoolhouse. I don't really know what the meeting was about. Perhaps we will be getting new books or materials. We certainly could use them. We never seem to have enough to go around, and the ones we have are well worn.

Mrs. Baglin is always talking about the new books that are being published for use in schools, and every year she tries to add a new one to our collection. Hopefully the scholars' parents will persuade the Board of Supervisors of our need, but I suppose all the schools have the same hopes of obtaining new textbooks.

### Monday, March 1

I awoke today to find a cloudy day. Because I was not feeling well, and Sarah had a bad toothache, Mother decided not to wash today. It could wait, she said, until everyone felt better.

Because I was feeling poorly, I did not go to school. Mrs Baglin would not want me to pass on some sickness to the scholars.

Because he had to work, Frank returned to New Milford early on the cars. Father carried him to the depot and then went to work himself so Mother, Sarah, Normie, and I were in for the morning.

I spent the day quietly, drinking hot tea with honey, and reading. Sarah's toothache finally subsided. She thinks it was caused by the cold weather. She said her face even hurt.

Mother did some housework in the morning instead of the wash and then prepared our lunch of chicken soup and fresh baked rolls. What is it about chicken soup that makes you feel better when you are sick? Even Sarah said it helped relieve the ache in her face. Perhaps it is the warmth on a cool day that has healing effects.

In the afternoon, Mother went up town to do some shopping and to take some letters to the Post Office. Sarah, Normie and I stayed near the fire in the parlor, reading and talking. Before his nap, Normie wanted a story so Sarah read from one of the books they had brought with them. He was soon nodding off, and she carried him upstairs.

I think Normie is confused with all the packing going on at his house and also being with us. Soon he will be in his new home with all his playthings in his room, and his life will be back in order.

## Tuesday, March 2

The weather was very pleasant today. It almost feels like spring will be here soon. I can't wait, because I always feel better when I'm warm. No matter how much wood Father brings in for the stoves and fireplaces, it never seems to be as warm as I wish it would be. I dress in layers to help keep the chill out and always sit as close as I can to the fire, without taking the risk of a spark to my clothing.

I wanted to go to the schoolhouse today, but Mother felt I should stay home and rest.

Mother finally decided to do the washing with Sarah's help. I tried to help but still felt so sick that I went upstairs to rest for a while, though I didn't sleep. I keep thinking about why I always seem to feel poorly. When I went down for lunch, Sarah had already hung the clothes outside and was helping Mother make lunch. She is so much help when she is here, but I feel guilty sometimes that I don't seem able to help very much anymore. I get so tired.

During the afternoon, Great-Aunt Emeline came to call. We had tea and cakes and talked for some time in the kitchen near the warm stove. She left after tea, and Father came home from work, bringing with him a letter from my friend Nellie Bronson, who is visiting friends in New Milford. Her letter was full of news of our mutual friends. She said she would be home soon.

After dinner, and after Normie was in bed, we played cards for a while. Father read us the paper so we heard the latest news.

I excused myself early to go to bed because I was so tired.

## Wednesday, March 3

Today was a very rainy day. After breakfast and after Father had left for work, I did the ironing. I still don't feel well enough to go to school. Normie is also not feeling well. He probably has what I have, and now Mother is also almost sick. It must be the grippe. Sarah made breakfast, lunch, and dinner because Mother and I did not feel well. Sarah is still not very strong so I hope she doesn't get sick again through helping us.

We took care of her, and now she is caring for us. That is what happens with a family, everyone helps when there is the need. Father helped Sarah by taking Normie into the parlor to read him a story. Normie wanted to play with his trucks, but he was soon almost dozing on the floor. Because he felt badly, Normie did not complain about going to bed tonight. I hope he is better soon. No one visited, and we retired early. I hope I will feel better tomorrow so I can go to school. I imagine Mrs. Baglin is hoping I will come back soon. I don't feel that I do a great deal for her, but it is less she must do. Keeping scholars of different ages involved during the school day and interested in learning is sometimes challenging for teachers and their helpers.

## Thursday, March 4

After lunch today, because the weather was not so cold, I felt well enough to go to the schoolhouse, but I was only able to stay part of the afternoon. My friends Emma and Carrie were there, so the time was enjoyable, but I still don't feel as well as I would like to be.

Later I walked home to learn that Father had gone up town to make some calls and to do some shopping.

Mother, Sarah, and I made dinner when he returned, and afterwards we sat before the parlor fire talking until it was time to retire for the night. Father had purchased a newspaper and we talked about local events. There is to be a social at the church Sunday after services, which should be fun.

I hope George will be there. It seems a while since I have seen him, but I suppose he is working hard in Danbury and, when he is home, he helps his father with chores around their place. There is always something to do. I feed the chickens every day and collect the eggs for breakfast. They aren't always glad to see me with my basket because they know I've come for the eggs. I try to feed them first so they are less aware of what I am doing.

Mother and Father, of course, do most of the work. I try to help, but I wonder if Father ever is sorry he didn't have a son instead of two daughters. I know he loves us, but some of our neighbors and friends have sons to help with chores.

### Friday, March 5

Though it rained in the morning, it was very nice in the afternoon. The school is closed today because Mrs. Baglin had to go out of town to her daughter's, so I spent the afternoon after lunch cutting out some pieces for my bed quilt. I also pieced one block.

Sarah and Normie took a walk in the afternoon. He is feeling much better now, and she has regained her strength. I still have some effects from my sickness, so I was happy to stay quiet in the warmth of the house.

Mother was busy baking for the weekend in case we have callers.

Sarah is looking forward to seeing Frank who will be coming from New Milford tomorrow. She must miss him very much. I wonder if I will ever find anyone who I will miss when he is away? I have not been anywhere where I have seen George, and he has made no calls or left his card. He must be very busy with his work in Danbury, and, because he is so friendly, I'm sure he has made friends there that he likes to spend time with. When he is home, I'm sure he has family obligations with his parents.

## Saturday, March 6

It was another cloudy day today. I long for spring, warm weather, and my flowers. I can't wait to put my hands into the warm soil, or to walk through the fields of wildflowers to the river. It is still too cold.

I am feeling sick again today. I want to get better, so I will feel like doing more to help Mother and Sarah and to play with Normie. I feel so tired sometimes, even though I might not have done very much to make me tired. Mother says it's because I have been ill, and that I need to rest just as Sarah did.

Father took the wagon to New Milford in the morning to bring Frank home. While he was gone, Mother made lunch, and Sarah and I made a shell box*.

After lunch, Great-Aunt Emeline called and spent some time with us. She had heard from Aunt Fannie and Willie and told us amusing stories from their letters. After she had gone home, Father and Frank arrived. Sarah and Normie were so glad to see Frank. He has been working plus getting their new home ready for them.

I feel like I have not been out of the house for so long. I really do want to get better soon. I miss my friends and school.

*Shell box: a small box for trinkets decorated with beach shells.

## Sunday, March 7

It was another stormy day with more snow. Because of that, we did not go to church, so I did not see George or anyone. No one called because of the bad weather.

After lunch, I wrote a letter to my friend Nellie, and then went through my schoolbooks to prepare lessons for tomorrow for the younger scholars. I also started reading a new novel by Mark Twain that kept me entertained through the afternoon.

We spent some time after dinner visiting with Frank and Sarah until all of us retired for the evening. I stayed awake for quite a while, listening to the wind and the snow striking the windowpanes. It made my room seem cold even though the fire still burned in the fireplace.

I feel like this winter is never going to end. I am so tired of the cold weather and the snow. Perhaps I don't feel better because I am always so cold. No amount of heat seems to make me feel warm. I long for the sun and warmth of summer. I vow I will not complain about the heat during the summer though I certainly have complained about the past few months of cold weather.

Even though the walk to the schoolhouse is short in comparison to that of some of the scholars, it takes me forever to warm up in the building because there has been no heat there all night, and it takes a while for the room to warm once I have the stove going.

I hope the snow will have stopped by morning or I will make sure I wear my boots.

## Monday, March 8

Today we arose early and found the day to be pleasant, though windy. It's March, with its wind and bluster.

In the morning, I helped Mother with the wash and hung it outside for her. I went back to school today and do feel better.

Father had done some chores before riding up to the Hollow where he heard that my grandfather, Hiram Tyrrell, was sick. Mother was concerned about her father, so she and Father rode over to see him and stayed the night with him and my Aunt Ruth and Uncle Charles.

For the first time in a long time, Sarah and I were alone. After Normie was put to bed, she and I talked for some time, about Grandfather and other members of the family. Grandfather, when he was younger, was a millwright, carpenter and joiner, and had built furniture for local homes and helped build several houses. He has been well up to this time. I hope he will be better soon, but I suppose when you get older you are more likely to fall ill than when you are young.

Perhaps that was not a correct statement. You don't have to be old to be sick. Even children are prone to certain illnesses, and our cemeteries tell the story when several children in one family may have died from one of those childhood illnesses that spread from one child to the other.

## Tuesday, March 9

It stormed almost all day. About 10 o'clock this morning Father and Mother came home from Aunt Ruth's. Since I had gone to the schoolhouse in the morning, I went home for lunch, so I could talk to them about how Grandfather is. They said Grandfather is not feeling very well, but that he is getting good care. The doctor has been to see him and gave him some medicine that perhaps will help him.

In the afternoon after I returned from school, Sarah and I finished the ironing, and she helped me with some hand piecing for my bed quilt. We sat on the floor in the parlor, near the fire, talking as we sewed. It's wonderful having her and Normie here, even if it is only temporary until their new home is ready.

Aunt Emeline came to visit in the evening. She is also concerned about Grandfather. We sat in the parlor and talked. After Emeline left for home, we went to bed early.

I didn't feel tired so I read for a while, then went to bed where it took a while to fall asleep. I was really concerned about Grandfather.

### Wednesday, March 10

Though it snowed some in the afternoon, most of the day was pleasant. After I returned from school, the weather was so nice that Sarah and I decided to ride up to the Hollow to visit Aunt Josephine. She had been to visit Grandfather and said he seemed to be feeling better today.

When we returned home later, our friend Nellie Bronson called, and we had an enjoyable time talking and drinking tea. She stayed for dinner and spent the night. Mother and Father had gone to the Hollow to visit Grandfather and returned home in time for dinner. They said Grandfather seemed better, but he is still far from well.

### Thursday, March 11

Today was another snowy day. When will it ever stop? I went to school and later in the day Nellie, Sarah, and I sat in front of the parlor fire and did some piecing on my bed quilt.

After supper, Father's friends, Wallace Hodge and Charlie Minor, called. Father rarely talks about the war, except when Mr. Hodge and Mr. Minor visit. Mother says it's because the memories of the war and its horror and his resulting facial injury are just too painful. She said he also feels such talk is not appropriate for us women.

However, from Mother and others I have found out that Father was discharged in 1865 because of a wound to the right side of his face that he received during a battle at Winchester, Virginia. I think that is why Father favors a beard and sideburns, to cover the scar from the wound.

Father was a first sergeant, and friends and family here in Roxbury and elsewhere still refer to him as Sergeant Nicholson or just "the sergeant."

Mother joined the men toward the end of their visit, and they talked about mutual interests and played cards while Nellie, Sarah, and I worked some more on my quilt.

They left about ten o'clock, and we went up to bed.

### Friday, March 12

No snow today, but it was overcast with no sun. I was up early to go to school, and Father was getting ready to go hunting with Mr. Minor.

School was as always, though we had a mathematics test that I helped Mrs. Baglin correct. The children seem bored. We need some nice weather with sun to chase away the cobwebs. I can hardly wait for warmer days. Winter is so long and often depressing.

It's depressing, too, because Grandfather is ill. He does not seem to be getting better.

After I went home from school, Nellie and I did some more piecing on our bed quilts. Sarah helped for a while, but Normie was very energetic today, and she spent a great deal of her time with him, trying to entertain him. He needs some sunshine, and to be able to go outside to play, just as our scholars do.

No one called this evening. Perhaps the winter gloom has overtaken everyone. I'm still not feeling too well. I need some sunshine. I'm already planning my flowerbeds in my head. I can't wait until it is time to plant. Perhaps Father will help me with some shrubs.

### Saturday, March 13

I arose today to another cloudy day. It seems as if the sun never wants to shine. I know I would feel better if the weather would be warmer and if there was sun.

Father and I took Bessie and the wagon and went around

the Pine Tree to carry Nellie home. Because I'm still not feeling well, Father then took me to see Dr. Kerrmann in Woodbury. He thinks I have a touch of the grippe that Sarah, Normie, and Mother had earlier. He said I need to rest more and stay warm. As if that is possible during these cold Connecticut winters. Sometimes I feel like I can never get warm. My room gets so cold when the fire has burned down during the night that even with blankets I'm shivering.

While we were gone, Mother and Sarah went up to Aunt Ruth's to visit Grandfather.

During supper, they said he didn't seem to be any better, but they were able to talk with him for a while. Aunt Ruth told them it doesn't look as if he is going to get better, and that he is dying of old age. It made me feel sad. Yes, Grandfather is old, but life goes by so fast, no matter what age you are. I remember that when I was sixteen time seemed much slower, but now that I'm older, it just seems to fly. Perhaps it is because I was a student then, and now that I am helping as a teacher, there is more to do, and time goes by faster.

It seems like not too long ago I was wishing to be sixteen and now I'm almost out of my teen years. What lies ahead for me? I wish I knew how and where I would spend the next few years. Will I still be living with my parents? Will I be a teacher? Will I be married, with a husband and children to care for?

## Sunday, March 14

Today was very rainy, and we did not go to church. Later, it seemed as if the day was crying with us, adding its tears to ours.

The day had turned very sad because late in the afternoon my cousin, Ernest, rode down from Aunt Ruth's to tell us that Grandfather had died at three o'clock. We were all very sad, but it was even sadder for Mother because he was her father. Although we will all miss him, she will miss him most of all. Her mother died after she and her twin sister, Laurie, were born and so her father was the only parent she ever knew. I feel so bad for her.

I know how terrible I would feel if something happened to her or to Father. I know it must happen someday, but I hope it's a long time from now. I can't bear the thought of not being with them.

After a light dinner, we all sat in the parlor, talking about

Grandfather and feeling very sad. Mother tried to tell stories about when she was growing up, but she kept tearing up and finally she and Father went up to bed. Sarah and I stayed in the parlor near the fire for a while but soon followed them upstairs. Normie was sleeping soundly, Sarah found, but we knew it would be a fitful, sleepless night for the adults of the house.

### Monday, March 15

At last a day with some sun, but we are so sad. I did not go to school because I needed to be home to be with Mother and Sarah. Mother was very quiet, feeling very sad because of Grandfather's death. Even though he was very old, a parent's death must be very difficult to accept, especially when he is the only parent you had all your life. I feel so sorry for her though she tries to appear as normal as possible.

Because of how Mother felt, we did not wash today, though for some reason Monday always seems to be wash day. Sarah and I did do some baking because there will be callers who will stop in to express their sadness over Grandfather's death, and we must be able to offer them some refreshment.

In the afternoon, Sarah and I took the buggy and called upon Aunt Josephine, where we took tea with her and Ernest. We were anxious about leaving Mother and Normie for too long, so we departed early for home.

When we arrived, we found that Father, who had gone in to work for a few hours, had left early to be with Mother and to help with Normie. In the evening, some of our neighbors stopped by to offer their condolences and to bring some baked goods and casseroles. The food was gratefully received because no one feels very much like cooking.

### Tuesday, March 16

Again, the rain is adding to our family's tears. Today was Grandfather's funeral. He is to be buried in Center Cemetery where our Grandmother, Laura, is buried. It is all so sad. Mother feels the loss of the only parent she ever knew. Though some of her sisters and brothers remember their mother, she and her sister were born just a few days before their mother died. I try to picture what it would have been to grow up without a mother, but Sarah and I are so lucky to have both our parents and will never know what that was like.

I pray that Sarah remains well so she will live a long and happy life with Frank and Normie and any other children they may have someday. She has said she would like to have daughters. I hope that happens for her. She said she even has ideas on what she would name them. One would be Eunice after me! That would be exciting, to have a baby niece named after oneself.

Sarah could not go to the funeral because she had to watch Normie so I stayed with her. Mother and Father went first to the church and then to the cemetery.

Aunt Fannie, Mother's sister, came up on the cars to attend the services. She stopped for tea with us after the funeral and stayed overnight. Dinner was quiet because both Mother and Aunt Fannie seemed engrossed in thought, probably about their father. We all retired early.

I for one had difficulty falling asleep. The room was cold, and it seemed like forever for me to feel warm under the blankets. I keep thinking about Grandfather and wished I had felt up to going to the funeral, but Mother said since I had been feeling poorly that I should stay at home with Sarah and Normie.

I keep thinking, as I often do, if there is a hereafter. Do we get to see our loved ones again, ones we lost throughout the years of our lives? Do we look the same? How could we when our bodies are put in graves, as Grandfather's was today. I sometimes have a difficult time believing some of the things that religion teaches us.

**Wednesday, March 17**

We're still in winter even though it is close to spring. More snow, but only squalls that did not amount to much in the afternoon.

Father and Mother and Aunt Fannie went up to Aunt Josephine's with the rest of the brothers and sisters and their spouses and stayed there all day. We had made a ham and pies for them to take for lunch and supper.

Sarah and I stayed home with Normie. I did not go to school.

George called on us to express his sympathy over Grandfather's death. He had attended the funeral where he saw Mother and Father but noticed that Sarah and I were not there so decided to call on us today. Since Sarah was here, he stayed and had tea and cake with us. We sat in the parlor for some time, talking about Grandfather and other matters. He left about five o'clock.

When Father came home later, we learned he had gone to the post office during the day and brought a letter for me from Willie. It was good to hear from him. He is at school, of course, and is at home with his father while his mother is here for the funeral. He said he is coming up on the cars Friday.

Aunt Emeline stopped on her way home from the gathering at Josephine's, and we had a nice visit.

No one called in the evening so after dinner Sarah and I played cards. Before Normie was put to bed for the night, I read to him for a while until he was sleepy and offered no protest when Sarah took him upstairs. I sat with Mother and Father for a while when they came home, but they were tired and went early to bed. I stayed for a while reading, but I had no interest in what I was reading so I soon followed them upstairs.

### Thursday, March 18

We finally had a nice day, though it was still cool. I went to school, and in the afternoon Aunt Harriet and Aunt Fannie were with us for tea. They were saddened and will be so, I feel, for some time. As I've said, it is not easy to lose a parent, no matter what their age.

Mrs. Seymour and Carrie also called at that time, and we had a very nice visit with them.

After the Seymours and Aunt Harriet left for home, we had dinner. Later, while Aunt Fannie and Mother and Father talked in the parlor, Sarah prepared Normie for bed and then came to my room and helped me piece on my bed quilt. It seems everyone wants to stay busy to keep sadness from overwhelming them.

It's difficult to think of never seeing Grandfather again. He has been a part of our lives for so long. My ferule is even more precious to me now because he made it for me. I hope that someday I will be the teacher that he always believed I was meant to become.

I know I would never be able to use the ferule for its purpose of disciplining female scholars. It's not that it's painful like the hickory stick for boys, which they tell me stings. The ferule used on the palm of the hand is more noise than pain, and I think it is meant more to scare than to inflict hurt. I don't think I would want to scare the girls, either. The ferule, I feel, will be more a keepsake, made for me by my special grandfather.

### Friday, March 19

There was more snow today. I don't think it will ever stop. The weather seems to match our moods. Mother misses Grandfather so much but is somewhat cheered because Aunt Fannie is staying with us for a while. They spend a lot of time talking about the "old days" when they were young with their brothers and sisters and how Grandfather took such good care of them. They also took care of each other, as, I understand, it is so often with large families. The oldest help the youngest.

I listen to their many stories with wonder. Times were much harder when they were younger, perhaps because they didn't have a mother. I wonder what it would be like to have several brothers and sisters. It's always been just Sarah and me. Perhaps we are so close because we only have each other. Sometimes Mother doesn't hear from some of her brothers or sisters for some time, and I know it hurts her that some have moved farther away, and she can't see them as often as she once did.

We had wanted to go to Uncle Thomas Tyrrell's today, but because the snow was so deep and the weather so stormy, we decided to stay at home. Uncle Thomas is Grandfather's brother, and he, too, is old now. Because he lives in Roxbury, we do see him often. He is a great storyteller. Perhaps it runs in the family.

I wonder if I could ever write stories like Uncle Thomas and Mother and Fannie tell, or, perhaps, poetry. I love my books of stories and poems. It would be wonderful to be able to put my thoughts on paper and even more wonderful to have others read what I have written.

Sometimes I wish I could put my thoughts about George down on paper. Perhaps that would help me sort out my feelings for him, though he has not said anything to me or to Father.

Willie came up on the cars today and was with us for dinner, but then Father carried him to Aunt Josephine's to stay with them.

### Saturday, March 20

The snow is very deep but some of the roads were passable for the buggy when I carried Aunt Fannie to the bridge where she met Uncle Oliver and Willie. Willie has been staying with Uncle Oliver and Aunt Josephine, so he could spend some time with Ernest before he and his mother return home to New York. Aunt Fannie was going to stay the night with Uncle Oliver and Aunt Josephine before they take the train tomorrow.

Uncle Oliver was also carrying Leana home. She had been visiting a friend in town. After leaving them, I stopped to visit Eliza Vose and Millie. We talked about the school and other children. Then I called at Mrs. Bronson's and took tea with her.

George called and seemed happy to see me there. We enjoyed talking about events at church and in town, but I could not stay very long because the snow was blowing, which would make some of the roads very difficult for Bessie to get through, and I wanted to be home before dark. George walked me out to the buggy and helped me in and then returned inside to visit more with Mrs. Bronson.

When I came home, Sarah and I played with Normie to amuse him because he could not go outside today. Sarah is sad because Frank did not come from New Milford because of the weather.

After supper with Mother, Father and Sarah, the night was uneventful. Sarah put Normie to bed early, and then we sat in the parlor by the fire and talked until she also retired for the night. I feel so bad because she is lonely for Frank, but they will soon be together in their new home.

I read the Bible some and mostly sat by the fire thinking about George and wondering what our relationship is going to be. He still has not said anything, so I have to believe we are just friends, as we have been since we were children. I went to bed early and had some pleasant dreams.

### Sunday, March 21

I rose early to find a more pleasant day than yesterday. It was still windy, and because the roads would be difficult to drive through, Father decided we would not go to church. Because of that, it was a more leisurely Sunday because we did not have to rush around getting ready to leave so to be on time for services.

Mother, Sarah, and I fixed a big breakfast of ham, eggs, and coffee, which we greatly enjoyed. We also had some bread, which Mother had made yesterday, and we sweetened it with her wonderful butter and strawberry jam. Then Father went out to the barn to care for the animals and to bring in wood for the fire while we cleaned up the kitchen and dining room.

Mother, Sarah, and I talked as we washed and dried the dishes and put them away. Then Mother started a fire in the parlor, so we could spend the morning sewing and talking. She asked about my visits with Eliza and Millie and Mrs. Bronson yesterday. I told her about seeing George at Mrs. Bronson's and how nice it had been to see him. Sarah looked at me with a little smile, but she didn't say anything. I think she is wondering if George would be calling on me as a suitor.

I don't think that is going to come to pass. I'd like to talk to Sarah about what I'm feeling about George, but I fear it would be for nothing since there doesn't seem to be anything to talk about.

The rest of the day I worked on my quilt and read some. No one called, probably because of the roads.

At night the roads were better so we went down to the schoolhouse for a meeting of the Board of Supervisors about scholar attendance.

## Monday, March 22

Today was also a pleasant day, but again very windy as was yesterday. The roads, however, are more passable so Father went up town to do some errands and to check the mail after taking care of the animals. He brought the mail home and then went to work.

Mother and I washed clothes and because the yard is full of snowdrifts, Sarah helped us hang everything on lines around the kitchen. The heat from the wood stove made them dry quickly, after which we folded everything that did not need ironing and put the linens and clothing away.

Normie was full of energy today. He needs to get outside to run around, but the snow is still too deep and drifted. He would disappear in a snow bank.

There is no school this week. Mrs. Baglin has gone away to visit relatives for the holiday, so I had more free time than usual.

I spent the day tidying my room and daydreaming. I know I'm being silly, but I find myself thinking more and more about George. I wish I knew what he is thinking. I wish I knew how I felt about him calling on me in a different way than as a friend.

No one called this afternoon or evening. Mother is keeping busy with some embroidery, but every now and then I see her just looking out a window or at the fireplace. She is probably thinking of her father. I know she misses him very much, and now with Aunt Fannie having returned home with Willie, she has no one to talk to about their various memories of how it was when they were growing up.

### Tuesday, March 23

It was a pleasant day for March, which sometimes seems like winter and other times like spring. I awoke early but lay in bed thinking about what I would do that day. Without school, the days seem long, but there are always things that need to be done.

I dressed quickly because my room was so cold and went downstairs to find Mother already at work making breakfast. I set the table in the kitchen, which felt so warm because of the stove. Sarah was dressing Normie there because it was warmer than the upstairs where the fires had long since gone out during the night.

After breakfast and after Father had gone to work, Mother began the ironing. I had dampened the clothes and started heating the irons. Then, while Mother was making bread and cake for supper, I ironed some, and Mother finished it after luncheon.

We stayed in all day, and no one called. I sewed some on a new dress for church, and Sarah helped me with the hem.

### Wednesday, March 24

It was another cold and windy day. March is being its wintry self today. After breakfast, Father went to work, and Mother and I cleaned up the kitchen and made the beds. After lunch, Father came home and we all went up to visit with Aunt Harriet and Uncle Henry and Ella.

We had a nice time. Ella, Sarah, and I played cards while the others talked. I would love to talk to someone about what I'm thinking about George, but I don't think that it should be Ella. She would tell her mother who would tell my mother. I don't think

Mother and her sisters ever keep any secrets from each other.

Whenever they are together, it's all talk about the family, those here in town and those farther away. I think Aunt Fannie, Aunt Laurie, and Aunt Lydia, even though they don't live here, are kept very informed about events in every family member's life. If I told Ella, it would be no time at all before Willie or Walter or some other of my cousins would be teasing me about my new beau, and I don't even have a beau. I think what I still have is a friend.

I believe if a man is interested in calling on a woman, he usually speaks to her father or to her parents first. If that had taken place, Father would have told me. I understand it can be a very formal process. I'm not sure I would be ready for such a change in my life, even with someone I have known for a long time. George is a very dear friend, and I would hope that he always would be, no matter what happens in the future.

We came home for dinner, and afterwards Sarah and I worked some more on my quilt. After Normie went to bed, we sat in the parlor for a while talking. Father read the paper out loud so we all knew what was happening in the area and the world.

## Thursday, March 25

Another windy day, but it was more pleasant than usual. I spent the morning helping Mother tidy up the house, and then spent the afternoon visiting with my friend Carrie. We had a nice visit.

Carrie is someone I could possibly talk with about my questions about George, but I am still reluctant. I'm afraid people will think I am just being silly, imagining something that isn't so. It's true, I have only seen him at social occasions and when he calls on our family, but I sense there is more than is being said at the present time. I wish I knew what to do. It's not ladylike to speak to him. I must wait, perhaps forever, for him to speak his intentions to Father, if indeed he has any. I wish I knew, and I wish I could make a decision about how I would feel about that.

There was some happy news today. Carrie told me that Ella Seattin had a baby. I wonder if I will ever be so lucky to have a husband and children. Or will I be an old-maid schoolteacher, living home with my parents or in someone's household until I am very old and cannot teach anymore? Then what would happen to me? What a terrible thought that is. I want to be like Sarah, to have a home and family of my own. Will I ever have that? I don't know. Perhaps falling in love, if that were to happen, would change these conflicting thoughts.

Sarah is very happy because Frank arrived this afternoon on the cars and will stay until Sunday afternoon. Father carried him home from the depot.

Dinner was a happy time with Normie so happy to see his papa, and I knew from the way Sarah looked at Frank, that she is very happy he will be here for a few days. He took tomorrow off from work so he could enjoy a long weekend.

Mother, Sarah, and I prepared dinner, and afterwards Mother and Father went out to return some calls to our neighbors. Sarah, Frank, and I played cards for a while, and then I put Normie to bed so Sarah and Frank could have some time together.

### Friday, March 26

Today I awoke to a very pleasant day. The sun was shining, and birds were singing. I can almost believe that warmer weather will soon be here. I can't wait to plant flowers and feel the good earth in my hands. It is also Good Friday.

We all gathered for breakfast in the dining room. It seemed as if it was a special occasion because we all were there. Mother had taken great pains to make an extra-special breakfast and to make the table look nice.

Sarah and Normie are so happy that Frank is here. I confess to a moment's jealousy when I saw them together at table, but I love Sarah and am glad she is happy. Normie sat between his parents, looking from one to the other, as if he couldn't believe they were both here with him. He misses his papa, but soon they will all be together in New Milford. Of course, Mother loves having Normie here and will miss him. For now, though, she dotes on him. Sarah says he is being spoiled, but I know Mother believes that loving him is not spoiling him.

Since Father did not have to work today, we were able to spend more time over breakfast, talking and just enjoying being together.

After breakfast, Sarah and I decided to paint Easter eggs with Normie. Of course, at 2 years old, he isn't able to do it himself. We prepared the eggshells for coloring, keeping them intact except for a tiny hole, and will use the eggs for baking later. Because it is a holiday, we can expect people to call and will need to have refreshments to offer them.

We had such fun doing the eggs, but very soon we were finished, and Sarah took Normie upstairs for a nap while Mother and I started baking. We made bread, cakes, and two apple pies, which made the kitchen smell so inviting.

After all the baking, no one visited this afternoon, and we had an early supper before retiring to the parlor where Father read some from the Bible and the newspaper. He said that the Tobacco Growers Mutual Insurance Company has incorporated in Connecticut. I'm not sure how that would affect small tobacco farms. After some conversation, we went to bed early.

### Saturday, March 27

The weather changed overnight, and when I awoke this morning my windows revealed a snowy day. Later in the afternoon the snow changed to rain and washed away the snow on the roads and pathways.

After breakfast, Sarah and Mother baked some more bread and cakes while I watched over Normie. He and I played with his train and created buildings with blocks on the parlor floor. We stayed as close to the fireplace as we could to ward off the chill that you could feel through the windows.

After luncheon, our baking came to good use because Aunt Josephine and my cousins Ernest and Elena called and stayed the night. Ernest and Elena are younger than I am, but fun to be with. They are full of energy. For supper, we grouped about the dining room table, talking about family matters and what was happening in town. There was so much to talk about so there was no problem keeping the conversation going.

Sarah and I played charades with Elena and Ernest, keeping them entertained while their mother visited with our parents. While Mother and Aunt Josephine cleaned up the kitchen, Father went out to the barn to care for the animals.

It was fun spending time with family. Later we were all in the parlor, enjoying some of Mother's homemade cider.

I felt tired so I went up to bed early but didn't sleep. I just lay there until Elena joined me later. We chatted for a while before finally going to sleep.

## Sunday, March 28

Despite it being a sunny day and Easter, we did not go to church because Mother and Father wanted to spend as much time with Aunt Josephine as they could because she and Elena and Ernest were going home tonight.

While our parents were visiting, Sarah and I took Elena and Ernest for a walk down to the river. It was not too cold, but Marchy, of course. Hopefully we will soon be rid of the snow and the wind. We saw some ducks enjoying the sun by the river, but they soon flew off when we came too close to them. When we returned to the house, we prepared lunch

After an early supper, Sarah carried them home and visited for a while with Uncle Oliver before returning. Mother and Father had gone calling, and Frank had returned to New Milford, so I was alone with Normie in the evening until Sarah returned. We played with his toy train and his toy soldiers for a while.

When Mother and Father returned from their visits, Sarah put Normie to bed, and the four of us played cards for a while. Sarah was quiet, probably because Frank had left to go back to work tomorrow. Soon she and Normie will be joining him in New Milford. Mother and Sarah will be going up to the new house to do some unpacking once Frank tells them all is ready and everything has been delivered. I will miss them. It's been so nice to have them here, and it reminded me so much of when we were young and spent so much time together.

## Monday, March 29

It was a nice day today but very windy. In the morning Mother and Sister did the wash while I was at school. Our scholars were very energetic today, and recess was filled with much activity and games. It was difficult getting them settled down when we came in, but the afternoon went by quickly, and I was soon on my way home, walking quickly because the wind was beginning to make the day feel cold.

Once I was home, I cleaned the north chamber upstairs. Later I finished my bed quilt. I can't believe it is finally done. It has taken so long to complete, even with all the help I had from others. Now I will be very warm in my bed even after the fire goes out. It will also make my room look very pretty.

Carrie came to call and had tea and cakes with us. After she went home Mother, Sarah, and I began preparations for supper.

Father came in from work, bringing the mail and a newspaper. After supper, we sat in the parlor, talking about items in the paper. Father said he heard that the Republican convention will be held June 2 to 8 at Exposition Hall in Chicago and the Democrat convention from June 22 to 24 at the Merchants Exchange in St. Louis, Missouri.

After discussion about who would be the likely candidates for president and vice president, we all went to bed early.

### Tuesday, March 30

It was a very nice day today, but windy like so many March days are. I went to school for half the day, but Mrs. Baglin didn't need me in the afternoon so I returned home and helped Mother do the ironing. I also finished cleaning the upstairs rooms. Spring cleaning is almost completed, and everything looks so clean and fresh.

I'm particularly pleased with how my new bed quilt looks. The colors make the room look so cheerful and welcoming.

During the afternoon, Aunt Harriet called and stayed for an early dinner. She was on her way to see Ella and the new baby.

For some reason lately, I feel very tired. I don't think I have fully recovered from the sickness I had. It was all I could do to stay awake after dinner. I don't think I should feel this tired just because I did some cleaning. It has never made me feel like this before.

After Aunt Harriet left, I retired early, hoping I would feel more energetic in the morning. I don't know why it is taking so long to feel better.

### Wednesday, March 31

Today was very nice despite being windy. It was a typical March day in New England. When I walked to school this morning, I could feel spring in the air despite snow still being on the ground in spots. Soon I will be able to start planting, though Father says the beginning of May should be the earliest that I can put new plants in the ground. I have some seeds started inside and can't wait to get some of the young sprouts planted outside. Some of them I will bring to school, so our scholars can learn about the joy of planting new life in the soil.

While I was at school, Father and Sarah took the cars to New Milford to see Frank for lunch and to do some shopping. Mother was also going to start some unpacking at their new house. I would have liked to go but they left early in the morning, and Mrs. Baglin needed me to help with some testing. Our scholars performed well today. The Board of Supervisors should be pleased with their progress.

Grandfather Squire, a friend of Father's, came to visit in the afternoon and Mother insisted that he stay to dinner. Dinner conversation was spirited and entertaining, and after enjoying apple pie with our tea for dessert, we spent some more time talking in the parlor until Grandfather Squire left for home.

We took turns reading from the Bible and then went upstairs to bed.

### Thursday, April 1

Today was a beautiful day. After school, I went to Emeline's for a visit. She wanted Mother to help her dye her dress, so I carried her home in the buggy. While she and Mother worked on the dress, I made tea and later, while the dress was soaking, we sat at the kitchen table drinking tea and eating rolls and butter. It was very cozy by the stove, which was still warm from baking.

Life can be so wonderful, especially when family members are together. I love listening to Mother and other members of the family talk about when they were growing up here in Roxbury. It wasn't easy for my Mother and her sisters and brothers because their mother died so young, but they all seem to remember those years fondly. It's so nice to be part of a large family. I can't imagine what our lives would be like without all these aunts and uncles and cousins.

Father was not home this afternoon. He had gone to South Britain to attend a trial.

After Emeline's dress was dry, Mother hitched Bessie to the buggy and carried Emeline home. I had begun dinner preparations when she returned so everything was ready when Father came home from the trial.

### Friday, April 2

After school, I walked over to Emma Beers' house and spent the afternoon with her. She is a friend of my mother's, but sometimes she seems much younger. I find that she and I have much in common, in addition to our mutual love for my mother. She fixed me some tea and little sandwiches, and they were wonderful. We talked for what seemed like hours. I had a very nice time. Later in the afternoon, Emma brought me home, just in time to find a horse and buggy at the front porch.

Mrs. Hodge had come to call. Emma and I joined them for another cup of tea in the parlor before Emma left for home to fix dinner for her family. Mrs. Hodge left soon after, and Mother and I cleared the table and washed the cups before starting dinner preparations.

We had a very quiet evening. After dinner, we spent some time reading in the parlor before retiring early for bed.

I am having trouble sleeping. Even with the fire going and my new quilt, I feel cold. Also, I can't stop my thoughts. I haven't seen George recently since there have not been many events to attend at church or in town, and he has not called. I suppose he is busy with work and activities at home.

### Saturday, April 3

I arose early to find a cloudy, gray day, but fairly warm. Mother, Father, Sarah, Normie, and I had breakfast, and then after the dishes were washed and put away, Sarah and I hitched up Bessie to the buggy and drove up to visit Aunt Josephine and Ernest, Elena, and Oliver. We were glad we took the buggy because it began to rain later.

While we were at Aunt Josephine's, George stopped to call. I was pleased to see him, as I haven't seen him for some time, it seems. I think he was very surprised to see me there, though Sarah said later she thinks he stopped because he recognized Bessie and the buggy at the gate, as most people in town would.

While we were having tea, I did notice Sarah looking at him in a very interested way, and I knew she was wondering what led him to call this afternoon.

George was very cordial to all throughout the afternoon, and I hope he didn't notice Sarah's scrutiny. Aunt Josephine served some lovely teacakes. I think we all ate too much.

While we were there, Frank came by. He had gone to our house and Mother had told him where we were. Sarah was very glad to see him, of course. Georgianna Squire also called.

We stayed until about 4 o'clock. Frank hitched his horse to the back of the buggy and took the reins on the way home. Sarah could not keep her eyes off him, and his being there kept her from saying too much to me about George's call at Aunt Josephine's.

Later, however, when we were setting the dining room table for supper, she wondered aloud about what had made George stop at Aunt Josephine's today and that perhaps he hoped I would be there.

Since he really did not have much to say to me, except pleasantries, I did not make much of his call and asked her not to speak of it to Mother and Father, unless they asked who was at Aunt Josephine's.

Dinner passed without any reference to our visit to our aunt's, and I was relieved when, after spending some time reading after supper, we all retired early. I fell asleep quickly and had several pleasant dreams that I was later unable to remember.

### Sunday, April 4

The rain that started yesterday continued throughout the night into this morning. Mother, Sarah, and I made breakfast while Frank and Father took care of the animals. After breakfast, Father took Frank part way to New Milford. There, Frank obtained a ride from a friend into town.

Because Father took the buggy, we did not go to church, so I was spared any comments from Sarah about George. I'm sure he was probably there. He rarely misses services. Even when we were children, he usually was always there with his parents. We are not as good, and often miss church, for various reasons.

I had received a letter Friday from Willie, so part of the afternoon was spent writing a reply that Father would mail tomorrow when he goes up town. Willie's letter was newsy and funny. I wish he lived closer. I so much enjoy his company. However, he must live where he is while he is in school.

Tomorrow Sarah and Normie will be leaving us for their new home in New Milford. I feel very sad, because I have become very used to her being here, and I love caring for and playing with Normie. We won't see them as much once they are in their new home, but I know it must be. Most girls do not stay with their parents for very long, but like Sarah, marry and have their own families.

I hope we will still see them often, just as we did when they lived in Danbury. She will make new friends in New Milford as well as continue seeing friends we know in Danbury.

### Monday, April 5

Today was a pleasant but windy day. But it was also a sad one for me.

Sarah left today to begin housekeeping in New Milford. Father carried her and Normie there in the buggy with her trunk, which she had spent last night packing. I offered to help her, but she said she could do it. I think she knew it would just make her departure more difficult for me.

I will miss her being here though I'm sure we will see her often. I know she is very excited about her new home and is anxious to begin keeping house there. Normie was so excited that he was going to be with his papa again that it was impossible not to feel glad for him. I will miss him, too. I enjoyed playing with him and helping Mother care for him when Sarah was not here.

I went to school but not even our scholars could take away my melancholy. It was very sad to come home after school and not hear Normie's sweet voice.

When Father arrived home, he put Bessie in the barn and then came in and changed his clothes before taking care of the other animals and barn chores. He brought in eggs from the chicken coop.

Dinner was quiet without Normie and Sarah. I pleaded a headache and went to bed early, but I know Mother and Father knew I just felt sad because Sarah had gone to her new home.

## Tuesday, April 6

The weather was very clear today, with a beautiful blue sky and hardly any clouds in the morning. When I came home from school, I helped Mother with the washing and then went up to the Hollow with Father. We saw several of our friends and neighbors at the Post Office and the store.

When we started for home, the sky had clouded over and there was a thundershower. I sat on the porch for a while, watching the lightning and listening to the thunder, enjoying the spring-like scent in the air. Soon it will be time to plant the gardens and the flowers. Father is insistent that we not plant until mid-May because of the chance of cool nights during April and early May and the chance of frost that would kill the new plants.

We had company at night. Mr. and Mrs. Squire and their family called in the early evening. We had coffee and cake in the parlor by the fire. Georgianna stayed the night, and even though she is younger than I am, we had a good time talking and playing cards and backgammon.

## Wednesday, April 7

It was a pleasant day today but very windy. It was almost like March, but the temperature was warmer.

I did not go to school today because Georgianna was here. Aunt Amelia also stopped by and helped me work on my new dress. It is a very light blue with a white lace collar and lace at the wrists.

We had a nice lunch, and afterwards Georgianna and I took a walk down to the river. The wind blew so hard that the tree branches were swinging rapidly back and forth. It seemed to push us down the road. It was cool by the river, but it was good to be out in the air without all the heavy clothes one must wear in the winter.

Other than this, I did not do much of anything. Aunt Amelia went home before supper, but Georgianna stayed another night.

## Thursday, April 8

The weather today reminded me of last month. It was very Marchy, cool and windy.

Mother, Father, Georgeanna, and I had a nice breakfast in the kitchen, and then Father and I went to Woodbury to see Dr. Kerrmann. Georgianna stayed with Mother, and was going to help her with lunch.

Since I had not felt very well since last month, Father felt Dr. Kerrmann should check me over to make sure I was quite recovered. I have been much better since the weather is warmer, and I have been able to get outside more.

Dr. Kerrmann agreed that warmer weather would help cure my ills. It was a very cold winter. I'm glad he did not propose any new potions or syrups to take because they really don't help my cough and seem to increase my fatigue. Perhaps Dr. Kerrmann is correct that the warmer weather should help me. I hope so. I'm tired of feeling poorly.

We arrived back home in time for lunch of ham and potatoes. After lunch, I went to school for a while to help Mrs. Baglin with our scholars.

Walking home after school, I felt chilled by the wind and was very glad to join Mother and Georgianna in our warm kitchen. Georgianna spent another night with us. We had such a good time talking and playing cards. It almost made me forget for just a little while how much I miss Sarah and Normie.

### Friday, April 9

This was another clear day but again very Marchy. After I came home from school, Georgianna and I went to visit the Finns and had tea and cake with them. After we arrived back home, Aunt Amelia called and stayed to supper with us.

Everyone went home after supper, and we were alone once more. It's always pleasant to have company or to visit friends and family. Now with Sarah and Normie in their new home with Frank, our house seems empty. I miss Normie's little laugh and playing with him. It seems strange not to see his toys in the parlor or to be able to visit with Sarah every day. Even though New Milford isn't so very far away, it seems like I never get to see them every often.

Of course, Sarah is busy settling into her new home, and Normie does take a great deal of her time. When she was here, she had us to help her. Now she must do everything herself or it doesn't get done. Frank is away most of the day, so he can't be of much help to her although when she was sick, he was quite helpful when he could be.

### Saturday, April 10

Today was very windy. Mrs. Hodge called on us in the afternoon. While we visited with her, Father took Bessie and rode up town.

It was not a good day for me. I am almost sick and lay abed for two or three hours. I feel very exhausted, though I did not do a great deal today. I was coughing some and hope I'm not having another bout of what I had in March.

Grandfather Squire came and stayed for dinner. He is always very talkative, and he and Father kept up a constant conversation, about town politics and farming as well as the hat industry. Father's major occupation is hatting, but like all our neighbors he is also a farmer. Father spends a great deal of time taking care of our animals as well as the fields and gardens. Winter is probably the only time he doesn't have work in the fields or gardens, but then there is the shoveling of snow and taking care of the animals as well as his work as a hatter.

I often wonder how he gets it all done. He also helps out neighbors when they need help, and they often come here to help him when he is putting in hay. It takes many hands to get farm work done, and Father has no sons to help him. Mother, Sarah, and I always try to help as much as we can, but we also have many chores that must be done to keep the house in order.

### Sunday, April 11

It was another Marchy day. We did not go to church, so I did not see George. I have also not been anywhere where I would have seen him. It would seem if his intention were to call on me, he would find some way to see me even if I don't get to church. This convinces me that he sees me as his childhood friend, someone to enjoy a sleigh ride or church supper with but not in a romantic way. Or perhaps he is just taking his time because we are young. I don't know how I feel. Sometimes I would like to have a suitor. Then other times, I'm happy the way things are. I think I'm not ready for the responsibilities that are part of being a wife and mother. It's fun to play with Normie but in the end it is Sarah and Frank who provide his care.

I am definitely sick again with a hard cold. I stayed quiet most of the day, either reading or resting on the sofa. I don't know why I keep getting these colds. It seemed that all I did today was cough.

Grandfather Squire came and stayed to supper but did not stay all night.

I went to bed early but could not sleep because of coughing. Finally, about midnight, I finally fell asleep.

### Monday, April 12

It was very clear today, but windy, as usual.

After breakfast, Mother did the washing, but I did not help. It is a long process that takes her almost all day. After putting the wash through a wringer to get out most of the water, she went outside to hang them to dry. The clothes smell so good when they are brought in after being out in the sun and wind.

I still felt poorly so I didn't go to school. My chest feels sore because of the coughing.

Father went to work, and then Mother and I were alone. No one called.

I spent the day reading "The Innocents Abroad" by Mark Twain. For lunch, Mother and I had chicken soup and biscuits, and then I laid down for a while.

I woke up in time to help Mother with supper, and after supper I went early to bed. I was so tired because I haven't been sleeping well. It seems as if I cough all night. None of my potions or cough syrups seem to help.

### Tuesday, April 13

It was very windy today. I am still not feeling very well, so I didn't go to school. Because Father is working at Mr. Seymour's today, Mother and I went to Woodbury to see the doctor. After he examined me, he said my cold seemed better but that I should continue to rest and eat well. After leaving the doctor's office, we called at the Lamberts where we also saw Mary Greene and enjoyed tea and cakes and good conversation with them.

Just after we arrived home, Grandfather Squire came to visit and stayed for supper. We had lamb stew with lots of potatoes and carrots from our root cellar.

Grandfather left for home a short while after supper, and Mother and I did the dishes and then spent some time reading in the parlor. I went to bed early because I was so tired. I wonder why I am always so fatigued. I remember going to parties and staying out late, and still getting up in the morning full of energy. It seems like it has been a long time since I felt that way.

## Wednesday, April 14

It was a wonderful warm day today. Even though I am not feeling quite as sick as I was, I stayed home from school.

Henry, our farm hand, helped Grandfather cut some wood while Father went to work at the Seymour's.

I am feeling low today. I am so tired of being sick. Even the warm weather hasn't helped me to feel that much better, though it is nice to feel warm. Mother has been making me soups and puddings that I can eat easily without hurting my throat. My cough is worse in the morning and gets better as the day gets warmer.

Grandfather stayed the night so our supper table conversation was lively. Father and Grandfather love to spar over politics.

I feel lonely. No one else called. I wonder about George, and why I haven't seen him. I don't know why I should care but in some way I do.

## Thursday, April 15

It was a beautiful day for a buggy ride. After finishing the breakfast dishes, Mother and I went to New Milford to see Sarah and Normie. We had a nice time. We went down on the green and walked about and then went back to Sarah's to have lunch when Frank came home. After he went back to work, we visited, and I played some with Normie. It was so wonderful to see them. We stayed so long we didn't get home until dark.

During the day, Henry went up town to get some supplies for spring planting, and Grandfather went home. Father had worked again at Seymour's.

We had a quiet supper. No one called, and we went to bed early.

## Friday, April 16

It was very rainy today. I stayed home again because I am still not feeling well. Perhaps I did too much yesterday. I lay abed part of the day.

No one called in the afternoon so after I had rested for a while I pieced some on the cushion for one of the parlor chairs. Once they are all finished, they will look very nice.

I helped Mother with supper, and then sat for a while in the parlor reading. My chest hurt some, but the coughing seems to be better.

## Saturday, April 17

It rained part of today. Since it was not very nice for an outing, I stayed at home, and that turned out to be a good decision because Katie and her brother Fred came up. Though Katie had another visit to make, Fred stayed to supper.

We had a very nice supper of stew, bread, and cake and good conversation. Then Katie came back, and she and Fred left for home.

I felt a little better today, but I did have some coughing in the morning. It seems to go away during the day, and then sometimes gets worse at night when I've gone to bed. Even though it is April, my room is still cold so that may be why I cough more then.

## Sunday, April 18

It was a very pleasant day. We all went to church where we heard Mr. Smith preach on the text of St. John 24.

George was there. He looked very handsome. After the service, he joined us outside in front of the church. When I was talking to some friends, I noticed that he was talking to Father. I wondered what they were talking about, though I wasn't close enough to hear. At one time, Father glanced in my direction and smiled, but he said nothing on the buggy ride home.

In the afternoon, George Squire and a friend of his came and stayed to supper. Aunt Emeline also called just before supper but didn't stay since she had to get home.

Father had brought me two oranges yesterday, which I enjoyed in the afternoon.

After we had supper and cleaned up, I wrote a letter to Aunt

Fannie and to my friend Ida. After Mr. Squire and his friend left, I read for a while and then went to bed.

Father never said what George spoke to him about after church services. It probably did not concern me, or perhaps because we had so much company today, Father decided to wait to say anything to me.

I find it very difficult to believe that George could be interested in courting me. He is very handsome and sophisticated while I believe myself to be plain and naïve to the ways of the world.

### Monday, April 19

It was cloudy and rainy today. I went to school, and in the afternoon, Mother and I did the washing. After hanging the laundry in the kitchen to dry, I sewed some more on a new dress I am making. It is a lovely color of blue.

John Kitcher, Emeline's husband, called in the evening, and we had cake and tea in the parlor. He stayed a while, talking to Father and Mother, and then left for home.

During the day and during the evening, I would catch Father glancing at me, and then he would look away. He and Mother were still talking in the parlor when I went to bed.

### Tuesday, April 20

It was rainy part of the day but it cleared off by the afternoon when I was walking home from school.

No one called in the afternoon before supper, so I did some stitching on my dress.

When Father came home, he came into the parlor where I was reading, and sat down on the chair opposite me. He looked very serious. He said he had talked to Mother and now wanted to talk to me. Meanwhile, I was wondering what this was all about.

He went on to explain that on Sunday George had asked him if he might formally call on me, and Father wanted to know how I felt about that before he gave George an answer.

I was speechless at first. I had been so sure that George still saw me as a friend and not anything more. Can it be true that he is interested in me as more than a friend? I didn't know what to say to Father. I admit I was a little embarrassed to be talking to Father about George as a possible suitor.

I like George. He's been my friend for what seems like always, since we were in school together. We have gone sleighing with other young people from church, we have been to the same church socials and private parties through the years. We have played parlor games together. But do I want him as a suitor? Am I ready for a suitor? Would I want to be engaged and then married?

Father saw my hesitation and said I didn't have to answer right away. He said to think about it for a while. If it is right, why do I hesitate?

When we went in to the dining room for supper, my head was filled with questions for which I had no answers. After helping mother clean up after supper, I went to my room where I sat on my bed and thought of everything Father had said.

George had spoken to him about calling on me. I went to bed amazed that what I had been thinking about for months had indeed become real. Did I want it to be real? That is indeed the question I need to answer.

### Wednesday, April 21

Today was a beautiful day. With my head full of questions that still had no answers, I went to school and then to High Bridge after school.

While I was gone, Father went up to the Hollow and brought home some geraniums that I will keep inside until they can be planted. We had quite a heavy frost this morning, so it is much too early for them to face the cold. They are such a beautiful shade of red. They make a very cheerful addition to the kitchen and the front hall.

After I came back from High Bridge, I made a cake and it was just in time because Mrs. Castle came to call.

I haven't talked to Father yet. I have no answer to give him because I'm not at all sure I want someone, even George, to call on me. I'm not sure I'm ready to take this step. But what if I say no now, will George find someone else? He probably will. He is very handsome, has a good job, and is from a fine family. And he obviously is ready to make a commitment to the future. What if his calling upon me becomes serious? Could it be that he is already serious?

As much as I would like to be married and have children in

the future, I'm not sure I'm ready to even think about it now. I love working with the scholars at school. I suppose if I married someday I could continue to do that, at least until I had a baby. But I don't know if I could stay home like Sarah does and take care of a house and children all day. She never seems to have any time for herself until Normie is in bed in the evening.

Then again, do I wait so long that I am considered a spinster, who lives at home with her parents or, God forbid they are gone, with a family of one of my students? I'm sure I would not want that. I wish I knew what to do. Why can't I make up my mind? For all that I have thought of this for some time, it seems very sudden.

### Thursday, April 22

This was a very pleasant day. When I came home from school in the afternoon, I found that Father had been plowing the garden and had gone to get a load of hay at the Castle's.

Despite how nice it was outside, I did not feel as well as I have, and went upstairs to my room where I covered myself with my quilt and went to sleep.

Later, Mother came up to see how I was and to tell me that supper was ready. I did not feel like eating, but I didn't want Mother to worry so I followed her downstairs where I tried to eat but was not very successful. She said what I needed was rest and wouldn't let me help with clearing or with dishes.

I went upstairs where I undressed and put on my nightclothes. It felt good to slip under the warm blankets and quilt. I soon drifted into sleep again.

### Friday, April 23

This was another pleasant day, and I was feeling better. After school, Mother and I went down to call on Mrs. Hodge and Mrs. Castle. While we were visiting there, Mrs. Rorraback stopped here. We found her card* when we returned. We will probably return the call in a few days.

Two days before church. I wonder if George will ask Father for my answer on Sunday. I'm still not sure what I want my answer to be. Why am I so confused? I need to talk to someone. This would be a very important step in my life. How I wish Sarah were here. Perhaps she could tell me how she felt when Frank asked to call on her. They are so happy, and they have Normie to love and care for.

Why do I hesitate? I know Father is wondering why I am taking so long to decide. If I say yes to George calling, it doesn't have to mean I will marry him.

*Calling cards: a social custom essential in developing friendships. The custom began in France in the 1800s. It became popular in the United States, especially New England, from 1840-1900.*

I don't even know if I could see him that way. He's always been my friend. Could I see him as my husband? Perhaps I am thinking about this too much. Calling upon someone does not necessarily lead to courting. All it means is that we will be spending more time together, and sometimes without a chaperone.

I sat in my room after supper tonight, trying to make up my mind as to what to do. Perhaps George doesn't expect an answer by Sunday. Perhaps I don't need to be this upset.

I'm beginning to feel poorly again. All this nervousness I feel is making me quite unwell. I must look at this in a positive way and not be so hesitant to make a decision.

But do I need to right now? I'm not sure what my future should be. I want to be a teacher, but I also would like to have a family. Can one do both? I don't think so because of the endless, repetitive work that is the role of a woman as keeper of a home. I have heard housework described as drudgery by many of my mother's friends. They sometimes complain about the laundry, ironing and mending, baking, and cleaning and other tasks that they must do day after day. In addition, some of them help their husbands on their farms.

Does the romance of courtship and marriage descend into such feelings? Since I spend so much time at school during the week and Father goes to work at the hat shop, it is obvious that Mother does most of the household and farm chores. How does she do it? I try to help her, but I know it is just a small bit of what she does every day. I know she is often very tired, especially when Father is unable to help because he has been called elsewhere.

I've read newspaper articles and magazines that set high standards for household tasks. I admit I enjoy baking when I have a chance to do it. There's nothing like the scent of an apple pie baking or hot bread or rolls fresh from the oven. But if I had to do it every day for a family, would I feel the same? Would it indeed become drudgery? It's fun when I go to Sarah's or help Mother, but do I want that for my life? Every day, would I want to care for children, make meals, and keep the stove and fireplaces burning? Then there is the sewing and canning, and cleaning, and other tasks too numerous to mention.

The chores seem unending for a wife and mother. But it has been our lot throughout history. Sarah is doing it, but it was difficult for her when she became ill. It was all she could do to keep up with Normie. She might not have gotten better if we had been unable to help her.

How would my life be different if I became a teacher? I could continue to live home, perhaps, unless my position took me to another town. Then I would need to live with some family, perhaps that of one of my students. What would be expected of me there if I taught all day? I would need to pay rent unless, of course, it was part of my monthly salary.

I would be a stranger in someone's home. There would be lessons to prepare, exams to correct, much more than I do now. I would need to keep the schoolhouse in good order. There would be other tasks to fill my day and night. But I would have no family of my own, like Sarah and so many other women I know.

Oh decision, you do not come easily.

### Saturday, April 24

It was cloudy and rained a little, a sour, mean day. Because it was Saturday, I did not have to go out, but helped mother around the house. I also finished the chair cushion.

Father went up town and brought back the mail. I received two letters, one from a friend of the family, Mrs. Haskins, and another from Carrie, which cheered me immensely and took my mind off other matters.

Because it was such a dreary day, no one called.

Tomorrow is Sunday. What shall I say to Father about George calling? Will George expect an answer tomorrow? I wish Sarah was here. She would know what I should do. George has been such a good friend to me, looking out for me when we were in school when someone would tease me. He's always been there for me. I just don't know if I'm ready to see him as someone who would call on me as a suitor. Could I love him? How do you feel when you are in love? Oh Sarah, why aren't you here?

I want to talk to Mother about this, but somehow can't bring myself to voice the subject. She knows about it, because father told me he had talked to her before talking to me. Why don't I feel comfortable about talking to her about this? Do I want to talk to her about the relationship between a man and a woman once they are married? Would I be too embarrassed if she brought it up?

I've heard my friends talking, but they are not married. They can't know how it would be. We are never alone with young men. There have always been adults at most of the functions we have attended. We are always with a group, I have never been alone with a man, not even George.

## Sunday, April 25

It was a much more pleasant day than yesterday. I rose early, apprehensive about going to church and seeing George. I have made no decision. Father said I could take some time, so I am hoping nothing more will be said today.

I bathed and dressed in the new dress I made for church, and then went downstairs to join Father and Mother for breakfast. Afterward I helped Mother by clearing the table and washing the dishes. Then we put on our outer clothing and waited while Father hitched Bess to the buggy. Then we set off for church. It's not a long ride, and I must admit I was very nervous all the way there. Father had not said anything at breakfast about George, so I was hopeful that my decision would not have to be made today.

There were several families arriving at the church at the same time and amid the confusion of tying the horses and people stepping out of their buggies, I did not know if George had arrived. Once in church I saw George's parents, but George was not with them. I felt relieved. No decision would be needed today.

Following the church service, we rode home, and Mother and I prepared lunch, after which we went to a meeting at the schoolhouse where we heard that Ella Clark had died that morning. It was very sad because she was quite young. Katie came home with us and spent the night.

## Monday, April 26

It rained in the morning today but cleared off by the afternoon. After I came home from school, Mother and I went down to Emeline's. Mother said Katie had gone home with Mrs. Rorraback, who had visited earlier that afternoon.

I hsd not said anything to Katie about George. I keep wondering why I am so unwilling to put my thoughts into words. Mother also has not raised the issue. Perhaps she feels I am too young. I am only 19. I feel too young. There is time in the future to think about courting, marriage, and children.

Sometimes I wish I could put it off forever. There is so much responsibility with a family. I see such changes in Sarah since she has had Normie. It's as if she is a different person now, and I suppose she is. She is a wife and mother, no longer a carefree young woman who lives with her parents. She has responsibilities.

Perhaps that is what concerns me. I want to stay as I am, living with Mother and Father, going to the schoolhouse to help Mrs. Baglin, and putting off for a while facing the inevitable events of being a grown up.

True, many of my friends already have suitors, and some have married. Their lives have completely changed, and they don't even talk about the same things any more. Now they talk about plans for weddings and children, and how they will furnish their homes. I feel like they are in a completely different place than I am.

I'm so happy in my pretty room at home that Mother helped me decorate. I just don't want anything to change, not any time soon at least.

## Tuesday, April 27

It was somewhat colder than yesterday. Mother washed clothes, and after I arrived home from school, I baked a cake and did some other work around the house.

Mother and Father went to Ella's funeral today. They said it was very sad. She was so young. Ella's mother said it just wasn't right that parents should survive their children.

I think all deaths are sad, no matter what the age of the person. It seems that the longer you had someone, the more difficult it would be to lose him or her. I miss grandfather, as I know Mother does. She sometimes is very quiet, and I think she is thinking of him. It must be so hard to lose one's parents. Mother never knew her mother because she died shortly after she and her sister were born, and I think that is very sad.

Today was as always at school. The younger children worked on their reading while the older scholars did math and geography. It was almost too cold to be outside at recess, but if the children don't get out and play and get some air, they get restless in the afternoon, so after lunch we all went outside. The younger children played hide and seek while the older ones had a tug of war.

Some of the boys were playing marbles while some girls played leapfrog.

## Wednesday, April 28

It was more pleasant today than yesterday. After school, I helped Mother do the ironing and baked a cake for supper. Then I worked outside for a short time, making flower mounds.

Emeline called late in the afternoon and brought us up to date on all the latest news of other members of the family. After she left, Father arrived home from work and brought a letter for me from Willie.

Willie's letter was full of news about school and his activities and his parents. He hopes they will be able to come to see us soon, but everyone is very busy studying and working. It won't be long, though, until school is out for the summer. Hopefully, he will be able to come for a visit then.

It was a quiet evening. No one called, and I spent it reading in the parlor by the fire. The nights are still not warm enough to not have a fire, and I was toasty warm curled up on the sofa.

## Thursday, April 29

It was clear this morning, but the wind blew up later and it commenced raining, so I was unable to work outside after school.

Because I didn't sleep very well last night because of coughing so often, I felt so fatigued that I was barely able to walk the short distance to the schoolhouse.

Mrs. Villey came and spent the day with Mother and visited with me when I came home. She had lots of news about her family and was very interested in hearing about Sarah and Normie and their new home.

In the evening, it rained very hard. After supper, I sewed on my bed quilt while Mother and Father read. No one called, probably because of the rain, and we went to bed early.

During the night, I awoke coughing, and it was difficult to get back to sleep because the rain was so loud on the roof over my head. My chest felt sore, and I found it difficult to find a comfortable position and get back to sleep. The cough medicines and potions the doctors have given me are not helping.

## Friday, April 30

After the rain last night, it was a cold windy day, just like January weather. I did not feel well so I didn't go to school. When I finally got to sleep last night, I had dreams, but I couldn't remember what they were about. I didn't sleep very well, so felt very tired all day.

Later in the day when I was feeling better, I sewed some and helped Mother with housework.

It was a cold, miserable day, and no one called.

As another Sunday approaches, I worry again that George will approach Father about my answer. I feel so confused about it all. I don't want anything to spoil the relationship I have with George now. We've always been such good friends. I don't want to lose that, and I think many things would change if he were to become serious about us having a future together.

I wish I knew what I want for my future. Becoming a teacher has always been very important to me. I look at the ferule that Grandfather made for me, and I think that it would be very difficult for me to give up that dream. From magazines and newspapers that I've read, it isn't as if a woman must marry these days. There are many new ways for a single woman to support herself. Times are changing, and women are becoming more accepted in roles other than those of housewife and mother.

## Saturday, May 1

1t was not a very pleasant day. It was much too cold to set out any flowers as I had planned. Instead, I stayed inside and did some sewing.

Father went up town, and while he was gone, Uncle Henry came to visit. He did not stay very long, and soon Mother and I were alone again.

When Father came home, he spent some time working in the barn, and then it was time for dinner. Father talked about who he had seen that day, including George, who he saw at the Depot. He said George was going to Danbury to see a friend and would spend Sunday there.

I was so relieved but at the same time wondered if the friend George was going to see was a man or a woman. Oh diary, what is wrong with me? Could I have been a little jealous? Is this the way you feel when you are jealous? I keep telling myself I want to remain friends with George, but is that only because I am nervous about a more serious commitment? I don't know. I'm just not thinking clearly.

Father started fertilizing the tobacco field today in preparation for when planting will take place beginning June 1. Father said an acre of land would yield 1200 or more pounds of tobacco that once harvested would be sold in New Milford.

### Sunday, May 2

It was cloudy this morning and commenced raining about noon. It was not a very pleasant day.

We got ready to go to church but finally did not go. Instead Mother and I spent more time than usual enjoying our lunch, drinking tea, and talking. I still cannot bring myself to say anything to her about George, and she didn't mention it. I think she believes that I will talk to her when I am ready, but I think I'm just nervous about talking about such personal feelings.

While I know she would understand, I think once I put all my thoughts into words, I might feel committed to something more than what I would want. I know Father and Mother won't rush me into marrying, but I remember how happy they were about Sarah and Frank. They were happy to see her settled, and now she has her own family.

In the afternoon, Millie Voss came and stayed to dinner. Later, I wrote to Carrie.

### Monday, May 3

It was a very pleasant day. In the afternoon Father and I went to Seymour's, and then Mother and I went up town to get the paper.

About 8:30, after supper, some friends of Mother and Father came to visit and told us that the file shop had burned down at half past seven. No one was hurt, but how sad for them. I wonder if it will be rebuilt.

Since I was still feeling unwell, I went to bed early, but Mother and Father and their friends talked well into the late hours. I had difficulty getting to sleep because I kept coughing. If I'm not better soon, I'll have to see the doctor again. I don't know why the syrups and tonics I've been given don't help. I feel more unwell in the morning, probably because of the coughing at night and lack of sleep, but as the day goes on I feel better, especially if it is warm. On cold days, sometimes I feel as if I can never get warm even if I sit next to the fireplace or stove.

### Tuesday, May 4

It was a beautiful day today. Because I have been feeling a bit poorly, Father took me in the buggy to see Dr. Hartwell and then we went to Sister's in New Milford where we stayed to dinner. Sarah was so glad to see us but lamented that Mother had not come.

Normie was also glad to see his doting grandpa and aunt. We had a good time.

Uncle Henry had also come to call and was also there for dinner, and we talked over our tea and cake until Father said we should leave for home.

It was a warm, delightful night to ride home behind Bessie, the clip clopping of her hooves and the bells on her harness echoing in the quiet of the night.

Mother was resting in the parlor when we arrived home, and was pleased that we had such a good time at Sarah's. I think sometimes she likes to be alone, to rest or do whatever she pleases at the time. All of us at some time enjoy our solitude. I know I do, especially on the days when our scholars have been more interested in play than doing their lessons.

I do know how they feel. When the weather is nice as it was today, it can distract you from what you need to be doing. It's days like this that make me anxious for summer and school vacation, but it won't be too long now. Time is really going by very fast.

## Wednesday, May 5

This was another pleasant day. Mrs. Baglin hasn't needed me this week, so I have been helping mother with spring-cleaning. There is so much to do. How do women do it without grownup daughters to help?

I started with my room. I took the carpet up, and Mother whitewashed. It made a beginning to cleaning house.

Tomorrow we plan to put up new wallpaper in my bedroom. My room is going to look so beautiful I don't think I will ever want to leave it. I just wish it could be warmer at night. Even with my new quilt, the room feels cold once the fire is out. Even though it is May, the nights can feel cool.

We were tired from our labors today so we all went to bed early.

## Thursday, May 6

It was a very clear day today. Mother, Father, and I had breakfast together before Father went to work at the hat shop.

After washing up the breakfast dishes, Mother and I papered my room and then worked hard all day with other house cleaning chores. There is always so much to do.

I often wonder what my chores would be if I didn't marry, and if I lived by myself or with another family. I don't think I would be able to live by myself. Spinsters often live with their parents, but what if they no longer have parents? What do they do then? Is it proper for a woman to live alone?

I know that times are changing, and that women are being accepted in many different types of work, but what is socially correct? I don't like to think about being alone, without my parents. I suppose I could live with Sarah and Frank if I would otherwise be alone. I love Sister, but how would Frank feel about that?

Why am I thinking about these things? I suppose it's because I am so confused as to what I want my future to be. Is it to be with George or someone else, perhaps? Or am I to be the spinster teacher, living with her sister or a student's family?

While I can't picture myself as a married woman with children,

I also don't see myself as being what people call an old maid.

Whatever should I decide about George? I haven't seen him recently. Perhaps he has changed his mind. If so, would he talk to Father about it? I know so little about these things.

### Friday, May 7

Today was not as clear as it was yesterday with many more clouds. Mrs. Baglin needed me, so after school I helped Mother paper her bedroom. I also took the kitchen carpet up and beat it. There was plenty to do all afternoon, and I felt more tired than usual.

We took some time between chores to have tea and some cake, and then went back to work, dusting and sweeping. I cleaned out some closets, making sure everything was neat and orderly.

During dinner of ham and baked potatoes, Mother, Father, and I talked about family matters and about the presidential conventions that will be coming up in June.

Father is quite interested in politics and enjoys going to town meetings where townspeople have the chance to speak their minds about local issues. He said sometimes those meetings get quite spirited and the monitor must bang the gavel to bring order back to the meeting. He said that is democracy in action, but it can become unruly.

After dinner, we cleared the table and washed up, then went into the parlor where we read and talked until it was time to go to bed.

### Saturday, May 8

Again, it was cloudy part of the day. We finished papering the bedroom and put away all the tools and stored the materials that were not used.

One of our horses had a colt. It is so sweet and is beginning to stand on its wobbly legs. It will be a while before it will be of use, but it will be fun watching him grow.

After lunch, when it was warmer, I went outside and set some of my plants in the ground. How good it feels to do this, to hold the warm earth in my hands. All winter I looked forward to planting.

Father said it is a little too early for some plants, and I have geraniums and other flowers that I keep indoors until there is no chance of frost.

Aunt Fannie and Willie arrived tonight, and we talked and talked, and had pie and tea. I can't believe it but none of us went to bed at all because we had so much to talk about and were having such a good time.

I imagine I will feel very tired tomorrow.

### Sunday, May 9

It was a wonderful warm day today. Sarah and Frank came over with Normie late in the morning. Because of all the company, we did not go to church, so I don't know if George was there or not. It's another week where I don't have to make a decision.

Even though I was tired from no sleep, after lunch with Willie and Aunt Fannie, Willie, Sarah, and I went for a walk and picked some flowers. We had a nice time. Later, Sister and I went for a ride up to the Squires and around by Emeline's, where we had tea and cake. Mother had been very glad to take care of Normie. I think she misses him since they moved into their new home.

Willie and Aunt Fannie went home at four and Sarah, Frank and Normie a little later.

After supper, Mr. and Mrs. Rorraback called as well as Ira Booth and his wife and Dwight Evans.

The day flew by because we had so many things to do and so many people to visit with. I admit I felt rather tired. It had been a very busy day. My cough is back despite the new tonic the doctor gave me. Nothing seems to help me feel better.

### Monday, May 10

While it was a nice day today, I felt dull and coughed as usual, so I didn't go to the schoolhouse. School is almost finished because the children are needed to help with planting on the farms.

Mr. Peet and his wife called during the morning, and we had tea and biscuits with them. After lunch, I felt better and helped Mother clean the front room. Father went up to get the mail and to do errands.

No one called in the evening, and I spent the night reading the Bible and one of Mother's magazines before going to bed.

### Tuesday, May 11

It was cloudy in the morning but cleared off later. After school, I cleaned and tidied the pantry. Then Father and I went around to Rorrabacks, and I called at Mrs. Jennings' house and had tea and conversation with her while Father did some errands around town.

I am still not feeling too well, but I don't feel any better if I stay at home so I might as well be active and get things done.

I'll be glad when school is finished for the year so I can stay at home without feeling guilty if I am feeling poorly. I can't seem to get over this cough, and it is worse at night, so I wake up feeling tired in the morning.

No matter what the doctor gives me, it does not seem to help my cough. Sometimes I cough so hard, it hurts my chest and back.

### Wednesday, May 12

Today was very pleasant but quite windy, though it was a warm wind, not like those icy winds of winter that made the air feel so much colder and chill your very bones.

Mother and I finished spring cleaning with the kitchen. After lunch, I put a few more flowers in the ground and then walked to the field where Father was planting corn. Soon it will be time for all the crops to be in.

School will be out soon because the older children are needed to help on the farms. I long for summer when perhaps my cough will get better.

I haven't seen George lately—has he changed his mind? Do I care? I don't know. Father has not said anything, so I think nothing has changed. George is still waiting for my answer to his request to call on me, but I'm so unsure of what I should say. I feel so confused. I have had no experience with this, but I suppose no girl my age would know what to do.

Father began plowing a new garden area. He is very proud of his new John Deere plough. He will soon be planting potatoes and early corn. He has also been cutting wood before spring farming chores begin. He has a large woodpile on the side of the house that is handy to the kitchen with a pile of cordwood and kindling. It is especially convenient in the winter because we don't have to go far to get more wood.

## Thursday, May 13

It was clear today but quite cold for May. Mother did the washing while I was at school. I helped by making dinner and managed to keep busy with some sewing and reading afterward.

No one came to visit, and we retired early.

I am still coughing, and this cool weather seems to make it worse. My room feels cold again, despite the warmth of my new quilt.

I am wondering if I will ever feel better. The pain in my chest makes it hard to breathe. Perhaps it will take the warm months to chase my ills away. I do hope so. Summer will be here soon, but not soon enough for me.

## Friday, May 14

I did the ironing in the morning. It is cold for this time of year, and we had a hard frost at night. I had thought to cover my flowers with newspapers, so they were protected from the cold.

Mother and I went up town and bought window curtains to spruce up the house.

We stopped at Mrs. Evans, also Julia Hull's, where we had tea and sandwiches.

I received a letter from Nellie Bronson. It's always wonderful to hear from friends. I will write a reply the moment I have a chance.

Later, George called and visited with Mother and me. He gave me a bracelet. It is very pretty, and very much like other trinkets he has given me through the years of our friendship. I did not feel there was any extra meaning to the gift. He did not make any reference to his discussion with Father, so I was very relaxed.

I have always felt close to George. After all, we have been friends all our lives. We went to school together in the little school where I now help teach. He was always very kind to me, even when we were young. Other boys might pull my hair, but George never did.

Perhaps our future is together, but there I go again. His calling on me does not mean we will be married. Somehow that comforts me at the same time I wonder what it would be like to know what your future would be and with whom.

## Saturday, May 15

It was another cold day, with also a frost at night. I finished setting out my plants but made sure to cover them in the evening. Later I put the kitchen carpet down.

Father set his eel lines and caught a nice mess of them that we will have for dinner tomorrow night. Father loves to fish. He and his friends often take a boat onto the river and fish half the day. While it is very nice that he enjoys it, if it pays off with supper, it's even better.

I received a letter from Mrs. Fabrique, who sent me a new necktie* that will look very nice with my new dress.

Since George was here the other day, I have been thinking more and more about what my answer should be to his calling on me. Father has not said anything, but I think he feels I'm being overly cautious in coming to a decision. How can I say no, I don't want someone calling on me, when the person who asked is such a dear friend? If I do say no, will George feel hurt? Will I lose him as a friend or would we be able to continue as we are?

We have been friends for so long. I would never want to do anything to cause him pain. Perhaps it is better to be friends first, before there is a more serious relationship. We certainly know each other well. There would not be many surprises, I'm certain, though shouldn't there be some mystery to a relationship or is it better to know everything about the person you will marry?

*Necktie: decorative piece of cloth worn with a gown or blouse and skirt.

## Sunday, May 16

For a change, it was a pleasant day, but still cool. We all went to church. George was not there. I wondered if he had gone to see his friend again. Could that friend be a woman? If so, I would imagine they are just that—friends. I would not like to think that he is seeing someone else now that he has asked to call on me. Oh diary, I fear that is a very jealous thought. I have made no answer to his request, so he is perfectly correct to continue his life as it is. Perhaps his friend is a man, and I have no reason to think otherwise.

We spent a quiet afternoon. I worked for a while in the flowerbeds, weeding and planting. We had the eels for dinner along with potatoes and vegetables. Mother had made a cake, which we enjoyed.

During the evening, while Mother and Father talked, I read through some of Mother's magazines, looking for possible remedies for my cough. Perhaps some kind of herbal extract would help me more than those the doctors give me. They don't seem to help but do make me feel sleepy. Unfortunately, I did not find anything that I felt would be beneficial.

I keep thinking I should talk to someone about my concerns about George. I can't talk to Father. I would be too embarrassed. I also don't want to talk to Sarah. I know she wouldn't tease me or in any way see my feelings as silly, but she is so happy with Frank and Normie that she might want me to have the same life she has. I'm not sure it's the life I want, at least not now. I don't know why I can't decide.

Perhaps I should talk to Mother. She's been married a long time and perhaps can look at life in a different way than Sarah. I need to think about this more or perhaps I am thinking too much about it so I'm getting more and more confused.

## Monday, May 17

It was another pleasant day. Mother did the washing, and I helped her some. Later I made dinner and was busy all day.

School is over for the year, and the summer lies ahead. Planting of crops is beginning, and Father has been to the store to obtain the needed supplies.

No one came to visit at night.

I went to my room early but was unable to sleep. I kept thinking about what I should do about George. I do care for him as a friend. If he officially calls on me, will that change to something more? I don't believe I can know him better because it seems like we have always known each other. Between school and church, we have always spent time together. Of course, that was always with other people. How would his calling on me be different from the past? Mother or Father would have to be here to chaperone. They are always here when he calls now. How would this be different?

The more I thought about it, the more I believe I should put aside my embarrassment and talk to Mother about my feelings and most of all about the questions that are nagging at me. How would this relationship be different? Would it necessarily lead to courting and marriage? Is it wrong to consent to his calling on me if I'm not ready for a more serious relationship? Is it fair to George?

### Tuesday, May 18

It was cloudy today, and though it looked like there would be a storm, it did not rain.

I did the ironing to help Mother and then sewed some on another bed quilt.

I also spent the afternoon working in the garden and picked some spring wild flowers for the kitchen table.

I love spring. I love to see the early flowers awakening from their long winter's sleep. I love to watch the trees as they leaf out to their full summer green. Autumn is beautiful with all the colors, but I think I like best that early green of the leaves in the spring.

I'd like to make a garden of wild flowers, including some that would bloom early in the spring and others that come along during the summer and fall. I think it would be very beautiful but would have to be planned so that there is something blooming all the time.

The first year would be the hardest because I would have to dig up the flowers and replant them each season. Imagine how beautiful the garden would be the next year. Some small shrubs that would stay green for the winter would be nice. They could go in now and the flowers be added as the seasons come.

I'm still not sure how I will begin my conversation with Mother about George. I need to do it soon. It will be more difficult the longer I wait, and he may want an answer before then.

### Wednesday, May 19

It was a very pleasant day. I went down to Emeline's and called at Mrs. Baglin's. When I returned home, I took a walk through the fields where I saw many of the early flowers I would like to have in my garden. I made a note to go back with a pail and trowel but first I must prepare the soil for the new flower garden.

Father said he would help me pick out some small green shrubs. He suggested I include a wild dogwood tree because many of the plants would require some shade.

Mrs. Castle called in the evening. We enjoyed her lively conversation and news of the town, and after she left for home, we sat in the parlor by the fire, talking. Since Father was there, I did not bring up anything about George to Mother. I need to pick a time when Father is out working in the fields or in the barn. She is often so busy during the day it is difficult to find the time I need. I'm not sure how I shall begin. I am so nervous; it is a very personal subject. I have no experience with someone calling on me or courting me. I don't know what to expect.

Even though it is George, I know things will change between us. I'm still not sure I want things to change. I would not want to hurt him so perhaps it would be simpler to just tell Father no, I'm not ready. Would George's feelings be hurt? Would he then look for someone else? How would that change our relationship? Would I care if he did find someone else? What am I to do?

### Thursday, May 20

It was very warm today. Mrs. Baglin came along, and I went up to the Hollow with her. Later, after she left, Emeline came up from Danbury and visited for a few minutes. She was on her way to New Milford to see friends. We had tea and sandwiches before seeing her on her way.

This seemed the perfect day to talk to Mother about George calling on me. Father would not be home for several hours, so I summoned up my courage and asked her if we might talk in the parlor. She did not seem surprised at my request, much as if she was expecting it.

I was uneasy as we sat down, but Mother was calm and waited patiently to hear what I had to say. I felt very awkward as I began talking even though I knew Father had talked to her about George asking for permission to call on me.

Eventually I became more relaxed. I don't know why I was so nervous. Mother is always willing to listen when I have a problem. I told her of my concerns about my relationship with George, no matter what my answer is. If I say yes to his calling, things will change; if I say no, I'm afraid our relationship will be greatly changed and not for the good. I told her how I'm uncertain how I feel, whether I'm ready to consider a serious relationship, with George or with anyone.

I told her I don't know what would be expected of me in a new relationship, especially since I feel I already know George so well. I told her that friends have told me that the reason men call on a woman is to get to know her better, to find out if she would be a suitable spouse.

Mother said she understood my concerns. I knew she would. I was just nervous about the subject. It's not like she and I have never talked about womanly concerns before, especially before Sarah and Frank were married and when Normie was born. But it wasn't about me. Also, my girlfriends have hinted about things such as the wedding night and being with child, making them sound scary. I was glad Mother had talked to Sarah and me about such things.

Mother said I had to feel good about the decision to have George call on me. If not, she said that I am young, and even though some of my friends are already married and have children, I should not let that influence my decision. Also, she said George would understand if I just wasn't ready for a more serious relationship. She said if he found someone else, then it just wasn't meant to be and that our relationship would change. I would hate for that to happen.

### Friday, May 21

It was warm and very dry today. Father went up town on some errands and came back with some boxwood shrubs. Uncle Philip and Winston stopped by on their way to New Milford and came back and stayed to dinner.

During the afternoon, I picked some flowers for the table. I started my new garden, gathering some spring-flowering wildflowers and planting them amidst the small boxwoods Father helped me plant. After Uncle Philip and Winston left, I sewed some.

I was feeling rather well today; no coughing or tightness in my chest. The warm, dry air seems to agree with me.

I haven't seen George, but I think that is just as well because, despite my talk with Mother, I still cannot seem to make up my mind about what I should do. Does my inability to decide mean that I should just keep our relationship as friends, that I'm not ready to commit to something more? Will George understand? He's always been kind to me, and a good friend, but would that change if I say no to his calling on me? Whatever is the matter with me?

## Saturday, May 22

It was a warm day. Father and I went again to Dr. Hartwell's, but he was not at home. Father has decided that he might have different cures for me than Dr. Kerrmann has. It was probably just as well he wasn't there because nothing any of the doctors give me ever helps my cough for long. It just seems to come back as strong as it was. One doctor even suggested that Mother make a poultice of hot potatoes to put on my chest to draw out the cough. It didn't help but had to be renewed often because it became hard or cool and was very uncomfortable.

We then went to Sarah's and stayed until five, then went up to Aunt Lydia's and stayed all night. We had a very good visit. My cousin Walter and his wife Amanda came by and had dinner with us. It was good seeing them. They have been married about two years now.

We spent the day talking and laughing and exchanging family news. Tomorrow we are going to stop to see Walter's sister, Esther, on the way home.

It rained some during the night. After a very busy day, we retired early.

## Sunday, May 23

It was another warm day. We called to Esther's and then to Sarah's, and stayed to supper, then came down to the doctor's and saw him, then came home about half past seven. Dr. Hartwell gave me another potion to try. I get very depressed sometimes because nothing I take for the cough seems to help.

Mrs. Seymour called during the evening. It was an enjoyable visit. She always brings us up to date on things that are happening in town. We had cake and tea. She stayed until 9 p.m. and then went home.

Mother, Father and I stayed up later than usual, discussing the various topics Mrs. Seymour had raised during our visit. She is a very smart woman and is active in town issues, though, of course, she cannot vote. I often wonder about that. In this country where all men are equal, does it mean that literally or does it include women? It doesn't seem fair that women don't have the same rights and freedom as men have. I wonder how George would feel about that. I know some women have been speaking out more often about women's rights. Even President John Adams' wife was said to urge her husband to remember women in his endeavors. I agree, as some women do, that we need the right to vote. I wonder if it will ever happen?

We finally went to bed about 11 o'clock. I still had problems getting to sleep because I was coughing again. The latest potion does not seem to be helping. Perhaps I'm just being impatient. I want so much to feel better and keep hoping that a new medicine will help.

### Monday, May 24

It was a very nice day. Mother did the washing, and I did the rest of the work. In the afternoon, I went down in the woods and got some wintergreen. I think I will plant some in a shadier part of my garden. It stays green during the winter. I know the berries are used medicinally. I would be able to make tea from the leaves. It is said it can alleviate rheumatic symptoms, headache, fever, sore throat, and aches and pains. Perhaps the tea would help my cough. I'm willing to try anything. I'm so tired of coughing all the time and not sleeping well at night.

I'm beginning to think I may never get better. None of the doctors have helped my cough at all. I wonder if they even know what is wrong with me? I am so tired most of the time. Instead of feeling this way, I want to enjoy the time I spend with Mother or working with the flowers in my garden.

It makes me wonder about George, also. When I see him, it's only briefly or if he calls at the house as he does now, I can excuse myself if I feel coughs coming on. He has never seen me on the days when I feel so tired that I just want to lay down. What if he came to call on me and all I did was cough every time I tried to talk? Sometimes my voice is so hoarse that I can barely speak at all.

## Tuesday, May 25

It was very warm and dry today. I did most of the ironing until I felt too tired to finish, then Mother finished it later. In the afternoon, Father went to Southville to get the horse shod, and brought me some candy. It tasted so good. I love sweets, though I never seem to gain any weight. Some of my clothing is actually getting too big for me. My friends say they envy me because they wish they could lose weight so effortlessly. They don't realize that I'm not trying to lose weight.

I probably shouldn't be concerned about my weight. I have never weighed more than 115 pounds, but it is strange for my clothes to seem too large for me now. I eat well, but then again, I am quite active, helping with housework and working in my garden. I also walk up to the center quite often when Father has the horse and buggy. I do all those activities as I have always done, but now I feel tired when I never did before. I remember when I never felt tired but could sleep well at night. Now I cough all night and don't sleep well and always feel tired.

I have done so much thinking since Father told me that George had asked to call on me. I have so many concerns about how our relationship would change. I know I don't want to lose George as a friend. As it is now, our relationship is not complicated. I am beginning to think that I will tell Father that I'm just not ready to have anyone, not even George, call on me, other than as a friend. I would feel much more comfortable if things went on as they are for a while. I know some of my friends will think it strange that I'm not looking forward to a different relationship, but I want to be sure of my feelings before I make such a commitment. I love George as a friend, but I'm not sure that anything more than that is right for me at this time.

I need to feel better physically before I think about having someone call on me with the possible outcome of marriage and a family. It would not be fair to someone, especially George, if I continue to be unwell.

## Wednesday, May 26

It was another warm day. Father and I went up town. I called at Mrs. Bronson's and bought some calico for a new dress and went down to Ella Pierce's and got a pattern. There was a shower at night. It's good for my flowers and for our vegetable garden, but I was glad it was nice during the day. I feel better when it's not damp and cold.

I keep thinking about what I have decided about George, and now I'm wondering if I have made the right decision. I know I want to feel better before making any changes in my life and, perhaps, that is what is most important now. Perhaps the doctors will finally find something to help my cough and my fatigue.

After dinner, I began laying out the pattern for my dress. Mother liked the material I purchased. It's very pretty and light in weight so it will make into a nice dress for summer gatherings. There will most likely be some family get-togethers, and the church will probably have some functions. Mother helped some with the dress, and then we sat in the parlor for a while, reading and talking. Father had gone to a meeting up town, so we were alone. and no one called.

### Thursday, May 27

It was warm and dry today, and I felt very well. This weather seems to agree with me. I don't seem to cough as much.

I cut out my dress with some help from Mother before she had to do some baking. Father worked at Mr. Seymour's today, so he was gone most of the day.

This morning I lay abed a while even though I slept better last night. I wasn't sleeping, though, mostly just enjoying being able to just lay there for a while listening to the birds outside and Mother moving about downstairs. I love when there is no school because I don't have to get up as early unless I want to. When there is school, there is so much to be done before the scholars arrive, and I need to have things ready. I don't have time to lay in bed and daydream.

Mother and I had a quiet lunch together. She hasn't said anything more to me about George since I spoke with her. I still am very confused as to what to do. I keep wondering why I sometimes feel so poorly and don't have my usual stamina. It's true that I feel better during the warm days and not so well during cold, damp days. My cough also seems worse in the morning than later in the day. Then it gets worse at night.

I know I am old enough now to have a gentleman caller, but I am still unsure if it should be George or if I am ready for any such arrangement with anyone. I am still concerned that if, for some reason, a closer relationship than friendship with George did not work out, that I would completely lose him as a friend. I know I would not want that to happen. I worry that my poor health sometimes would interfere with a new relationship. If George and I continued just as friends, I could feel more comfortable and not hurt his feelings if I had to beg off from social activities if I was not feeling well. I would not want to hurt him in any way, and, in this way, our friendship could continue as it always was.

I also wonder if we would remain friends if he were to call on someone else as a suitor. Perhaps, no matter what I do, our relationship would change in the future. From what my friends say, a new wife might resent her husband having friends who were women, especially if they are unmarried.

### Friday, May 28

It was somewhat cooler today. After breakfast, I sewed some on my new dress. Late in the afternoon Aunt Harriet came and stayed for dinner. In the evening, we had just settled into the parlor for tea and pie when Mrs. Castle came to call. Later, while Mother and Father, Aunt Harriet, and Mrs. Castle played cards, I read some of Mother's magazines. I keep hoping to find some medicine that will help my cough.

After our company left, Mother and Father joined me in the parlor for a while before going up to bed. I didn't feel like I would be able to sleep so I stayed for a while, mostly thinking of all the feelings I have been having about George. I know I must tell Father something soon. He keeps looking at me as if he wants me to decide though he hasn't said anything directly to me.

I seem totally incapable of making any decision. I am so indecisive that I sometimes wonder what is wrong with me. Any girl would be proud that a man such as George was interested in her as a possible wife. Am I just not ready? Are my fears about my health just an excuse for not taking a forward step? I just don't know why, but something just seems to tell me to go slow, to not make a decision that might not be right for me or for George.

Finally, I went up to bed, where I lay awake for some time, counting the chimes of the Grandfather clock as it announced the hours passing. Finally, sometime around three a.m., I must have fallen asleep.

### Saturday, May 29

It was a pleasant day today, though I admit I felt rather tired though I did sleep later than usual. After breakfast, Mother and I went up town and did some shopping and visiting. I was very glad to come home for lunch because I felt so tired and my chest hurt from coughing. I felt almost breathless from all the exertion. Mother kept glancing at me with a worried expression when I would have a spell of coughing. I don't want to worry her, so I try not to make much of it, but it does make me so fatigued.

Emma and Carrie came up in the afternoon and stayed about two hours. Though I wanted to join in all the conversation, I found that I couldn't speak very loud. I was almost relieved when they left so that I could go up to my room to rest.

I guess I fell asleep for a while because Mother had to come up to wake me for dinner. I really wasn't hungry, but she would not hear of my not eating something. She made me some soup and soft toast that went down easy, but all I really wanted to do was sleep. She kept watching me to make sure I ate. I know she is worrying about me.

It is not like me to not be happy to see Emma and Carrie. I hope they don't think I was rude, but I just was so tired from not being able to sleep last night. I don't know if my room was too warm for a change, but I felt so hot several times during the night. I got up once and opened a window, thinking I would feel cooler if there was a breeze.

All I could think about all night was the need to decide about George calling on me. I wish I knew what to do. I'm so afraid that if I say no I will lose the friendship we have had for so many years. I don't know if I could learn to love him in any other way than as a friend. My concerns about my health also seem to plague my thoughts recently. I wonder if it is wise to change anything now. Sometimes I wonder if I will ever feel totally well. Would it be fair to George, or anyone, if I never felt better?

## Sunday, May 30

It was a rainy day and night so we all stayed at home. I really did not feel up to going to church, and I think the weather discouraged Mother and Father from going. It was just a very sour day, and it was so much nicer to stay snug inside. I wonder what any minister would say about such thoughts.

It was Decoration Day, and though no one died in our family in the war, Mother wanted to go to the cemetery to put flowers on Grandfather's grave, but because of the rain she decided to go tomorrow.

I wrote a letter to Mrs. Fabrique that Father will mail tomorrow. That letter was about all I accomplished today. Most of the day I just sat about reading or just resting on my bed. I found myself hoping that no one would call and was thankful when no one came. The rainy weather was keeping everyone close to home.

I do feel worse today than ever, can't speak loud at all. My voice is just a whisper, and my chest hurts when I cough. I don't know why I can't get over this. Nothing the doctors give me helps. Everyone is very kind, bringing me soups, oranges, and light desserts, but I don't feel much like eating.

I wonder if George was in church today. He must be wondering why Father has not spoken to him regarding his request to call on me. I sometimes think it is very strange to use the term to call on me when George has often been in our home on one occasion or another, or just visiting with his parents and some of our other friends. We have often set out from here to go to social events. Of course, Mother and Father or some of our friends have always been with us at those times.

## Monday, May 31

It was cool and nice today, and surprisingly I felt better after feeling so bad yesterday. I felt so good that I went with Father up to the Hollow. Earlier he had taken Mother to the cemetery to put flowers on Grandfather's grave. They said several people had been there to mark the graves of veterans with flowers and flags.

I am still very hoarse, but it felt good to be out in the air. I feel less well when the weather is cold or rainy.

Father and I visited with some friends in the Hollow, and afterwards came home in time for me to help Mother prepare dinner.

I went out to the garden and picked some early greens for supper and afterwards sewed some on a shirtwaist* to wear to school in the fall. No one came to visit, but Carrie sent me a tie that will look very nice with some of my clothing.

I went to bed early because I had begun coughing again. I was glad I had my quilt because my room was cool. None of the medicines are helping, and the coolness seems to add to my coughing.

If the weather is good, Father will probably begin planting the tobacco plants in the field next to the barn. They have done well in the house, and it is time for them to go in the ground.

*Shirtwaist: A tailored blouse or shirt worn by women, first recorded in 1875-1880.

## Tuesday, June 1

It was a cool day so again I felt quite poorly. I wish the weather would get warmer because I feel so much better when it is warm, and the air is dry.

Mother had done the washing in the morning and hung it outside, and I sewed some before helping her fold clothes and put them away. I don't seem to have much energy lately, though I try not to complain because I know Mother and Father do worry about me.

Father was helping one of our neighbors with some work, so Mother and I were alone. We enjoyed a quiet lunch together. Mother played the piano for a while, and that was very restful.

No one called in the afternoon, but Mr. Hodge came to visit in the evening after dinner. He and Father talked about possible exhibits to be entered in the New Milford fair in the fall. It's not even summer yet, and they are talking about fall. I don't want to think past spring and summer. I want the warmer weather to last, and don't want to think about the cold again because I feel so much better now, at least better than I did in the winter. I can't bear the thought of fall and winter.

While they talked, I crocheted on a doily for my bedroom dresser. It will look very pretty with my comb and brush set.

Mr. Hodge said that as soon as they had some strawberries, he would bring me some. That will be very nice. Strawberries are among my favorite things, and Mother makes the best shortcake. I look forward to it every June.

### Wednesday, June 2

It was cloudy part of the day so I did not feel as well as I did yesterday. I did some sewing in the morning on my new shirtwaist.

In the afternoon, Mrs. Squires and Leona came to see me and stayed a while. After they went home, we had dinner and then spent some time reading and talking in the parlor.

It rained very hard at night. I think I listened to it most of the night because I couldn't sleep. It seemed at one time I was hot, almost perspiring, and throwing off the quilt; then I got cold and pulled the quilt up around me. My chest felt tight, and I was coughing and felt breathless.

I spent a lot of time thinking about George. I must address his request to call on me. I must talk to Father to speak to him on my behalf even though I know I will have to face him eventually about my decision. I know it isn't fair to say yes now because I don't feel well enough to take on a new relationship, especially when I am very happy with the way it is right now. I admit our relationship will probably change anyway if he calls on someone else. I would miss his friendship. I suppose that is all part of growing up.

Summer is coming and there will be many social gatherings that I will attend with George and other male and female friends. I want that to continue. At the same time, if I don't feel well, I would not feel guilty if I had to say no to some activity.

I think this decision is for the best, but, in a way, I feel a little sad. I wish I were like some of my friends who eagerly embark on new experiences, such as having a gentleman friend call on them and getting married and having children. Unfortunately, I don't feel ready for such a commitment. I will talk to Father, so he can speak to George when he sees him Sunday at church. Hopefully, George will understand my concerns and things will not change between us.

## Thursday, June 3

It was cloudy some in the afternoon. I was feeling worse today, so I did not do anything. Mrs. Hodge came in the morning and visited with Mother and me. We had some tea and cake, after which she continued on her way. Later Mother and I had some lunch, and I spent the afternoon resting on my bed and looking at magazines.

When Father came home, he brought a letter for me from Willie. It's always good to hear from him. His letter was lively and full of news of Aunt Fannie, Uncle Phillip, and him and his sisters. His letter gave me incentive, so I wrote to Sarah. Even though she is in New Milford and not so far away, it seems I don't see her very often. I know she is very busy with Normie and her new house, but I do miss her a great deal. When I feel better, I hope to go up to see her, Frank, and Normie. I hope that is soon because it seems like I haven't seen her in a long time.

Father began planting tobacco plants this week. It is a very lengthy process. He once planted each plant by hand, but now he uses a tobacco setter, which is a low wagon pulled by our horses. We all help, plus family members and friends often join us. One person drives the team and up to four others sit at the back to set the plants in four rows at a time. A large tank on the setter supplies the water for each plant. It usually takes about a day and a half to plant an acre of land. But this is only the beginning of the work involved.

The most time-consuming task is pulling off suckers that grow on the plants after they have been topped so not to get too large. The suckers, if not removed, sap strength from the plants. I always hated that job, but someone has to do it or we will lose the crop.

Father also worries about heavy rains that can also destroy the crop. Now that the plants are in the ground, they need sunshine as well as light rain in order to flourish.

## Friday, June 4

It was clear and cool today. After lunch, since I was still feeling poorly, Father and I went to Sandy Hook to see Dr. Brown, then we did other errands, so we did not get home till almost night. I was exhausted by the time we got home. Dr. Brown said I should continue to take the medicine he gave me, but I feel it is hopeless.

None of these potions help my cough or make me feel better. I think I sometimes feel more poorly after taking them. I think they are part of why I am always so tired.

Dr. Brown recommended exercise and a nutritious diet, but Mother certainly makes nourishing meals and my household and farm chores, gardening and the walks I take are more exercise than some people do. One of the other doctors I have seen said the very opposite, that my health problems are caused by overwork. He didn't quite say it, but implied that my ailments were the result of a nervous disorder and fretfulness. Mother and Father were not happy with what he said, so I don't see him anymore.

I was unable to help Mother with dinner, and just curled up on the parlor sofa until it was ready. Later, Mr. Hodge came to call, and stayed quite late visiting with Mother and Father. I excused myself rather early and went up to bed, but had trouble getting to sleep. I was worried that Mr. Hodge would think I was rude, but I was so tired from our busy afternoon I felt I could not sit up any longer. I'm sure Mother and Father would explain if he questioned why I went to bed so early, though I don't think he will.

My concern over my health has made me feel confident about my decision about George. I seem to have so many bad days lately. The night sweats continue even on cool evenings, and my cough continues to trouble me, even in the mornings. No one seems to know why I am feeling this way.

I intend to speak with Father tomorrow night after supper, so he can speak to George on Sunday. I want to make sure Father speaks of my concerns that I am not ready and that I feel I am too young to make such a commitment at this time.

### Saturday, June 5

Today it was cloudy and still quite cool. Where are the warm days? I know it is not officially summer yet, but I long for the warmth of the sun. I was sick today and sat up in bed most of the day. Mother fussed over me, making sure I ate breakfast and a light lunch. After lunch Father went up to Seymour's to work. When he came home for supper, he brought me a letter from Sarah. It was full of news of Frank, Normie and her and their new home. She is still doing some decorating.

I am so happy for her. I know she has always wanted her own home. I wonder if I will ever want a home of my own. I know I'm not ready for a relationship that could lead to marriage. Perhaps I will never have what Sarah has. She is so happy, and I would like to have that happiness someday, but not now, not until I feel better and only when I feel more comfortable about taking on a new relationship.

I felt better later in the day, so I went downstairs to have dinner with Mother and Father, and afterwards I asked Father to sit down with me in the parlor. I knew I had to talk to him about my decision about George calling on me. I don't think he was surprised at my decision. I suppose he believed if I had decided in favor of it, I might have had an answer sooner. I did take a long time coming to this decision because I was so unsure of what I should do.

I don't want to hurt George's feelings. Hopefully he will understand.

### Sunday, June 6

It was rainy in the morning but cleared off later. We did not go to church, so Father was unable to speak to George. This will give me more time to talk to Father, to emphasize that he speaks to George in a way that he knows that I am honored by his request but that I feel I'm too young and not ready for a more serious relationship than friendship.

When I talk to George after Father speaks to him, I want to be sure he knows I would like our friendship to continue as it is, but that if he is really ready for a more significant relationship at this time, I will understand if he looks for someone who is also ready. I would miss his friendship if that comes to pass, but I feel strongly that I have made the right decision for me, and perhaps for him, also.

I want to feel healthy before I commit to anything more than friendship. It wouldn't be fair to anyone if I were sick all the time like I am now. I hope I will be better soon, and the doctors will find something to help my cough and fatigue. Perhaps then I would be more interested in looking to the future.

After lunch we had company. Willie Vose came as well as Emeline and Mrs. Land.

## Monday, June 7

The weather was clear and warm today. I was feeling better, so Mother and I went up to Mr. Eastman's. If I could feel like this all the time, I would think I was getting better. But I fear that is not going to happen.

Father is working in the tobacco field. It's that time of year. He is very busy with the various crops as well as working at the hat shop.

I look forward to the warmer weather. Sometimes June can be cool and July and August very warm. I always feel better then. In addition, I'm looking forward to working outside in my flowerbeds. I have already transplanted some wildflowers that should bloom soon and others that will blossom during the summer. Soon I will be looking for those that bloom in the fall. I can't wait until the first year when I see all the changes in my flowerbeds as the seasons change. For winter, the shrubs Father helped me plant will look very pretty if I keep them properly pruned.

I love to garden. I would hate to not be able to do it. That's why I am so happy that I usually feel much better in the summer when most of the work of caring for my flowerbeds must be done.

Soon berries will be in season, and we will be canning strawberries and blueberries for the winter as well as enjoying them with shortcake and in muffins and breads. I enjoy working in the kitchen with Mother. I hope I will be able to continue to do it.

## Tuesday, June 8

It was a cloudy and warm day. I did not do much. No one came to visit. No, I am wrong. Katie and Mary Botsford came. I had forgotten because they arrived late in the afternoon when I was working outside with my flowers.

We had a nice visit, but they didn't stay very long. We offered them tea and cake, but they said they had to get home to make supper for their family. It was still light outside when they left so I returned to weeding my flowerbed until Mother called me in to dinner.

Afterwards Mother and I washed and dried dishes and cleaned up the kitchen before joining Father in the parlor. It was a little cool so the warmth from the fireplace felt good. I am still looking through magazines, hoping to find some medicine that would help me feel better, so I will be able to enjoy the parties and other activities that will take place this summer in town and at our church. There will be picnics, I'm sure, and even boating on the river.

I'm sure Father is looking forward to more fishing on the Shepaug and Housatonic with his friends. Of course, everyone also has more work in the summer, cutting and raking hay, weeding the gardens, putting away produce toward the long winter. Because of that, we all look forward to the fun times. I try not to think about winter. I feel so much better when it is warm.

Another Sunday is looming ahead. Will Father finally be able to talk to George? I hope so. Now that I have made my decision, I'm anxious to have it behind me. Hopefully, George will understand, and our friendship will continue as it has all these years.

### Wednesday, June 9

Today was a cloudy day and it, looked very much like it would rain, but did not. After lunch, Katie came, and we had a nice visit. Mother was in the field helping Father in the tobacco field. She tries to help Father as much as she can because he has so much to do with working at the hat shop as well as taking care of our animals and farm and helping his friends.

I know Father appreciates her help and knows just how much she does for our family. I often think of how hard she works, both in and outside the home, as well as in the community, providing food for church suppers and get-togethers and for those who are ill. I don't wonder why she is often fatigued. She also sometimes helps prepare the altar for church services, with other ladies of the church.

Thinking about church makes me aware that Sunday is almost upon us. I hope that the question of George calling on me will be resolved that day. I have talked to Father, and he understands my decision though I think he and Mother are disappointed because they like George so much. Hopefully George will also understand.

I wish I could be like other girls, looking forward to a gentleman caller, but for some reason I don't fully understand I am unlike them. I suppose I don't like change. I want things to stay as they are, although I know that cannot always be. I want to spend the summer with my friends, including George, going to parties and picnics and other gatherings. I want to work in my flowerbeds and watch them change as the seasons change.

I want to go back to school in the fall to learn more, so I can become a teacher in the future. I love what I have been doing at the school, even though it is often hard work in preparing our scholars for their futures. When you are young, you don't realize how important it is to have an education, so we try to make our lessons as interesting as possible, so the children will want to learn.

No one called in the evening, and we retired early.

### Thursday, June 10

It was another cloudy day, but it did not rain. Ella Pierce called and spent part of the afternoon with Mother and me. It was an agreeable time.

Father is working at Seymour's. After Ella departed, I went out in the meadow and picked some wild strawberries. They are so sweet. I admit I ate some on the way back to the house. Hopefully Mother will make strawberry shortcake tomorrow with real cream that we will all enjoy. We sometimes have it for Sunday supper. With coffee or tea, it is enough after our big meal following church services.

Writing about church services reminds me that hopefully this Sunday Father will be able to speak with George about my decision that I am not ready for a gentleman caller, even if it would be George. I want to be well when I come to that decision, and right now I do not feel well enough for changes in my life.

I wish I knew what was wrong with me. Mother and Father do not speak of it often. I don't think the doctors even know why I don't get better. I've certainly been to several, and all they do is give me different potions for my cough, none of which have helped very much.

For supper, Mother made strawberry shortcake topped with thick cream. I don't know why my clothing is getting big for me. I should be getting fat, especially the way I eat cake, pie, and other sweet things.

## Friday, June 11

Today was very cloudy, but no rain. I feel about the same. The warmer weather, even though there is no sun, makes me feel better, at least for a while every day.

I arose early and helped Mother with breakfast while Father was in the barn taking care of the animals. Following breakfast of eggs, bacon, and leftover strawberries, I worked in my flower beds for a short time. They are looking so good, I can't believe it was only a few months ago that I thought about transplanting wildflowers every season. I still need to dig up and replant flowers that will bloom during the summer and look for others for the fall. I love all the seasons, and it is wonderful to see them reflected in my flowerbeds. The shrubs will look cheerful during the winter, despite the absence of flowers.

George Squire and Georgianna visited in the afternoon and stayed to dinner. After dinner, after cleaning up the dishes, Mother, Georgianna, and I played cards while Father and Mr. Squire sat in the parlor. We could hear them talking about the results of the Republican National Convention in Chicago. From what I know from Father reading the paper out loud to us, there was a fight between the Stalwart faction, which supports the party patronage system, and the Half Breeds, who favor reform. Apparently, this resulted in a compromise ticket of James A. Garfield, a Half Breed, for president, and Chester A. Arthur, a Stalwart, for vice president. The Democrat National Convention is to be held from June 22 to 24 in St. Louis.

Father loves to talk politics, but I don't really understand them. I often wonder why anyone would want to be president, especially after what happened to President Lincoln. But the men get involved because they can vote and try to make a difference. Sometimes it seems like it is all talk and things they promise don't happen or, as Father said once, the other levels of government don't let it happen. I think he was talking about Congress particularly, especially when the two parties don't agree.

Later, after our visitors left for home, we spent some time reading in the parlor before going to bed.

## Saturday, June 12

Finally, it was a clear day. We need the sun for the gardens as much as we need rain. In the afternoon. Libbie Booth, Katie, and Mary Tyrrell called. Ella Pierce also stopped by and brought me two oranges. What a treat they are. Libbie brought me some strawberries.

I was glad for the company because it kept me from thinking about Father talking to George tomorrow after church. I don't think I will attend. It might be better if Father just goes alone or with Mother. I don't think I could stand it if George became upset or insisted upon talking to me right there. I would be so embarrassed. Perhaps Father will invite him here before they talk. I could stay upstairs in my room. Then if George takes it well, I could go down and talk to him about the reasons for my decision.

I'm still so afraid I will lose him as a friend, but I cannot agree to him calling on me as a possible suitor just because of that fear. What will happen will happen, and I must live with the consequence of the decision I have made. We've always been comfortable with each other but that would change if circumstances were changed. George is obviously ready to make a commitment to someone, and I'm sure many of my friends believe it would be me. I don't think this would surprise them, but my decision would. I know I probably will regret this if he is no longer willing to be my friend, but I think I'm doing what is best for both of us. Perhaps we would continue as we have in the past until he begins calling on someone else.

I had a poor spell tonight, probably because I am so worried about tomorrow. Perhaps George won't be there again. This decision took a long time to make, but it has become even longer because sometimes we didn't go to church and other times when we did George wasn't there. Perhaps it is fate that it has taken this long, so I could change my mind if I regretted my original decision. I don't regret it. I feel so poorly sometimes that I don't think it would be wise to move ahead with my life until I know I can be perfectly well.

## Sunday, June 13

It was a pleasant day, but there was a shower in the afternoon. I did not feel well this morning probably because of restless sleep last night. I was so aware that today might be the day that Father and George would both be at services, and Father would tell him my decision. I was afraid to know what George said, but I was also fearful that today I would see the end of a cherished friendship. As it was, I was correct in my feeling that today would be the day I had looked forward to as well as dreaded.

When Father and Mother returned from church, they both looked sad. It was a difficult day for them also because I think they had always thought that George and I would be together someday as more than friends. I also know that they are concerned about my health. There have been so many trips to doctors, all to no avail, as nothing seems to help. If I am depressed at times about that, then how do they feel?

While Mother made lunch, Father asked me to join him in the parlor. Why is it that important discussions always seem to take place in the parlor? I went in, feeling sad, knowing that now George knew about my decision, and I would have to face my fears.

Father said he and George had a lengthy conversation after the service, mostly because George had many questions. Father said he explained my reasons for not entering a more serious relationship at this time because of my youth and that I felt my health needed to improve before I even thought about the future. But then Father said that George had asked if he could speak to me. I wasn't surprised because I realized he would want to talk to me. Father said he told him we were expecting guests that afternoon, so it would be better if George called on us tomorrow evening after work.

I was so relieved that I would have a day in which to prepare myself. I had no idea what George would say to me or ask. My mind was taken away from these thoughts when Amelia and Grandfather Squire came and stayed almost all day. Dwight and George Evans also came by during the afternoon. No one stayed to dinner, so we had a quiet evening. I was so tired from the company and having to keep a happy face despite what I was thinking about the next evening. I went to bed early as did Mother and Father, though I could hear their voices in their room, but was unable to understand what they were saying. Were they talking about me? Was it because my decision about George was now final?

## Monday, June 14

It was a very nice day today. Mother did a large wash and hung it outside on the line. Despite the warmth of the day, I was not feeling well. Perhaps I was apprehensive about seeing George tonight. I did not sit up much during the morning, but spent most of it in my bed mulling over what might transpire later. After lunch, Cordelia and Aunt Fannie came and spent the afternoon and brought me some wine. Libbie sent me more berries, which I enjoyed later at dinner, though I didn't eat much of anything else. I was so nervous. Father said I need not be nervous as he and Mother would be with me, but I was afraid of what might be said, and that my friendship with George would be over.

It was, however, as Father had said. George arrived about seven, and he seemed his usual self, friendly and polite. There was no anger. However, he did tell me that he was both disappointed and saddened by my decision but understood my reasons for it. He said there was no reason to rush into any decisions at this time. We are young, and there is time to consider another relationship in the future. Meanwhile, he said, we could go on as we are because he did not want to lose my friendship.

George was also genuinely concerned about my health, saying he hoped that I would soon feel much better. The warmer weather would probably help, he said, and he hoped Mother, Father, and I could attend many of the activities that are being planned this summer. I could feel myself relaxing. It seemed we could be as we always had been.

Following dessert and coffee, George left for home. Father and Mother were pleased that all had gone so well. However, I was a little concerned about his mentioning a relationship in the future. Did he mean with me? Or, perhaps, did he mean both of us with someone else? It is possible he could ask to call on someone else as a suitor. While I think I would be upset by that, I'm not sure of my future. If my health doesn't improve, how could I be married and have children? Why shouldn't George look to someone else in the future?

Later, as I sat at my bedroom window, gazing out at the dark, I felt my future is also as dark.

## Tuesday, June 15

It was cloudy and rained in the afternoon. I still felt apprehensive about the night before. What did George really mean? I suppose I will find out soon, especially if things change between us despite his referring to seeing me at the summer activities. I was very quiet at breakfast, and Mother and Father spoke quietly to each other when he was leaving for the hat shop. I suppose they are worried about me and concerns I might have about what was said last night.

I didn't have much time to really spend worrying about it because we had visitors almost all day. Mr. Hodge called in the morning, and Mrs. Hodge came in the afternoon. She brought me some cake which we all enjoyed with tea. Aunt Harriet also called in the afternoon in time to join us for refreshments.

While Mrs. Hodge left to make dinner for her family, Aunt Harriet stayed for dinner, and there was much talk about family matters. I always enjoy listening to Mother when her sisters and brothers visit. It must have been great fun to be a part of such a large family. My grandfather did a very good job raising the children, and it is always obvious they all loved him very much. Some, including Mother, do not remember their mother, and I think that is very sad.

After Aunt Harriet left for home, we cleaned up the dining room and sat for a while in the parlor. While Mother and Father talked, I tried to read, but my heart wasn't in it. My thoughts kept returning to last night and the things George had said. I suppose only time will tell how things will be in the future.

## Wednesday, June 16

It was a very nice day today, and, warm, and, probably because of that, I feel a little better. I always seem so when it is warm. I have continued to mull over what George said to me the other night but cannot come up with any answers about what it could mean. Perhaps I am reading too much into what he said. He certainly seemed interested in seeing me at the various events planned for this summer. I suppose I won't know until we attend some of them and see how George is at that time. Oh Diary, I would not blame him if he sought a relationship with someone else.

Certainly, I would want the best for him. I hope I would not be sad or jealous about it.

I did not have much time to think about my concerns because we had some company today. Mr. Smith, the minister, came and had tea with us. He and Mother talked in the parlor before he left to make other calls. Then Sarah, Frank, and Normie arrived late in the morning, and stayed all day. Sarah helped mother with the ironing since I was too tired to be of much help. I watched Normie while they talked in the kitchen. When he was put down for a nap, I answered Willie's letter, so father can mail it tomorrow.

Some neighbors also brought me some berries today, which I will enjoy at breakfast tomorrow. It was very good of them to think of me. I haven't felt up to going berrying, though I know there are wild strawberries in the field near the stone wall. Perhaps tomorrow I will walk there to see.

After Sarah, Frank and Normie left, we had a quiet dinner, and then spent some time in the parlor. Mother played the piano, which I find very restful. I always sleep better after I hear her play. It feels almost like when we sing to Normie to get him to sleep.

## Thursday, June 17

It was a very nice, pleasant day, so I really felt quite well and was glad to see some of my friends who called in the afternoon. Ella Pierce also stopped in for a few minutes to bring me some strawberries. I was very pleased to receive them because I didn't have time to go up to the field to see if there were strawberries there. I'm concerned, though, as to why so many people are bringing me food and beverages. I suppose they know I have been sick for a while and want to help me to feel better.

Frances Hull and Mary Barnes stayed almost all afternoon, and we had a good time talking about when we were schoolgirls together, which wasn't very long ago. It seems like yesterday that I was walking down the road to the school as a student, not as a grown person learning to be a teacher. I haven't mentioned anything to my friends about George. I never feel comfortable talking about his request to call on me, and, because of my decision, I feel it was not something people other than family needed to know.

Later, when I was reading the newspaper that Father brought home, I found it very interesting to know that the town of Watertown is 100 years old today. I wonder what it was like to live in this area 100 years ago. It's too bad we are not in school now because this would be a good topic for our history lesson. Perhaps I will bring it to Mrs. Baglin's attention when school begins again.

### Friday, June 18

It was somewhat warmer today. Summer and nicer weather are on the way. My flowers are doing well. We have had just enough rain, so I have not had to water them.

After breakfast, I went out to pull some weeds in the flowerbeds. It always makes me feel better to see the pretty gardens I have made. Once I get flowers in them from all three seasons, they will look even better, and with the green shrubs, they will also be attractive in the winter.

In the afternoon, Aunt Fannie and Huldah and Clara called to see me. Kattie also came by and brought me some peas and other early vegetables. Carrie also came by later in the afternoon and called on us. Mrs. Hodge sent me some fish for our supper that her husband had caught. Fresh fish will taste very good tonight. Father has not had much time for fishing, but I know he is looking forward to it with his friends. They often take a boat out on the river instead of just fishing from shore.

Our evening was quiet once everyone had left. Mother fixed the fish for supper, which we very much enjoyed. Father said he would have to make time to do some fishing himself within the next week or so.

### Saturday, June 19

It was a warm day today. I worked outside for a while until I got tired. Then I went inside to have lunch with Mother and Father. After resting for a while in my room, I returned to my flower beds. The weeds are growing as fast as the flowers, and it is hard to keep up with them.

Later in the afternoon, Mrs. Bronson and Mrs. Squire came to see me and brought me strawberries and cherries. Fresh berries and fruit always taste so good.

After they had left, Mrs. Baglin and Emma Beers came to see me, as well as Katie, who brought me some beer. It tasted so good on this warm day.

Just before supper, Miss Higgins sent me a bouquet of peonies from her garden. They are such pretty flowers. I think I should include some in the rear of my flower gardens. They grow taller than the flowers I have planted and will serve as a colorful background during the summer. I would have to remember to stake them before they get too tall because the blooms get so heavy. If it rains very much, they would fall over on the other flowers I have planted. Several of our neighbors called in the afternoon and some stayed for tea and cake. Dinner was a quiet time, with no guests, and after cleaning up the kitchen and dining room, we spent time in the parlor reading and talking about some of the events that are to take place in town and the area in the next two or three months.

### Sunday, June 20

It was a very pleasant day today. We went to church, and after lunch we had company almost all day. Grandfather Squire came and spent the day, and Ella Pierce stopped by after church with a bouquet of wildflowers for me. Ellen Baldwin brought a bouquet later in the day, and Charlie Booth brought me some strawberries from his garden.

Aunt Harriet and Uncle Henry stopped by to visit in the afternoon, and Maggie and Pete came by later in the afternoon.

Everyone has been wonderful to me this summer about visiting because I haven't been out and about very much. I am still coughing at night, feel very hot, and always so tired. I suppose everyone knows I have not been feeling well since school ended. I miss the scholars though I have seen Mrs. Baglin quite often and some of the children at church or the store. Even though I love the summer, I am still looking forward to September when we will return to school. I hope I will feel well enough by then, though no one seems to know what is wrong with me, even the doctors, or at least they haven't told me.

I often wonder if Mother and Father hear more from the doctors than I do. I know they are very concerned about my health, and I know it has upset them that I did not feel up to having George call on me. They understood my concerns, but I think they hope my health will improve so that George and I would have a future together.

George has always been part of my life, and I hope that he will continue to be, but that remains to be seen.

### Monday, June 21

It was a pleasant day, but very windy. Our morning was quiet, but after lunch Dr. Brown came to see me and then stayed for dinner.

Dr. Brown asked Mother and me how my health had been since I saw him last. He said there might be a new potion he could give me to help with my coughing, but it might increase the fatigue I feel. I don't want to be more tired than I already am. I have not been able to help Mother very much around the house, and my gardens are full of weeds because I tire so easily. They are still beautiful, but I feel bad that I can't work in them more. I don't think any of the doctors Mother and Father have taken me to know what is wrong with me.

After an early dinner Father carried Dr. Brown to the depot to get the cars, and then went on to New Milford to see Sarah, Frank, and Normie. When he returned, he brought me some strawberries from Sarah's garden.

I am so lucky to have received so many gifts of fresh fruit and berries, plus other treats. I think everyone believes the food will make me feel better, and it does. When I don't feel like eating very much, I still enjoy fruit, especially oranges.

I received a letter from Carrie today, with many stories of family and friends. She writes just the way she talks, and many of the stories were very humorous.

### Tuesday, June 22

It was a beautiful, clear day today. Because I felt very strong, I helped Mother clean the house in the morning and after lunch Mrs. Haskins and Robert and Nellie Bronson called and stayed for a while. After they left, Bertie came over to bring me a cherry pie Mrs. Hodge had made. We enjoyed it later with our supper.

When I went up to my room later after reading for a while in the parlor, I thought about all the gifts I have received recently. I thought about how I have been feeling. I don't think my health is improving despite all the potions doctors have given me. It was a very difficult decision about George calling on me, but I had to make it, because it was best for both George and me. It would not be fair to George if my health doesn't get better.

Our friends and neighbors and my family have been very kind to me, bringing desserts, fruit, berries, and other gifts. It raises my spirits knowing so many people care about me and want to help me get better. I do want to get better, but sometimes I don't feel that I will. I find myself wondering what is wrong with me, and why the doctors and all their potions don't seem to help. What if I never get better? What if what is wrong with me can't be cured?

I went to bed wondering what lies ahead for me. I'm so young, I should be thinking about my future, but I wonder if there is one for me.

## Wednesday, June 23

It was a warmer day today. Mother, Father, and I had an early breakfast, and then Father went to work after taking care of the animals. Mother and I helped by feeding the chickens. I always laugh when I walk into the pen with a bucket full of grain, and they all come running toward me. I have found it is best to throw the food in different directions so the birds head for the food instead of to me. The sight of all those clucking beaks coming toward me was always scary when I was a child. I admit, diary, that they still scare me a little.

In the afternoon, I received some cherries from Mrs. Hodge. We enjoyed the pie she sent yesterday, and there is still some left for tonight's dinner. Mother made bread in the afternoon. I don't think there is anything that smells as good as bread fresh from the oven.

I worked for a short while in my flower beds until I began feeling poorly with a headache, probably from the heat. I came up to my room and sat by the window where it was cooler and eventually the headache went away.

Father came home after work with his hand bandaged. He said his horse kicked him. It wasn't Bess, but the new horse he recently purchased. Bess is a sweet animal. I have never been afraid of her. I often take her pieces of an apple and sit up in her feed box while she eats them. She is always very gentle when she takes them from the palm of my hand. Father said the new horse, which isn't named yet, will settle down once he gets use to us.

Some of father's friends came over after dinner and played cards in the dining room. I was in the parlor reading, but I could hear them discussing what might be the outcome of the Democrat National Convention that began yesterday.

They were still playing cards when I went upstairs to bed.

### Thursday, June 24

A warm day. Having recovered from my headache yesterday, I was feeling a little better, so I spent the morning helping Mother around the house and did some baking. I collected eggs from the hen house and made a custard pudding for supper.

After lunch with Mother, I worked in my flowerbeds for a while, weeding and clipping. I cut some flowers for the house and arranged them in a vase. My gardens are looking very fine. I am very happy with them and can't wait to see them when the summer flowers bloom. Last year these gardens were just a dream, and the wildflowers I planted in the spring are at their fullest flowering now. The shrubs that father helped me plant have provided some greenery for year-round color, and I have planted some annuals that hopefully will last through the fall. However, my favorites are the wildflowers. I'm looking forward to the Queen Ann's Lace, black-eyed Susan and other summer flowers I will add to the gardens.

Mother worked for a while in the vegetable garden. As soon as some of the fruits and vegetables are ready, she will be canning so we will have them for winter meals. We usually have canned applesauce, peaches, and some berries, as well as vegetables. It's like having a bit of summer all year long.

In the afternoon Mary Oliver called to see me, and then Wallace Hodge stopped in and stayed for dinner. Father and Wallace talked town politics and farm concerns while Mother and I prepared dinner. My pudding was a great success, as well as our freshly baked bread.

After Wallace left we sat outside on the porch for a while. The evening was cooler, the sky clear with bright stars, and there was a slight breeze.

I almost felt I was well, but when I went to bed the coughing began again, bringing reality back into my life.

### Friday, June 25

It was somewhat warmer today than yesterday. Father worked in the barn before going to the hat shop. Soon it will be time to cut the hayfield, so the animals will have food and bedding for the months to come.

Mother and I enjoyed a quiet breakfast of porridge and coffee with buttered bread and jam. Later I read for a while in the parlor, but the ticking of the grandfather clock was distracting. I wondered what time has in store for me.

All the food and gifts I've been receiving from relatives and friends have been wonderful, but they have made me wonder why I have received them. Is my sickness worse than I realize? Oh diary, the future lies ahead but will it be there for me? It is obvious I am losing weight. Recently, I have had to take in some of my skirts, dresses, and shirtwaists so they will fit better. My nightshirts are big, also, but they are more comfortable that way.

I need to talk to the doctor soon about what is wrong with me, and why I don't get better despite the potions I take. If Mother and Father know what is wrong, why don't they tell me? Perhaps they don't want me to worry. But I worry anyway. Perhaps the doctors don't even know what is wrong with me.

### Saturday, June 26

It was a warm, dry day. We spent a quiet breakfast but had company in the late morning. Ellis Baldwin called and brought me a cake, pie, and some strawberry jelly his wife had made. Mrs. Hodge also stopped by with one of her wonderful cherry pies. We had some of the desserts with dinner later, and the jelly will be delicious on buttered toast for breakfast tomorrow.

After everyone left, I went up town with Mother. We stopped at the post office, and I was happy to receive a letter from my friend Mary Greene. While we were gone, Father said neighbors brought me two bouquets.

The flowers are lovely, but again I thought about all the kindness I've received. I question what my future holds. Will I be able to continue with my hope to become a teacher? I have felt ill for months now. Some days I feel almost well, then I will have days of coughing and fatigue from not sleeping well. I try to be positive, so I don't worry Mother and Father. I know they are concerned about me. Do they know more than what I've been told about my almost constant illness? If I were to ask them, would they tell me? Or would I just give them more reason to worry if I tell them of my concerns?

I am even more comfortable with my decision regarding George calling on me. It would not have been right to accept his intentions and perhaps not be well enough to someday have a husband and family.

## Sunday, June 27

It was another warm day today. Mother, Father and I had a late breakfast, after which we went to services. As I expected, George was there and sat with us, and after services we talked outside the church for a while.

I had taken special care in dressing and my appearance this morning and was glad I did. Instead of my hair hanging down my back with curls in my bangs, I wore my hair up. I think it made me look more elegant. Mother said it made me look older than my years, and that I should not rush my young years because they are gone all too soon.

George was his usual self, friendly and outgoing, talking enthusiastically about some of the upcoming events in town. We had to leave because Father had to attend a meeting at the schoolhouse, but we promised George we would see him at the summer parties. Mother also invited him to call whenever he could, though why she said that, I don't know, because he seems to be coming around much more often. I know she likes him, and I think she still hopes that he and I will have a future together.

Riding home in the buggy, listening to the bells on Bess's harness jingling merrily, made me feel good and forget my problems, at least for a while. I was so happy that my friendship with George did not seem to have changed.

When we arrived home, Father took the buggy and went on to his meeting. I have often wondered why only men attend these meetings. Don't women have opinions? I suppose because they cannot vote, they just don't bother to go. Mother never seems particularly interested in town politics when Father talks about what is happening or reads the newspaper out loud to us. Perhaps it is because in the end she has no say in what happens, just as other women don't. I hope some time it is possible for women to vote. I know some people are already advocating voting rights for women, but I believe it would be a long process. I think some men would be reluctant to allow women to vote because they would see it as relinquishing some of their power.

Mother and I enjoyed a light lunch, and later in the afternoon received callers, Mrs. Baglin, Leona and Lavinia Squire, and Emeline. We enjoyed tea and cakes and the conversation. Mrs. Baglin is enjoying the months off from school, but all too soon it will be time for the scholars to return to their books and us to our tasks of teaching them.

When our guests were leaving, Father returned from the meeting, and Mother and I began preparations for dinner. All this company had kept my mind off my troubles. Perhaps the answer is to keep my mind and hands busy, so I don't think so much about my ailments. Sometimes, though, it is very hard to ignore the coughing and, most of all, the fatigue. The question is, how do I resolve my concerns about the future and what I might be doing then.

After dinner Father said there was a great deal of talk about the results from the Democrat National Convention. The delegates nominated Winfield Scott Hancock for president and William H. English for vice president.

### Monday, June 28

It was another warm day. Since Mother was going to New Milford to see Sarah and Normie, she asked Maria Pettit to come to do the washing. Ordinarily I would have done the wash but lately I have not been able to help Mother very much because I get so tired.

My good feelings of yesterday vanished this morning with a fit of coughing upon rising. I slept poorly last night because all the concerns I have about my future had returned after dinner. I was sitting in the parlor trying to read some from Mark Twain's book, The Innocents Abroad, about his travels in Europe and the Middle East, hoping it would keep my mind off my problems. My mind kept wandering to whether I should talk to Mother and

Father about concerns for my health. As wonderful as the book is, it could not hold my interest because I need to decide what to do.

I think I take so long to make decisions because I want to make sure they are correct. In this case, I fear I may add to my parents' concerns. I know they are trying very hard to help me be well. Mother always makes sure I eat well, and I try to get enough sleep, but sometimes the coughing keeps me awake at night, so I am very tired the next day. I know they hear me coughing and are concerned. I find I must take rests in between chores now where I once was able to go from one to another with no sign of fatigue.

I just don't know what I should say to Mother and Father. Perhaps it would be better to just leave it for a while.

## Tuesday, June 29

It was another warm day. Mother ironed, and I worked in my flowerbeds. I went inside for a while because there was a swarm of bees in a tree by the barn, but they finally went away. When I went outside again, I planted some summer flowering plants that will highlight my gardens until it is time for the fall flowers.

When I went back indoors, I canned one can of raspberries and then it was time for lunch. Following lunch, I sat in the parlor crocheting the dresser scarf for my room. I have only recently learned how to crochet. When I was younger, I was too active to sit and pay attention when Mother tried to teach me. I always preferred to be outside, walking to the river, sitting on the front porch and daydreaming about my future or reading. Sometimes I would take a book and walk up to the meadow or to the river and sit there for a while on the grass, reading. Mother finally managed to teach me to crochet this past winter since the snow and cold kept us inside more. I started it when I was staying with Sarah, and it is almost finished. It will look very pretty in my room.

As far back as I can remember, I always wanted to be a teacher. Now I wonder what I will become if I am unable to do that. I even wonder if I will have the strength to go back in the fall. The scholars can be very active, especially at recess, and I might not be able to help Mrs. Baglin as much as I have. She might want someone else to help if I'm unable to because of health reasons.

Sometimes I can't help feeling depressed. It seems as if my hopes, dreams, and plans for my future may be out of my grasp.

I've always wanted to be a teacher, but ever since Sarah was married and had Normie, I have dreamed of someday having my own family and home. I know I am young, and I don't need to think about these things now, but what if they don't happen? Oh diary, I don't like feeling depressed, but sometimes I feel like I have little hope of having what I would consider a normal life in the future. I try not to think about it, but what if I never get better or even have more sickness in the future.

Even now I don't feel up to doing so many things. What if I didn't feel well enough to go on outings with my friends? What if they stopped asking me to join them at parties and other gatherings? What if my health kept me from accepting invitations?

## Wednesday, June 30

Today was somewhat less humid than yesterday so I spent the cooler morning hours working in my flowerbeds. Since I was still concerned about my future, I decided to write to Dr. Kerrmann to see if the next time I see him we can talk about my continuing health problems and what he thinks is wrong. I don't know if I will know anything more by doing this, but I don't feel comfortable talking to Mother and Father because I'm afraid to upset them.

Father worked at Seymour's during the afternoon and Mother finished the ironing, so it was a good time to write a letter. After I finished, I walked up to the post office to mail it. I don't know what I will say if he responds to my letter, and Father will see it if he picks up the mail that day. Perhaps I should tell them I wrote to him. They don't have to know how troubled I am. I could just say I want to get another potion to try that he has talked to me about in the past.

I was exhausted when I returned home from mailing the letter. I had decided to wait and see if he writes to me. I wonder if he would stop by the house. Then I would have to explain to Mother and Father why he came, though he has stopped by in the past.

I can't take back the letter, so I will just have to see what happens. Perhaps I should have thought about this more instead of being so impulsive. It's just that I want to feel better and wonder if I will ever be as I was before. I'm just too young to feel this way.

After dinner we sat in the parlor talking about some upcoming events. Father was particularly interested in entering some of our vegetables in the New Milford Fair in the fall. The gardens are doing well and by then the apples will be ready for picking. I might want to enter some of my flowers in the fair. Perhaps I would win a ribbon.

After father read some passages from the Bible, we went to bed.

### Thursday, July 1

Today the weather was clear through the day, but it rained quite heavily at night. I did not sleep very much last night because I was coughing so often. I was so tired this morning that I felt groggy and tried to stay in bed longer, hoping I could sleep some more. However, since I always wake up early, particularly when I must be at school, there was no extra sleep. I finally got up, washed and dressed, and went downstairs for breakfast.

Following breakfast, Mother and I did the dishes and put them away and cleaned up the kitchen. While Mother did some baking, I went outside to work in my flower beds. The summer flowers are coming along nicely, considering I had just transplanted them. I keep them well watered at first, so they get a good start, then I count on the rain and sun to help them grow. I was very pleased with how they looked.

Mother had made plans to make some calls today so after lunch we set off in the buggy, with calling cards in our purses in case our neighbors were not at home. What usually happens is that we come home to find calling cards left in the basket on our porch, some from people that we might have tried to call upon.

This time when we returned we found a neighbor's card in the basket. Mother decided we would walk the short distance to visit her. We found her at home. We enjoyed the conversation and had some tea and cakes, which were very good.

We walked home in time to begin preparations for supper. Father returned from the hat shop, bringing the mail. Of course, it is too soon for the doctor to write, if he was to do that, but I was nervous nevertheless. I am almost sorry I wrote to him, because Mother and Father will surely wonder why I did. I'm still hoping that the next time I see him, I can talk in private with him, but Mother always stays. I suppose it's because she believes a young, single woman should not be alone in a room with a man, but he's a doctor.

Sometimes I feel like I'm being overly sheltered. After all, women are now working alongside men in many occupations. Times are changing, with most colleges and hospitals now open to women.

### Friday, July 2

It was a warm day today, and we had some rain last night, which is good for my flowers. The annuals I added to the gardens are doing well, but I love the wildflowers that will come back every year. Even if I don't do anything about planting annuals, I know the flowerbeds will look lovely with all their wild beauty.

When I'm not weeding or planting in the gardens, I have been working on my new silk dress. I purchased the dress pattern last week for 20 cents. It is to have a pointed neckline, with a trimmed collar. It's a day dress and will have a pleated skirt and a fabric draped bustle. Emeline came by and helped with the stitching. I asked her about my idea to cover a fan with the same fabric. With the warmer weather, a fan often helps make you feel cooler, even for a little while. She thought it would be a nice touch to go with the dress. Some women still use parasols for when they are in the sun, but I love the warmth of the sun after a long, cold, snowy winter.

Afterwards, we joined Mother for some tea and cakes that she had baked that morning. It was a nice leisurely day, and my cough seemed much better today, perhaps because of the warm temperatures.

After Emeline left for home, I walked out into the meadow and picked a few berries. The wild blackberries are doing well this year as well as the raspberries. They will taste good on my porridge mornings.

Father came home from work and brought the mail. No letter as yet from the doctor. I think I should tell Mother and Father that I wrote to him. I don't like thinking they might not have approved of my writing it, but I need to know why I'm not getting better. Surely, they will understand my need to know something so important to my future. How can I plan on being a teacher or having a family someday if I don't know what is wrong with me? Perhaps the doctors don't even know. There is still so much mystery about so many diseases that I don't know how doctors can tell one from another.

After dinner, we sat in the parlor reading. I have been reading about the Barnum and Bailey Circus, and particularly about General Tom Thumb. I would love to go to the circus. I have been to several local fairs but never to the circus. I would like to see all the animals, and, I am told, there are many interesting events as well. I have also begun reading The Song of Hiawatha. I think it would be wonderful for our scholars to read this in the fall.

Here it is only the beginning of the summer, and I'm already projecting into the school year. I hope I will be well enough by then to continue helping Mrs. Baglin with our young scholars.

### Saturday, July 3

It was a nice cooler day today but still warm. I arose early because I needed to help Mother with baking in the morning. Saturday is the day when we can expect company to stop by, so we need to have something to offer them.

While Father was in the barn caring for the animals, Mother and I had a quiet breakfast and then set about making piecrusts and cake batter. While the cake was baking we prepared blueberries for the pies. There is something so pleasant about the scents of cakes and pies baking, which Father mentioned when he came in the door. I could see he was looking forward to an afternoon of company, but was it mostly for the blueberry pie? Father does love his desserts, yet because he is so active he stays slender.

Mother had put on a little weight over the winter when we were less active, but she is back to her regular self now with all the activities we need to do in the gardens.

After lunch, neighbors began to arrive to visit, and Father got to have the piece of blueberry pie he was hoping for. Dr. Brown also came up from Newtown to visit. Though Father and Mother have taken me to see Dr. Brown in the past, most of the time I have seen Dr. Kerrmann. I didn't say anything to Dr. Brown about the letter I wrote, but I did wonder if the two doctors talk to each other about their patients or asked advice about certain ailments. I wish I knew more so I would feel more knowledgeable when I spoke to them about my condition.

Dr. Brown had walked down from the cars, but when he began to depart, Father offered to carry him there, so he didn't have to walk back.

Later, I found that I was coughing badly, just like most days. After everyone had left, I rested in the parlor until Sarah arrived later. She had left Normie and Frank at Aunt Harriet's for a visit, then Aunt Harriet and Uncle Henry brought them here to visit with us. We all had dinner together, then a short time after they all left for their homes.

## Sunday, July 4

The holiday was pleasant with company almost all day. Following services and a small get-together afterward, we arrived home to find that Frank, Sarah, and Normie had arrived to share the holiday festivities with us. Then Emeline arrived, bringing me a bouquet of flowers, and Uncle Henry stopped by in time to join us for lunch.

Father and Mother always observe the Fourth of July with the flag flying and a picnic lunch on the porch. Father remembered his Civil War comrades during prayers, noting their actions helped keep the union together.

After lunch, which included lots of lemonade and cake, we all played croquet on the lawn, with Sarah, as usual, winning the first game. For a while I entertained Normie, pushing him around in his pram and making him laugh. Then he wanted to get out and run around, and after chasing him for a while, I had to catch him and sit down. I was out of breath from all the activity. Meanwhile, it looked like Frank might win the second croquet game, until Sarah sent his ball into the weeds at the side of the yard. It took him several strokes to get back into the game, and by that time, Sarah had won again.

Father and Mother were laughing so hard because Sarah was doing a little victory dance in front of Frank, who tried very hard not to laugh at her antics. Even Normie was amused, even though he probably didn't really understand what was going on between his parents. He is so cute. I can't wait until he is old enough to play. Then croquet will really be fun.

## Monday, July 5

It was a pleasant morning, but rained later in the afternoon when Father, Mother, Sarah, Frank, Normie, and I set off in the buggy for Aunt Harriet's. Father was not staying after dinner because he had a meeting later at the Town Hall, and since he didn't need us at home, Aunt Harriet asked us to stay the night, which we did.

Aunt Harriet said I was looking very thin and insisted that I be weighed. Much to everyone's surprise, but not mine, I weighed 100 pounds, about 15 pounds less than usual. This, of course, is why all my clothing has required the alternations I have been making continually the last few months. I have to admit that knowing the exact amount of weight loss made me more than ever want to know what is wrong with me. I can hardly wait to talk to the doctor.

Mother was troubled by the results of my weighing. I now believe I need to talk to her and Father about my concerns about my health and go to see the doctor soon. I want to know how I will be when school begins again. Will I be able to follow my dream of being a teacher or can I expect only more illness in my future?

I could tell that Sarah was also troubled. I felt bad that I was causing them concern, but it has been obvious to me that I have been constantly losing weight despite the amount of food I eat.

After dinner, we spent some time in the parlor talking or reading the Bible. We were a somber group, all of us, when we later went upstairs to our bedrooms. I know I was the cause of concern.

## Tuesday, July 6

The rain cleared off this morning but began again in the early afternoon when we were leaving Aunt Harriet's after an enjoyable luncheon.

Aunt Harriet had started to bring us home, but we met Father on his way to us so we rode home with him. Sarah and Normie are going to stay with us for a few days so she can help mother with some of the chores that I have been unable to do. After a short time at home, Father carried Frank home to New Milford because he has to work tomorrow.

Since I could not work in my gardens because of the rain, I took my book of Longfellow's poetry into the parlor and curled up on the sofa. Though it is July, the room was cool because of the rain. I seem to feel cold more often now, so I had a small quilt around me rather than starting a fire in the fireplace.

Mother had said nothing on the way home about my weighing, but she seemed deep in thought and when Father came home, I heard them and Sarah talking in the kitchen, but was unable to hear what was being said. Mother was probably telling him of my weight loss.

I have not said anything about it, but Mother was aware I was altering some of my clothing. However, I don't think she realized how much I was taking in my skirts, and because of our long skirts and long-sleeved shirtwaists, even I wasn't aware of how much thinner I have become.

I lost interest in reading, and just looked around the room. It is a pleasant place. The dark-stained furniture is polished weekly. The floor is carpeted, and when we were little, Sarah and I often played on the floor with our dolls. Family portraits are on the walls, and there are drapes at the windows. It is a place where our family comes together nightly to read, talk, or just relax, which is what we did after dinner tonight after Sarah had put Normie to bed.

Mother and Father talked to me about seeing Dr. Kerrmann in Woodbury or having him come here to see me. It was then that I told them of the letter I had written to him. They were surprised, of course, and questioned why I hadn't come to them before doing so. Father was particularly upset. As head of our family, he thinks he must know about everything before anything is done. I apologized for not telling them, but said I was tired of taking syrups and potions that don't help, and that I wanted to know what is wrong, so I could know what the future holds for me.

After considerable more conversation, during which Father was still upset that I had taken matters into my own hands, I again apologized. I had acted in haste without thinking it out and regretted doing so but could not undo it. They agreed that I should see the doctor as soon as possible. Father will contact Dr. Kerrmann, and see whether he would come to our house or we go to him in Woodbury. Perhaps he could combine a visit here with others he might have.

## Wednesday, July 7

It was a clear day today after all the rain yesterday. I rose early as usual, even though I didn't sleep very well last night. I felt I had caused Mother and Father to become upset as a result of not only my weight loss but about my letter to the doctor that I didn't tell them about.

I feel sad to have caused them pain. It hadn't been my intent. After I wrote the doctor, I knew I had done wrong, but it was too late to do anything about it.

This morning at breakfast both Father and Mother were quiet, which is not like them. I know they are upset with me. There's nothing I can do to undo it. Father was particularly unsettled. I kept feeling his eyes upon me and, when I would look at him, he would look away. He looked sad. Is it possible he is worried about me and that is why he was so somber? Perhaps he is not so much angry with me as he is concerned. He did say he would contact Dr. Kerrmann within the next few days so that he can either come here or we can go to Woodbury to see him.

I am nervous about seeing the doctor even though that was my intent when I wrote to him. There has still been no reply, but he is probably too busy with other patients to reply to letters from nervous young women.

After breakfast, I helped Sarah clear the table and do the dishes. Mother was busy baking bread and cake for the next few days, so the kitchen was a very busy place. Later, after lunch with Mother, Sarah, and Normie, which was still very quiet except for Normie's chatter, I went out to my flower gardens. I always feel more at peace there, and the flowers are flourishing. I was pulling weeds when Sarah came out, saying she was going cherrying and raspberrying in the orchard while Normie was napping, and did I want to go with her. I declined, saying the rain had put me behind in the flower beds, and I wanted to finish the weeding. I really declined because I didn't want to talk about yesterday with Sarah. She had been casting worrisome glances toward me all day, and I just wanted to forget about everything until I see the doctor.

Sarah had good luck in the orchard, and we can expect Mother to make a cherry pie and some raspberry jam.

## Thursday, July 8

It was a warm day today. In the morning, Mother was churning butter and Sarah was ironing. Then she went berrying and had good luck again. She said it was warmer today than yesterday, so she was thankful for the lemonade we had made when she returned from the orchard. Because of her efforts, we will have plenty of raspberry jams and jellies to share with her and her family in the winter months. It will seem like a little bit of summer during the cold weather.

Mother made a cherry pie for supper, which smelled so good that we were all tempted to dip into it while it was still warm. Mother said if we wanted some sweet cream for it, we would have to wait for dinner. That is worth the wait, and we all enjoyed it later.

In the afternoon, I took Normie to the barn to play with the cats. We have four that live in the barn and catch mice, but we also let them come in the house during cold weather. There is one gray cat that I particularly like. Perry loves to play with strings and sometimes when I have a ball of yarn, he can be very entertaining, rolling on the floor with it or getting all tangled up in it. He also likes ribbons and can get into trouble at Christmas when we are wrapping gifts. He wants to play, and we need to get our wrapping done. He would lay on the floor and roll around in the ribbons and bows. Once Sarah tied a ribbon around his neck, and he didn't like that at all, but it didn't stop him from playing with the ribbons.

There was a musical program at the church tonight that we all attended after dinner. It was good to see some of our neighbors and church members. George was there and sat behind us with his parents. I love the piano, and it was wonderful to hear some classical offerings as well as current and religious music. It was cooler in the church than outside, with a slight breeze through the open doorway. Following the program, we spent some time outside talking to friends and enjoying refreshments. George came and talked to me for a while. Everything seems to be normal between us. Our friendship does not appear to be changed.

The ride home in the buggy was cooling. Mother and Father seemed more relaxed than they had been the last couple of days, and I think the music calmed them. They even seemed cheerful when we arrived home. Mother plays the piano, but she also loves to hear others play. After some time reading in the parlor, we all went to bed.

### Friday, July 9

The day was pleasant and warm. After breakfast with Mother and Sarah, I spent some time in the parlor answering a letter from Ida, then worked for a short time in my flowerbeds doing some weeding. It's always amazing to me how I can pull a weed one day and come back the next and it seems like another has taken its place very close to where the other one was.

Sarah went berrying again after lunch and returned with a pan full of blueberries. I felt sad that I didn't feel up to helping with the berry picking. The walk to the orchard has begun to tire me, and I have found I feel better just working in the gardens where I can sit on the grass and pull weeds. Sarah said she has to get to the berries before the birds or we will not have any for jam and pies. Mother spent the afternoon sitting on the front porch with some mending.

I spent the afternoon on my bed reading, but sometimes I was distracted from the dime novel I bought at the store last week. I kept wondering whether Father would go to Woodbury to see Dr. Kerrmann to make an arrangement for him to see me. In some way, I am sorry I wrote to him, and since he has not replied, I'm not sure he will have time to see me for a while. While I want to know what is wrong with me, I wonder if he even knows. Sometimes it seems as if doctors rely too much on tonics and syrups because they really don't know what is wrong. It's obvious that these things have not been of much help to me, and I wonder if they help anyone

After dinner, we all went to our neighbor's house for the evening. George was there and some of our other friends. We played charades and some card games. George and I as usual were partners in charades and did very well with our subjects. Refreshments included cake and lemonade just before we left for home. George walked out to the buggy with me, and we had a very pleasant talk. From some things he said, I think he hopes I will someday change my mind about a change in our relationship. We do get along very well, but that might change with a new relationship. I know I can't make any decisions for my future until I am assured my health will be better.

It was late when we arrived home so we all went right up to bed. I couldn't sleep for a while because I was thinking about the evening and the fun I had with George. I am so happy we are still good friends, but I do wonder how long it would last if he met someone he was interested in calling on or courting. I also wondered how I would feel if that occurred. Would I be jealous? Would I regret my decision? Oh, diary, I'm not sure if I could ever love George in the way a wife should love her husband. We have always been friends, but that would change with courtship and marriage. Between my health and concerns about a change in my relationship with George, I am sure I made the correct decision.

### Saturday, July 10

It was a warm day, but we had a hard shower in the afternoon that continued into the evening so it was not possible to work in the gardens. I could just imagine the weeds growing.

After breakfast, Sarah took the buggy to go to New Milford to bring Frank here to help Father with some barn chores. Father had hoped to do some haying tomorrow, but it will probably be too wet because of the showers.

Mother and I watched Normie while Sarah was gone. After a busy time with Normie during the morning and an early lunch, I felt very tired and retired to my room for a rest until I heard the buggy's wheels coming up the gravel road. Sarah had returned with Frank.

Sarah said they had run into showers all the way from New Milford, and it did not look like it was going to stop in time to do much outside. After Frank took care of Bess and the buggy, he joined us in the kitchen for some tea and cake.

This is why I sometimes like a rainy day. It brings us all together, to talk about family concerns and to just enjoy being together, dry and cozy inside, while the rain keeps coming down. It has been so wonderful having Sarah here to help Mother because I have been unable to do very much of the work I usually did. I get coughing and my chest hurts, then Mother insists that I rest for a while between chores, so I don't get over tired.

We had an early dinner and spent some time in the dining room playing cards. No one called today, probably because of the sour weather, and we all retired early.

## Sunday, July 11

There were no outside chores today. It was warm enough, but it rained off and on until night when it cleared off. Frank had helped Father yesterday with cleaning the barn and taking care of the animals, but with the rain continuing today, we all spent most of the day in the house. As usual, Father and Frank took care of the animals and did some milking. The animals need to be fed and watered and their stalls cleaned every day despite what the weather is. A farmer's work is never done. Father is concerned about haying because of all the rain we are having. He hasn't cut it yet, but if he had, the crop might have been lost if it wasn't put in the barn soon enough.

Sarah helped Mother with meals and dishes so I did not have very much to do. Because I wasn't feeling very well, I spent the time reading Longfellow's poetry, and I have started Ben Hur: A Tale of Christ by Lew Wallace. It is quite interesting, and, because it was Sunday and we didn't go to church, Father led us in reading the Bible after lunch. Normie was napping so it was a quiet time for us to be together and discuss what we had read.

It was so peaceful that we could hear the church bells as services ended in the center as clearly as we could hear the ticking of the grandfather clock in the parlor. Later we played whist, which has become a popular card game of our family.

Later, Mother and Sarah did some crocheting while I read to Normie. No one called, probably because it was a good day just to stay inside and enjoy some quiet pursuits.

Father is also concerned about the tobacco crop because of all the rain. If it rains heavily, it could damage the plants.

## Monday, July 12

We had clearing during the day, but rain returned in the evening. After Father arrived home from taking Frank to New Milford for work, I went up town with him and Normie.

While we were away getting the mail and a newspaper, Sarah helped Mother with the wash. Then she went up in the back field to do some more berrying. We will have plenty of blueberries and blackberries for jam and pies to bring to the many social events that will be taking place in town and at the church.

We always like to have cakes and pies ready for when our friends and members of our family come to call. Mother is a wonderful cook, and Sarah and I do our best to help her prepare for our guests. I enjoy these hours spent together in the kitchen. I have found I enjoy making pies, no matter what kind. Today it was blueberry pies. I sat at the table and rolled out the dough for the piecrusts while Sarah prepared the filling. We use recipes passed down in the family, and I imagine the pies we make are just as good as those my grandparents enjoyed. The kitchen smelled so good when the blueberries were simmering on the stove. It was even better once the pies were in the oven.

It is so nice to be a part of a family that has a long history. We have always enjoyed our times together with so many aunts, uncles and cousins. As I've written before, dear diary, Mother and her sisters and brothers have always been close, and they either come to our home or we go to theirs. Every year we have a big summer reunion when everyone comes. I'm looking forward to it though no date has been set. There are always plenty of games, food, and family chatter. It's a wonderful way to learn what everyone has been doing during the time we have been apart.

Early in the afternoon, Ella Pierce came to visit, and we all enjoyed a piece of pie and tea. Ella told us about some activities planned at the church this summer, such as musical nights, luncheons, and dinners. We are looking forward to all of them.

## Tuesday, July 13

It was cloudy today but for once it did not rain. It was a good feeling to get out of the house and be in the fresh, warm air. Since I felt stronger today, I took a short walk down the road to the schoolhouse and back. Of course, I was tired when I arrived home, but it was just cool enough that the walk had been enjoyable. I wonder if I will be able to do that every day once school begins again. I want so much to be a teacher, but am I being unrealistic? Perhaps I will not be able to continue my work at the school in preparation for becoming a teacher. When I think about that possibility I feel so sad.

Despite being tired, after lunch I worked in my flower gardens for a while. Since Father did not have to work today, he and Uncle Henry and their friends, Charles and Ambrose, went fishing and had good luck. We will all enjoy a meal of fresh fish tomorrow with some of the vegetables from our garden.

I am feeling very nervous about Father going to see Dr. Kerrmann to arrange for him to see me. I'm so sorry I wrote to the doctor. It was a wrong thing to do. I should have talked to Father before doing something so rash. It was just that I was feeling so bad and nothing the doctors give me helps me. I'm so afraid that the doctor will tell me bad news about my condition. Why was I so hasty about finding out something that I might not want to hear: I am trying very hard to eat well and exercise, but just like today I get so tired whenever I do anything too active. I don't think I will be much fun at croquet and lawn tennis this summer. I have always enjoyed those activities at the church and neighborhood events. George and I always paired up for tennis, but I wonder if I will be able to play this year. I wonder if George will understand if I don't feel up to playing.

If that happens, will our friendship change? I would not blame him if he sought another partner for tennis. During croquet, when it's not my turn, I can always sit on the grass, but tennis is very active, and I wonder if I will be able to do it. I don't want to disappoint George, and most of all I wonder how I would feel if he was playing with someone else.

### Wednesday, July 14

It rained a little today, but Father had some clear weather later in the day for working in the tobacco field. Sarah also went up to the orchard and picked some more blueberries. They taste so good when they are fresh from the bushes. I have to admit when I would go to pick them, some of them didn't make it back to the house. Mother always teased me that she could tell from the blueness of my tongue that I had a snack on the way back. It was just too tempting not to indulge.

It seems so long since I went berrying or did anything too strenuous. I'm sure Dr. Kerrmann is going to say I need to do more exercise to keep up my strength, and I do try but I get so tired.

Father said last night that if he can leave work early tomorrow, he will go to Woodbury to see Dr. Kerrmann. I'm beginning to dread that more every day. Why did I ever write that letter? If I hadn't, I would never have had to tell Mother and Father about it, and they would not be making arrangements for me to see the doctor. I want to know what is wrong with me, and then another side of me doesn't want to know, especially if the news is not good.

I did write the letter so now I must go through with this. I try to remember how frustrated I was at that time because of how sour I was always feeling. It made me do something that I would not ordinarily do by not telling my parents I had written the letter until it was too late to do anything about it.

I have had to make so many decisions recently, and most were with Mother and Father's knowledge, but I hurt them by writing that letter without telling them of my concerns for my health. I usually try to put a brave face on, so they don't worry, but by doing this, I caused them pain anyway. Since then they have been more concerned about me than ever, and I notice how much Mother is relying on Sarah now to help her with some of the work I once did.

### Thursday, July 15

It rained a little in the morning but cleared off in the afternoon when our folks went fishing. Father was unable to leave work early today, so he wasn't able to see Dr. Kerrmann. I was relieved, but I know it's only been postponed until Father can get away early enough. It only gives me more time to lament my action in writing the letter to the doctor. I just wasn't thinking but acting out my frustrations over never feeling well anymore. There are so many things I once did that I enjoyed that I feel unable to do now. I love to take long walks to the orchard or to the schoolhouse, but I always come back so tired that I find it difficult to do much else that day.

It's good that I love to read, because I don't have to do anything strenuous for that. I've also been checking books Sarah and I enjoyed as children, so I can introduce them to the children once school begins again. I am determined I will be able to go back to school.

One of my continuing comforts is the work I do in my gardens. There, I can sit on the ground and weed or plant. I am still transplanting some wildflowers into the gardens that will bloom in the fall. It's not as easy as it once was to go into the field and dig up the flowers, but I am determined to do it. Sarah has said she would help me, but she is already doing so many of the chores I once did. She comes here to help Mother and isn't able to do as much at her own home. Luckily Frank is here a great deal to help Father with the tobacco or haying, so it's not like she is not with her family.

Normie continues to be a joy for me. He keeps me company when I'm in the garden, and even helps water the plants, though sometimes they don't need water because it has rained. But he likes to help, so I let him, plus it gives Sarah time to help Mother without worrying about what he is doing.

We had an early dinner tonight and spent some time in the parlor reading. No one came to call so we went early to bed.

**Friday, July 16**

It was clear this morning, but though it looked like there might be a shower in the afternoon, it never rained. Father said this morning at breakfast that he hopes the rain holds off long enough for him to get some haying done when Frank is here tomorrow. He also has to do some work in the tobacco field. Uncle Henry may come by to help with the haying.

I played outside with Normie this afternoon after lunch and before he went in for his nap. Then while Mother watched Normie, Sarah and I took Bess and the buggy up town and around by the hollow. We had a nice ride, and then met Frank at the cars. It felt good to get out in the warmth, especially since there was no rain. I always enjoy going with Sarah because it gives us time to talk. She is very concerned about me, I can tell, and she tries to keep me talking and laughing to keep my spirits up. Sometimes I laugh so hard my chest and back hurt, but it's good to have this time alone with Sarah.

There is a social at one of our neighbor's tomorrow night. I am looking forward to it. Perhaps George will be there. Some of my friends will be going. It will be good to see them.

Mother said she will take a couple of pies to add to the dessert table as well as some baked chicken for the meal.

Sarah, Frank and Normie will stay the night tomorrow so they can attend the social. Frank is going home early Sunday morning to take care of chores there and to get ready for work the next day, but Sarah and Normie will stay with us.

We had an enjoyable dinner together with much conversation about family and chores that need to be done in the fields. Father said he was hopeful that tomorrow he and Frank would get some work done in the tobacco field. Hopefully the hay field will dry out from the rain, so some haying will also get done. Father said he would wait and see what tomorrow brought as far as fair skies.

### Saturday, July 17

It was a pleasant day, and though there was a brief shower in the afternoon, it did not prevent Father and Frank from finishing their chores in the hayfield and tobacco fields.

During the afternoon, Mother baked the chicken and Sarah and I helped with the pies we will take to the social. Though I felt a little tired, I was looking forward to seeing everyone later, and it was a wonderful gathering. Many from the neighborhood were there as well as relatives and friends from the area. Mother's chicken was very popular and was soon gone as well as the pies we had made. After dinner, some of us played lawn games while others sat about on blankets or on the porch talking. George and I paired up for lawn tennis, and then took part in a game of croquet, which, of course, Sarah won, as usual.

Normie was very happy because there were other children to play with. They chased each other around or tumbled about on the ground playing with toy trucks, successfully getting both their clothes and hands dirty. I became tired from playing croquet and retired to the porch where I enjoyed watching their fun. Sarah was a little concerned because Normie is younger than some of the children, and thought he might get hurt, but he was fine.

Some of the older children played hide and seek, leapfrog, or tug of war. I can remember playing those games when I was young and just recently with the scholars in the schoolyard.

When it became dark, it was time to pack up and go home, with Frank carrying a very tired little boy. I think Normie was glad to go to bed after Sarah had successfully cleaned him up. He fell asleep soon with one of his toys tucked under his arm. He was so tired.

## Sunday, July 18

Today was a clear day, but not as warm as yesterday. Sarah left early after breakfast to take Frank to New Milford, and we did not go to church. I would have liked to go, but just didn't feel up to it. I think the social last night was a little too much for me. I felt very tired this morning, and I think Father and Mother did also.

Normie was even more quiet than usual and went for his morning nap without any disagreement. I think he was worn out by yesterday's games and the fun he had with the other children. He's a very social child and was very happy with all the attention he received because of being the youngest child there.

I spent the morning reading the Bible and some of Mother's magazines, curled up on the parlor sofa. It was quite a while before Sarah returned, so Mother, Father, Normie, and I had lunch together. I read to Normie for a while afterwards, and we played with his wooden soldiers and blocks on the parlor floor. I also took some yarn and did cat's cradle with him. He loves that. I am also trying to teach him to count, though he is a bit young for that. He can recite one to five, though, but loses interest for anything more. He would just rather play.

Sarah came back later, and Father went out to put Bess and the buggy away. She said she was later than she thought because she decided to stay for lunch with Frank. I think they enjoy time alone sometimes. They love Normie, and I know they would like to have more children, but, as Sarah always says, once you have children, your time is not your own, so you have to find time to spend with your husband.

Sarah said the roads are a little rough and bumpy because of all the rain we have had recently so her ride was not very comfortable.

In the evening, no one called so we spent time in the parlor reading and talking, and later all of us were glad to go to bed because it had been a busy two days.

## Monday, July 19

It was a pleasant day today. Sarah did the washing while Mother did the housework. Not needing to help them, and not feeling well enough, I worked for a while sitting by one of my flower gardens, weeding and snipping back the flowers that needed it. Normie played outside and kept me company as I worked. He was so good that I said he could bring his Mama a flower. After he picked out a bright yellow daisy, we went indoors for lunch with Mother and Sarah.

Sarah, of course, hugged and kissed Normie when he presented her with his flower choice, saying it was her favorite color. He just smiled and smiled and was very good during lunch.

After lunch, Sarah put Normie down for a nap, and we sat on the porch for a while until it became too warm. Because of our tall trees, the house is shaded and feels cooler than outside.

Mother decided to make some more blueberry jam. Sarah is in a race with the birds to pick the rest of the berries and went up to the orchard after lunch. I sat in the parlor reading for a while, enjoying the quiet as Mother had gone outside to pick some vegetables for dinner.

When Father came home, he brought me a letter form Aunt Fannie. I always enjoy her letters, but this time she mentioned her concerns about my weight loss, the news of which has traveled from family home to family home, it seems. In a large family, there are no secrets or no taboos on what can be discussed, even if you would prefer it not be. Even in New York, they heard about it. The Post Office must have been very busy with all the Tyrrell family letters going back and forth.

I admit I was a little unnerved by all the attention I have been receiving. It's not as if I'm trying to lose weight; it has just happened. I don't know why, but perhaps I will once I see Dr. Kerrmann, whenever that will be.

Since the evening was cooler, following dinner we took a short walk outside with Normie and Father. Then after Normie was put to bed, we played cards in the dining room until quite late.

## Tuesday, July 20

It was rainy most of the day today. At breakfast Father said he was leaving work early today to see Dr. Kerrman in Woodbury.

This upset me, though I had hoped to see him when I wrote the letter. I have had a while to consider the action I took and am sorry I have so upset my parents and sister and the rest of the family. Everyone is so concerned about me, and I know this is because they care about me, but I'm not happy about all the attention I have been getting from friends as well as relatives. I can only hope that Dr. Kerrman is able to see me soon, and that the news will be good.

Despite my concerns, our day went on as usual. During one of the breaks in the showers, Sarah went berrying, and then came back and did the ironing. Mother and I folded clothes and linens as Sarah ironed, and soon we were done, and everything was put away. Laundry takes so long that it fills up a great deal of a day. It can be very tiring, but many hands do make light work.

After lunch, Maggie Casey came to see me. It was good to see her because we did not have much time to talk at last weekend's social. Possibly because of the weather, my throat felt a little sore, and I was coughing. We probably talked too long, but it was so nice to see Maggie. After she left, I rested on the parlor sofa with a magazine.

I read an article that discussed wages earned by teachers. It seems that women make about $33 a month compared to $42 for men. Why is this? Is it because men have greater responsibilities at home for a family and women don't because in most cases they are not married? I found this quite upsetting. With colleges now more open to women students, why shouldn't they be paid an equal wage to that of men if they have the ability?

I think it is so because men are in important positions in government and business, and they look out for each other. Who looks out for women? Possibly the women in the suffrage movement, but they are primarily concerned with getting women the right to vote. They may be correct, though, because if we could vote, we might be able to obtain action on our concerns, such as equal pay.

I have often wondered, too, why women who are married are unable to be teachers. Is it because they would keep a man from obtaining that position? Or is it because men believe women should care for the home and children and not work outside the home at all? I wonder if couples who are to be married discuss this concern or if the woman takes it for granted that she would not be able to work out of the home.

### Wednesday, July 21

It was cloudy part of the day today. After breakfast, Father carried Sarah, Frank, and Normie home before going to work at Rorrabacks.

Father did see Dr. Kerrmann yesterday, and he said he would try to see me within a week or so when he is here in Roxbury seeing other patients. Of course, this news made md feel very apprehensive because I'm afraid of what he will tell me. I really wish I had never written him and started all this. Perhaps he will be able to help me with some new tonic but none of his potions have helped in the past. I still cough and have pain in my chest and am always so tired.

After lunch with Mother, I worked in my flower garden for a while until Ella Pierce came to see me. Also, it was a sad day because Aunt Betsy Brown was buried today. While Mother was at the funeral in Southbury, I visited with Ella and after she left, I picked some berries.

I felt stronger today, but the walk to and from the orchard was tiring so I rested in the parlor while Mother was making dinner. Father brought the mail when he returned from work, and I received letters from friends in Danbury.

During dinner, Mother talked about Aunt Betsy's funeral. Mother is very sad because she and Aunt Betsy had been friends for many years. Though she was not related to us, she always seemed like family. We often visited her, and she also called on us. It must be very difficult to lose a life-long friend, one who knew you as a child and as an adult. I know I would be very sad if any of my friends were to die.

### Thursday, July 22

It was very rainy today so there was no work that could be done outside in the flower gardens, though Mother did go out to gather some vegetables for dinner. The gardens are doing well this year because we have had just enough sun and rain to nurture them. I am so pleased with my flowers and look forward to transplanting some more of the fall wildflowers from the fields and by the road. I hope tomorrow is nice, so I can do some weeding.

After lunch, Mrs. Hodge and Frances called, bringing me a bouquet of flowers and some honey.

Mother and I enjoyed their visit, serving blueberry pie and tea, and catching up on the news of the town. They left for home shortly before Father returned from work. He had brought me some peaches and an orange from New Milford. I had the orange for dessert with some berries. It tasted so good. I think I will have some peaches with my breakfast tomorrow.

I love fruit and think I could just live on that, if there was enough. I think Mother might frown on that because it would not be nourishing enough just by itself.

After dinner and cleanup, we spent some quiet time in the parlor. No one called so it gave us time to talk about our day and the company we had entertained that afternoon. Father read some from the Bible before we all went to bed.

**Friday, July 23**

It was very cloudy today, but it did not rain as expected. After breakfast, Father and Uncle Henry left for Seymour's where they worked for half the day, then were home for lunch.

I did manage to work in the gardens for a while this afternoon before company arrived. About two o'clock, Ella Lattin and her husband arrived, and Susan Minor and her husband brought me some peaches. I will have quite a bit of fruit for a while. The peach trees are producing well this year. Mother said she would probably make a peach pie. I just love peach pie, and she knows that.

I felt well today and thoroughly enjoyed the time with our callers. There are many socials being planned throughout the summer that I hope we will be able to attend. A Tyrrell family reunion is also being planned by Aunt Harriet. It will be sometime in August at our house. Mother is helping her by asking members of the family to bring a main dish, vegetables, or dessert. There are so many in Mother's family that it is a big job to get them all together, even once a year.

Of course, we see mother's sisters and brothers who live locally very often, and especially at holidays, but others, such as Aunt Fannie, who live away from the area, need early notification so they can make their plans, especially if they will be traveling by train.

### Saturday, July 24

It was a pleasant day, no longer cloudy, but I didn't enjoy it. I was quite poorly again today and didn't even feel up to working in my gardens. I spent most of the morning reading in the parlor while Mother did some baking in the event we would have callers today or tomorrow. I wanted to help her, but I just felt so fatigued, and she insisted that I rest.

It was good that she baked because our minister, Mr. Smith, called early in the afternoon when I was sitting outside on the porch. He and I talked for a while, then Mother brought out lemonade and peach pie for us.

Mr. Smith stops to see me often and is always very concerned about my health. I try to put on a brave face for him because he has so many people to worry about. I don't think he believes me when I say I am feeling well. He knows I was always very active in the church, and during the winter and spring I did not attend many of the meetings or socials because I just didn't have the strength. It's been easier now that the weather is warmer, and I have enjoyed the entertainments that have been held and the socials at neighbors.

After Mr. Smith left to visit other parishioners, Emma Beers called around tea time, and we had tea and peach pie with her in the dining room. Then she left to go home.

Father had been to New Milford to see friends and returned in time for dinner.

### Sunday, July 25

It was a very warm day, but not uncomfortable. We had breakfast early, then attended services at the church where we saw several people we had not seen recently. After many conversations with them after church, we returned home. After Father put Bessie in the pasture, we spent some time sitting on the porch reading the local paper and discussing upcoming events we had heard about at church.

I feel better when there is warmth, but not if it is muggy. The air was very clear and fresh this morning. After lunch I worked in my flower gardens for a while, then took a short walk down the road toward the river.

When I felt tired, I returned to find that Mr. Hodge, Millie Vose, and Emeline had called. We again sat on the porch enjoying the clear day and conversation.

There is a meeting at the schoolhouse tonight that Father and Mr. Hodge are to attend. I don't know if it is about the school or whether it is a town issue. I find it difficult to keep up with town events, and, even if I could, what could I do about it. Only the men are able to vote. Mother only attends meetings when something is being discussed about the schools, so I think tonight's meeting must be about an issue before the town. Neither she nor Millie and Emeline appeared involved in what Father and Mr. Hodge were discussing. I know I wasn't paying much attention to what they were saying.

When Father and Mr. Hodge took a walk out to the garden, Mother and I had time with Millie and Emeline to talk about other things, such as a music program next Sunday at the church. When they returned, Mother and I served lemonade and peach pie, and after a while they all left for home.

After dinner Father saddled Bessie and left for the meeting. Mother and I spent the evening reading in the parlor and doing some crocheting.

## Monday, July 26

It was another warm day today. I have felt better the last two days, probably because there is no dampness or mugginess to cause me pain. The weekend was restful, with both visitors and quiet time so I was rested.

Mother washed clothes in the morning and hung them outside to dry. After breakfast Father went up town on some business before going to work.

Mrs. Castle called after lunch, and later in the afternoon Mr. Rorraback visited with us until Father came home. After enjoying some tea and pie, Father and Mr. Rorraback went out to check on the hay that needs cutting. They expect to do that in the next few days if there is no rain. It takes some time to cut it, stack it, and then put it on the wagon for storage in the barn.

When Father came home, he told us he had seen Dr. Kerrmann in town. He said he was very busy but hoped to see me tomorrow if all goes well with his scheduled visits. I immediately became nervous, the thought of seeing him bringing memories of how all this started when I wrote to him without telling Mother and Father, and then had to tell them why I acted so impulsively. I'll never forget how I felt about deceiving them and causing them additional worries. I would have become much more depressed, but George stopped by on the way home from work and spent some time with us before dinner. It brought back memories of his request to call upon me and my refusal.

It was good seeing him, but I felt there was something different about him, or is it just because I am so afraid our friendship will change because I did not accept his calling upon me. I think he understands that I want to be sure I am well enough to make plans for the future. At this time, I don't even know if I will feel well enough to help at the school in the coming months. Mrs. Baglin counts on me, and I don't know if I will be of much help if I keep feeling as poorly as I do. The school day is long, from eight in the morning to four in the afternoon, and I don't know if I will be up to it. Hopefully Dr. Kerrmann can give me something to help.

**Tuesday, July 27**

Another warm day. I can almost believe I am better. Seeing George last night gave my spirits a lift. Mother and Father like him and have known his parents for years. We grew up together, spending time as families at each other's homes. I think they have always hoped we would have a life together some time in the future.

It's always wonderful to see him because he never seems to change. I think my anxiety yesterday was caused by my feelings that things could change if he began calling on someone else. There is no agreement between us, and he is free to do so. Even though I feel I'm not ready for such an adult decision, I think I still wish that my health had not caused me to hesitate about considering a different relationship. At times, though, I remember my reluctance wasn't all about my health, but about whether I was ready for such an arrangement and to give up my dream of becoming a teacher.

Speaking about my health, Diary, we expected the doctor today, but he did not come. His schedule must have been too busy. Perhaps he feels I am overly concerned about my health, and that I am just a silly young woman. He's always been kind to me, but I think I overstepped when I wrote to him without first telling my parents.

Mother, Father, and I began the day with a nice breakfast, then Father left for work. Mother did some chores, and we had lunch with Frank, who was passing through town on his way home from Danbury where he had been on business.

During the afternoon Mr. and Mrs. Bronson called. We had a nice visit with them, and after they left, Frank, Mother and I went to Mrs. Hodge's. Frank visited just a short time and then went home to New Milford. While I was there, Mrs. Hodge weighed me. I have lost more weight, and now weigh 98 ½ pounds.

I became very tired, but I didn't want Mother to have to leave so Bruce offered to bring me home in their buggy.

At night, I read some from a book by George Eliot that Mrs. Bronson gave me, and because no one called, we all went to bed early.

## Wednesday, July 28

It was cool and nice today. I was awake early, so I prepared myself for the day and went down to help Mother with a breakfast of eggs, toast, and coffee.

After breakfast, Father left for work at Rorrabacks, and Sarah and Normie arrived from New Milford. While Sarah played outside with Normie before his nap, Mother and I cleaned up the kitchen. I swept the floor while Mother washed the dishes, and then I wiped them and put them away. There are always chores that must be done to keep the house looking clean and tidy. Mother does not like an untidy kitchen and always cleans up after we finish a meal.

I found myself to be overly concerned about another loss in weight, but my mind was taken away from these thoughts because we had several visitors today.

In the afternoon, Uncle Philip and Aunt Fannie came up on the cars from New York and will stay the night. At tea time, Aunt Harriet, Mrs. Crofut, Mrs. Seymour, and Emeline came to call so we had a full house and wonderful conversation while enjoying Mother's blueberry pie. I found it a bit tiring with so many people here, but I was very happy to see them.

After Mrs. Crofut and Mrs. Seymour left for their own homes, Aunt Fannie, Uncle Philip, Emeline, Mother, Sarah, and I sat in the parlor and talked about the upcoming family reunion that will take place on August 22 following services. It seems that everyone will be there,

Of course, everyone will bring their best dish for the evening meal, and Mother and Aunt Harriet will make sure there are sandwiches, beverages, and desserts for luncheon. Hopefully there will be some freshly churned ice cream.

There will also be games for all ages. For the small children, there will be hide and seek, ducks and drakes, tug of war, leapfrog, and blind man's bluff. For the older people there will be croquet and lawn tennis. In the evening, there will be charades and card games, such as whist.

I'm sure the fun will last from morning to night, and everyone will have a good time. I'm always sorry to see the day end because, though we see most of the family throughout the year, this is the one day everyone comes together. It's then we hear the family stories about when Mother and her brothers and sisters were young. I never get tired of hearing them.

Father arrived home from work in time for dinner. It was like old times with all of us gathered around the dining room table. After dinner, Emeline left for home after helping us with the dishes. After everything was put away and Sarah had put Normie to bed, we joined Father and Uncle Philip in the parlor for cards.

**Thursday, July 29**
Another cool day, just perfect for working outdoors in my flower beds. We enjoyed breakfast with Philip and Fannie, then later in the morning they left to get the cars to return home.

After lunch, Mother, Sarah, Normie, and I went up town and stopped at Huldah's and stayed to tea. Huldah gave me a nice bouquet from her garden. She has beautiful day lilies and roses. She said when she separates the lilies, I could pick some to include in my gardens. I think the lilies would be an especially beautiful addition and would add to my wildflowers.

We have wild rosebushes along the stone walls in the meadow, but I don't think I would have any luck with the beautiful ones in Huldah's garden. She is a wonderful gardener and knows just what to do for her roses. I suppose she would be happy to help me if I decided to include some in my gardens.

When Mother and I returned home later, I put my bouquet in a vase and then went outside to weed and snip in my gardens, which are not as wonderful as Huldah's, but are of great joy to me. I have worked hard in them, and most of the flowers I have transplanted are thriving. I've had a few losses, but nothing too serious. I think sometimes I failed to get all the roots when I was digging them up and that may be why they died.

After all the visitors we had yesterday, today was very quiet with no callers. Sarah and Normie left for home after dinner, and Father, Mother, and I spent some time reading in the parlor and talking about the upcoming reunion.

**Friday, July 30**

It was another cool and pleasant day, with a lovely breeze. We spent a quiet morning doing chores and baking pies and cakes for the weekend for any callers who might arrive.

It was not a good day for me. I felt tired and my right side ached. While I am afraid of what Dr. Kerrmann may tell me, I almost wish he would come soon. Perhaps he can give me some new medicine to help with the fatigue and the pains I seem to be getting more and more often. I worry about the cost of having him come to see me, but Father said he can afford the dollar or two he will charge for the visit.

I find it hard to help Mother with the baking. I can't seem to stand very long so I have been sitting at the kitchen table making pie shells and rolling them out while she prepares the filling. This morning we made blueberry and peach pies and shortcake to have with some sweetened peaches and cream.

No one called today so the afternoon was very quiet. Father had gone to work early this morning and did not return until just before dinner, but he brought me a surprise. He had stopped at the post office, and I was pleased to have letters from two of my friends in Danbury. I will write them a letter tomorrow and ask Father to mail it the next time he goes up town.

## Saturday, July 31

It was warmer today than yesterday. It was a good thing that Mother had baked because we had visitors almost all afternoon. Aunt Lydia and Uncle Amos arrived early in the afternoon and will stay overnight. Later Mr. Smith called at tea time, and we all enjoyed pie and tea on the porch.

Aunt Lydia brought me a cake, pie, and some strawberry jelly, which I know I will enjoy. Aunt Lydia is an excellent baker.

We had an enjoyable dinner with Uncle Amos and Aunt Lydia. Despite my weight loss, I found I had a good appetite, and we all sampled Aunt Lydia's spice cake for dessert.

Mr. Hodge arrived in the evening. He, Father, and Uncle Amos went out to check the tobacco field while Mother, Aunt Lydia, and I visited in the parlor. Of course, there was more talk about the reunion plans because Mother and Aunt Lydia will be taking care of luncheon foods.

I felt very tired. It has been a busy few days, with people coming and going. While Mother and Aunt Lydia discussed possible lunch menus, I read some more of the book Mrs. Bronson gave me, but found that my eyes kept closing and I finally excused myself and went upstairs to bed.

## Sunday, August 1

It was very warm today, a typical August day, with barely any breeze to cool it. Uncle Amos and Aunt Lydia went home after breakfast, and later after church services and lunch, Dwight and George Evans and Emeline called.

Father spent some time in the tobacco field this afternoon. He plans to begin harvesting it this week. Every year, some of our relatives as well as Father's friends, help him to string the ripe tobacco leaves on strips of wooden lathes in the field. Then they load the lathes on the wagon and take them to the tobacco barn where they will be hung in four tiers to dry.

Once finished with our field, Father and the others will move on to another farm to harvest the tobacco crop there. Before they leave that final day, we will prepare a supper to thank them for their help. Sarah will be here to help us prepare the food, and the wives of the men also bring their best dishes to add to the feast.

Once harvested, the tobacco is hung in the tobacco barn to dry for several weeks. To protect the crop, the barn's sides are made of hinged boards that can be open for air circulation but that can also be closed to protect the tobacco from harsh wind.

After dinner, we attended the music program at the church. It was very entertaining and was followed by refreshments. We returned home quite late, and I was happy to go right to bed.

### Monday, August 2

It was a pleasant day. I did not feel well in the morning, so I was happy to see Dr. Brown when he called in the afternoon. Mother and I talked to him about my concerns about my health. He said he had talked to Dr. Kerrmann and was aware of my recent weight loss. He asked Mother about my appetite and suggested foods that might help me to gain weight. He said exercise and fresh air are important, for my cough, and that it is good that I try to walk some every day and work outside in my flower beds. However, he stressed that I should not overdo exercise because that would only increase my fatigue and the pain I am experiencing. He said I should start with short walks and slowly add to that as I was able. He said Dr. Kerrmann plans to come to examine me and see what could be done in the way of a cough syrup or some other medicine.

Upon leaving, Dr. Brown refused any payment because it had not been an official medical visit. After he left, Mother and I took a buggy ride near Jack's Brook and then stopped up town to get some groceries. By the time we got home, Father was home from work, and Mother and I began preparations for dinner, after which we played cards for a short time. Father then read some from the Bible and then we went early to bed.

### Tuesday, August 3

It was a rainy day today, a good day to stay indoors and read or do other indoor activities.

Breakfast had been quiet. Father had left early to take the cars to work in Danbury, and Mother and I dallied over our eggs and bacon before cleaning up the kitchen. I did some dusting in the parlor and then swept the kitchen and front hall. Then I was tired, so I turned to crocheting and reading.

I spent some time in the morning crocheting a collar for one of my shirtwaists. It will make it look very nice. After I tired of that, I read some more from George Eliot's book.

Aunt Harriet and Uncle Henry called in the early afternoon, and then he left to go to Hartford.

Plans for the family reunion are on-going, and Mother, Aunt Harriet, and I spent the afternoon deciding what foods to serve for lunch and dinner. Aunt Harriet is coordinating main dishes, vegetables, and desserts among the family members, but we need to know there will be enough for everyone that is coming.

Since the gardens have flourished this summer, I'm sure we can expect some very good recipes will be enjoyed that day.

Some of the family members will be arriving on Saturday, the 14th. Aunt Fannie, Uncle Phillip, and Nellie, Willie, and Winston will be staying with us Saturday and Sunday night, so we will have a full house for those days. Others who live away from here will come in on the cars on Saturday and will stay with other members of the family. Sarah is planning to help with that as she has an extra bedroom in her new home.

Aunt Harriet spent the night with us.

### Wednesday, August 4

It was another mean day, and we had rain most of the time. Aunt Harriet stayed a while until Uncle Henry came to carry her home late in the morning. He said he had spent most of yesterday in Hartford and was anxious to get home to catch up on chores there.

In the afternoon, Emeline called for a short time while on her way to other calls. She said she will be making pies for the reunion. It is only about two weeks away, and I am looking forward to seeing everyone. This yearly event always gets good attendance. Everyone is very busy all year long, but they always manage to save time to come to the reunion. Mother has been very busy cleaning the house in the event the weather is sour and we need to be inside. She has been washing windows and mirrors and polishing the furniture, so they shine. She has also been making some room in the pantry for all the food that will be arriving that day.

I'm hoping for a sunny day for the reunion, but not too warm, but it is August so we can't expect too much in the way of a cool day. No one will mind the heat. They never do because all our relatives will be so busy catching up on everyone's lives and taking part in games and other activities that they won't notice the weather. If we do have to be inside, our house is large enough to accommodate everyone.

Sadly, Stanley Squire died yesterday and will be buried on Friday. Mother and Father will most likely attend the funeral. They have known him for several years, and he has often called upon us here at home, and we have gone to his.

When Father came home today, he said he had seen Sarah, and she would like to have me come and stay with her for a few days. I think I will enjoy that. I'll be able to walk about the green and visit some people we know in New Milford. Father will take me in the morning and then go to work.

### Thursday, August 5

It was cloudy in the morning but it cleared off later. Father and I went to New Milford but found upon arriving that Sarah and Normie were not home. I felt very tired from the long drive and was disappointed that Sarah was not there. She was expecting us, so she left a note that she was nearby at Amanda's. Father went after her, and soon she, Father and Normie joined me. I was excited about staying over and looking forward to being with her, Frank, and Normie for a few days.

We had a nice lunch with Sarah, and then Father left. While Normie was napping, Sarah and I talked for a while about the upcoming reunion. We are both so excited because we will be seeing several of our cousins who we have not seen for a while because of school and work schedules. Sarah has been helping Aunt Harriet with contacting everyone about what to bring for food. She is also counting on the younger people bringing things for games during the day, such as croquet, and board games for after dinner.

My favorite parlor game has always been charades. It will seem strange this time without George. Perhaps Willie will be my partner or Amanda.

While Sarah was doing some work, I rested in her parlor and read to Normie when he woke up from his nap. He is so sweet and cuddly when he wakes from his nap, but after a quiet time with me reading, he was ready for more active things to do. He brought out some of his toys and played on the floor near me and proudly showed me all his treasures.

Frank came home after work and after taking care of his horse, he took Normie outside for some exercise before dinner. After dinner, we spent time talking and reading, then Sarah put Normie to bed, after which we played cards for a while before going to bed.

## Friday, August 6

It was a pleasant day today. Though I was tired yesterday when I arrived, I feel no worse for my ride. I did not cough last night, so I had a restful sleep. Normie woke me early by coming into my room and patting my cheek. Wake up, Aunt Eunice, he said. He was anxious for his breakfast so once he saw I was up, he was on his way to the kitchen where Sarah was cooking breakfast. Frank was enjoying a cup of coffee when I joined them.

I helped myself to coffee and joined Frank and Normie at the table. Sarah asked how I had slept since it was the first time I have stayed over with them in New Milford. It hadn't seemed as noisy as when I stayed at their place in Danbury. They are near the green so there are quite a few people around during the day, but not as many during the evening except if there are activities at the churches.

After Frank had left for work, I helped Sarah clean up the kitchen. Working together, we soon had the room tidy. Normie was playing with his train in the parlor so I went in to watch him while Sarah made beds and swept. Sarah was kept busy most of the morning and then before lunch we took Normie down on the green in his pram. It was very nice walking about and seeing people I haven't seen for some time.

I told Sarah that Stanley Squire was to be buried today and that Mother and Father would be going to the cemetery. Sarah said she was sorry to have heard about his death and would send a note of sympathy to his family. After lunch, Sarah and I talked for a while. Then I read to Normie from one of his books before she put him down for a nap.

I felt a little tired after our walk on the green so I went to my room to rest for a while before dinner.

No one called, and after dinner, after Normie was put to bed, Sarah, Frank and I played whist and backgammon before going to bed.

## Saturday, August 7

Today was another pleasant day. We are having a spell of good weather after the rain on Tuesday and Wednesday, though Father would say we still need more for the crops and the vegetable gardens.

Mrs. Welton came to see me in the morning, and after lunch I walked out to call on her. She gave me an orange, which was very nice. I will have it with my breakfast tomorrow. Later in the afternoon Mrs. Thayer called on Sarah and me, and we had an enjoyable time. She was full of news about New Milford and the fair, which will be in the fall.

Many people enter their flowers, fruits, and vegetables in it as well as home-made pies and other food items. We usually go to the fair, but I'm not sure if I will feel well enough. Mother and Father will be disappointed if I don't go with them. We always meet Sarah, Frank, and Normie there and see friends that we don't see very often. Everyone is so busy during the week days that a fair is a perfect place to spend time with family and friends. Our friends in Danbury always come and sometimes stay overnight with us. It's a long trip back to Danbury, not one to do at night.

After dinner, we spent some time in the parlor. Frank was reading the paper, and Sarah and I took this time to talk. I told her about how Dr. Kerrmann is supposed to see me sometime soon, and hopefully will be able to give me some new remedy that might help my coughing and pain. I try to be optimistic that eventually I will find something that helps me.

When I told Sarah how much I was looking forward to going back to school to help Mrs. Baglin, she said she didn't want to upset me, but some people believe that I might not be well enough to take on the scholars and the long days in the school house.

I told her how much it would upset me if I couldn't go back. Some of my best memories are of the time I have spent there, as a student and as a young woman learning to be a teacher. I particularly look forward to the nice days in early fall when I take the younger scholars outside for lessons. We sit under a tree, and they take turns reading out loud. I always believe that gives them confidence.

I was so upset I couldn't talk about it more and went to my room feeling saddened that people are saying I won't be able to continue my work with Mrs. Baglin. I wonder how much they talk about me and about my future.

## Sunday, August 8

Another nice day. We had breakfast together early. I shared my orange with Normie. I don't know if he has had one before, but he wasn't sure he liked it. I found it wonderful, a real treat, and encouraged him to try it. When he did, he nodded his head and smiled so I knew he liked it. After breakfast, we cleaned up, and went up on the Green to church where we saw many people we knew.

Later, we spent a quiet morning reading the papers and talking. Later, Mother and Father came and spent the day. After lunch, we went up on the Green for a short time, walking and meeting some of our friends who were gathered there.

When we arrived back at Sarah and Frank's house, we spent some time in the yard admiring her flowers and a small vegetable garden she and Frank are tending. Normie loved running around in the yard, chasing butterflies and tumbling around on the lawn. Sarah picked some vegetables for our dinner, which would be earlier than usual, so Mother and Father can be home before it gets too dark.

We had a nice dinner together, though Father said he wasn't feeling well. He needs to go to work tomorrow, plus take care of the animals before he leaves in the morning, so a short while after dinner, Mother and Father left for home.

I will miss them this week, but I'm looking forward to the time I will spend with Sarah. Even though she has brought up some unsettling ideas about my future, it is still good to be here. When she comes to our house now, she spends a great deal of time helping Mother with chores I once did and am now unable to do. It doesn't leave much time for her to spend with me, just talking or playing cards, which seem to be the only things I can do without getting fatigued. I appreciate the help she gives Mother, but she also must take care of Normie and go home and take care of her own household duties.

Sarah has always had a great deal of energy and it certainly has been put to the test over the past few months. Sometimes I feel so guilty because I can't do the things I once did, but I am trying to get better, so I can go back to helping at the school in January. If I do too much now, it might not be possible to help Mrs. Baglin with the scholars, and, Diary, I so much want to do that.

## Monday, August 9

Today was a beautiful day, but I was coughing more. Mornings are very hard, but I usually feel better by lunch. I sleep on two pillows at night that seem to help my breathing, so I don't cough quite as much. I just don't sleep well enough so that I feel rested in the morning. I've tried to go to bed earlier but it doesn't seem to make any difference.

In the afternoon, I was feeling better, so I went out to walk and called on Mrs. Welton, the Beaches, and Thayers. The walk was tiring but it was good to see our friends. By the time I arrived at the Thayers, it was tea time and I joined them for tea and cake, and then walked back to Sarah's.

While I was gone, Sarah had washed and hung out the clothes and linen in the back yard. I felt guilty about not being there to help but I was able to sit quietly and fold the items that did not need ironing while she prepared dinner. I played with Normie for a while, then Frank came home, so we sat down to dinner, after which we spent some time in the parlor reading the newspaper he had brought home.

No one called in the evening so all of us went to bed early. I was so tired from my walk that day that I almost immediately had fallen asleep.

## Tuesday, August 10

It was cloudy in the morning, but pleasant in the afternoon. During the morning, I spent some time with Normie in the backyard, playing catch with a small ball while Sarah ironed. It's a long process so I needed to keep him busy, so she would have time to get it done. Normie is not too good at playing catch at two years old but enjoys running with me to chase the ball after he misses it. I thought it would be more fun if we kicked it around, and he thought that was great fun. I love how he laughs when he is having a good time. He's a very cheerful child and very seldom cries so Sarah is very lucky he is so good.

We walked around looking at the flowers, and I tried to teach him the names of the different plants that Sarah has in her garden. He seems to like everything that is yellow so even goldenrod was of interest when I pulled it out. I told him it didn't belong there, was just a weed, and would just spread where we don't want it. Of course, he had to take some into his mother, along with some vegetables we had picked. She thanked me for picking the goldenrod before it goes to seed and comes back next year.

After lunch, Mrs. Welton came to see me, and Mrs. Lathrop brought me some fish for my lunch. After they left, Sarah returned to her ironing, which can be a full day's work. I spent most of the afternoon playing with Normie so Sarah could get her chores done as well as do the baking that was needed. While he was napping, I read for a while out in the garden.

It was a lovely day, and I felt better than I have over the past few days, though thoughts of what Sarah had said about my going back to the schoolhouse still troubles me.

### Wednesday, August 11

It was rainy in the morning but cleared off, then there was a shower in the afternoon and a rainy night. I was glad I had spent some time outdoors yesterday because it was not a good day to be outside today.

In the afternoon, Mrs. Welton brought me some apples, and Mrs. Lattin stopped by with some more fish. Mr. Lattin must have had a great deal of success with fishing this week.

I felt sick after dinner, and though I went to bed early, I did not sleep very well. I seemed to toss and turn a great deal. I miss my cozy bed at home and my airy room. At night if it's not too cool I keep the windows open and the sounds of the night are soothing and restful. New Milford sometimes seems busy at night because we are so close to the Green. My home near the river in Roxbury is far away from noises from people coming and going in buggies and wagons and on horseback. The most I might hear is a frog croaking or an owl hooting.

After dinner Sarah, Frank, and I had played cards for a while. I read to Normie before Sarah put him to bed. He had fallen asleep on my lap as we sat in the rocker by his crib, looking like the little angel he is. He can get into mischief sometimes, but he is so sweet it's difficult to be upset with him. Sarah says we all spoil him. I know Mother hopes Sarah will have more children for her to spoil, and I always tease Sarah about it. Sarah always smiles and says she would like at least four children. I can't imagine how busy she would be with four children, but some families have even greater numbers of children, and I think the oldest help take care of the youngest. That is the feeling I have had when listening to Mother and her sisters and brothers talking about their young days without a mother. It was necessary for the older children to help care for their younger brothers and sisters.

I don't know how I would feel about having children someday. I love children, such as Normie and the scholars at school, but I don't have to take care of them as a parent. When I become a teacher, I won't want to get married for a while because I would have to give up teaching to take care of a family, which is one of the reasons I was not ready to have a suitor, not even if it was George. I am just not ready to have that responsibility.

**Thursday, August 12**

It was rainy in the morning but cleared off about noon. I felt worse this morning but was better after breakfast. I feel a little homesick. I miss Mother and Father but am also glad to be spending some time with my sister.

Sarah was busy as usual with her household chores so after lunch when the grass was dry, I took Normie outside to kick the ball around. He really seems to love that, and he was so cute running around on his little short legs to try to beat me to the ball, all the time laughing.

In addition to playing kickball, we sat under a tree for a while and I read to him from two of his books. He also likes me to tell him stories, and I enjoy making up fairy tales for him that are not scary. I always did that for the younger scholars at school. I hope I will be able to do that again, so I'm practicing my imagination by telling Normie stories. He's young so I keep them simple. The scholars like scary stories, but they are older and know the things

I tell them are not real, while Normie might be afraid if I told him the same ones.

I sometimes think I should write some of my stories down, so I can just read them to Normie or the scholars. If I couldn't be a teacher, I think I would like to be a writer, like George Eliot.

I keep looking forward to being back in the schoolhouse helping Mrs. Baglin but I get depressed sometimes when I think it might not happen. My health does not seem to improve no matter what I do. I try to follow the doctors' instructions and eat well and exercise more, but sometimes it is so difficult because I seem to be losing more weight and become more fatigued following exercise.

I haven't seen Dr. Kerrmann yet though Mother said he had stopped by one day after I had gone to Sarah's. She said that he took that as a positive sign that I was feeling better. Oh, if that only were true. I have been walking more since I have been in New Milford and that may be why I'm coughing more and feeling tired.

I was so tired after playing with Normie in the afternoon that I took a short nap while he was sleeping.

Later, after dinner, some of Sarah and Frank's friends stopped by and visited. It had been a busy day, and I was glad when it was time to go to bed.

### Friday, August 13

It was a clear day and very enjoyable. I walked down to Mrs. Welton's and to Mrs. Thayer's. She gave me some lemonade. Later, Mrs. Welton stopped by and brought me some peaches.

Everyone is always so kind to me. I know many of our friends are concerned that I have been losing weight, so I think that's why they are always bringing me fruit and baked goods to tempt my appetite. You would think that because I am less active than I ever was that I would be gaining weight. I think I may have to take in my clothing again because several of my skirts and dresses are too big for me.

Mrs. Emma Warner was buried today. It seems that several people we have known have died recently, and I find myself wondering what it is like to die. It's one thing if people have lived a long time, but it is sad when younger people pass away. Grandfather wasn't young, but it was very sad for my family, especially Mother and her sisters and brothers. I miss

Grandfather, too. It's hard to think about how one death can change a family, but how a birth can bring such joy.

Every time there is a wedding in the family, the first thought that comes to many minds is how long before there will be a new baby to spoil. I know Mother keeps hoping for more grandchildren, though I think Sarah sometimes feels overwhelmed by all she must do as a young wife and mother. It's no wonder that most women don't work outside the home because there is plenty to do in it, what with housekeeping and child caring tasks.

That's why I would like to be a teacher for a while before I thought about marriage and children. I have seen enough of the responsibilities a married woman and mother has. It is not an easy job. I wonder if husbands and fathers realize how much work it takes to keep a house clean and tidy and to care for children.

### Saturday, August 14

It was cloudy today and rained some most of the day. This will be my last night here because Frank and Sarah will be taking me home tomorrow after an early dinner.

Mother and Father came over and spent the day and took Normie home with them for a short visit. Father brought me an orange and some peaches.

Mrs. Latten, Mrs. Thayer and Mrs. Welton called early in the afternoon and Aunt Lydia and Uncle Amos came in time to join us for tea and cake.

We certainly have had a great deal of company since I have been here. It was also enjoyable to be able to take the short walk to the green and see people there. I will miss that when I get home. It's a longer walk to Roxbury's center from our house, and I am barely able to make it to the schoolhouse at the end of our road, much less up to town.

After everyone went home, I went to my room to rest before dinner and found myself thinking about my future and wondering what it would be like not to be able to go to the schoolhouse and prepare to become a teacher.

My health is not better, as I had hoped it would be. I seem to tire more now, and I often wonder if the doctors have told me everything about my illness. I often wonder if they know what I have. If I keep losing weight, what does that mean? The coughing, pain, and fatigue are with me always, no matter what I do to get better. I wonder, could I have something serious? Could I be dying?

I have been reading the Bible more and reading prayers from my prayer book. I keep hoping to find some peace there. One anthem that is sung in church reads "I am the resurrection and the life, saith the Lord, he that believeth in me, though he were dead, yet shall he live, and whosoever liveth and believeth in me shall never die." What does that mean? I've also heard "dust thou art and unto dust you shall return". Clergymen say we all have a soul that doesn't die when the body dies. Where does it go? When I was younger, I found it easy to believe that when we die we are reunited with loved ones who passed before us and are waiting for us. Now I know their bodies are in a cemetery, and I find it hard to believe I would see them after I died.

Is religion just a beautiful story? Is there anything ahead for us after we die? I know if I voiced these thoughts to our minister or even to my parents, they would be shocked. Every night Father reads from the Bible. He truly believes in God as does Mother, but as for me, I'm not sure what lies ahead.

I feel I'm becoming too morbid after being sick for so long and not feeling any better despite all the potions and cough syrups the doctors give me. I'm sure Mother and Father would truly be shocked if they knew what I am thinking.

### Sunday, August 15

Another pleasant day. It will be my last day staying in New Milford because Frank and Sarah are taking me home today. Sarah and Normie will also be staying with us so she can help Mother get the house ready for the reunion next week.

In the afternoon, Dr. Brown came up and stayed to dinner, then after he left, we came home.

I had my picture taken in the afternoon. It is a time-consuming process, and you must hold very still so the photograph will not be blurred. I wore one of my new dresses that I had made for social occasions. The photographer was very patient with me, because it is so difficult to remain still. I don't often like to have my photograph taken because I think I always look too stern, but that's because of not being able to move. Sarah, Frank, and Normie also had their photograph taken together. Mother and Father have had their photographs taken in the past when the photographer was in the area.

We had some treats of candy and other sweets during tea time after the photographer left.

I realized something last night. I am getting too morbid with thoughts of death and dying. Perhaps it is about Grandfather's death. We all miss him very much. The reunion this year won't seem the same because he won't be here. I'm sure many in our family are having similar thoughts, though perhaps not as morbid and questioning as mine.

Many members of my family have faith in God, and regularly attend church. I don't know what they would think if I ever voiced my concerns about what lies ahead for each of us. They truly believe in Heaven and Hell. Why am I different? Because I wonder where these places are. Is Heaven somewhere above the clouds? Does our soul leave our body and go to Heaven? Will I see Grandfather there?

I need to stop having these thoughts, particularly about what happens when you die. I need to have faith and believe, but it is so difficult to imagine.

After Frank left for home and Normie had been put to bed, Mother, Father, Sarah, and I read for a while in the parlor, but my mind kept wandering from my reading. Since no one called in the evening, we went early to bed.

**Monday, August 16**

Another pleasant day. I awoke to the cheerful chirping of birds outside my window. It was a new day, a new beginning, and I was determined that I would be more positive and less questioning about my future. I must take a lesson from Mother and Father and have faith in God's plan for me.

If I am to become a teacher or not is in His hands. I so want to believe that we are born for a purpose, and I believe that mine is teaching. It has always been so, since I was a little girl, which I know was not so long ago. It was just a short time ago that I sat with the scholars. My dream was just a dream then. I didn't know Mrs. Baglin would ask me to help her after I completed my studies in our little schoolhouse, and I have so much enjoyed my work there and what I have learned from her. She has supported my dream, and I have to believe that I will be able to see that dream become reality by learning more from her and going on to be a teacher myself.

After breakfast, Sarah helped Mother with the wash and hung it out on the line. Then they began to clean the house in preparation for the reunion. Unused bedrooms were aired and cleaned thoroughly. I wish I could have helped them, but they insisted that I helped by watching Normie and entertaining him while they were busy. I enjoy playing with him, so I really don't look upon it as helping them so much as enjoying myself.

After lunch, I took Normie outside for a while before his nap, and, while he was napping, I did some sewing on a new dress that I hope to wear during the reunion. Sarah said she would help me if I didn't think I would have it ready in time, but since I don't have chores to do, I can get a lot done on the dress while Normie sleeps. He still takes two naps, one mid-morning and one about two in the afternoon so it is ample time to get other tasks done, such as working on my dress.

In the afternoon, some of our neighbors called and had tea and blueberry pie with us. I have no idea why I am not gaining weight because of all the sweets I eat. One of Mother's friends brought me some candy that I later shared with Mother and Sarah. Sarah doesn't like Normie to eat too many sweet things because then he won't eat his meals.

It was not very difficult to be cheerful today with Normie around. He is such a good little boy. Before dinner I took him for a short walk toward the river, though we didn't make it all the way because we both became tired. His little short legs were trying to keep going but I had to carry him back because he kept sitting down in the road to rest.

Following dinner, after Normie was in bed, Mother, Father, Sarah, and I played cards. No one called.

### Tuesday, August 17

It was very warm today, much more so than yesterday. It was not a good day for ironing, but Sarah was busy most of the morning helping Mother. Together they finished the clothes and linens and put them away.

I was surprised they did so much today because they didn't feel well, and my side aches worse, though that may be from carrying Normie home from our walk yesterday. He is getting too heavy for me to carry. I think I should start taking him out in his pram, so he doesn't have to walk and get tired. Then, perhaps, I could take a longer walk to get ready for walking to the schoolhouse.

I am trying very hard to be positive about being able to feel well enough to return to school and help Mrs. Baglin with the scholars. She has called several times but doesn't talk too much about the school year starting soon. Of course, there is still time to plan before school starts.

In the afternoon, Frank came from New Milford and he and Father went to Mr. Seymour's to help with the haying. Frank doesn't have to work tomorrow so he will be staying over tonight. Tomorrow he and Father and two of Father's friends plan on going fishing. If they have luck, we will have fish for supper tomorrow night.

I did take Normie out in his pram. It was much easier to push him than to carry him. Then we went up to the meadow where he saw the sheep grazing there. On the way back home, we stopped at our garden, and I showed him the vegetables that are doing so well. There are cabbages, squash, and carrots, among others, as well as melons. Normie was excited about the pumpkins that are growing so big that he can almost sit on them.

Dinner was fun with all of us together. I always like it when Sarah, Frank, and Normie stay with us. There is always a lot of conversation and laughter. I did not find it difficult to stay cheerful and positive. With so much activity going on, it's always enjoyable. Talk centered about the upcoming reunion and the hope that the weather will be fine, but even if it isn't everyone will have a wonderful time.

### Wednesday, August 18

It was clear but cooler today than yesterday. Mother and Sarah did some more housecleaning after breakfast while Father, Frank, and their friends went fishing.

I don't feel quite as well today as I have. My side still aches, and I have been coughing again. I expect I will see Dr. Kerrmann after the reunion since he hasn't been able to come since I have been home from Sarah's. I hope he will have some new cough medicine that will help me and make it possible for me to return to help Mrs. Baglin when school starts.

After lunch, Katie came over and stayed until tea time. Early in the afternoon Father and Frank returned with several fish that we will have for dinner tonight. Fish are always a welcome change from chicken and other meat dishes.

My determination to stay positive and stop worrying all the time about school and the future seems to be getting some positive attention. Katie said I seemed happier than I have been recently. She said it is obvious I am feeling better. I wish that were true, but I have been trying to do more walking to gain some strength and not to dwell on my aches and pains. It's not always easy to do because, while I can try to ignore the pain, I can't always ignore how fatigued I feel. It's those days when I find myself on my bed or on the sofa in the parlor while others are being busy or having fun.

I haven't seen George for a while. He hasn't called and sometimes he is not at church. His mother told Mother that he sometimes stays in Danbury to see friends on Saturday and Sunday. I understand his family also has other family members there so, perhaps, he stays with them when he doesn't come home.

I often wonder if I made the right decision about George calling on me. I even feel a little jealous sometimes that he might be calling on someone else and that's why he doesn't come home as often. Oh, diary, I think I made the right decision based on my age and the state of my health at the time. Those things haven't changed but I do miss what once was when I was well and could go with other young people to social events and have a good time.

Hopefully he will stop over during the reunion.

### Thursday, August 19

It was a cloudy day. I received a letter from Willie. He, too, is looking forward to the upcoming family reunion. They will be coming up on the cars on Saturday and will spend the night with us. I know Mother is looking forward to having Fannie help with preparations.

Aunt Fannie is always so cheerful and is very quick to see what needs to be done and sets about doing it.

Mrs. Castle and Mr. Hodge called in the early afternoon. Then Father left us for a while to call upon Dr. Downs, who later called to visit with us at tea time. Mother and Sarah had made peach pies that we all enjoyed. After he left, I sat out on the porch for a while reading but caught myself thinking about the prospect of school starting soon. I imagine many mothers are busy making new clothes for their children or shopping for new shoes or boots. I remember well Mother doing those things for Sarah and me. It was not that long ago that both of us were walking to and from school together. But since I have been helping Mrs. Baglin my best memories are of the time I spend with our scholars.

Once school starts, it seems like summer is over, though it really isn't. Some days are very warm in September. It's then that we sometimes sit outside under the trees where it is cooler and read short stories and poetry. If it isn't too warm, we often walk down to the river to count the number of birds we see, and any signs left by other animals, such as hoof prints of deer. The scholars like being outside, and, of course, the younger children would rather play games, but we insist that even outdoors they continue learning.

**Friday, August 20**

Another cloudy day. Ella Pierce called, as well as Mary Bates and Eleana, Mary Botsford, and Lavinia Squire.

Sarah had the chills badly today. I hope she is better in time for the reunion Sunday. She won't have a good time if she doesn't feel well. I will be helping with Normie so that should make the day easier for her.

Because I am coughing so much more today, I had to take more cough medicine. It didn't really help, but I'm hoping it will help me sleep better tonight. I will still wake up coughing, but I will have slept better, I hope.

Mrs. Baglin stopped by. She is talking about school beginning soon. I need to do some preparation if I am to help her again this year. There are days, though, when I wonder if I will be able to do so. She didn't speak about my helping her but perhaps takes it for granted that I will.

I try to walk every day because once school begins, I will have to walk every morning to the schoolhouse and every afternoon to come home, no matter what the weather. I hope I will be able to do it. It's been my dream ever since I was a little girl that I would be a teacher someday, and it's difficult to think I might have to give up on that dream because of my health concerns.

I need to put these negative thoughts away, so I can enjoy the reunion Sunday.

### Saturday, August 21

It was clear in the morning, but there was a shower in the afternoon. I hope the weather is better for the reunion tomorrow. Our house is large enough for everyone if we have to be inside, but it is so much more fun when we can be outside for the games during the day. I don't mind being inside in the evening, but I always look forward to being outside with all the cousins.

Mrs. Elwell and Mrs. Gillett came to see me in the afternoon. Mr. and Mrs. Merimem. George Squire and Mrs. Bronson and Ellen also called. Mrs. Merimem brought me a bouquet of flowers from her garden. She knows how much I love flowers. Mary Bates and Kate and Elena also stopped by and brought me candy and peaches, which I look forward to enjoying.

This afternoon everyone arrived that are to stay the night. Father went to carry everyone who came on the cars, and I was looking forward to seeing Aunt Fannie and Uncle Philip, Nellie, Willie, and Winston. Later, after they arrived, our side field began to fill up with buggies and wagons of friends who came by to see all of us, and we all had a good time visiting with friends and family. After our friends left, Sarah and I finished readying the bedrooms and Aunt Fannie helped us make bread and pies while Mother began dinner.

I expect tonight will be as much fun as tomorrow because we will have more people around the table at dinner, talking and laughing. Then later we will most likely play cards or some other games.

### Sunday, August 22

The reunion day is finally here, and we were all very busy getting ready for everyone else to arrive. Sarah is feeling better, so she was able to enjoy herself. I did not cough very much last night so I slept better. Following breakfast, we attended services, then came home to put together lunch for everyone who would be arriving at that time.

Father was in the barn early in the morning, making sure that everything was ready for the other horses that would need to be stabled or put out in the pasture. There is enough room in the meadow for all the buggies and wagons. Most of our family members live in the area, such as in New Milford, Southbury, and, of course, Roxbury. Most of them arrived early to attend church with us. We filled up a number of pews.

All our neighbors know we have this yearly reunion, so they were not surprised to see so many Tyrrells in attendance. George did ask if he might stop by in the afternoon as he knows many of the people who will be here. Father said he was sure everyone would like to see him. I, of course, felt glad that he would stop by. I was thinking he and I could partner in lawn tennis games as we always do. My friend Carrie also stopped by and visited with us for a while.

It was a very warm day, but that did not stop any of us from having fun. After lunch, which Mother, Aunt Harriet and Aunt Fannie prepared, we all went outside to have some fun playing games, such as croquet and lawn tennis. The younger children played tag, hide and seek, leapfrog, and other games that kept them busy all afternoon. Mother and Father and all the aunts and uncles joined in the fun when they were not watching the smallest children. Normie had so much fun playing with everyone and, of course, loved all the attention because he is one of the youngest children in the family.

George did come by and we played some serious games of lawn tennis against some of the cousins. I became very tired at one time, and Amanda, my cousin Walter's wife, took my place for a game while I rested in the shade. They did really well, but George came over to me after the game to see how I was, and if I wanted to play again. We have always been a good team.

George stayed to dinner, which was served outside under the trees since it was so nice. Everyone had brought something to add to the feast, and there was so much food. The best part, of course, was the desserts. Pies, cakes, puddings, fruit; there was something to everyone's taste.

At night, as expected, indoor games began. Whist and other

card games and charades led to much fun and laughter. It was very late when all those who were not staying left for their homes.

Frank left for home because he has work tomorrow, but Sarah and Normie stayed to help Mother with some work around the house after everyone has left. I heard them talking about George and how much everyone enjoyed seeing him. I know many in the family still believe that George and I will have a life together in the future. I heard Mother say that she wasn't sure that George had accepted my answer to his request to call on me as a suitor.

I sometimes wish things could have been different, but it appears my decision was correct. My health would need to be much better for me to consider any other relationship but friendship.

## Monday, August 23

It was another warm but pleasant day. After breakfast, family members who had stayed over left for home.

Mr. Rorraback and Father are cutting tobacco today, which is very warm work but must be done. They were very pleased when Sarah and I took them some cool lemonade and biscuits warm from the oven.

Mrs. Veilly stopped by in the morning, and Mother, Sarah and I spent some time having an early lunch with her before she left for home. Mother took lunch out to Father and Mr. Rorraback so they could take a break from the work. They decided to eat outside at one of the tables that had been set up for the reunion. Later Father began putting some of the tables and benches away for storage until the next occasion when they would be needed.

After Normie got up from his nap, Sarah gave him his lunch and then we took him for a walk to the river. He always loves to throw small stones into the water. Sarah told him someday he will be able to go fishing with Grandpa, perhaps even in his boat.

When we returned, Mary Bates and Elena had arrived and were visiting with Mother on the porch. They spent the afternoon with us and stayed for tea.

While we were preparing dinner later, we enjoyed talking about the reunion and how wonderful it had been to see everyone all in one place at one time. We see all family members often but it's this one day in the summer when everyone tries to come.

With everyone gone, it seemed so quiet, and we spent time reading in the parlor after dinner, and then went early to bed. I was very tired after all the activity the past few days.

## Tuesday, August 24

A very warm day. I love this warm weather. In the winter, it is so hard to feel warm, even with layers of clothing, but in summer you can always cool off under the trees, especially if there is a soft breeze, or in the house where it is cooler.

Mrs. Bates and Elena called in the afternoon, and George Beers stopped at tea time.

I don't feel as well as I have, and Sarah is sick again with the chills. We hope Normie isn't going to come down with it, whatever it is. Mother said it is only a summer cold and that Sarah will be feeling better soon. I wish my cough was as easy to identify as part of a cold, but it is with me always, especially early in the morning and at night. I try to keep positive thoughts that one of my doctors will find some medicine to help me, but their potions and cough medicines have not helped me very much.

No one called in the evening, so we spent time reading and Mother played the piano for a while. We love to hear her play, and Father particularly enjoys it, saying it is restful after a busy day. I spent some time thinking about whether I would be able to go back to the schoolhouse when the scholars return. I try to walk some every day, so I am up to the walk to the school, but then there is the whole day with recess and helping Mrs. Baglin and then the walk home at 4 o'clock. I hope I am up to it. I don't want to give up on my dream. I really enjoy helping Mrs. Baglin, and I am learning so much from her about how to be a good teacher.

## Wednesday, August 25

It was a warm day but partly cloudy, and there was a shower in the afternoon. I worked for a while in my flower gardens before the rain began. I am very pleased with how the flowers have flourished since I transplanted them. The annuals I planted are also doing nicely.

Mother and Sarah did the washing in the morning and hung it out so it was dry before the shower began. I helped with folding what did not need ironing.

At tea time, Carrie and Eve Hurd visited with us, and Wallace Hodge also came and stayed a while. Mrs. Castle also visited for a short time. Those who had not been to the reunion were eager to hear about how much fun we had.

Father and Mr. Rorraback are continuing to work with the tobacco. It won't be long before it will be ready for sale. It will also be time soon for the final hay crop of the season. Once it is cut and raked into piles, Father will throw it onto the wagon where Mother or one of Father's friends will stack it. Frank usually helps if he is available. Then it is stored in the barn until needed for the animals. It is important to get all these chores done before the weather becomes too cold with the potential of snow.

The garden is doing well, and we will have many vegetables to can or to store for winter use. Sarah took a hoe and went up to do some weeding while Mother was baking much needed bread. She brought back some tomatoes to further ripen on the window sill.

I'm surprised we didn't have some leftovers from the reunion feast, but most of the food was eaten between Saturday and Sunday by all our hungry family members, who had played so hard during the games and enhanced their appetites.

We snacked on the desserts after dinner that day so there wasn't much left over and what was, we shared with callers and during tea time. The blueberry and peach pies were enjoyed by all.

It will be apple picking time soon, and Mother will be busy canning applesauce for the winter. Best of all will be her apple pies. She also plans to can some of our peaches.

This is why I wonder how I still lose weight because I do love the sweets that Mother bakes.

## Thursday, August 26

It was cooler today than yesterday but still warm. My chest hurt some and my cough was worse in the morning, but I went out to walk so I could keep up with my goal that I would make it to the school and back without having to rest. No one I know that is my age seems to have any problems with their health and certainly don't have to plan activities, so they don't get tired.

After lunch, I wrote a letter to Aunt Fannie. It was so good to see her last Saturday and Sunday. We don't get to see them as often as we would like because they live in New York where Uncle Phillip works.

Ella Pierce called in the afternoon and brought me some things. Mrs. Baglin also came. She talked about school starting soon. It doesn't seem possible the summer is almost over, and the weather will be getting cooler. I wonder if I will be able to help her as much as I did last year. She didn't mention too much about it, but I think about it all the time.

I so much want to be a teacher, and have learned so much from Mrs. Baglin, but whether I will be able to continue, I don't know. I'm not even sure she still wants me to help her. Is she afraid that whatever ails me might infect the children? I would never want to do anything to harm them. Should I ask her outright whether she wants me to continue? Oh, Diary, I wish I could find the answers to so many questions. Why do I keep losing weight? Why do I lack stamina for walking and doing chores? Sarah comes more often to help Mother because I get so fatigued when I try to help. How I wish the doctors would find something to help me.

**Friday, August 27**

It was pleasant today but cooler. The summer feels like it is slipping away, bringing cooler nights and signs that cooler weather is just around the corner. School will be starting soon. Will I be able to help Mrs. Baglin? I need to talk to Mother to see if she thinks I should ask Mrs. Baglin about continuing to help her with the scholars. Or should I just attend as I usually would on the first day and see what she will say?

Sarah and I went up town to get wallpaper for the kitchen. Mother was going to watch Normie and put him down for a nap after we left. We had a nice buggy ride, and it was fun just being with Sarah. We saw some of our friends on the way and stopped and chatted for a while. I miss the days when we would walk to school together and play games after school. I know it's normal that our lives change, but I miss Sarah, especially when I need advice.

The wallpaper we picked out will make the kitchen look so nice. Sarah will help Mother with it before she goes home.

I was in my room in the afternoon when Sarah came up to tell me that Dr. Kerrmann was here. My heart felt like it stopped. He had finally come. Though I had expected he would, I wasn't ready to hear what he might say to Mother and me. I took some deep breaths that started me coughing as I followed Sarah downstairs.

I was particularly concerned that he would be upset with me because I had written to him. I was afraid he might think that I thought he was not taking good care of me. That was never my intent. It's just that all the medicines and potions all the doctors have given me have not helped.

Sarah left me at the parlor door where Mother was already talking to him. Why is the parlor always the place where serious discussions take place? I suppose it's because it provides more privacy.

When I entered the room, Dr. Kerrmann stood, greeted me, and led me to a chair next to Mother. I was almost speechless from fear. Mother took my hand and patted it, and I felt more relaxed with her support.

Dr. Kerrmann asked me how I was feeling. Did I think I was better? Were any of the medicines of help? I told him about the pain, night sweats, coughing, and the feeling of breathlessness. I mentioned my concern I could not walk very far or do chores because of feeling fatigued.

After examining me, he said he would bring some medicines that I could take more often without any harmful effects. He stressed eating and sleeping well and moderate exercise to keep up my strength. But it was what he said upon leaving and the sadness I saw on his face that truly upset me. He said that while he understood how much I enjoyed helping Mrs. Baglin, it might be better if I took time to rest and see how I am feeling before going back to the schoolhouse, perhaps until the New Year.

While Mother was showing him out, I remained in the parlor in tears. This was what I had feared all the time I was waiting for his visit. What was I to do now? Do I tell Mrs. Baglin what he said? Does she have a right to know?

### Saturday, August 28

It was warmer today than yesterday. We should have warm days through September, but the nights are cooler, reminding us that summer is waning and in just a few weeks will be gone. I always hope for warmer weather in September and October, but by November it is usually obvious that autumn is upon us and that the Thanksgiving and Christmas holidays are near with the cold of winter not far behind.

When I awoke after a restless night, I was struck immediately by the memory of Dr. Kerrmann's visit yesterday and the way he looked at me before he left. I know he talked to Mother before as well as after he examined me. Why do I feel he is not telling me something that perhaps he told Mother? He certainly didn't look very cheerful when he left.

I arose from bed, feeling tired from not sleeping very much, and took longer in making my bed and getting washed and dressed. I almost didn't want to go downstairs because I'm not sure if I should ask Mother what he said to her, and I'm afraid of what she might tell me.

I attempted to put a pleasant expression on my face as I went down stairs. I could hear Mother and Sarah in the kitchen making breakfast, and I was reminded of all the happy times the three of us had spent there making meals or enjoying our time around the table with a cup of tea and some pastry. I could hear Normie's voice as he asked his mother when his breakfast would be ready, and her cheerful answer—soon.

When I entered the kitchen for a moment the conversation stopped, but then Mother and Sarah said good morning and Normie ran to give me a hug. I was surprised he hadn't come into my room to wake me, but perhaps he had been told to let me sleep. If only I could have. I thought Mother and Sarah looked tired also, so perhaps they didn't sleep very well either. I couldn't help but feel that my efforts to be more positive about things, such as my health and future, had taken a downturn yesterday with Dr. Kerrmann's visit.

During breakfast, the usual conversation did not come easily for me. There was too much on my mind, and I kept losing track of what was being discussed. Even Father seemed quieter than usual and somewhat distracted. Politics and town issues that are usually part of his mealtime discussions seemed to have escaped his attention today. I think Mother must have told him about Dr. Kerrmann's visit and his recommendation that I take time off from helping Mrs. Baglin at the school.

Later Mother and Sarah papered the kitchen walls. The new paper looks so fresh and clean and makes the kitchen bright and cheery, but it didn't seem to lift anybody's spirits very much.

Sarah had the chills again in the afternoon and after lunch went upstairs to rest. Mother and I entertained Normie until it was time for his nap, and then Mother did some baking.

Normie is developing a taste for peach pie, though he doesn't like other berry pies. I suppose children's taste for different foods needs to be developed just as we help them expand their minds through reading, recitations, and other class room activities.

Father worked at the Rorraback's, helping pick tobacco. Very soon he and all the neighbors will be taking their tobacco to New Milford for sale or auction.

Later in the afternoon, Mr. Hodge and Mrs. Thomas called, and we enjoyed tea and peach pie with them. They enjoyed seeing Normie and were glad that Sarah was still with us to help Mother.

After they left, Mother and I spent the afternoon playing cards and entertaining Normie. Sarah is still not feeling well and will be staying over again tonight. Frank will come tomorrow to carry her and Normie home.

I wanted to ask Mother about what Dr. Kerrmann might have said but there was never any correct time to bring it up. She was either busy or caring for Normie or we had visitors.

### Sunday, August 29

Today was very warm and showery all afternoon and into the night when it rained very hard. We were glad our reunion had not been set for today. We would have had to be inside all day and that would not have been as much fun without the outdoor activities.

We did not go to church and no one called in the afternoon. I haven't seen George since the reunion, but he is probably busy at work.

I was glad it was a quiet Sunday because I did not feel very well. I have not spoken loud for a few days and my throat hurts. Perhaps I have whatever illness Sarah has had. Last night I had some night sweats, but perhaps it was because it was warm with no breeze.

When we were out the other day, we stopped in some stores. I am looking for a new dress pattern and material for the fall. The dress patterns cost about 20 cents, and I did see some material I liked. I also need to do some work on my other clothing since I have lost weight over the summer.

I did not walk outside today because it was showery, but I intend to keep doing it often so I am able to make the walk to the schoolhouse despite what Dr. Kerrmann said.

I still have not talked to Mother about what the doctor said to her because I'm afraid of what she might tell me. I don't want to let go of my dream to be a teacher, and feel that by taking time off from school, I would be giving in to my illness rather than trying to get better by staying busy and involved with school work.

I haven't determined how to approach Mrs. Baglin about my helping at school, but I fear Mother will tell her what the doctor has recommended if I don't. I'm sure Mrs. Baglin will most likely agree with the doctor, but it's difficult to admit that any decision I would make about school would most likely be taken out of my hands. Mother, the doctor, and Mrs. Baglin will be of one mind, I am sure.

After lunch, Mother, Father, Sarah, and I played whist while Normie napped. Then Frank came to take them home. Before she left, Sarah and I talked for a while, both of us ignoring any reference to the doctor's visit and what happens next.

After dinner, Father and Mother retired early because he has a busy day planned for tomorrow. I read for a while, but had trouble concentrating on my book. I felt lonely. It had felt good to have Sarah and Normie in the room next door, but I know Frank must miss them. It's very nice of him that Sarah can spend so much time here since I am unable to be of much help anymore, which troubles me, but when I attempt to help I get so tired I need to sit down.

## Monday, August 30

Another hard, rainy day so we were confined to indoors all day. Mother was very busy as she usually is on Monday. She didn't do the laundry as she usually would because of the rain. It was warm, so she didn't want to start a fire in the kitchen to dry the clothes. Instead, she papered the hall and moved the stove out to clean.

Mother must be missing Sarah now that she has gone home, but Sarah has responsibilities there, plus she was still not feeling well when she left yesterday.

She told me she was sorry she was unable to stay to help Mother. I do feel some better, but I have days like this when I do, and then the next day I have pain and cough all the time so my chest and back hurt. I need to talk to Mother about what the doctor said when they were alone in the parlor. I keep remembering how he looked when he left. I think he felt sad that he had to tell me to take time off from school. Or was there another reason for the way he looked at me? Again, I wonder if he knows more than what he has told me. Perhaps Mother knows. But will she tell me if what he said is not good?

It is getting closer to when school will begin, and Mrs. Baglin has not said anything about helping her again this year. I have been afraid to ask her when she has called, and she didn't t talk as much about the school as I think she might have ordinarily.

Father has been cutting wood for the winter, and there is a pile of cordwood and kindling that is growing by the week. He's also been helping neighbors with their tobacco picking as well as working as a hatter. He is always very busy, but there is much that needs to be done to keep us warm this winter, and to keep our crops producing. Father also must take care of the animals before work in the morning and after work, so it is a long day for him. I wonder if he sometimes wishes he had sons, but he has always been a loving father to Sarah and me.

In the afternoon, Mrs. Castle called. Father came home as she was leaving. He was very tired. After dinner, he read for a while and then went to bed, leaving Mother and me playing cards in the dining room. This was my opportunity to talk to her about Dr. Kerrmann's visit, but my courage failed me. Perhaps tomorrow there will be an opportunity.

### Tuesday, August 31

It was a nice day after all the rain. Mother did the wash and hung it out to dry, then she brought in the linens when they were dry and folded them and put them away. Tomorrow she will do the ironing, too. I wish I could help her. I feel so useless.

After lunch, I went down to Mrs. Baglin's, and walked for the first time in a long time. I must admit that I was tired when I got there. I did not mention anything about helping with the scholars this year, and Mrs. Baglin was silent on the subject. I wonder if she is considering not having me help her and is unsure about how to tell me. I haven't talked to Mother about my concerns, but I think I must because school will be starting soon, and I need to know what I am to do.

Mr. Smith called in the early afternoon, and Emeline stopped in time for tea. Mr. Smith, who is our pastor, has been visiting more often recently. I think Mother finds his visits comforting, but I feel as if he comes to see how I am, and if I am better or still ill. I try to put on a brave face, but sometimes I just feel so bad that it's hard to keep people from knowing. I cough more often now, my chest hurts, and I have a feeling of fatigue most of the time.

I wonder what lies ahead for me. No one seems to know what is wrong with me, but many of our neighbors have been calling more, and often bring me gifts of food, candy, and fruit.

Mother is so concerned about my weight that she tries to make me eat more to keep up my strength. Our breakfasts are always hearty, usually ham, eggs, or porridge, and sometimes donuts or biscuits with our coffee. I try to finish it all, but I don't seem to have the appetite I once had. It's difficult to have a good appetite when you don't do anything.

### Wednesday, September 1

It was very cloudy today but it did not rain. I went up to the hollow with Father when he came home from work. We saw Mrs. Baglin at the store for a few minutes, but nothing was said about school starting soon.

In the afternoon, Dr. Brown and his father came to see me. Dr, Brown said he agrees with Dr. Kerrmann that I should start off slowly if I am to help Mrs. Baglin this year, and when I start in January, only staying until after lunch each day, then I could come home and rest before dinner.

I am beginning to feel that Mrs. Baglin is putting off talking to me because she is not sure how I will take it if she says I won't be able to help her. She knows how much I want to be a teacher, and she has been very kind in helping me toward that goal.

I know Mother, Father, and Sarah are concerned about me, and I often find them looking at me with what can only be described as sadness. I know I am not as I was before I became ill. Sometimes the fatigue is so strong that I have all I can do to walk down stairs in the morning after a night spent without enough sleep. I know some of my lack of sleep is worrying about my future and if I will ever achieve what I most want in life.

I continue to receive gifts of food from neighbors and friends. Liza Pierce sent me some cake and plums today, and Mr. and Mrs. Rorraback called in the evening and brought me some peaches. Everyone is so kind, and I am so thankful to have so many caring friends and a loving family. Mr. Hodge also came by. I'm sad that I cause my family so much concern, but I can't seem to summon the strength to appear better for their eyes.

## Thursday, September 2

It was very warm today, and because of that I am feeling better, so I helped with some of the less strenuous household chores.

I commenced filling the oil and kerosene lamps in preparation for when it turns dark earlier through the upcoming days. We also have made several candles and put them away for use later. Father has been busy working at increasing our wood storage for the fireplaces and the kitchen stove. The woodpile outside the house has been growing steadily from his efforts.

I don't like to think about the colder weather that is sure to come within a couple of months. While the late fall and winter bring holidays that bring our family together to celebrate Thanksgiving and Christmas, I regret the cold they also bring. I never seem to be able to get warm, even though I wear layers of clothing when outside and even when I am in the house. Unless you are next to a fireplace and keep it burning, you never seem to be warm once you step away from that heat.

Mary Green and Eva Hurd came and stayed about three hours this morning, and Eliza Jennings called in the afternoon at tea time.

Father had a meeting at Town Hall tonight after dinner, so I summoned what courage I could to talk to Mother about Dr. Kerrmann's visit. I believe she was truthful with me, but I still wonder if there is something I don't know. She said Dr. Kerrmann talked to her about increasing some of my cough medicines and other potions to help my pain and said some of them could be adding to the fatigue I feel. He also discussed with her about my not helping Mrs. Baglin at the schoolhouse until January when we will see how I am feeling then.

## Friday, September 3

It was a very warm day. Our folks are getting tobacco. Sarah is feeling better and returned today with Normie so she can help Mother. In the early afternoon, Sarah and I went up to the lot and back twice to bring the workers some lemonade and sandwiches.

I was very fatigued after my second walk, so I spent some time in the parlor reading. I dozed off once, only to wake and realize I had been sleeping for a while and had dropped my book on the floor. I couldn't remember what page I was on, but then remembered and commenced reading again.

Mother came in mid-afternoon to check on me before she began preparations for dinner. The men who are helping Father with the tobacco will be staying so she and Sarah had extra work. I helped some by setting the table and preparing the vegetables, while Mother prepared a chicken for baking.

The men worked late in the afternoon and then trooped in for dinner, obviously fatigued from their labors. During dinner, conversation centered about the price of tobacco this year and whether it is economical to continue planting it every year. I suppose it depends on the amount of tobacco available to the buyers and what they are willing to spend to make their cigars. Father doesn't depend on his income from our farm as he works most of the time as a hatter, but many of our neighbors depend on all their animals and crops being profitable. We have chickens, but the eggs are for our own use unless someone in the neighborhood needs some.

After the men left for their homes, Sarah and I helped Mother by clearing the table and washing up. We then spent some time sitting outside on the porch, enjoying the warm night air. It's difficult to think that just within a month it will most likely be too cool to sit out like this.

Normie was happy running around in the yard with his papa. Frank had come down after work and he, Sarah, and Normie will spend the night and tomorrow with us. He always helps Father with chores when he is here. I think he enjoys being with Father. Frank is older than Sarah and both his parents are deceased so the only father he has now is his father-in-law.

## Saturday, September 4

This was another warm day, and we had a nice breakfast with Frank, Sarah, and Normie. After breakfast, Father went to work at Seymour's since Frank was going to do the chores here before leaving for New Milford. Sarah and Normie will be spending another night with us, then Father will take them home tomorrow after lunch.

I feel better today because of the warmth. I dread the upcoming months of cold, snow and ice. I try not to think about it, but it is difficult not to because I have so much pain during the cold weather. I try not to let it stop me from doing things, but some days I have so much pain in my chest I can barely breathe.

I am being more and more concerned about my duties at the school. I wonder if Mrs. Baglin will understand why the doctors think I should take time off once school starts next week? I hope she will be willing to let me come back to help her if my health improves.

By this time last year, she was talking to me about what she expected me to do to help her and to prepare to be a teacher in the future. She has been here several times, and I have seen her at the store and church, but nothing has been said. Perhaps nothing has been said because she expects me to remember my duties and the training that goes with them.

Mrs. Baglin has visited with Mother when I wasn't here. Perhaps she has said something to her. I know I'm not in as good health as I was last year. I wish I could feel better, but instead there are many times when I feel less well than before. I'm concerned about the weight loss and am constantly having to take in my skirts and shirtwaists.

Carrie called in the evening, as did Robert Haskins. We had a nice visit and enjoyed coffee and some of Mother's peach pie with them.

After our visitors left, Mother, Father, Sarah and I played cards for a while before going early to bed.

## Sunday, September 5

It was warm and dry today. We all went to church, which I always enjoy. Mostly I love the music and hymns. Sometimes the sermon is too long, and it is difficult not to let thoughts wander during that time. Somehow Mother and Father always know when someone in the family is not paying attention. I always wonder about that. How do they know? Perhaps because they remember how they were at our age.

Normie was good in church today, though sometimes Sarah might have to take him out because he is making too much noise or crying.

After church, we had some refreshments in the parish hall. George was there and came over to talk to me. We walked outside while we waited for our parents. It is always wonderful to see him. I wish things could be different, but if I'm even hesitant about my ability to help out at school, how could I enter a more serious relationship at this time. George is always so attentive, and it doesn't appear that he is calling on anyone seriously with marriage as an objective. However, he has given no sign that he expects my decision to change, so we remain as we were, friends.

When we were about to get in our buggy, Mrs. Baglin approached and asked Mother if she might stop by this afternoon. We had no other plans, so Mother said yes, but it caused me a fright. I knew this may be when I must tell her about not being able to help her this year. All the way home, I was afraid she would say she wasn't willing to have me back in January even if my health is better.

After lunch, Father carried Sarah and Normie home to New Milford. While he was gone, Wallace came over and stayed a good while. Aunt Harriet and Uncle Henry also called. I was so nervous that it was difficult to pay attention to our callers. It was shortly after they left that Mrs. Baglin arrived.

Mother offered Mrs. Baglin tea and refreshments, but she said she could only stay a short while, and she wanted primarily to talk to me. She was very kind, but it was as I feared. She said she felt I should take some time to see if my health would improve enough to allow me the activity level that is required with our scholars, particularly during more active parts of the day, such as recess when I spend time with them outside playing games or during walks to discuss what we would see in nature.

Mrs. Baglin agreed with the doctors that I take a few months to see if I would feel better by the New Year, at which time we could talk again if my health had improved. I protested, of course, saying I had been walking more recently and gaining strength. However, she held fast to her conviction, saying I have not been well for several months and my weight loss and fatigue have been obvious to anyone who has seen me.

I felt such pain inside. It felt as if all my hopes for my future were shattered. If I couldn't continue training to be a teacher, there is no hope of being a teacher in the future. I tried to be polite, but I could not stay talking to her any longer without crying. Though I knew it was rude, I ran upstairs to my room before throwing myself on my bed and bursting into tears.

Shortly after, I heard Mother on the stairs, and she knocked gently on my door before entering. Mrs. Baglin had left, she said, feeling very dispirited because she didn't want to hurt me, but only wanted what was best for me now. She told Mother I need to take the time to heal whatever "wasting" illness I have, and that I should rest, eat well, and get better.

I am so depressed, Diary. How will I fill my days without school, without looking forward to the future as a teacher, if that may never be possible.

When Father came home, he called me down to dinner, but I wasn't hungry. Instead I went early to bed.

## Monday, September 6

I was awake early because I had not slept very much during the night. My mind kept going over and over what Mrs. Baglin had said. Did she say I could have a wasting illness? I have heard of this before when other people were ill for a long time, but never thought I could have one. The doctors have never said it to me or to my parents. I think they would have told me if they had or maybe not if they thought it would upset me. I would want to know, at least I think I would.

I felt listless as I prepared for the day, washing and dressing before going downstairs. Mother was in the kitchen preparing breakfast for Father, who was in the barn caring for the animals before leaving for work. Mother came away from the stove to give me a hug and said I should not worry, that things will be all right.

It was then that I broke down again, crying into her shoulder like I often did as a child. But this was not a skinned knee to be easily treated. Months stretched ahead of me without school, without learning from Mrs. Baglin, without interaction with the scholars. What was I to do, especially through the winter months when activity outside is limited? There would be no flowers to tend, no walks to the river, no playing outside with Normie.

Under Mother's watchful eyes, I ate breakfast though I had no appetite. Father patted me on the hand, urging me to clean my plate like a good girl. I felt like I did when I was 10 and never wanted to sit still long enough to eat. Oh, to have that energy and zest for life I once had to run and play. All I seem to have is pain and fatigue and, now, I feel I have no hope for the future.

Father left for work at the hat shop. Dwight worked here today in the tobacco field and the gardens. It will soon be time for the harvest.

It was not as warm as yesterday. To prove something to myself, I went up in the field to see the colt and down in the lot but had a poor spell and coughed more as a result. Perhaps Mrs. Baglin is correct in thinking I need time to rest and get better. But will I get better? Again, I question why the doctors don't seem to be able to help me. Could there be something seriously wrong with me?

### Tuesday, September 7

It was cloudy and rained a little in the morning. After work today, Father began cutting tobacco.

Since I felt better than I did yesterday, I helped Mother by canning ten cans of pears. We will also be making applesauce soon. Mother made an apple pie today which we enjoyed when Mr. Hodge called in the afternoon and took tea with us. No one else came.

Dr. Kerrmann sent me a stronger medicine yesterday. I hope it helps because my cough seems worse and my chest feels tight and sore. I have tried so many potions and syrups in the past few months and none have seemed to help. Perhaps this one will prove more helpful.

I can't seem to overcome the hopelessness I have felt since Mrs. Baglin's visit Sunday. School started today, and I was not among those in attendance. January seems a long way in the future. I don't know how I will fill the time. If I'm not in better health at that time, it appears I would not be able to help her.

I wonder who will be helping Mrs. Baglin in my absence. It will probably be one of my friends who also hopes to be a teacher in the future. I wonder if the scholars miss me or if they even notice I'm not there because they are kept so busy in the classroom and the schoolyard. I miss them and Mrs. Baglin. I miss their smiles and laughter and the fun we have during the noon hour recess.

I often look at the ferule that Grandfather made for me. I see it as a keepsake, not an instrument of discipline for girls. I don't think I would ever be able to strike a child, even lightly. Sitting in the corner seems ample punishment in some cases. Mrs. Baglin has used the hickory stick on boys, but only if they have been very bad. Mostly she makes them stay in at recess and clean the blackboard or sweep up.

## Wednesday, September 8

It was a sour, cloudy day, much like I have felt since talking to Mrs. Baglin on Sunday. It's so difficult to think of the scholars in the schoolhouse and not being there with them. I have always wanted to help children learn, from the time when I was a little girl. I used to line up my dolls and pretend I was their teacher. I would read to them and do sums.

In the afternoon, Ella Pierce came and brought me a watermelon. It tasted so good, cool and fresh. We did not grow watermelons this year, so this gift was very welcome. Our pumpkins are getting very big. I see pumpkin pies in the future, though it is a lot of work to prepare them.

Mother washed and hung the clothes and linens on the line despite it being cloudy. The breeze will get everything dry. Later I helped fold the clothes and linens that don't need ironing. If there is one chore I'm glad I don't have to do, it is ironing. It is such a lengthy process.

My side hurts worse because I had coughed last night and today. I just couldn't get to sleep last night. After coughing so long, I feel breathless and then I'm afraid to go to sleep.

Mother came in to see if I was all right and had me take a spoonful of the new medicine. It helped some, but the coughing didn't stop, only didn't seem as strong. Sometimes even honey can stop the coughing because it is very soothing though even that hasn't helped me lately.

Ella was the only person that called today. I spent the day doing some sewing and helped Mother some until I got tired. I spent some time in the parlor reading, and then Father came home from work and it was time for dinner. We had some more of the apple pie for dessert. I don't seem to have lost my appetite, especially for desserts, though my weight loss doesn't seem to stop. Mother makes the best pies.

### Thursday, September 9

It was cloudy in the morning, and it commenced raining at noon and continued throughout the afternoon and night.

Mr. Hodge called in the afternoon in time for tea and cake that Mother and I had made that morning after she had finished ironing. I wish I could help her the way I once did, but I get so tired doing more than lighter chores. Ironing is hard work and takes a long time.

I already miss going to the schoolhouse to help Mrs. Baglin. It was such an important part of my days. I find it difficult to have this free time after having those days that were so fulfilling. I hope that my new medicine helps and that once January comes Mrs. Baglin will see I am so improved that she will want me to come back to help her. I don't say this to Mother because she will think I am getting my hopes up for a fall if I am not better.

I want to maintain positive thoughts and try not to feel like I have lost hope because I haven't. I try to eat well, I'm walking as much as I can to keep up my strength, and I'm reading newspapers and magazines to keep in touch with what is happening in the world. Plus, these activities help pass the time.

No one called in the evening. We spent some time in the parlor reading, and Mother played the piano for a while, which I find very soothing before going to bed. Perhaps because of that I will sleep better tonight.

### Friday, September 10

It was rainy in the forenoon but cleared off in the afternoon. After lunch Father went up to Uncle Henry's to work.

I slept better last night than I have the past few days. I think

I'm more resigned about not being able to help Mrs. Baglin for a few months, but I still must find things to do here at home that will keep me prepared to start helping out again in January.

I'm trying to keep positive thoughts that I will be able to help her again in the future. Though I'm not able to help Mother as much as I once did, I try to do as much as I can without getting too fatigued. Until the weather gets too cold, I intend to continue walking as much as possible to keep up my strength and to eat well to try to stop the weight loss.

Mrs. Castle came and spent the afternoon with Mother and me. She is always such good company and brings us news about neighbors' activities and town events. After dinner, George stopped by for an hour on the way home from work. He is well liked by my parents, and they are always glad to see him. He had some lemonade with us and talked about his day. He said he is thinking about getting lodging in Danbury where he works because of the time it takes to get to and from there, but his parents also need him to help with chores. He said he is torn between being more independent and the needs of his parents.

After he left, I went to my room, thinking about what it would be like not to have George here in town. I don't see him all the time, especially since I turned down his request to call on me as a suitor. I think he was hurt, even though he understood my reasons at the time. I also find myself wishing I could have made a different decision, but at the time and even now, it seemed the only decision I could make that was best for both of us.

I know my parents still wish things were different, but they respect the decision I made and know very well how poorly my health has been this year. My condition seems to get worse instead of better, but, as I said, I keep a hopeful attitude.

### Saturday, September 11

It was a nice cool day, and I feel quite well today, only my cough seems worse. I don't know why I can't have something to cure it. It occurs almost every day and night, and no matter what syrups or potions I take, they don't seem to help.

Father is working at Uncle Henry's today in the tobacco field. It will soon be time to sell the crops, and all the neighbors help get them ready.

Mother made lunch for us and then went out to the garden to gather some vegetables for dinner. She made a stew because she knows Father likes them, and that he would be very hungry when he got home.

I worked on some sewing and embroidery while sitting outside on the porch this afternoon. I found myself thinking about what George said last night, about possibly moving to Danbury. I would really miss him though I know he would stop by when he came to his parents to help them with chores. It might not happen because he appeared to be concerned about his parents if he did move. Now he is home every night if they need him, but that might not be possible if he was living in Danbury.

I know my decision was the correct one, but every now and then I wonder what it would have been like if I felt well and had accepted his request to call on me as a suitor. Will I be what they call an old maid? I know I would like to have a family, but when I see how hard Mother and Sarah work every day, I don't think as I am now that I could do it. It seems like there is a sad future for me in that regard if my health does not improve. I remain hopeful, however, that a few months of rest may help.

Sarah comes more often now to help Mother, and I think often of how lucky we are to have her. It's a big help to Mother, but also for me because I don't have to feel so guilty that I'm not able to do the chores I once did.

### Sunday, September 12

It was warmer today than yesterday, and I felt better in the warmth. We did not go to church. I miss attending services. I love the music most of all, and Mother often plays the hymns on the piano, especially on Sunday when she has more time.

I love to listen to her play and often regret that I did not learn how. Mother offered to teach me when I was about eight, but I was more interested in playing outside with my friends from school. To have to practice an hour a day seemed to be a large part of my day back then, but Mother said that would be the only way I would learn. She said I would regret not learning someday, and I sometimes do because it would give me something else to do during the day. Perhaps I could still learn if she was willing to teach me. It would be something we could do together.

While I was sitting on the porch this afternoon, Mrs. Hodge stopped by to visit and brought me a cake and pie and a bouquet that was fresh out of her garden and so beautiful. Everyone is being so nice to me, and I very much appreciate their kindness in thinking about me. Many of them tell me they are praying for my recovery. Later in the afternoon, Mr. Hodge called just in time to see Father returning from Uncle Henry's. They sat out on the porch, drinking coffee, and talking. Then Mr. Hodge left for home.

After a dinner of Mother's wonderful stew, I wrote a letter of thanks to Dr. Brown, who has been very kind to me. He and Dr. Kerrmann are trying very hard to find some remedy for me that will cure my cough and the pain in my chest and back.

## Monday September 13

It was clear in the morning but commenced raining at noon and was rainy all day and into the night. When it rains, it seems like my chest has more pain. After breakfast, I was very glad to curl up on the parlor sofa with a quilt and read. I felt cold even though it was quite warm outside.

As on so many other Monday mornings, Mother washed, but was unable to hang the clothes and linens outside. On days like this she strings clothesline in the kitchen near the stove and hangs the wash there to dry.

Father went to work and when he came home, he went to the pasture and discovered that our cow got hurt by stepping in a hole. She was not seriously hurt, but he brought her into the barn and bandaged her leg to give her more support when standing. I don't think she liked it too much, but she could have broken a leg and might not have been able to be helped.

On the way back to the house, he went to the garden and brought in some near ripe tomatoes to further ripen on the windowsill. They may be ready for lunch in a couple of days.

After dinner, we sat in the parlor reading and talking, then I was glad to go to my bed because I still did not feel very well.

**Tuesday, September 14**

Cool but clear today. It was just right to work outside so after breakfast I took up some of my plants. Mother was ironing so later I helped her prepare lunch for us. We had expected Sarah to come today to help Mother with the ironing, but she didn't. She is probably busy with Normie and her house.

After lunch, I returned to my flower beds and did some weeding. It won't be too long before frost, and the flowers will be gone. I enjoy my time in the garden knowing that too soon I won't have it. I don't look forward to winter. I love the warmth of spring, summer, and early fall, but winter seems so long with its cold and snow, and I always feel more pain during the cold. I always find myself hoping for spring in February, but knowing it is weeks away becomes depressing.

I did not sleep very well through the night last night. I kept thinking about George possibly moving to Danbury. I know how much I missed Sarah when she and Frank moved first to Danbury and now to New Milford. It just takes longer to get to see her, but her house in New Milford is closer than the one in Danbury because we can take the horse and buggy instead of the cars.

Traveling by horse and buggy or wagon is quieter than the cars, but there are bumps and turns in the road and when we go over bridges there is a lot of noise if planks are loose. It certainly makes the bells on Bessie's harness jingle, which is a cheerful sound.

**Wednesday, September 15**

It was a cold, sour day, and rained some. Despite the bad weather, however, Father spent the afternoon digging potatoes. It is time to put them in our underground cellar along with other root vegetables, such as carrots, beets, and onions.

Mother went out and checked on our other vegetables, which are still doing well. The corn was very good this year, and Mother will can some pickled relish and pickles for the winter. She will also can tomato sauce for use in stews. There is a lot to do to prepare a supply of food for the winter. I usually get the job of going to the root cellar and I often need a lantern to see in there. It has a door on it, so animals can't get in, but it doesn't stop the spiders and other creepy things. When I was little, I hated that job, but I quickly learned that the faster I got it done, the better.

Mr. Hodge called in the afternoon, and Father took a break from his labors to take tea with us. Mother had made an apple pie so we all had a piece.

Later in the afternoon I wrote a letter to cousin Nellie, which Father will post for me tomorrow. After dinner, we played cards until it was time for bed.

## Thursday, September 16

This was a rainy, bad day, which is probably why I felt worse today and coughed more.

After breakfast, I read for a while before helping Mother with some baking. We needed bread and rolls, and she made a cake in case we had callers, which turned out to be a good decision because Bertie Hodge called in the afternoon and spent some time with Mother and me. His family lives near to us, and I have known them all my life.

It did set to storm hard just before he left, but he had brought an umbrella so he would not get too wet on the way home. Most of the time he rides over on his horse, but this time he decided to walk, but he doesn't live too far away.

Father came home after work, and Mother and I prepared dinner while he was in the barn taking care of the animals and cleaning up.

After dinner Mother played the piano for a while, then she and Father played backgammon before going to bed.

I stayed up a little longer, listening to the rain, and thinking about how I spent the evenings a year ago. I would have been preparing some reading for the younger children. On nice days, we would go outside while Mrs. Baglin taught the older scholars. We would sit in the shade of a tree and read from one book, with each child taking a turn to read out loud. It helps give them confidence to read in front of others.

Recess after lunch was always fun in good weather. We would play tag, hide and seek, and tug of war. The boys sometimes bring their marbles and play with them while the girls might work on puzzles or cat's cradle. How I miss those days. It was with a sad heart that I finally went to bed where sleep was disturbed by coughing and thunder from the storm.

## Friday, September 17

We got frost last night, but it was a great deal warmer today than yesterday. As the month goes by I guess we will see more cool days than warm ones.

I went over to Aunt Josephine's with Father after he came home from work. On the way there, we stopped at the Post Office. I received a letter from Dr. Brown. He inquired of my health, and if there was anything he could do to help. He and Dr. Kerrmann have been trying to find some new potion or syrup that would help my cough, but so far nothing has helped.

Because Mother had a meeting at the church, when Aunt Josephine stopped in briefly in the morning, she invited Father and me to come for dinner. We had a very nice time, talking about family concerns and events. Grandfather's tombstone has been placed at his grave and includes the name of his wife Laura, my grandmother. I never knew her because she died long before I was born. It was difficult for Grandfather to raise my Mother and her brothers and sisters, but I think he did a good job. They are all upstanding, caring people, and are well liked and respected.

After a wonderful dinner with Aunt Josephine's rice pudding for dessert, we spent some time playing cards until it was time for us to leave for home. When we arrived home, Mother was just getting in from her meeting, so we spent some time talking about that until bedtime.

## Saturday, September 18

It was a very warm day today, which made me feel very well. I don't seem to ache so much when the weather is warmer. After breakfast Father went to New Milford. I suppose while he is there he will stop at Sarah's and probably have lunch with her, Frank, and Normie.

Mother and I had a quiet lunch together, after which I went to Mrs. Hodge's and was weighed. I'm now 96 pounds. It doesn't seem to matter how much I eat because I still lose weight. I once asked Dr. Kerrmann if he thought I had what they call a wasting disease, where a person loses a great deal of weight. He said I might, but he wasn't sure. I don't think doctors always have all the answers to why a person is sick.

Bertie brought me home in their buggy. He said he misses me

at the schoolhouse, and it made me feel good that he told me because I have wondered if any of the scholars have asked why I wasn't there anymore. He said it is too early for the leaves to begin falling, but the younger children are already getting excited about playing in the leaves during recess. We always had a good time making huge piles of leaves and then taking turns jumping in them. Perhaps you never get too old for these simple enjoyable things.

After I arrived home, I took a short walk and saw some pheasants in the cornfield. They better be careful because Father is a great hunter.

Mrs. Castle called in the evening, and we played cards after having tea and cake. After Mrs. Castle left for home, we talked for a while in the parlor and then went early to bed.

### Sunday, September 19

It was a very nice day, not too warm and no rain. That's good because Father and the other men have a great deal to do in the fields to get in the crops before there is a severe frost.

We went to church where we heard some sad news. Mrs. Bixby's boy died. It was very sad. He was very young and not yet in school.

When we got home, Mother set about making some food to take to the family. It seems that we hear about so many deaths at a young age. It must be very sad for the families. My Grandfather always said that it's not right that parents should outlive their children, but I suppose that it is God's will. Perhaps He needs more angels.

We had some visitors today after church. Mr. Hodge called in the early afternoon, and Mrs. Fuller and Ella called at tea time. Mother had made two apple pies, one for the Bixby family and one for us that we shared with our callers.

George stopped by later in the afternoon and had some lemonade with us. He told us he has decided not to move to Danbury as it would be very hard on his parents not to have him here. He will continue to live with them until he can perhaps find a house or rental apartment closer to Roxbury, such as in Newtown. I was glad to hear his decision because it means I will see him more often than if he was in Danbury. Our friendship seems to be the same as it has always been.

After George left for home, I helped Mother with dinner preparations. Father was working in the barn, so he would have less to do in the morning before going to work. After dinner, we played cards for a while, but we were all tired, so we went to bed early.

## Monday, September 20

A warm and pleasant day. The longer the weather stays warm, the better. I dread the thought that cold weather is not very far away. Then the aches and pains will be more severe, not only for me, but for Mother, who always says that the injuries she had as a child have led to her pains today.

She often laughs about tripping over things and falling, getting kicked by a cow when she ran through the barn, or getting thrown by a horse when she was young, but she says she is paying for those things now. The most serious thing that has happened to me is I sprained my ankle a couple of years ago. I hobbled around for a while, but it doesn't give me any trouble today, though perhaps it will when I get older.

We butchered chickens this afternoon, and later went up town with Father and stayed to Aunt Thomas' for tea. We had a nice time. It is always wonderful to see members of our family. There are always stories about growing up in Roxbury. Aunt Thomas is older than Mother, but she has many of the same memories. Things have not changed very much through the years in Roxbury. Probably the only thing that changed the town in some way is the railroad coming through. It caused some dissention among some who had to give up some of their land, but I think it has become more important as people used the cars to go to work in places like Danbury and New Milford or even farther away.

No one called after dinner, so we played cards for a while before going to bed.

## Tuesday, September 21

Today was a nice cool day, but not too cool. It was just right for some gardening, which I set about doing while Mother went to the funeral for the little boy. It must be so sad for his family. I have read enough history to know that childhood illnesses often took the lives of several children in families. I have been to cemeteries for funerals or to put flowers on graves and have often seen rows of tombstones of children from the same family. How do the parents ever get over these losses? Do they lose their faith? Do they question God? I don't believe God made illnesses, but I often wonder why He can't do something to stop them. I suppose a minister might say that God gives us free will, and it is up to someone here to discover ways to prevent or heal these illnesses. Perhaps someday someone will.

These thoughts troubled my mind even as I took up some of the wildflowers and divided and transplanted them. It was busy work but allowed my mind to wander to the loss of that little boy. The wildflowers do grow very well and would spread to take up the whole garden if I didn't move them.

After lunch, I canned one can of peaches, and when Mother came home, we went up to Mrs. Castle's and took tea.

Dinner was a somber time as we all spoke our concerns for the family of the little boy. I didn't know him because he wasn't in school yet, and he would probably have gone to another of our local schoolhouses. Ours is just one of several here. They are located so children can walk or ride horseback to school.

I was tired from working so long in the gardens today, so I went to bed early.

## Wednesday, September 22

Another nice, cool day. There was almost a frost last night. Father and the other men are getting our crops in just in time.

Mother did the washing, and I took up some more of my plants to transplant them.

I feel better. The weather is not too cool to cause me pain so I also walked up to the schoolhouse around lunch time, so I could see the scholars at play. They all waved to me, and some of the older students came to talk to me for a while until the bell rang. Some of them are very close to my age, and we were fellow scholars just a few years ago. Some of them have lived in town all their lives, as I have, so we have known each other's families for a long time.

Father picked apples after supper before it got dark. He hopes to make some cider in a few days. Fresh cider tastes so good. I can't wait. We will also have it to offer callers when they come to see us.

Father has almost finished digging potatoes and storing them in the root cellar. He has also been chopping wood to keep the wood stove and fireplaces going in the cold weather that is sure to begin soon. Haying is mostly finished and Father and some of his friends have stored the hay in the barn, so the cows will have bedding and food during the winter. He has also purchased grain for all the animals.

### Thursday, September 23

Today was quite cool. There was a little frost last night. Father is very glad most of the crops have been harvested. Mother and I will have many vegetables and fruits to can for use during the winter. It's a lot of work but must be done so we have plenty put aside for our use. I particularly love the applesauce that Mother makes as well as the canned peaches and pears.

It was a quiet day. Most of my gardening work is done except for some more dividing of plants and keeping weeds from springing up. Most of the wildflowers have been re-located, and I think next year I will have flowers blooming from spring to fall. It gives me a great deal of satisfaction that I have achieved this with help from Father, who planted flowering shrubs and forsythia for me. It took a lot of planning as to how to set out the gardens, but they have looked wonderful and will be even better next year.

Mother and I had company this afternoon. Carrie came early so we could have time to talk. Sarah and Normie, who had come to see friends earlier, were here to tea, and Delia Bates and Eliza Jennings also called later in the day.

I have decided to let my hair grow longer. I have noticed that women with longer hair, in addition to wearing it in a bun, also let it cascade down the back of their neck. I like my bangs and my hair is quite long, but I always thought a bun would make me appear older. It might be helpful to wear it that way when I become a teacher, if that happy time should come someday.

### Friday, September 24

A pleasant day. It was another good day for working in the garden, not too cool. I have finished taking up my plants and separated and replanted them. Now all I have to do is cut some down to allow for regrowth and keep the weeds out until the cold weather is upon us. Then I will be very happy to stay indoors near the fire to ward off the cold.

My cough seemed better today. Perhaps being outdoors in the fresh air makes a difference.

In the afternoon. I canned tomato pickles. Mother also canned tomato sauce that we use in stews and soups during the winter. It is very warming in cold weather to come home to hot soup or stew. I always like to have Mother's chicken soup when I'm not feeling well, which lately seems all the time. I keep hoping that the doctors will find something that helps me, so I can go back to the schoolhouse in January, but I feel that is unlikely. It's very difficult to remain positive when every day I don't see any improvement in how I feel, no matter what medicine I take or how well I eat or exercise.

Father bought a new pocket watch and some shoes when he went to Danbury today.

While Mother was making dinner, I went to the henhouse to collect eggs so we will have them for breakfast tomorrow. Saturday breakfasts are always special because we have more time to be together without Father having to go to work. I hope Sarah, Frank, and Normie will visit tomorrow or Sunday.

## Saturday, September 25

It was a warm day today, and very pleasant. I felt almost well today, and, because of that feeling, took a walk up to the meadow where Father and Mr. Rorraback were finishing up some haying. Mr. Rorraback was driving the horses while Father piled the hay in the wagon. It is heavy work, and they looked hot and tired. I was glad I had taken them some lemonade and sandwiches, so they could have a few minutes to rest.

Of course, I was too optimistic about my ability to do the walk. On the way back, I felt quite weak and kept coughing. There was still some lemonade in the jug, so I drank some and felt somewhat better the rest of the way home. When I got there, I rested for a while in my room before lunch.

After lunch, I felt better and helped mother by cleaning up the pantry, making sure we have all the supplies we will need for cooking and baking for the next week or so. The number of jars of canned goods is growing, and that is good news for winter.

Mother has been very busy picking and cooking the vegetables from the garden.

About tea time, Mary Seymour called and brought me some sweet pickles. They were so good. She had been canning some for her family and thought to bring some to me when she called. We enjoyed the afternoon with her. After she left, Father and Mr. Rorraback came back from the meadow and were storing the hay in the barn while Mother and I prepared dinner. Mr. Rorraback stayed for dinner, and then left to go home.

After tidying up the kitchen and dining room, Mother and I joined Father in the parlor where he read the Bible for a while. I was disappointed that Sarah had not come, but perhaps tomorrow.

### Sunday, September 26

I had a bad spell today so Father took me to see Dr. Brown, who said I had probably done too much yesterday, what with walking up to the meadow and helping with cleaning and canning. I can't just not do things. It's a long day when all you do is sit around. I can't imagine what it would be like to be so sick that you could not do anything enjoyable. He gave me a new cough medicine to see if it would help. I don't like to be pessimistic, but none of the others have helped so this one probably won't either.

Despite having to see the doctor, it was a pleasant day for a ride in the buggy.

When we got home, Mother had prepared lunch and done some baking in case we had callers, but no one came, not even Sarah, Frank, and Normie. I suppose they were busy today or had company themselves. I know she has made some new friends since moving to New Milford.

After dinner, Father went down to the schoolhouse, but he returned very soon, saying there was a note on the door that the meeting was cancelled. While he was gone, Mother played the piano for a while, and I read a magazine.

There was an advertisement showing dress patterns, and I was interested in some of the new styles. I don't need as many clothes now that I'm not helping at the school, but it would be nice to have a new dress. The patterns cost 20 cents each, plus whatever material I would need. There was also a pattern for a jacket for a child. That might be something I could make for Normie for Christmas. I'll ask Sarah the next time she is here if he needs a winter coat.

When Father came home, we played cards for a while before going early to bed.

## Monday, September 27

It was cloudy part of the day but cleared up by afternoon.

When Father came home from work, he and I went up town. We stopped at the Post Office, where I received a letter from Ella Lattin. I miss seeing my friends, even though they do call on us sometimes but it's not the same as having fun with them at parties at their homes or socials at the church. I just don't feel up to these activities lately. I keep hoping I'll feel better soon, but so far nothing has changed.

When we arrived back home, Mother was visiting with a friend of Father's, Charles, who greeted Father as "Cy Nick, the great hunter." We all laughed. Father is known for his ability to hunt rabbits and other game and receiving bounty payment for capture of foxes that are often after people's chickens. One of his friends has a fox hound, and last January they captured several in three days.

Father also loves to fish, either alongside the river or in a boat he and his friends use in deeper waters. In the spring, they are always busy remodeling and preparing their boat for the fishing season. Father seems happiest then, and we enjoy the eels, sunfish and bullheads he catches.

Mother never minds the time Father spends hunting and fishing, and always says it is good for him to be with his friends after working so hard at work and at home. It is true there is not much time spent away from his daily chores, but when he does, he seems more rested when he returns home.

## Tuesday, September 28

It was cloudy and rained a little. It was not a very good day for any work outside because of frequent showers.

Despite the weather, Mr. Rorraback is working here today to help Father with some of the field chores, such as fixing fences. Most of the hay is in the barn now, as is the tobacco. Most of the vegetables have been put in the root cellar, and Mother has been busy canning and filling up the pantry shelves. There will be apples soon for applesauce that we will be able to enjoy all winter.

The New Milford Fair commences today. I don't know if I will be up to going this weekend, though I want to. I'm sure Sarah is looking forward to all of us coming. Mother will want to go as she has entered some baked goods and vegetables in hopes of getting a blue ribbon or two.

I enjoy seeing the exhibits, but mostly for me it's always fun to go because I see so many of my friends, particularly those I haven't seen for a while. That's especially true for this year because I wasn't well enough to be very active at church or social events, so I don't see them as often as I once did.

We had sad news this week. A friend of my parents, John Barry, died. Father learned of his passing when he was up town yesterday after work. I expect they will be going to the funeral later this week.

Father and Mr. Rorraback came in later in the afternoon, wet from a quick shower that passed through while they were on their way back from the meadow, and enjoyed coffee and apple pie near the warmth of the kitchen stove.

I spent my afternoon in the parlor reading. I try to keep up with current events from the newspaper and magazines so if I return to the schoolhouse in January, I will be up to date on what has been happening in the world.

### Wednesday. September, 29

It was windy and quite cold all day. Father and I went up town for a while, and. I stayed with Mrs. Bronson and took tea while he did some errands. While I was there several of her neighbors joined us, and it was an enjoyable time.

I feel quite well today despite it being so cold. Perhaps the new medicine is helping some. I don't seem to be coughing as much, but this has happened in the past, and I can't be sure this good feeling will last. Sometimes it lasts for a few days, but then I begin coughing again and having trouble with breathing and pain in my chest and back.

Mr. Rorraback is working here again today. Father has taken some time off from the hat shop to finish up the crops.

Our tobacco crop is now thoroughly cured, and Father and his friends will take it off the lathes, sort it for length and color, and place it in wooden crates or bundle it to be taken to New Milford where it will be sold.

Father is debating whether to sell it to Stuart Halpine or to Warner. There is also an auction barn owned by the Green family near the railroad tracks on Bridge Street. He will have to make up his mind soon as to where it will be sold. I suppose he is trying to determine where he would get the best price.

It is a very profitable crop, and many of our neighbors in town also raise tobacco in addition to other crops, but tobacco is the only one that is usually sold as a cash crop. We know of neighbors who paid off their mortgages just within a few years with money earned through selling tobacco.

I went to bed early because tomorrow Father and I are going to New Milford so he can attend the fair.

### Thursday, September 30

It was a cold day and there was a frost at night.

Father and I went over to New Milford after breakfast, and I stayed with Sarah while Father went to the fair. He was interested in seeing any new farm equipment that might be on exhibit and to meet with some of his friends from town and New Milford. We also brought some items for exhibit in the hopes of winning some ribbons or cash prizes. He said our baked goods and vegetables looked very good and may be able to win some prizes.

When he returned to Sarah's later, Father brought us some candy and fruit and vegetables from the fair. He said it had been a little cool for his liking, but within tents it felt warmer than just being outside. I'm glad I didn't go because I don't like to feel cold. Perhaps tomorrow will be a better day, and I will feel up to going. I know Sarah is looking forward to it, and Normie is very excited. I'm sure Father and Mother will buy him some treats or toys.

Father left for home later in the afternoon and will return with Mother tomorrow. When Frank came home from work, Sarah and I began dinner while he took care of his horse and barn chores. When they were in Danbury, Frank had to take the cars to go to work in New Milford, so it is more convenient for him to be living here. Sometimes he can walk to work depending on where his work takes him that day, and sometimes he even can come home for lunch.

Normie loves that because now he can see more of his papa. Sarah also looks very happy to be in her new home, especially now that everything is in place. It took a while for her and Mother to unpack all the household items after the move, but now she is really settled in.

After dinner, we played cards for a while, and then Sarah had to get Normie ready for bed. I went to my room and read for a while and then went to bed. Tomorrow we go to the fair.

### Friday, October 1

It was a nice day today, just right for going to the fair. Father and Mother came over early with Aunt Fannie, who had surprised Mother yesterday by coming up from New York to attend. It was so good to see her, and she is always so much fun. Willie was not with her as he had school.

We were all in good spirits as we set off for the Green. It was surprising that there were so many people there since it was a week day.

We went on a hayride around the Green, and watched some pie eating and watermelon seed spitting contests. There were games, such as tug of war, sack races, and pony rides, for younger children. There were also some older children there who should have been in school. I imagine that Mrs. Baglin was among other teachers who were missing some students today. Teachers often complain about absences when there is a town fair and will lament the loss of a day of learning.

The exhibits were very interesting. Father was mostly interested in the cattle and horses for sale. He is thinking about getting another horse and possibly another cow at some time, but finally decided to wait to see if any of our neighbors would be selling any of their animals.

We had sandwiches and lemonade for lunch and for dessert hand dipped caramel apples.

Father bought an applesauce cake to take home.

We all had a nice time, and I stood it well and wasn't too tired when we went back to Sarah's. We had a light supper with Frank and shortly after Father and Mother went home, leaving Aunt

Fannie and me to stay the night with Sarah and Frank. Aunt Fannie intends to stay the weekend, so she can see her brothers and sisters and some of her friends before going home Monday on the cars.

### Saturday, October 2

It was another nice day, but I was very tired after spending all day at the fair yesterday. I wasn't sure if I would be able to go today, but Father and Mother were coming again so I decided I should go rather than worry them.

Aunt Fannie helped Sarah with breakfast and dressed Normie so Sarah and Frank could get ready to go when Father and Mother arrived.

We all went up on the street, except for Fannie who volunteered to watch Normie while we were gone. He was tired from yesterday and didn't make a fuss about not going. He's too young to enjoy it. When he is older and can have a pony ride or play games, then he will be more eager to go. Aunt Fannie said she would make sure he napped later in the morning.

There were more people today than yesterday because it is the weekend. We made the tour of the tents, and Mother checked whether the judging had taken place for the baked goods. It had, and her apple pie won a blue ribbon and will be auctioned off later in the day. She was so happy, but I wasn't surprised. Her apple pie is so good. Father hinted he might come back and bid on it. He said the applesauce cake he bought yesterday was very good. He had a piece of it with his breakfast this morning.

Before we left for Sarah's house, she bought a watermelon for dessert after dinner tonight. As it turned out, we left in time for lunch at Sarah's because she was not feeling well. After lunch and some watermelon, Father took Fannie to see one of her friends where she will spend the night. She plans on seeing family members later tomorrow before she leaves Monday.

Because Sarah feels poorly, I came home with Father and Mother after helping make dinner at Sarah's. I was glad to be home after two very busy days and went early to bed. I didn't sleep very well, though, because I coughed quite a bit during the night.

### Sunday, October 3

It was a pleasant day today. Some of the trees are starting to change their leaves to more vivid colors. It's a pretty time of year, but I hate the thought of the cold weather that follows all this beauty. Once the leaves drop, everything is so dismal.

When we were children, Sarah and I loved to jump into the piles of leaves that Father had raked. Then he would have to rake them again. I think Normie will enjoy that fun for the first time this year. I'll make sure Father saves a small pile for when Normie visits.

As adults, this time of year is spent in preparation for the cold weather, with canning vegetables for use during the winter and storing grain for the animals.

Carrie came here after church and stayed to dinner. There was to be a social at the church following the services, but we did not stay for it. I noticed that George and his parents were not in church. It seems it has been a while since I have seen him. He must be very busy, or perhaps there are other reasons.

I don't know why I feel this way, when it was I who turned down his request to call on me as a suitor, but I didn't mean I didn't want to see him as a friend. I suppose it is unfair of me to expect to see him as much as I previously did, especially because of that decision.

No one called in the afternoon, so Carrie and I played cards for a while, and we enjoyed the chestnuts Father roasted in the evening. Shortly after, Carrie left for home.

After dinner, Mother played the piano for a while, which is always very soothing. It is a wonderful way to spend the time before bed. It always helps me to relax so I can sleep better. I think Mother knows that, and it is her way of helping me to rest more so my health will improve.

### Monday, October 4

It was clear most of the day, and as usual on a Monday, Mother did the wash. I tried to help when she was hanging it out on the line, but I don't feel as well today. She finally told me to go back indoors and take my medicine because I was coughing more.

When Father arrived home in the afternoon, he went up town to see some friends. He is still looking to purchase another horse and perhaps a cow, and since he didn't purchase any at the fair, he is keeping in touch with neighbors to see if anyone has any to sell.

After lunch I felt better, so I went outside again and picked up some butternuts from our tree before the squirrels get them all. How they get those nuts out of their thick outer covering I'll never know. It must be because they have sharp teeth. We like to use them like walnuts in desserts, but it's hard work to separate the nut from the shell.

Since it was so nice, I tried to walk down to the river, but I grew tired half way there and turned around to come home. I am trying not to walk past the schoolhouse because it hurts to see the scholars playing outside or hear their voices reciting inside. I miss being involved with their education, and still hope that I will be able to return to the school in January, but it is up to Mrs. Baglin and the doctors as to whether I can.

After dinner, I spent resting on the sofa in the parlor. I didn't even feel like reading because I was so tired from my activities today. I finally excused myself to Mother and Father and went to bed.

## Tuesday, October 5

It was rainy in the forenoon but cleared off in the afternoon.

When Father came home from work, he went up town to do some errands and to pick up the mail at the post office. I got a newsy letter form Aunt Fannie with a few sentences from Willie included. It was good hearing from them. Willie is very involved with school work, of course, and Aunt Fannie has been baking and preparing canned vegetables and fruits for winter meals. However, living in a big city, she has more things to do socially than we do here in Roxbury, so she has been busy since she was here for the fair.

Mrs. Beardsley, Mrs. Baglin, and Maggie called at tea time. Mrs, Baglin doesn't talk about school very much anymore. I think she feels it would make me sad to hear about it, and she is correct, in that I miss it more and more every day. I'm hoping so much that my health improves soon so I can return to help her with the scholars. I love being home with Mother during the day, but I can't help her like I once did, so it can be boring.

When Sarah and Normie are here I feel better about being here instead of at school, but she comes mostly to help Mother with tasks that I once did before and after school.

I try to keep up with the news, so I don't fall behind on knowledge of what is going on in the world, but it is not as fulfilling as helping with the scholars. I understand that the population of the United States is now over 50 million. Imagine how many of them live in the big cities.

I think I would always want to live in a small town, but, as I've never been to a big city, I really don't know what living in one would be like.

One reason I enjoy being home is it's nice to be here when we have callers. I often missed their visits when I was in school and would come home as they were leaving. It seems we have many more visitors lately than we once had, but that may be because I wasn't here to know how many called previously. Of course, Mother often went calling to friends and neighbors while I was in school, so I didn't get to see them.

## Wednesday, October 6

It was clear but quite cold today, and there was a hard frost last night. The trees are really beginning to turn color now, and I dread when the leaves fall and the hard cold will be on us.

I had some pain in my chest and back last night. Even with my new bed quilt, my room is beginning to get quite cold, especially in the morning when I first wake up. I always wash and dress quickly so that I can go down to the kitchen, which will be warm and toasty from the stove.

Mother always is awake early, so she can make breakfast for Father before he leaves for work. She is a firm believer in a hearty breakfast to start the day. I find it difficult to eat as much as she puts in front of me, but I try my best because I know she worries if I don't eat.

Father had helped me several times to transplant some of my flowers so most of that is done. I'm glad, because I'm never happy when I must work outside when it is cold. Of course, when I was younger, and felt better, the cold didn't bother me as much as it does now. I always liked to walk to school on brisk cool mornings, if dressed warmly. Now, even though I might dress for the cold, I still feel cold.

My cough is worse. Since I was feeling poorly, Father went to Stepney with Charlie Minor and got me some medicine.

In the afternoon, I wrote to Ella Lattin and read some magazines. I helped Mother set the table for dinner and to wash up after, but then I felt tired again. The fatigue is what bothers me the most. I wonder if I will be able to walk to school, and if I can't, then I think I probably won't be able to help Mrs. Baglin.

It's so easy to say why me? I don't want to feel sorry for myself, but I wonder why I have these troubles. Other girls my age are having fun, going to parties and church socials, and sometimes I can barely walk upstairs at night just from what activity I have here at home. I enjoy the parties and socials and try to put on a smile, but I often am very happy to come home. I like it best when Mother and Father entertain here so I don't have to go out. Here, I feel comfortable, and can feel more at ease. I admit that sometimes I would just rather go upstairs and lie down when we have guests, but that would be rude, and I wouldn't want to upset Mother and Father.

### Thursday, October 7

It was cold and windy today. When he came home from work, Father asked me if I wanted to go up town with him, but I was very happy to stay near the fire where I could feel warm.

Later, after Father arrived home, he took up the honey, but unfortunately it was but little. It has not been a good year for the bees. I don't know why.

Today was one of those rare days when no one called. Perhaps others felt the cold on such a windy day. Instead, we had tea and some cakes in the afternoon. Then Father went out to do some chores in the barn and to feed the animals.

I tried to help Mother with dinner, but I coughed worse, and she told me to sit by the fire in the parlor where it was warm. The stove warms the kitchen once dinner is being prepared, but it takes a while for the room to be comfortable.

I wrapped myself in a quilt and curled up on the parlor sofa with a magazine and the newspaper that Father had brought home from up town. I enjoy reading about the events going on in the world that are so different than here in Roxbury. In small towns like ours, events center about the Grange, church, schools, and families. We spend a great deal of time just taking care of our homes and farms and look to our neighbors and the churches for what entertainment there is, such as musical evenings and social gatherings.

Even though I still feel poorly, I can enjoy all the activities and would miss them if I was unable to attend social gatherings. Sometimes it is difficult to keep smiling when I am in such pain from coughing so much.

### Friday, October 8

It was a nice day, with no wind.

Father and Mother left early in the morning to attend the state fair at Danbury. I stayed at home. Eliza Jennings stayed with me, and she was good company. When I began coughing, she made sure I took my medicine and then fixed me some tea with honey. It soothed my throat so some of the coughing stopped for a while.

I know my parents love the Danbury Fair, and I have enjoyed going to it in the past. It is much larger than the New Milford or other local fairs, and the cars can take you directly to it. I have always gone with them in the past but didn't feel up to it today. I don't know if they will go on any other day when I might feel better.

Mother and Father returned late in the afternoon, tired and happy. They had seen several of our friends and neighbors, so it was obvious they had a good time. Father also brought me some oranges and peanuts.

Father said the main building was full of exhibits from people from the entire area. Mother didn't enter anything this year. I hope it isn't because she didn't have time to prepare anything because of the extra work she has. Sometimes I feel so guilty that I am becoming a burden for my parents at a time when I should be helping them more. I'm young, but I don't seem to have the strength I once had. Just walking to the river or to the schoolhouse takes what energy I have. I am trying to keep walking, hoping that it will help me grow stronger, but for right now it seems it is not helping.

## Saturday, October 9

It was a nice day today. Bruce and Father took up the honey in the tree, and Father gathered apples.

I felt a little better today so I walked up to the bee tree and watched as they went about gathering the honey. Then I walked to the meadow to see the fall flowers in bloom. The fields are full of them right now, but soon they will all be sleeping during the winter.

Those I transplanted to my gardens are doing well. I'm so glad I did that work, so we will have flowers for spring, summer, and fall. The shrubs Father helped me plant will remain green in the winter and will give the house a welcoming look during that season. Perhaps at Christmas we can decorate them in some way, perhaps with popcorn garlands. I imagine the birds would like that.

During the afternoon, Dr. Richards, a friend of our family, called to see me. At tea time, some of our neighbors called and brought me some jellies and puddings. Everyone is so kind.

My friend Carrie called as some of the neighbors were leaving. I had never told her about George asking to call on me because it was never to be because of my decision. At the time, I thought of talking to her, but it would not have made any difference in what I decided.

Even though she doesn't know, I wondered why she asked me if I had seen George recently. When I thought about it later, I realized it's been quite a while since I have seen him, and all our friends know he and I have been friends since we were small. I expect she thought I would know why he has been absent from some of the socials and gatherings in town and at the church. I realized he has not called and hasn't been in church when we were there.

She wondered if he was calling on someone from out of town. She said she and her mother were at the Danbury depot the other day, waiting to come home on the cars after shopping. As they were boarding, she saw George getting on the cars with two women, one an older woman, and the other, younger. When they arrived in Roxbury, she watched as he led them to his parents who were there with their horse and buggy to take him home. She said she was surprised when they all left together.

I tried to be calm so Carrie wouldn't think I was over-reacting, but it was quite upsetting to hear. It was probably some family members, I said, who were coming to visit his parents. Carrie didn't think so. The young woman was very attractive, she said.

After Carrie left for home, I found myself going over our conversation. I was surprised about how I was feeling about Carrie's news. I don't think she meant to be unkind because I'm sure she thinks of him as one of our friends and nothing more. She was just interested in knowing if I had any information that she didn't. It wasn't like we were gossiping.

I think Mother would think it was in very bad taste to talk about someone the way we did. He obviously had not seen Carrie, or he might have introduced the visitors to her and her mother.

### Sunday, October 10

Another nice day with sun and a gentle breeze, and not very cold. A nice Indian summer day, a perfect day for the fair.

Mother and father went to church, but I stayed home. I didn't feel like going because I didn't sleep very much last night. I seem to be coughing more than usual, and the medicines as usual don't seem to help.

After lunch, Maggie Divine called and visited with us. She had brought me some cake, which we all enjoyed with tea. It seems as if our neighbors and friends are always bringing me things to eat. Perhaps it's because I have lost so much weight since I have been sick. I know, because my clothing is getting bigger on me again, so I'm sure some have noticed.

We had some good conversation, but then Maggie said she had seen some new people in church that morning who were obviously visiting with George and his parents. I looked at Mother and Father because they had not said anything about seeing them, but knowing how Mother feels about it, I suppose she did not want it to appear she was gossiping. Apparently, from what Maggie said, George and his parents and their visitors left immediately after the service without speaking to anyone except the minister and deacon.

After Maggie left, I went to my room to read for a while and to think about what Maggie had said. I wasn't sure if I should say anything to my parents because Maggie obviously didn't know the women, just as Carrie hadn't.

Perhaps they were relatives or maybe George knew them from Danbury and had brought them to meet his parents. Even though I still believe I made the right decision when George asked permission to call on me, I could not help but feel a little sad if things are beginning to change and our friendship will not be the same. I don't know if I'm ready to face that yet. However, while I have always loved George as a friend, I had a difficult problem trying to see how that relationship would have been if I had been able to say yes to his request to call on me.

Should you ever marry someone because you feel comfortable with them because you have been friends for years? Shouldn't you feel something more than that? Or is it possible to grow to love someone in a different way if you were to marry? I know so little about married love, but I do think it is better to love someone you marry rather than think of him as a friend that you will learn to love later.

### Monday, October 11

It was very warm and nice today, so Mother did the wash and hung it out on the line.

I felt very low today. Though I slept better last night than I have lately, my cough this morning was much tighter and my chest and back hurt from coughing so much.

I spent the day on the sofa in the parlor pretending to read but mostly thinking about what Carrie and Maggie had talked about.

Mother was concerned because I didn't eat much lunch and kept coming in to check on me. She brought me a piece of cake from yesterday and tea, but I didn't feel like eating anything but took a few bites and sips, so she wouldn't worry.

After lunch, Mother brought in the dried clothes and linens and sat with me while she folded and readied clothing that would be ironed the next day. We talked some, but Mother still did not refer to whether she had seen the women who were with George and his family, so I didn't bring it up, for fear she would think I was gossiping.

After Mother put the clothes and linens away, she began to make dinner, and I went back to my pretend reading as I continued to mull over who the women could be. It does seem strange that George and his parents didn't stay for the social hour after church but left directly after the service. Perhaps their company had to return home today on the cars. I wondered if George would escort them back to Danbury. Would he stay somewhere in Danbury since he needs to be to work there the next day? I know he has friends who have homes there.

When Father came home from work, he picked some quinces in the orchard and brought them inside. Perhaps Mother will make some quince jelly or jam, or perhaps a quince tart. They are the strangest fruit. They are bright yellow but when they are cooked they turn pink. When I was a little girl, I tried to eat one raw and soon realized they were much too tart to eat that way. They do make a dessert look pretty and taste much better after being sweetened and cooked.

Father went out to the barn to take care of some chores before dinner. I so much wanted to ask him and Mother if they had seen George and his family's guests at church and if they knew them. I would think if they are relatives, Mother and Father might know who they are. Again, Mother probably doesn't feel comfortable talking about them or perhaps she feels it might be painful for me.

### Tuesday, October 12

It was a nice forenoon but was windy and rained a little in the afternoon. It reminded me of how restless our scholars could be on rainy days because they were not able to go outside at all.

We had some callers after lunch, and Mrs. Hodge called later in the afternoon and spent some time sitting on the porch with Mother and me. She was concerned about my health and how I felt about not being able to help Mrs. Baglin at the school. I know she didn't mean to be hurtful but talking about it did make me feel sad. I miss the scholars and helping them with their lessons. I even miss correcting papers and helping to clean up the school room at the end of the day.

After Mrs. Hodge left for home, the rain had stopped so I went out and got some chestnut leaves to use with other leaves and berries in a wreath for the front door. I enjoy doing these things and look forward to the Thanksgiving and Christmas holidays and the planning and decorating we do for them.

I hope I will feel better by Christmas and will be able to tell Mrs. Baglin that I am ready to come back to the school to help her. She has called several times but does not say much about the scholars or the school. Perhaps she knows it would make me feel sad. I miss the children, particularly the small ones, who are just beginning and are so eager to learn to read and do their sums. True, some children come to us already reading because their parents have helped them prepare. It makes our job a little easier because there are so many new things for them to learn.

My favorite was always reading, and it didn't matter what I read, whether fiction, poetry, or history, I loved them all and still do. These things help me pass the day when I feel unable to do anything more strenuous.

## Wednesday, October 13

It was cooler and windy today. Already the nights are cold. There is a nip in the air that tells us that colder days are on the way.

Emma Beers came by at tea time and brought me some peaches. Eliza Jennings stopped by after school and brought home some of my books that I had loaned the older scholars.

I don't feel quite as well today, and I can't help but wonder why I'm not doing better. I take my powders and potions as directed by the doctor, eat well because of Mother's good cooking and baking, and try to exercise as much as possible. The walks to the river or up to the schoolhouse are not always easy, but I try to make it all the way and back because I know they will keep up my strength for when I will be able to do it every day for school.

I am trying so hard to keep positive thoughts because I know it is not good to think in the negative all the time. I have been through such times, when it was difficult to think in a positive way, but I sincerely want to believe that I will return to the schoolhouse to help Mrs. Baglin and that someday I will be a teacher like her.

Father has been picking corn and apples after work as well as finishing digging up the potatoes in the garden. We have a wonderful supply of food already set aside for future use in the cold weather. Mother has been canning applesauce and corn relish, and the jars are starting to fill up the shelves in the pantry. During the winter Father and others will butcher hogs and the ice house will hold a fine supply of pork and bacon.

Mother baked yesterday, and I had a warm piece of buttered

bread with strawberry jam with a cup of coffee this morning. Mother makes sure that I eat well.

## Thursday, October 14

It was a very pleasant day today. When Father came home from work, he and I went up around by Mr. Minor's and up town.

Jennie Minor gave me some peaches, and she and I had a nice visit while Father and Mr. Minor went to sell our quinces. When they came back, we had tea and cake, and then Father and I returned home.

Mother was preparing a stew with dumplings for dinner, and the house was filled with the wonderful aroma. I can't understand why the doctors don't think I eat enough. I do, I just don't seem to gain weight and continue to lose. How that happens when Mother is such a good cook and baker, I don't know. I certainly eat very well, even though sometimes I am not very hungry. Mother watches very carefully that I eat all she gives me, so hungry or not, I eat. I don't want to make her worry.

After dinner, I retired to my room. The drive this afternoon tired me, and I didn't feel like playing cards or board games or even reading the newspaper Father had bought while he was up town selling the quinces. As I lay on my bed, though, I did not sleep because my mind kept coming back to the two visitors George escorted home from Danbury and to his parents' house. I have heard nothing more about them. Even Carrie hasn't said anything since she first mentioned it, though she has stopped in to see me a few times since. She never stays long so perhaps she had heard something and forgot to tell me.

I don't know why it bothers me so much. It was me that turned down George's request to call on me. He is not my suitor because of my decision for the two reasons I raised at the time. I wasn't ready for any new relationship, not even with George who I know so well, and because of my concerns over my health. Since then I have felt no doubt about my decision, but I know Mother and Father still hope that things would change in that respect if my health improved. So far, that does not seem to be happening, and I have become more certain that I made the right decision.

I have some regrets, yes. I would like to be like other young women my age who look forward to courtship, marriage, and a family of their own, at least someday. However, somehow being a teacher has always seemed more important to me in the immediate future.

I also regret not sharing my decision with Carrie, who is such a close friend. She would have understood and been a comfort these last few months that I have carried this decision alone except for my family. They have been supportive, but I should have included Carrie in my decision.

I suppose it's not too late to tell her, but nothing would have changed even if she had known.

**Friday, October 15**

It was warm today, just like summer. In the morning after breakfast, I helped Mother make quince sauce and jelly, more jars for the pantry shelves.

I feel better than I have in a few days. Yesterday was very tiring, what with our drive to town and visiting with Mrs. Minor. Even though I rested after dinner, with all my thoughts about George and the two women and whether I should talk to Carrie about my decision, I did not sleep as well as I had hoped. My head was just full of all those thoughts and would not let me rest. Once in the night, I got up from bed and sat by the window, looking out at the dark.

I'm not sure, but I think it is much too late to talk to Carrie about my decision about George. It would probably only make her feel sad for me. As it is, she is concerned about my health, and she and her mother are always bringing me good things to eat. I should be getting fat, not thinner, and she has wondered why I'm not getting better now that I'm resting more because I don't go to the schoolhouse.

I have heard that two of the older girls, who have been doing well in their studies, are now helping Mrs. Baglin with the younger children. I'm glad she has found help because it is difficult to keep the younger scholars involved while she is testing the older ones.

No one called so it was a quiet day. It was just as well because I felt very tired and even a little depressed because of all the thoughts that have been going through my brain since I was told about the two women with George.

I need to put those thoughts away. I did what I did because of very good reasons, one about my age and the other about my health. If I get better, I may want a relationship someday, but I must concentrate on getting better so I can continue training to be a teacher. That is my purpose for agreeing to take a few months to rest, and I can't think about anything else.

If someday, I would want a relationship that would lead to marriage and a family, it would be long after George had found someone else, I'm sure, so I can't worry about him calling on other women. His life will go on, and I knew our friendship would change.

After dinner tonight, we stayed in the parlor for a while to read and talk and then we all went early to bed. I hope I can sleep better tonight.

### Saturday, October 16

It was partly cloudy, but it didn't rain. I had expected to go up town but did not because Mother was unable to go with me, and I did not feel well enough to go alone. Bess is easy to drive, but I felt I might arrive somewhere and not feel well enough to get home. Then someone else might become inconvenienced by having to drive me, and I would not want that to happen. It was better not to go at all.

Perhaps Sarah, Frank, and Normie will come tomorrow and Sarah and I can make some calls together in the afternoon while Frank and Normie visit with Mother and Father. I would feel much better if I had Sarah with me in case I had a poor spell.

In the early afternoon, Ella Pierce called and brought me pie, cake and candies. They all looked wonderful, and I'm sure we will enjoy them in the next few days.

Mr. Hodge came to visit in the late afternoon and stayed to dinner, after which we played cards for a while. After he left, Mother and Father read quietly in the parlor while I did some needlework. The doilies I am making for my bedroom are looking fine.

I keep thinking I should probably talk to Carrie about George's request to call on me, and my reasons for declining. It would give me someone to talk to that would understand my reasoning. Carrie has said she is in no hurry to have a suitor and to marry, so I think she would be more understanding than some of my other friends, who can't wait to get married. Carrie is also very aware of my concerns about my health and has often wondered why I don't seem to be getting better now that I have been resting more.

### Sunday, October 17

It was cloudy in the morning and rainy through the afternoon and tonight, a dismal day to do anything outside.

Despite the rain, Father and Mother went to church. I did not go though I dearly wanted to hear the music and the sermon. My cough and pains seem to be worse when it is not only cool but rainy. I was happy to stay by the fire in the parlor and work on my needlework and do some reading. When they returned from church, they were full of news of upcoming socials and musical programs that will be held at the church before the holidays.

I couldn't help but wonder if I would feel well enough to attend any of them. This respite from the schoolhouse is not helping me feel better. I really thought I would be better by now, but no, it was not to be.

Later we heard the clip clop of a horse's hoofs on the road, and were so happy to see Sarah, Frank, and Normie. Sarah ran carrying Normie through the rain and into the house while Frank unhitched the horse and led him to the barn

Normie was laughing so hard over their sprint into the house that we all just had to laugh, too. He didn't mind at all that they got wet, but thought it was great fun. It seems that Frank does not have to work tomorrow so they had come to spend the night.

When Frank joined us, Mother and Sarah made some lunch for us, with Ella's apple pie from yesterday for dessert. It was very good with some sweetened cream.

Since the day was so dreary, Sarah and I did not make any calls, but since she will be here tomorrow, perhaps we can go then. If it's a nice day, I may feel better. I just could not seem to stop coughing today. None of the potions and syrups seem to help.

### Monday, October 18

It was clear but quite cold, and despite my hopes that Sarah, Frank and Normie would stay longer, they went home early in the morning. I had hoped she and I could do some calls today, but she expected some friends for lunch and wanted to be home to prepare. They are making a quilt together that will be sold at a church fair before Christmas.

I feel I was being selfish because they had been here from lunch time yesterday and overnight so it's not like we didn't spend time together. It's just that most of the time when she is here, she is helping Mother and doesn't have much time to spend with me. It's been a while since I made any calls on our neighbors and friends, and, while I don't often feel well enough to do so, I felt it would be something Sarah and I could do together.

After they left, Mother washed the clothes and linens, and in the afternoon hung them out to dry. It was sunny but cold when I went out to help her take them off the line later in the afternoon. They were cold to the touch, and there was a real scent of fall in the air. Leaves are beginning to come down and will soon need raking. I always enjoyed raking, making the yard all neat again, but I don't know if I have the strength this year to do it.

Father said he would help me put some in the flower beds to protect the flowers during the winter. How I dread the thought of cold weather. I'm sure the flowers will be fine because they are mostly wildflowers, which always seem to thrive, no matter how cold the winter is.

Mother knew I was disappointed that Sarah left so early, but while I know she has her own house to take care of and calls to make to her friends in New Milford, I just wanted her to stay long enough so she and I could have some time together that didn't have to be shared with Mother and Father. We were always so close when we were younger, but now I must share her with Frank and Normie as well as Mother and Father, and I just miss the times when we were just two young girls sharing secrets and fun times together.

### Tuesday, October 19

It was clear but cold today. We probably can't expect too many more warm days as we draw closer to November. How I dread the cold. I always feel as if I can't get warm, no matter how warmly I dress or as close to a fireplace or stove I sit.

I helped Mother make jelly in the morning. It's something I can do to help her that doesn't make me feel fatigued. Several more jars were added to the pantry shelves. We shall have plenty to eat this winter as Mother and Sarah have been busy canning vegetables and fruits and berries.

Mother and I had a nice quiet lunch, after which she made a cake, and I went into the parlor to read and work on my doilies next to the fire.

In the afternoon, Mrs. Fabrique and Mrs. Eastman called, and Dr. Brown was here quite a long time. I felt his eyes on me often, probably thinking that I look thinner than ever, and it's true. My clothes are getting too large for me again and I must take them in. I don't think I am fooling anyone by taking in my skirts and shirtwaists, so they appear to fit me well. I'm afraid it is well noticed I am losing weight.

I know that Dr. Kerrmann and Dr. Brown are trying to find some medicine to help me, but their efforts have not been successful. I don't think they even know what is wrong with me. There are so many illnesses that have the same symptoms.

They stayed to tea, and we had some cake as well as some interesting conversation about town news and what is happening in political campaigns. Dr. Brown did not say anything to me about my health, I'm sure, because he was here on a social visit, not as a doctor. When he was leaving, he did tell Mother that he and Dr. Kerrmann are discussing some possible remedies for me to try.

After Mrs. Fabrique and Mrs. Eastman left, Mother did some housework while I read in the parlor. Then I helped her set the table for dinner and peeled some potatoes and carrots.

### Wednesday, October 20

It was a nice day, somewhat warmer than yesterday. Despite the warmer temperature, however, I don't feel near so well today. My cough is worse.

In the morning, Mother did the ironing, and I spent some time working on the doilies for my room and reading the newspapers that Father brought home yesterday.

It appears the campaigns for president are in full swing as well as those on the state and town level. Father often goes to meetings at the Town Hall or the church that involve politics. He says he wants to hear about issues himself rather than rely on the newspaper.

It is too bad that women cannot vote. I would also be interested in hearing the speakers at those meetings, rather than reading about what they said later. I wonder, as I have before, if women will ever have the right to vote and have their voices heard at the ballot box.

Mother and I had a quiet lunch. I was hoping Sarah might come today, but I suppose she is busy with Normie and preparing for her church fair. We did have company, however, this afternoon. Then after Mother's friends left, she went back to doing her chores. It was then that Carrie arrived, and because it was warm outside, we went out on the porch to talk. Seeing her made me realize I needed to tell her about George's request to call on me and its outcome.

She was not too surprised because George and I have always been good friends since we were children, but I think my decision and the reasons for it did cause her some concern. She said she understood how much I have wanted to be a teacher ever since we were little girls, when we would play school with our dolls instead of playing house.

She agreed I was right about concerns about my health. However, she also wondered if I had been too hasty in my decision and might regret it in the future if my health improved, especially if George had found someone else to marry. It was then I told her one of my concerns was that I would lose George as a friend, but that I felt my decision was the best for both George and me, and that I would have to accept whatever happened in the future

Before Carrie left for home, she gave me a big hug, whispering that I could always talk to her and that she would never tell anyone else about what we had discussed. She has always been my friend since we were little girls in school.

I felt better after talking with her, knowing she understood the reasons for my decision.

### Thursday, October 21

It was clear today until night, when it clouded up, but it did not rain until Mother and I returned from New Milford later in the afternoon.

Mother and I had gone to see Sarah and Aunt Fannie, who was visiting from New York for a few days. Mother had recently purchased a pattern and material for a new dress, and they helped Mother cut it out and pin it, so Sarah could bring it to our house later in the week to have Mother try it before final sewing is completed.

While we were at Sarah's, Ella stopped in and had lunch with us. Later, Mother, Sarah and Ella went down on the street to shop, and I stayed with Fannie and Normie.

After we put Normie down for a nap, Fannie and I talked for a while in the parlor. Of course, she was concerned about me, asking if my health was improved since I was no longer going to the schoolhouse to help Mrs. Baglin with the scholars and Sarah was helping Mother more with chores.

Aunt Fannie is always so caring and easy to talk to. I didn't want to worry her, but felt I needed to talk to someone about my frustration about not feeling better, no matter what medicines the doctors give me, and my concerns about what my future might be. I don't like to worry Mother and Father, so I rarely talk about these concerns at home.

I told her how much I miss going to the schoolhouse and how I try to keep up with reading and current events, so I will be ready to return to school. I was almost in tears when I admitted to Aunt Fannie my concerns that I might never be well enough to be a teacher and what would happen to me in the future.

Aunt Fannie sat next to me on the sofa and held me in her arms, comforting me as she had so many times when I was child, after falling and scraping my knees or facing some disappointment. Nothing back then compares with how I feel about not being able to help at the schoolhouse or becoming a teacher in the future.

She said I must keep taking my medicines and listening to the doctors when they suggest some new remedy because it might be able to help me to get better and follow my dreams. A positive viewpoint is important, she said, so I must steer myself away from any thoughts I might have that would have me lose hope.

I felt better for having talked to her, as I have so many times before. By the time the others returned from shopping, Normie was awake and entertaining us with his toys and books.

Sarah brought me some candies, which we enjoyed during tea time. Shortly after, Mother and I left for home.

## Friday, October 22

It was a rainy day and night, and because of that, I don't feel as well as I did yesterday. My cough is worse, and so I did nothing much today.

We had no callers, probably because of the rain, but Aunt Fannie, Sarah and Normie did come in the late morning, bringing Mother's new dress for her to try on before the final sewing is done.

I left them to take care of that and was happy to spend the day by the fire with some books and magazines and watching Normie play with his toys. I read him a story, but he was more interested in playing with his train and soldiers. It was just as well because my throat hurt when I talked too much.

We had a nice lunch together, and afterwards Sarah got out the machine to finish sewing Mother's dress. It did not take her very long, and by mid-afternoon, when Normie was just getting up from a nap, Mother had a new dress for church and social occasions, except for some ornamental touches that they will take care of tomorrow.

Sarah wanted to get home before dark so about an hour later, she, Aunt Fannie, and Normie set out for New Milford. I always hate to see Sarah leave. I have so little time with her it seems. She is so busy with her family, the church fair, and helping Mother when she can that there is no time for sisterly talks. I miss that, but I don't let her know how I feel because I know she would try to make more effort, which, I think, would take away from the time she would have with her own family. I just need to keep that in mind when I start feeling sorry for myself and being selfish that I don't have as much attention from Sarah as I once did.

I was in the parlor reading when Father came home early from work so he could clean out the well. There are so many chores that need to be done before cold weather comes so there is always something for him to do after work and on weekends.

After dinner, we played cards for a while and went early to bed.

## Saturday, October 23

It was rainy by spells and cloudy most of the day. My voice is worse. I whisper most of the time because my throat hurts so much. I wish I could say this was something that would go away, but it only seems to get worse. I was also feeling feverish.

In the morning, Father went up town to get the mail and to do some shopping. He brought home more canning jars for Mother to continue putting together vegetables and fruit for the winter.

Later Sarah and Aunt Fannie came by to help Mother with the finishing touches on her dress and stayed for lunch. Normie did not come because he was spending some time at home with his papa. It was nice to have more time with Sarah. I love Normie, but he does require a great deal of time and attention from his mother.

Sarah fixed me some tea with honey that she said might make my throat feel better. It was very difficult to carry on a conversation because my throat was so sore, and I also had some coughing spells. I get so tired being this way. I want to have fun, to go to social events, or shopping with Mother, Sarah, or my friends, but I never feel quite able to do any of those things anymore.

When Sarah and I were alone for a while, she asked me if I had seen George lately. I had to think of when I had seen him last. It seems like such a long time since he has called. I told Sarah I thought he had been here sometime early in September, and was taken aback when I realized that was over a month ago

She must have noticed how that upset me because she quickly changed the subject after noting that he was probably very busy with work and helping his parents. We talked of other things, but my mind kept going back to thoughts of George and that he hasn't called since early September. I usually would have seen him and my other friends at church or social events, but most of the time I don't attend because I have not been feeling well enough.

I miss church and my friends, but unless they come here to visit, as some of them have since I haven't been going to church or the schoolhouse, I don't see them. I miss the fun we always had, especially this month with Halloween parties. There will be no dunking for apples for me this year.

I wonder what is keeping George so busy. Mother and Father have not mentioned seeing him at church or around town, so I have no idea. Perhaps things are already changing between us as I felt would happen eventually. Is it because of the young woman Carrie saw him with?

After Sarah and Aunt Fannie left for New Milford, I helped Mother with dinner preparations. It is one thing I can do to help her. I can peel potatoes and scrape carrots and set the table without getting fatigued, but anything more than that is usually difficult to do.

After helping to clean up after dinner, I went to my room to read, but my mind kept going to George and wondering why it has been so long since he has called. The only answer that kept coming to mind was that things have already begun to change regarding our friendship. I suppose if he is calling on someone, it would not be appropriate for him to see other women, even if they have been friends for a long time.

**Sunday, October 24**

It was cold but clear today, but we did not go to church. Father was busy with chores in the barn and Mother was canning tomato sauce for stews during the winter.

I miss not going to church, and often wonder if Father and Mother don't go as often as they once did because they don't want to leave me home alone. Father still reads the Bible aloud to us in the evening, especially on Sunday, and we discuss the passages afterward.

I miss the music, though I can't say I always enjoy the sermon, especially if it is overly long. When I was a child, I would almost doze off during it, but Sarah would poke me to keep me awake so Mother and Father wouldn't notice. The minister's wife sits near the front of the church, near the altar, and is often seen looking at her watch and then looking at him. Does she send him a silent message that the sermon is getting too long?

There was a meeting at the schoolhouse in the afternoon that Uncle Henry and Father attended. I think it was a political meeting, and not one about the school. It is getting closer to the election so there were probably candidates giving speeches about town and state issues. Sometimes I feel like I would want to know more about our government, but since women can't vote, it hardly seems worth the trouble to try to keep up with all the issues.

Ella Pierce and Emma Beers came to see me in the afternoon, but otherwise we had no other callers. I keep wondering why I didn't realize how long it had been since I had seen George. I keep thinking about that young woman he was with when Carrie saw him. Perhaps he is seriously courting her.

## Monday, October 25

It was clear but windy today. Mother did the washing and then hung it outside to dry. It didn't take long with the sun and the strong wind.

I don't feel very well but better than yesterday.

No one called so it was a very quiet day. In the afternoon, Mother went out to make some calls at our neighbors and while she was gone, I read Sunday's newspaper and a magazine and spent some time doing needlework. The house seemed so quiet. I could have gone with her, I suppose, but I just didn't feel well enough to spend time with other people. I was content to stay on the sofa in the parlor with a quilt around me to keep me warm.

I have noticed that we don't seem to receive as many visitors as we once did. I wonder why that is. Could it be because I have been sick, and they don't want to intrude? I still wonder what is wrong with me that I don't get better. When I look in to my mirror, I now see a very pale young woman who a year ago was well and happy and looking forward to the holidays because of all the social events. How things have changed.

When Mother came home, I forced myself to get up and help her in the kitchen. I set the table for the three of us and prepared some vegetables while she fixed chicken for dinner. Father came home from work a short while later and after he had taken care of chores in the barn, we sat down to eat. Mother had made a custard pudding for dessert, which went down well even though my throat was still sore. Because it is so windy, my pains seemed more severe today. I ached all over.

After supper, Father read from the Bible, and he and Mother discussed the passages he had read. I was content to just listen because my voice was almost a whisper. After listening to Mother play the piano for a while, I went early to bed. Hopefully I will feel better tomorrow.

### Tuesday, October 26

It was cloudy and rained some in the afternoon, bringing down more leaves that will need raking again. Soon all the bright colors will be gone.

Ella Pierce called in the afternoon and brought me a loaf of cake, which we shared at tea time. It was good seeing her, and she stayed for about an hour.

I have not lain down today at all for the first time since I was sick. Every day for a few weeks now it seems that I spend some time on the parlor sofa or on my bed napping. It's probably because I don't sleep through the night because of coughing and the pain I have in my chest. Despite all the rest I am having from not going to the schoolhouse, I don't seem to be getting any better. I would rather have gone to the school, so I would have something to do.

It seems a long time since I felt well enough to be at the schoolhouse helping Mrs. Baglin, then hurrying home in the afternoon to help Mother with supper or other chores. I don't do much of anything now without getting tired, but today I didn't nap and wish I could believe this is a sign of a change in my health. But I know in my heart it's not. I don't know what to expect in the future, but I do know that I made the right decision when I declined George's request to call on me as a suitor.

I know there are times when I have regretted that decision because of my fear that I would lose George as a friend. But our lives would be different if I became a teacher and lived and worked somewhere else. I still cling to the hope that someday I will be able to go back to the schoolhouse and later become a teacher myself. I look at the ferule that Grandfather made for me and remember how much he supported my goal of becoming a teacher. I cannot give up on that. I need to believe I will get better.

### Wednesday, October 27

It was a nicer day today than yesterday, which was gloomy and rainy.

I felt better today, so much so that I helped Mother by making some pickled onions. There are now more jars sitting on the pantry shelves in preparation for winter. How I hate the thought of the cold weather that is sure to come. It's such a grey time of year, with no leaves on the trees. If it snows, it is prettier for a while, but after a while I get tired of the snow. It was more fun when we were young and did more sledding and skating, but once I was working at the schoolhouse, I didn't always have time to really enjoy the outdoor events, especially since it gets so dark early in the evening.

Sarah and Normie came by early this afternoon. She left Normie with Mother and me and went out to the yard to do some raking, so Father and Mother would have less to do. I always did the raking in the past, and when Sarah and I were little we would rake the leaves into a big pile and then jump in them. Then we would have to rake them up again. It was so much fun.

Sarah came in after a short while to get Normie, and I watched from the window as the two of them jumped in the leaves. I opened the window, so I could hear his cute little laugh as the leaves flew around him. When Sarah started to rake again, Normie continued to jump and roll about in the leaves, slowing down the process of getting the yard cleaned up. Mother finally went outside and took Normie for a walk so Sarah could finish up the task at hand. I admit to a little jealousy. I wanted so much to join them, but I knew the increase in activity would only get me coughing again and would take away from how much better I felt today.

Sarah and Normie stayed for tea and cake, and then headed home to New Milford.

When Father came home, he had been to the Post Office, and brought me two letters, one from Carrie, who has been staying in Danbury with family friends, and another from Mary Greene. Carrie expects to be home this weekend, but I will answer Mary's letter tonight so Father can post it tomorrow.

### Thursday, October 28

It was a nice day today, and I was feeling better so later in the morning I went down to see Mr. Rodgers.

Mother ironed in the morning while I was out, and when I got back, Mother and I had a quiet lunch. No one called in the afternoon. Of course, it is a work day, and most of the women we know use this day to clean and bake in preparation for the weekend when there is the likelihood that family or friends will visit.

I took some time to write to Dr. Kerrmann, telling him how I have been feeling better the last few days. I know it is probably only a respite before I again have pain and coughing, but it did my spirit good to write about it. It helps keep me in a positive mood. I also answered Mary Greene's chatty letter. She and I attended school together, and she is currently teaching school, something I still hope to do in the future when I am better.

I am hopeful that some medicine the doctors give me will eventually help me so that I can go back to the schoolhouse and prepare for my own teaching life.

Some people might think I am being overly optimistic because of the bad days I often have, but I cling to my hope that everything will eventually work out. Yes, I have my bad days, when I can hardly get up from the parlor sofa or find it difficult to even walk a short distance, but I will not give up and fall into doubting thoughts.

Mother is beginning to talk about Thanksgiving. It seems the month of October is just flying by, and November will be here in a very few days. I expect that Aunt Fannie and her family will be coming for Thanksgiving plus some of Mother's other sisters and brothers. It's always a day for family, with church services in the morning. Then we usually have a light lunch followed by outdoor activities that raise the appetites of all for the wonderful dinner we will enjoy later. Aunt Fannie and Uncle Philip, as well as Nellie, Willie, and Winston, usually stay over until they leave again on Sunday for New York. It's very much like a second reunion.

### Friday, October 29

It was a very cloudy day, but it was made cheerful by Carrie, who came by early in the afternoon and brought me some books. Mrs. Hodge came, also, about tea time. Afterwards, while Mrs. Hodge and Mother talked in the parlor, Carrie and I played cards at the kitchen table. It was warm and cheerful there with the air punctuated by the scent of bread baking in the oven.

Carrie said that while she enjoyed visiting relatives in Danbury, she was glad to be home. I was glad she has returned. She has been my best friend since we were little girls, and now that I have told her about what happened with George, there are no secrets between us.

We talked and laughed until it was time for Carrie to leave for home. After she left, I found I was not able to talk very loudly. Perhaps I was too optimistic in my letter to Dr. Kerrmann, which Father took to mail today. Mother and Father are no longer upset if I write to my doctors because I always tell them what I have written. I should never have written that first letter to the doctor without telling them. I was just so upset about not feeling better and the biggest blow has been that I have been unable to go to the schoolhouse.

This respite is supposed to help me get better, but I know that is not happening. I have some good days but it's getting so that there are more bad days than good, and the doctors still have not found something to help me. Perhaps they never will or perhaps they have not told me what they think is wrong with me. There are so many illnesses that seem to have the same symptoms.

### Saturday, October 30

It was rainy all day and into the night, a very dreary day when we usually have several callers.

Mrs. Hodge did come in the morning and had coffee with Mother and me, but she didn't stay long because she was expecting some family members to arrive in the afternoon. No one else came. I suppose the dreary weather kept them warm and dry at home.

Despite the bad weather, today was one of my good days. I did not lay down at all today, and the coughing was not as hard as it usually is. Perhaps it was because I did not go outside at all but stayed in the house. I read for a while in the parlor after Mrs. Hodge left, and after lunch with Father and Mother, I helped Mother clean up the kitchen, after which she and Father left to pay some calls.

I wonder why I have days like this, when I really can believe that I am indeed getting better, but then a day comes along that convinces me that this type of day is more the exception than the rule.

I wish I could go to the schoolhouse. I miss the scholars and Mrs. Baglin, but I promised to wait to see how I would be in the New Year, and so I must be content with that and hope for the best.

I wish Carrie had come by today, but since she was here yesterday, I'm sure she is spending today with her parents or visiting other family members here in town after being away in Danbury. I wrote a letter to Elizabeth, a former school friend, who is now living in Southbury.

### Sunday, October 31

It was rainy in the morning but cleared off and was a windy day.

No one went to church. I seldom go now, though I miss it, but it is a rare Sunday when Mother and Father miss services. Mother helps with preparing the altar, and sometimes serves coffee during the social hour after the service. It is a good time to spend with friends and family, and for the women to plan future social events.

Most of the men spend their time talking about their farms, businesses, or politics. With an election coming up, that is usually well discussed during the coffee hour. I think I would like to be part of that conversation, rather than worrying about social activities that can sometimes be boring, even though the organizers may have thought them exciting. You may not be interested in playing cards or going to musical entertainments, but they are activities that women involve themselves, in addition to their interest in their children's school work and tending their homes.

I think it would be much more interesting to be involved in politics, helping to have a candidate elected to whatever office is sought. Unfortunately, even if women could help a candidate, they could not vote for him, since women cannot vote. Perhaps someday.

No one called this afternoon. Perhaps the rain and wind deterred them from making the customary calls. I certainly was happy to stay in where it was dry and warm.

### Monday, November 1

It was clear today but quite windy. There is no snow in sight, which according to who you are and what you like to do could be upsetting. Those of us who always enjoyed sledding or sleigh rides in the snow may be disappointed, but it is a little too early for any snow.

I imagine the scholars at the schoolhouse are anxious to make snow angels and have snowball fights during recess. Last year I was among them. It doesn't seem so long ago and yet it seems I have been away from the schoolhouse for a long time.

I was very tired today because I did not sleep much last night. My cough was worse, and it seemed as if I coughed almost all night. Mother came in once to give me some of my medicine and it helped for a while, so I did get a few hours of sleep.

I spent much of the morning on the parlor sofa reading, or at least trying to read, while Mother did the washing. Most of the time I was just thinking of all I was missing this fall. Mother and Father insist that I rest, but there is just so much of that I can bear. I want to do something, but my body tells me I can't. As soon as I begin walking about or try to help Mother with some chores, I get weak and tired and then must rest some more. Some days, like today, I am even too tired to read.

I found myself thinking about George and wondered if Carrie had seen him when she was in Danbury. If she had, it seems she would have said something, plus he was probably working during the day, so she wouldn't have seen him when she was out and about. It seems a long time since I have seen him, and I wonder, diary, is this what I feared? Perhaps he is now calling on some young woman, maybe even the woman Carrie saw him with in Danbury and then here in Roxbury.

Perhaps he feels awkward about calling on us because things have changed, and he's not ready to see me because he doesn't want to hurt my feelings. I had long ago accepted that if he was seeing someone, our friendship would change. I know the decision I made was right, but it doesn't stop me from missing George and his friendship.

### Tuesday, November 2

It was a pleasant day for the beginning of November. I do not feel quite as well today but did a little work while Mother ironed.

I did not mail my letter to Elizabeth until yesterday because I kept adding to it as things came to mind. I haven't seen her in a long time so there was much to ask and to tell. I hope I receive a letter from her soon. I feel so separated from my friends. I am no longer able to harness Bessie and drive to see them or take the cars to Danbury or New Milford to do some shopping. Just doing the little work I do around the house seems to tire me out. I keep hoping that I will get stronger and be able to do all the things I enjoy again.

Not many of my friends come to visit any more, except Carrie, who is so loyal. I suppose they are all busy with social activities or work, and I would probably seem very boring in comparison.

Since I have so little to occupy me now, I find myself remembering all the fun events I enjoyed in the past, playing with the small scholars during recess or reading with them while sitting in the shade of a tree during the fall and spring. In the winter, they loved making snow angels and snow men during recess or having a good-natured snowball fight. It was such innocent fun, but we always had such a good time.

I remember the socials I attended, the callers we received here at home, and the many Christmas Eve parties by the tree in the parlor when members of our family and neighbors joined in celebrating the holiday. The holidays are coming again, but will they be the same for me? I fear they won't. If I don't feel better and stronger, I will not have the schoolhouse to look forward to in January. Then what will I do?

### Wednesday, November 3

It was a nice day, and probably because of that I was feeling quite well today. I was able to help Mother make jelly.

Mr. Smith came to see Mother and me as part of his duties of calling on his parishioners. He always asks about my health, and I try to be optimistic, but I think he sees the truth before him. I am thinner than I was even a week ago and my clothes are again becoming too big for me. I had a bad coughing spell at night and didn't sleep well so I probably looked tired even though I did feel better.

Mr. Smith stayed for tea during which Father arrived home, bringing the newspaper with the results of the national election. Discussion quickly turned to politics. According to the newspaper, Garfield defeated Hancock in a close presidential election, winning the electoral vote 214-155, but the popular vote was much closer, 48.27 percent to 48.25. His Republican party gained 19 seats in Congress, while the Democrats lost 17. According to the paper, the Democrats lost their majority in the House and the two major parties were tied in the Senate.

When Mr. Smith left, Father walked him out and they stayed by Mr. Smith's buggy for a few minutes talking more about the election, I would imagine. When Mr. Smith left, Father went into the barn to take care of the animals. Meanwhile, I helped Mother clear the tea plates and cups and took them to the kitchen while she began preparations for dinner.

After dinner, I helped Mother clear the table and wiped the dishes as she washed. We then joined Father in the parlor. He read some passages from the Bible, Mother played the piano for a short time, and then we all went early to bed.

## Thursday, November 4

It was clear in the morning but turned cloudy in the afternoon. Mother and I had a quiet morning, with no callers.

In the afternoon, Mrs. Hodge brought me a bouquet and some pineapple, which was a real treat. The only time we have pineapple seems to be at Easter when we have a ham Mother prepares with pineapple slices and whole cloves. It is always so good. Then we have the leftover ham to enjoy with eggs the morning after. I always take some of the cooked pineapple slices to add to the morning feast.

After Mrs. Hodge departed for home, I wrote a reply to Aunt Fannie in New York. She always asks about my health, but I try not to worry her by telling her about all the bad days I have. Instead, I tell her about days when I feel much better. I'm not really lying, but only telling her part of the truth. I feel bad enough that I am worrying Mother and Father.

I have always felt close to Aunt Fannie because when she and her family come to visit, they stay with us most of the time and visit the other siblings for shorter periods of time. Because of that,

I am also closer to Nellie, Willie and Winston than I am to my other cousins. I will have Father post the letter tomorrow.

**Friday, November 5**

It was a rainy, dismal day. I spent it fixing one of my dresses that has become too large for me. I also felt well enough to help Mother more around the house, dusting and sweeping in preparation for the weekend when we usually have more callers than during the week. Mother baked the customary cakes, pies, and bread.

Even though my cough was bad at night, and my voice is almost gone, I felt better otherwise.

Father has been busy the last few afternoons readying the tobacco for sale to Warner in New Milford. He hopes to get a good price because we raise prime tobacco that is used for cigars, and we had a very successful crop this year.

I always wonder why men like to smoke cigars, but some of my more adventuresome girl friends have said they would like to try one to see why men like them so much. What a strange idea when it is not deemed proper for women to even smoke cigarettes. I think if they tried one, they would never want to do that again. I think they are smelly and disgusting, but that is my opinion. I'm sure some of my uncles and Father would disagree. Father favors a pipe usually, which doesn't smell as bad as cigars.

Mother doesn't let Father smoke even his pipe in the house since I have been feeling so poorly. I feel bad that he must go outside or to the barn to enjoy his pipe, but I know I have a hard cough after men have been smoking while visiting. On the other hand, smoke from the fireplaces also makes me cough, so it is very hard to avoid these things.

Father was very happy during dinner this evening because he is looking forward to tomorrow's sale in New Milford. Uncle Henry is going with him to help unload the tobacco, and they will be leaving early in the morning.

**Saturday, November 6**

It was cloudy and rainy all day. Father and Uncle Henry left after breakfast to go to New Milford with the tobacco crop.

Mother and I spent the morning quietly. No one called before lunch, but several of our neighbors came in the afternoon. Carrie did not come, but her parents brought the cake and jelly she had prepared for me. They said she would probably call on us tomorrow after church.

I will enjoy the jelly with my toast in the morning.

We were still having tea and cake with Carrie's parents when Father returned from New Milford. He had sold all his tobacco, and at a good price. He was very happy all the hard work had paid well.

After Carrie's parents left, Father went up town to see some friends and while he was gone Mrs. Hodge called and stayed for about an hour. She and Mother are helping to plan a social at the church next week so while they were talking in the kitchen, I read for a while in the parlor.

I can't wait to see Carrie tomorrow. I hope nothing happens, so she is unable to come.

Father returned from up town, still very cheerful after his tobacco sale today. We had dinner and then played cards for a while before going early to bed.

### Sunday, November 7

It was very windy but clear for most of the day. Mother and Father went to church, but I stayed home near the warmth of the parlor fireplace. The wind, when it is as strong as it is today, takes my very breath away and I usually avoid going outside when it is like this.

I read some, but most of all I thought with anticipation of Carrie's visit today. If she went to church, as her mother thought she would, she no doubt will have things to tell me as to who was there and who was not.

I was thinking particularly about George. Mother and Father don't ever mention him if they see him, though I think more and more he is probably staying in Danbury on Saturday and Sunday unless his parents need him here.

I remember how he wanted to move closer to his work, so he wouldn't have to take the cars every day, but after talking to his parents, he decided they needed him here during the week.

I wonder why he hasn't called in what is now weeks. I know I would not change my mind about his calling on me as a suitor. I still believe my decision was best for both of us, but I feel badly when I think it may have cost me his friendship. And yes, Diary, I knew that might happen, especially if he began to call on someone else. It would make our friendship difficult, if impossible.

In the afternoon, Dwight and George Evans called, as well as George Rorraback and Frank Castle, and joined us for tea and cake. Later Carrie arrived, and I could tell she had something to tell me. When Mother asked her to stay for dinner, she gladly accepted. After dinner, while Mother cleaned up the kitchen and Father went out to the barn to check on the animals, Carrie and I took our tea and went into the parlor to talk.

Carrie said George was in church today with his parents, and the same two women were with them as well as another gentleman. During the social hour after services, Carrie said they were introduced as friends from New York City. When George went to get coffee, Carrie went also, and she said he asked about me and if my health was better. He said he had not been in town very much on weekends recently because he was working on Saturdays as well as showing his parents friends around Danbury. It seems they may be moving here, or at least have a summer home in the area, Carrie said.

Carrie said George did not appear to be overly attentive to the younger woman. I know Carrie thinks that I will change my mind if my health improves and that George is waiting to see if that happens. I think she is being fanciful, because if I do get better, I will go back to the schoolhouse and continue preparing to become a teacher. George is a friend and hopefully will remain so if I do get better.

### Monday, November 8

It was clear and nice today, and I felt better because I had slept more with not as much coughing. Because I slept more, so did Mother, and she looked more rested today than she does when her sleep is interrupted. She always comes in and makes me take some medicine, and I think she has trouble getting back to sleep because she is worried about me.

Because I felt so good, I made some jelly before going into the parlor to read some.

Mother washed as she usually does on Monday and hung the clothes and linens out to dry. Later I helped her prepare the clothing for ironing and folded the linens.

No one came to visit at all today, and it was just as well, because by mid-afternoon I no longer felt as well. Perhaps I did too much, but my cough was tighter. Mother insisted I take some of my medicine, but none ever seems to help. After dinner, Father read some from the Bible and the newspaper, and then we went early to bed.

### Tuesday, November 9

It was a beautiful day. When Father came home from work, I went up to the hollow with him and stayed at Aunt Josephine's while he did some errands.

My cough was bad, and my chest felt tight all day. It was one of those days when I feel as if I will never get better, at least not in time to return to the schoolhouse in January. If I don't return then, I don't think I ever will. By then, Mrs. Baglin will have someone else helping her so they, too, can become a teacher. What will I do then? Just stay home with Mother and try to help her as best I can at that time?

Aunt Josephine fussed over me, making me comfortable on her sofa until Father was ready to return home. She made me tea and toast with warm milk on it that made it go down easily without hurting my throat. I ached all over, and though I had taken some of my medicine before leaving home, it was not helping as usual. I get so depressed that nothing I do seems to make any difference. It makes me wonder why I even try.

Aunt Josephine tried to keep me entertained with news of some of the other relatives and what was going on about social and church activities. I tried to be polite and make suitable comments and ask questions, but clearly my heart wasn't in it. It is no fun to hear about activities that I know I will not be able to attend. I don't have the strength I once had to attend social gatherings.

I was quite ready to go home when Father returned. It was near dinner time, and while I was not very hungry, Father was. He bundled me up in the buggy with blankets and soon we were home where Mother had dinner waiting for our return.

During dinner, I just picked at the chicken stew Mother had made. I once enjoyed such meals on cool days, but more and more I seem to have no appetite, though Mother tries to prepare things that have always been my favorites. I particularly like her custard pudding, which we had for dessert, and I did manage to eat all of it.

I know Mother is concerned about my lack of appetite, but I don't do very much to feel like eating. I rarely get outside to walk to keep up my strength because the cold bothers me so much.

After dinner, I excused myself and went to my room where I read for a while before going to bed.

## Wednesday, November 10

It was another beautiful fall day. Late in the morning Mother and I went over to Sarah's for lunch, so Mother could get the dress Sarah had finished sewing for her. Sarah is a very good seamstress, much better than I. Oh, I can make things, but I'm not as creative with a needle as she is. She always adds something to make the dress more attractive.

Even when I was younger, I didn't have the patience to do the handiwork that Sarah enjoys so much. I can knit and crochet, but my work never looks as nice as what Sarah has done. Sarah spent a lot of time years ago learning from Mother and some of our aunts, and the time has proved to have been worthwhile. I always preferred to be outside taking care of the gardens, especially flower gardens, or just walking to the river and back.

Mother went up on the Green for a while and made some calls, then departed for home, leaving me with Sarah and Normie. I'm to stay for about two weeks, I think mostly to give Mother some time to rest. I know Sarah is concerned about me, but she is also concerned about Mother, who must do so much more work now that I am unable to help her.

Sarah still comes to our house every few days to help, but I am sure she is concerned that Mother doesn't sleep well because she is worried about me. I know my coughing at night awakens her, but my powders and tonics don't help very much, if at all.

My cough is very tight. If not for that, I otherwise would be as well as usual, though that is nothing like I once was. I wish I could go back in time when I was well and went to socials and church activities, had fun with my friends, and helped Mrs. Baglin with the scholars. I fear those days are over. I try to keep a positive attitude, mostly so not to cause Mother and Father any concern. I also know that they can hear me coughing and can see that I am losing more weight. My clothing keeps needing alterations, and that keeps me busy sewing, though I try to do it when they are away making calls or are busy with chores.

### Thursday, November 11

It was rainy in the morning but cleared off in the afternoon. My cough is still tight and hurts me worse.

Today is my birthday, and I am now 20 years old. How quickly those 20 years have gone. It seems just like yesterday that I was well and happy, going to socials and spending time with my friends. I look back at the years I spent in school and remember how much I enjoyed learning. I still do and try to keep up with current events by reading the newspaper. Sometimes Father reads it out loud, and I enjoy hearing the news and his opinions about certain issues.

It must be wonderful to be able to participate in government functions. Uncle Henry goes often to Hartford to meet with our representatives in the Legislature, and while it is a long trip for a day, he seems to enjoy it very much.

Sarah is making me a cake for my birthday, and Mother and Father are coming to have dinner with us. I suppose I will receive some presents. I particularly would like some oranges and some candy. These always taste so good, and I do think the oranges help my throat.

It does seem strange not to be at home for my birthday. Usually some of my friends would call, and we would enjoy cake and tea together. Sometimes they would bring me a book or some candy. I admit I have a sweet tooth and am particularly fond of the homemade ice cream Mother always makes to go with the cake.

I'm sure I will have more to write about my birthday tomorrow, though I'm sure it will be quite different from that of other years.

### Friday, November 12

It was colder and very windy today. Even so, Sarah did some wash and hung it out to dry. It dried very quickly because of the wind, but everything felt so cold when I was helping her fold and prepare laundry for ironing.

I am about the same. My chest feels so tight from all the coughing. I hope I didn't keep Sarah and Frank awake last night. I know I didn't sleep very much myself. Normie seems to sleep through any disturbance because he plays so hard during the day. He still takes naps, but not as easily as he once did. He wants to stay up and see who calls or play with his toys, plus he has learned that there are treats he likes during tea time and he doesn't want to miss them.

While Sarah did some baking in preparation for the weekend, I crocheted for a while. After lunch, Mrs. Weldon called. She told us she had heard that a French actress, Sarah Bernhardt, had made her New York debut at Booth's Theater.

I think I would like to see a play. When I was in school, we sometimes acted out scenes from books we had read. I loved Little Women by Louisa May Alcott, and always wanted to read the part of Jo. There are so many books I have enjoyed. It must be wonderful to be an author and see your words in print.

Despite my concerns that my birthday would be different than other years, it turned out to be wonderful. It was a great surprise when Carrie arrived with Mother and Father for dinner. We enjoyed Sarah's cake with some ice cream Mother had brought from home. Luckily it was cold, so it didn't melt too much on the way here.

Carrie brought me a book that I have been wanting to read, Mother made me a new skirt and shirtwaist, and. Father gave me some candy and magazines to help me pass away the time. Sarah and Frank gave me a beautiful music box which I will always treasure.

Before he went to bed, I read to Normie for a short time. I hope he will grow up to love books and become an educated man. Perhaps one day he will go to college. I certainly will encourage him, but I am beginning to wonder if I will be here to do that. I feel I'm not getting better, in fact the days I feel well are becoming fewer and fewer in comparison to those when I feel poorly.

## Saturday, November 13

It was a cloudy day but did not storm. Frank had to work this morning, so he left early. Sarah, Normie, and I enjoyed a leisurely breakfast.

Later, while Sarah was ironing, I did a little work in the kitchen to help her, but then rested in her parlor while she finished the ironing and then helped her store everything away.

After lunch, she and Normie went down on the green and made some calls. When she came home, she brought me some candy, which one of her friends had given her for me. Everyone is always so kind. I hope someday I can help others as I have been helped. Someone is always bringing me something to eat or flowers because they know I love them so.

We had some callers, friends of Sarah and Frank, around tea time, which was enjoyable. I felt a little better today because I slept better last night. I hope I will do so again tonight because it certainly helps me feel better the next day.

Frank came home in time for dinner and after Normie was put to bed, we played cards for a while. No one called in the evening, though there was more activity on the green than usual, Frank said. One of the churches was probably having some social activity.

I went to bed early, hoping I would sleep well.

## Sunday, November 14

It was a nice day, but I don't feel as well, though I rested better at night.

I am concerned there doesn't seem to be any planning for Thanksgiving. Sarah said Mother has been talking to Aunt Lydia, but apparently most of our family members will either be staying at home that day or going to be with friends. Even Aunt Fannie and her family don't appear to be coming. I guess it will just be us and Sarah, Frank, and Normie.

Of course, it's not like Christmas when everyone seems to come on Christmas Eve and then again on Christmas Day for dinner after church services. I wonder if it will also be different this year. Is it because of me? Is it because I have been ill? I have noticed that neighbors and friends don't call as often as they once did, but perhaps it is as Sarah says, that they are concerned about the additional work Mother has to do because I am no longer able to help her.

I want to help, but I tire so easily that I often must take rests in between chores. I have been trying to help Sarah with some household chores, but she seems to appreciate it if I watch Normie when he is playing so she can do her chores more quickly. It is fun to watch him, and I often read to him before his naps and, if I feel well, we play with his toys.

No one called at Sarah's today, and Sarah and Frank went to church while I stayed home with Normie.

I'm looking forward to going home in time for Thanksgiving. I love Sarah, Frank, and Normie, but I miss Mother and Father. Sarah said they will probably take me home that morning, so she can help Mother with the dinner. She intends to make the pies that we will have for dessert that day. I love pumpkin pie, and Sarah said she will make one as well as an apple pie. While my appetite is not always good, I'm looking forward to the desserts.

### Monday, November 15

It was clear most of the day but snowed a little just at night, just enough to make the scenery less bleak. It's so drab during these fall and winter months with no flowers or leafy trees.

My cough was a little looser than it has been most days. I spent the morning watching Normie while Sarah did the wash and hung it outside to dry.

After lunch, I felt better so I walked down to Mrs. Thayer's and to Mrs. Welton's. I enjoyed tea with Mrs. Welton and some members of her family who had also called.

When I returned to Sarah's later, I found that she was not feeling well. I hope she didn't catch a chill while hanging out the laundry. Since I was having such a good day, with little coughing or tightness, I helped by fixing dinner. She set the table while I prepared the chicken and vegetables, and by the time Frank came home from work, dinner was ready. Sarah had baked on Saturday, so we had bread with our meal and cake for dessert, which made Normie very happy. He seems to have my sweet tooth. Even when I don't feel hungry, I can always manage to eat candy or baked goods.

I know my doctors would not approve of that, but I just can't resist sweet desserts. No matter how much I eat, though, I don't gain any weight and still appear to be losing. I just finished taking in some of my skirts and shirtwaists. I hope I don't have to continue to do that. I'm so afraid I have what some people call a wasting disease, for lack of a better name for it. If that is the case, I fear I won't have to worry about my future.

I know Mother and Father would be upset if they read these words, but if I don't get better by January, I know I will not be going back to the schoolhouse. Ever. I try to stay positive but it's becoming more and more difficult to do so.

**Tuesday, November 16**

It was a pleasant day, but quite cold, according to Mrs. Welton, who called in the afternoon. I did not go out at all today. When it's this cold, my cough seems worse and pains in my chest more intense.

Sarah ironed in the morning after breakfast while I watched Normie in the parlor. He is very easy to watch because his toys keep him very busy. He was tired after a while, so Sarah put him down for a nap after lunch. He seems to only take one nap these days. He is becoming more social and loves to visit with callers when they visit so it's often difficult to get him to take an afternoon nap unless it is right after lunch.

I didn't do much today, although I felt more rested than I usually do. After lunch, I wrote to Dr. Brown, my friend Mary, and George. Frank will post them tomorrow for me.

I haven't seen George in what feels like a long time, and it felt strange writing to him rather than seeing him. I know Carrie saw him recently at church, but he still hasn't called on us. He told Carrie that he had been very busy and hadn't seen many of his friends when he was in town.

I felt nervous about writing to him, but perhaps he will come to call as a result. I kept the letter as from one friend to another, with nothing written that he might think I had changed my mind about his calling upon me as a suitor. I just want to remain friends, even though I know if he eventually marries, that will not be possible.

We enjoyed a quiet dinner after which we played cards for a while before going to bed.

### Wednesday, November 17

It was a cloudy, dark day and rained some. Despite the lack of sunlight, we were all up early, including Normie, so we had breakfast together before Frank left for work. Usually he has left by the time I get up, but I guess he felt today was a good day to sleep a little longer.

Days like this can be very depressing, with no sunlight, and showers off and on throughout.

I felt very well today, despite the weather, but my powders are gone. It's good I'll be going home soon because I will need to get some more from Dr. Kerrmann. I think they help me somewhat, and I don't want to be without them.

Later in the morning I helped Sarah with a little sewing. Some of Normie's clothing is getting too short for him, so we have been making him some new. I often wonder why we put little boys in dresses for a while. I suppose it's easier to change their diapers if they don't wear pants like the bigger boys. He is almost trained, so I imagine we will be making him some pants and shirts before long.

Frank took my letters to the post office on his way to work. I still feel nervous about having written to George, but it was just a letter from one friend to another, nothing that would make anyone think I was being too forward.

Another week and I will be getting ready to go home. I love visiting with Sarah, Frank, and Normie, but I do miss Mother and Father so much. I don't think I would ever be able to go far away from them. Women who marry men from other states rarely see their families. Women still do not travel alone very often, and because their husbands work, it is difficult to return home for even a visit.

Of course, Aunt Fannie is an exception to this. She is very modern in her habits, and Philip doesn't seem to be concerned that she comes here by herself. I'm going to miss her on Thanksgiving. It just won't seem the same.

### Friday, November 19

It was clear and nice today, much better than the dreary day yesterday.

Though she isn't coming up for Thanksgiving, I spent some time helping Sarah sew on Fannie's new dress for the holidays. As

I've said before, Sarah is a much better seamstress than I, but I did help her a little by doing button holes and attaching a collar.

I feel about the same as yesterday, not better, not worse, just the same. I miss my powders because they do seem to help.

I wish I could feel like this all the time. It would be as if I was really in good health again, but I know it will not last. I am beginning to accept that I will not be able to go back to the schoolhouse in January. I would have to be doing exceptionally well by then to make that possible.

I miss the scholars and Mrs. Baglin so much. I'm sure she probably has already arranged for the girl helping her now to continue if I don't return.

Sarah and I had a quiet lunch with Normie. He had taken a nap just before, so he didn't take another after lunch. He was probably hoping we would have callers, so he could visit with them, but no one came. Everyone loves to see him, too. I think it won't be long before naps will be a thing of the past.

I can't imagine what Sarah will do when and if she has another child. I know Mother is looking forward to another grandchild, perhaps a girl, in the future. With two (or maybe more) small children, Sarah would be even busier than she already is.

## Saturday, November 20

It was another rainy, dark day. November can be so bleak. There hasn't been much snow, so the landscape just looks grey except for the green pine trees.

Despite the weather, I feel very well today. Perhaps I was getting too dependent on my powders and other remedies the doctors have given me. Maybe it is them that make me feel so tired so much of the time. I am finding it increasingly difficult to do any long walks, though I have made several calls recently to our friends here in New Milford. Visiting with them gives me time to rest before walking back to Sarah's.

To help Sarah, I sewed some on Aunt Fannie's holiday dress. I had hoped she and her family would be coming for Thanksgiving and would get the finished dress at that time, but it appears that no one is coming with us except our immediate family. It will be quite different from other years.

We need to have the dress ready soon because at some time Aunt Fannie will come to get it. It's going to be very pretty on her. She has a very busy social life in New York, so she is always having new dresses made for parties and other occasions.

While I was working on the dress, Sarah did some baking. We were low on bread, cake, and pie. We always must be prepared on the weekends in case anyone calls.

After I finished what I could do on the dress, I wrote to Father. I will be so happy to see him and Mother Thanksgiving morning.

No one called in the afternoon. Sarah, Frank, and I enjoyed our tea and a piece of pumpkin pie. Later we had an early dinner after which we spent some time in the dining room playing cards.

### Sunday, November 21

It was a very cold day and the temperature was so cold last night that the last of Sarah's flowers had a hard freeze. Winter in all its cold and snow will soon be upon us. I dread the thought of it because I always feel less well when it is cold and damp.

Despite the cold outside, I slept very well last night and felt very warm under one of Sarah's quilts.

After breakfast, Sarah and Frank went to church while I stayed home where it was warm and watched Normie. He is a little young to go to church and would not understand anything about the service. He would like the singing, I think. Sarah sometimes sings when she is working or when she is putting him to bed at night. She has taught him to sing the A, B, Cs, but sometimes he mixes up the x,y,z.

I read to him for a while, then we played some with his toys. About late morning, he was yawning so I put him down for a nap. He was soon sound asleep.

To help Sarah, I prepared some lunch for when they returned, then went into the parlor to read for a while.

After lunch, during which Sarah and Frank discussed the minister's sermon to great length, some of Sarah's friends called, and we enjoyed talking with them. They had no sooner left, when Aunt Josephine and Ernest arrived in time for tea. They were on their way to New Preston to see friends and stopped for just a few minutes.

After they left, no one else came. We had an early dinner and spent the evening reading because Frank does not approve of card playing on the Sabbath.

## Monday, November 22

It was another cold day. I suppose we can expect this to continue now that we are in the end days of November. Our warm days are most likely over until spring. Soon it will be snowing.

I did not go outside at all today. On cold days, I am happy to spend my time inside where it is warm. I did some sewing on Fannie's dress and some clothes for Normie.

Sarah as always did the Monday ritual of the wash. I often wonder how that became the day that most women do laundry. Of course, Sarah does it more often since she has had Normie. He can get his clothing quite dirty, and he is also outgrowing most of it.

Frank left for work earlier today because he had to go to New Preston. Sarah was up early with Normie so she made Frank some breakfast before he left, then she, Normie and I had a leisurely breakfast together. Normie played with his food like always. He makes what he says are roads in his oatmeal. Where do the roads go? I asked him. To Grandma's house. I think he is looking forward to seeing Mother and Father as much as I am. Only three days until Thanksgiving.

Sarah will be making pies to take with us on Thursday. I don't know what Mother is planning for dinner. Because we usually have company, she always bakes a turkey, but for just us I don't know what she will make. Perhaps chicken. Anyway, Thanksgiving won't be the same. I'm just looking forward to more pumpkin pie. She also makes what is called Indian Pudding, which is made with corn meal, milk, molasses, and spices. It is the best part of Thanksgiving, especially when topped with Mother's whipped cream. I imagine we will have lots of vegetables, which have been stored in our root cellar.

After lunch, Sarah took Normie and went up on the Main Street to do some shopping and make some calls. I stayed near the fire and read until I found myself starting to doze.

When Sarah and Normie returned later, I woke from what was a sound sleep. I rarely nap during the day no matter how tired I am because then I can't sleep at night. Shortly after, Uncle Amos stopped in to visit. He was our only visitor today.

Frank arrived home in time for dinner and later we spent time reading the newspaper he had brought home.

## Tuesday, November 23

It was a very cold day that felt like winter had already begun. How I dread these cold days that will last for months until spring comes again. The only highlights of the winter are Christmas and New Year's, but I wonder if I will be able to take part in the social activities of those holidays.

I did not feel quite as well today. My cough was somewhat tighter than usual. I took my cough medicine, but it didn't help very much. I tried to help Sarah with some chores but I kept having coughing spells, so she made me take a rest on the parlor sofa. I don't like giving in to my ailments, but sometimes I just need to rest so the coughing stops for a while.

Frank came home for lunch today as his work had him close to home. He had stopped at the Post Office and picked up the mail. I was surprised by a letter from George, in answer to the one I had sent to him. I opened it quickly and took it into the parlor to read.

His letter was much like mine to him, a letter from a friend to a friend. He apologized for not calling as often but noted his work had been very busy and his parents had also needed him to help them ready their home for the cold months ahead.

I know from watching Father and Frank just how much must be done to lay in enough firewood for the winter and to make sure that the house, barn, and outbuildings are prepared for the cold weather. Father has already been preparing the sleigh in the event of an early snow and has been making sure there is enough food and bedding for the animals who would not be able to be out grazing in the meadow once the snows come.

I enjoyed reading George's letter. He said he had seen Father at the Post Office one day and found out I would be home for Thanksgiving. He said if all goes well he may call that afternoon or perhaps on Friday. I look forward to his visit.

## Wednesday, November 24

It was another cold day but warmer than yesterday. It was an especially wonderful day because plans for Thanksgiving have changed somewhat and for the better.

Mother came over in the morning, and I went home with her and Aunt Fannie, who had surprised Mother by coming up on the cars yesterday. She wanted to surprise me, plus Fannie needed to pick up her holiday dress. It's good Sarah and I finished it in time. She was very pleased with it and thought she might wear it for dinner tomorrow.

Uncle Philip, Nellie, Willie, and Winston being with us will make this weekend special, especially after I thought it would be very dreary, without any callers. Though it will be a smaller dinner party than usual, I am so glad Aunt Fannie and her family will be here.

Before we left, Sarah and Mother went up street to do some shopping, and while they were gone, Fannie and I played with Normie and read him a story.

The buggy ride home was uneventful. Normie was excited to be going to Grandma's house and to be staying over. Frank is to come tonight after he is finished with work.

## Thursday, November 25

It was cloudy and snowed some today, and there is quite a lot on the ground. It is Thanksgiving today, and Fannie's family arrived in time for lunch. Mother, Fannie, and Sarah were busy preparing for Thanksgiving dinner later in the day.

Sarah had made pumpkin and apple pies, which we had brought with us yesterday. All arrived safely, unlike one Thanksgiving when I was carrying a pie from the kitchen to the dining room and tripped and dropped it. What a mess, but, luckily, we had others.

Mother has made her wonderful Indian pudding, which I love. I can't wait for dessert. It's the best part of Thanksgiving. While waiting for dinner, I read two letters I received yesterday from friends.

No one called during tea time, and though George had said he might stop in, he did not. I was disappointed because I thought he would come by in the afternoon, but I suppose his family needed him at home or perhaps they had company and he couldn't get away. I keep hoping he will come sometime over the weekend, but we shall see. Though this made me sad, I put on a happy face, so no one would know I was upset.

Dinner was very festive. Sarah had set the table with a lace tablecloth, a centerpiece of fall flowers and colorful leaves, and Mother's best china. Sarah is always so creative. Her home is always cheerful with colorful flower arrangements and holiday decorations. I wonder if I would be as creative if I had a home of my own. I help Mother with decorations, especially at Christmas, but I'm not like Sarah. I don't seem to have an eye for decorating.

## Friday, November 26

It was cold but clear today. I have got a cold.

I canned some fruit and made jelly, which will be used throughout the winter. It took some effort on my part, and I was very tired when I finished. I wish I could get over the fatigue I always feel after doing even the smallest of chores. Whatever is wrong with me does not seem to be getting better.

Fannie and her family are still here. Uncle Phillip did not have work today, so they won't need to go back to New York until Sunday. Father also had the day off. We had a very nice lunch of leftover Thanksgiving fare. It always tastes as good the second day as it did the first.

Despite that most people do not work today, no one called in the afternoon. Fannie and Mother and Sarah and I played cards for a while. Father and Uncle Phil of course had to take care of the animals and cleaned the barn.

Normie was the center of attention as always, and Willie, Nellie, and Winston took turns playing with him to keep him entertained while we played cards.

I had hoped that George would stop by, but again dinner time came, and he did not come. I should not have counted on him stopping by but hoped that he would be able to visit before having to go back to work on Monday. There is still tomorrow and Sunday and many of our neighbors and friends make most of their calls on those days, but I won't get my hopes up about George.

## Saturday, November 27

It was a pleasant day and warmer, but there is still snow on the ground. I didn't feel very well today. Because the day was so nice, we did have several callers after lunch, and at tea time George's parents called, but he was not with them. I was disappointed, but I am learning not to count on his visits since he hasn't called for so long.

I had a bad cough and excused myself to go to my room to take some medicine. When I was returning downstairs, I heard George's name mentioned by Mrs. Webster. I paused on the stairs rather than interrupt, but I could not help hearing George's mother say that he has been calling on a young woman in Danbury, a daughter of their friends that visited here a while ago. I turned around and quietly returned upstairs so it would not appear I had been listening to their conversation. It suddenly occurred to me that it might be the young woman that Carrie saw with George at the train station.

While I have been expecting this, I couldn't help but feel stunned. What I have feared is now coming true. George is moving on with his life since I did not answer favorably to his request to call on me. I still feel my answer was for the best for both of us, but truly, diary, I did not expect this to happen so soon. No wonder he has not called here in some time.

He probably doesn't know how to tell me, but now his mother has told Mother and his secret is out. I wonder if she will tell me or if it was told to her in confidence. I know Mr. and Mrs. Webster, as well as Mother and Father, had always thought that George and I would someday be a couple. Mother had told me they were very disappointed about my decision, but that they understood my reasons.

When I returned down stairs, Mr. and Mrs. Webster were preparing to leave so I said my good bye and returned upstairs to my room to think about what I had heard. Mother made no effort to talk to me, so she may be waiting for a better time to do so or perhaps she feels it is up to George to say something to me.

## Sunday, November 28

It was cloudy all day and rained towards night. Despite the weather, we had several callers in the afternoon.

Carrie came and was here to dinner. George Evans and Dwight and Mary Bronson called after dinner, and they and Mother and Father played cards for a time before we had some refreshments later in the evening.

Carrie and I spent our time in the parlor by the fire, talking. I wondered whether I should say anything to her about what I had overheard when Mother and Mrs. Webster were talking yesterday. I decided to wait to see if Mother would tell me, so I could be able to discuss it openly with Carrie without asking her to keep it secret. Sooner or later I think everyone will know, but for now it doesn't seem that anyone other than the Websters and their friends know. And Mother, of course.

After Carrie left for home, I went to my room and read for a while, but I couldn't keep my mind on the book. My thoughts kept returning to what I had overheard yesterday. I wish I could talk to Carrie about what I heard, but Mother has not said anything, so I guess I will just have to wait and see if George tells me himself. I can't really say anything to Mother without letting on that I came downstairs in time to overhear her conversation with Mrs. Webster. I don't want Mother to think I had purposely eavesdropped on their conversation.

Aunt Fannie, Uncle Philip, and Nellie, Willie, and Winston left for home during the afternoon. The house seems very quiet because Sarah, Frank, and Normie also returned to New Milford. I miss them all, but we will all be together again over the Christmas holidays.

### Monday, November 29

It was a cloudy day but did not storm. The weather seems to be getting gloomier as we get towards the end of the month and the beginning of December. How I hate this time of year. The trees have lost most of their leaves and now we only have the greenery to color our vistas.

Emma Beers was here to see me in the afternoon. We talked for some time, and then had tea and cake with Mother.

After Emma left, I wrote two letters to friends I haven't seen for some time. I am going to fewer social events, and when one also doesn't attend church services, you see fewer people. I miss going to church, especially because of the music. I love the organ and the hymns. Mother and Father are very involved and attend regularly. I once was involved by taking care of some of the small children while their parents were upstairs at services, but that, like so many other things I enjoyed, is no more. It was fun to sit on the floor and read religious stories to the children or play games with them. I wonder if I will ever be able to do these things again.

I felt a little better today. I didn't have as much coughing as I usually do so I felt stronger. I helped Mother with dinner. Wallace Hodge visited late in the afternoon and stayed for dinner, during which there was much conversation and laughter. Mr. Hodge has been Father's friend for a long time, and they enjoy many of the same activities, such as fishing, hunting, and talking politics.

### Tuesday, November 30

It was a very pleasant day but, unfortunately, I didn't feel very well in the morning. I couldn't enjoy it as I once would have. On a day like this, I would have enjoyed a brisk walk. I often would see friends and neighbors along the way and would enjoy our conversations. Today was a day that reminds me of the early days of autumn and makes me forget that the cold days of winter are only a short time away.

One of the high points of the day was when Carrie called in the afternoon and stayed most of the day and was here to dinner. I always feel better when she is around. Her manner is so comforting, but she doesn't coddle me. She refuses to accept that I'm not the same as I once was and have limitations as to what I can do. She convinced me to go outside for a short time, and though I knew Mother was concerned, I did manage to walk about a third of the way to the river.

I enjoyed being with Carrie, and, when I became tired, we turned around and walked back to the house. The air was crisp, but not too cold, and the breeze light and refreshing. Carrie said the walk had put some color in my cheeks. She always says I'm much too pale because I don't get enough sun.

I had not coughed at all and the pains in my chest that had concerned me in the morning seemed to be less. I wish I could feel like this every day. If so, I would believe that I will be able to return to the schoolhouse next month.

But while my heart hopes, my head tells me this good feeling will only be temporary, and I try to enjoy these good days when I can.

After dinner, Carrie and I played cards for a while and then she left for home.

## Wednesday, December 1

It appears winter storms are already upon us, so days such as yesterday will soon only be memories until spring. It was stormy today, with hail and a cold rain, and it snowed some last night. I suppose we can expect this to happen more often now.

I helped Mother by canning two jars of applesauce to add to the pantry supply.

No one was here through the day but Frank Carter, one of Mother and Father's friends, stopped by in the evening to visit. While they played cards in the dining room, I read for a while in the parlor, wrapped up in an afghan since the room was a little chilly.

I'm having a difficult time getting excited about Christmas this year. It will be much different than last year when I was in good health and participated in all the parties and church events.

I took my good health so much for granted, but it wasn't too long before I realized I wasn't feeling as well as I once did. It was during that time that George approached Father and asked his permission to call upon me, and I made the decision that led George to calling on a young woman friend of his parents that I'm not supposed to know about. Apparently, George's mother asked Mother not to tell me, and Mother always keeps her word., but I wonder when I will be told.

Most of all, about this time last year was when I started to have concerns about whether I would ever be able to become a teacher. As the time approaches for when my doctors will say yes or no to returning to the schoolhouse, I am feeling less sure that it would be possible.

If my health improves, I pray I will never take it for granted again. I know now that life can change quickly, and you have no way of controlling that. All the syrups, powders, and potions the doctors give me have so far been unsuccessful.

Mr. Carter stayed quite late, but I said my good nights to my parents and him, and went early to bed, though my concerns about my future kept me sleepless for some time. My nightly prayers failed to calm my concerns.

## Thursday, December 2

It snowed part of the day and was clear later in the afternoon when our minister, Mr. Smith, called. I did not feel as well today. Perhaps it was because of the weather. I did help Mother in the morning by making some quince jelly.

Mr. Smith seems to come more often now and spends time talking with me and reading the Bible. He is always considerate about my health, but I know he is also concerned about my soul. It's true I haven't been to services very often since I have been feeling poorly, but I have never mentioned to him how my beliefs have changed since I was a little girl.

Just a few years ago, I would never have questioned anything I read in the Bible or hear in his sermons. However, as I have grown older, I have a great many thoughts that conflict with what religion teaches us.

When I was little, I knew people died but never questioned why people said the deceased was in a better place, in Heaven with Jesus. I remember picturing all these deceased people praying and singing around Jesus, as we do in church every Sunday. I suppose that is some solace to those left behind but is it true?

I heard it more recently when Grandfather died, but I did not find it comforting. Now I find myself wondering if all those who have died will never be seen again by their loved ones and are not in a better place of heaven. I suppose Mr. Smith would be shocked if I ever spoke to him about my conflicts over religious beliefs. Even as I say my prayers every night, I find myself wondering. Is anyone listening? If there is a heaven, where is it?

Before he left, Mr. Smith spent a few minutes talking with Mother. I don't know what they talked about. Was it about an upcoming social event, church business, or was it me?

## Friday, December 3

I rose early today to find a day that would be good sleighing weather. I know several of my friends are probably looking forward to a day of fun on one of Roxbury's snowy hills. I wished I could be with them. We enjoyed sliding down a hill on sleds or toboggans, until we were too tired to pull them back up the hill. After an afternoon of fun, we would go to someone's home where we would have tea and refreshments. We never wanted to have the day end.

I remember one time when I was a little girl that our toboggan turned over and my hand got scratched. Mother bandaged it up when I got home, but it didn't pain very much.

Today, Father seemed to know how much I missed the activities I would ordinarily have enjoyed so when he came home from work, he took me up town in the sleigh. It was cool and crisp, and Bess had no problem making it through the small snow cover. As we drove along, with the bells on the harness ringing merrily, we saw many of the neighbors' sliding down the hills on their property. I wished it could have been me among them.

When we returned home, Aunt Harriet and Uncle Henry were here to dinner and until 8 o'clock.

## Saturday, December 4

It was a nice day, so some of the snow is already melting. Father says the sun is still strong enough early in December to clear away a small amount of snow, but by January it is usually a very different story, with colder temperatures keeping large amounts of snow around longer.

It's not unusual to have the wind causing large drifts, particularly around the buildings and even in the roadways. It can even effect travel on the cars.

While snow does make the landscape appear more appealing than leafless trees, it sometimes makes travel of all kinds more difficult.

I didn't feel as well today as I did yesterday. I spent most of the day by the fire in the parlor, reading the newspaper Father had brought home and some of Mother's magazines. I couldn't concentrate enough to read any of my books because my chest and back hurt so much.

Later in the afternoon, Dr. Brown called and brought me a new cough syrup. It wasn't a usual house call, but he said he was in the area and thought I might benefit from taking it. I wish I could believe that it would help but I have had so many that didn't. Dr. Brown did notice that I was thinner than when he last saw me, so it seems that altering my clothing only seems to emphasize my weight loss.

Mother sees that I eat well, even when I don't feel hungry, but I keep losing weight rather than gaining. Dr. Brown suggested that I try a little more exercise to increase my appetite. I just don't have the strength I once had. The walk with Carrie the other day is the most walking I have done for some time, and I was very tired following it.

Dr. Brown stayed for tea before leaving to see some friends in town, and I returned to my reading. Mother and Father left to make a few calls before returning later for dinner.

It was a quiet evening and no one else called.

## Sunday, December 5

It was a hard, rainy day, one I will never forget, on which I had to face the knowledge that my friendship with George would never be the same again, that what I had heard by accident when his parents called recently was now reality. I always knew it would be only a matter of time before I would have to face the news that I had carried secretly inside me since that day.

When there was a knock on the door earlier this afternoon, I opened it, and there, standing with his hat in hand and a somber expression on his face, was George. I tried very hard to remain calm. I didn't want to have it appear that this day was any different from any other. But I knew it was, and the sight of George after so many weeks without any visits from him put my nerves on edge

I welcomed him, took his coat and hat, and showed him into the parlor where Mother and Father were reading while awaiting any callers who might come by.

While they exchanged pleasantries with George, l went to the kitchen for the tea pot and the pastries Mother had ready for callers. While I prepared the table in the dining room, my mind immediately went back to my decision that led to this day.

I know very well why I declined George's request to call on me as a suitor. I wanted so much to be a teacher and knew that if I put aside that dream, I would probably never achieve it. Being a teacher is what I have wanted ever since I was a little girl when I would line up my dolls and play school.

There was also my concern about my health at that time, and because of all that has transpired since, I still believe the decision I made was the right one despite how sad it makes me feel. Now it doesn't seem I will ever reach my goal of being a teacher, much less think in terms of being married someday and having a family.

At that time, Mother, Father, and George joined me in the dining room, and we had a pleasant conversation over tea and pastries. But later, Father excused himself to go out to attend the animals while Mother, George, and I returned to the parlor.

I don't think Father was comfortable with the reason for George's visit. He must have known from Mother why George was here after so long an absence. Father always liked George and hoped that he and I would someday marry. I know he was very disappointed with my decision despite understanding my reasons.

Once in the parlor Mother took a seat apart from us and resumed her reading so that we could talk somewhat privately. George said he was sorry he hadn't called sooner but that he needed to tell me something and had found it difficult to decide how to go about it. He said we had been friends for so long and he had always thought it would progress into something more. He told me, as he had before, that he had been very disappointed with my decision but understood my reasons at the same time he had hoped with time it might change.

However, he said it has been obvious that nothing has changed, and he knows our friendship will change because he is now seeing a young woman in Danbury whose family has been friends with his for several years.

I told him I always knew things would change, but that I always felt my decision was best for both of us. My uncertain health, which continues to keep me from the schoolhouse, will most likely continue indefinitely. Despite the sadness I felt at finally hearing what I had always expected, I wished him well and kept myself from crying until he left for home.

It was then that I turned to Mother, who held out her arms and held me while I cried until there were no more tears to shed, only sobs.

Later Mr. Hodge came up and stayed for dinner, but I had no appetite for taking part in dinner conversation, which included that Frank Castle had broken a limb. I ate very little, then asked to be excused and returned to the parlor where I attempted to write a letter, but I had no heart for it. I felt too sad, not because I regretted anything that brought about today's visit, but because I know George and I will no longer have the friendship we once had. I have lost one of the best friends I have ever had.

**Monday, December 6**

Though it was a pleasant day, I did not feel well at all, probably because I did not sleep well last night.

I kept replaying in my mind the events of yesterday. I awoke this morning, after a short, restless sleep, knowing in my heart there will never again be a pairing with George for charades at parties and other social occasions or lawn tennis at our annual reunion. Someone else will be at his side, that is even if he attends any of these events. She might have altogether different interests in which he would be engaged.

Sadly, I went about preparing for the day, and tried to smile but failed miserably when I joined Mother and Father for breakfast. It was difficult to seem unaffected by yesterday's visit. I hugged and kissed them both, knowing they were also feeling sad while trying to act cheerful on my behalf. I love them both so much, and when I made my decision about George all those months ago, I knew it would hurt them, but I knew there was nothing else I could do.

George has always been a good friend. However, I think that the feeling you have for a future husband should be more than just the care you have for a friend. Oh, I know all about how there are often "arranged" marriages, but do they ever learn to love each other as husband and wife? I'm so glad that my parents made it possible for me to decide for myself.

After a very quiet breakfast, Mother and I cleaned up the kitchen while Father went out to the barn to strip some tobacco before going to work.

After lunch, Amanda called, and we had tea and cake with her. No one else came, and the three of us played cards after dinner and then went early to bed.

## Tuesday, December 7

It was cloudy today but did not storm. However, it is very slippery for travel on the roads. Father left early for work, and Mother spent the morning baking and doing household chores. I tried to help, but soon felt very tired. I think I haven't recovered from the loss of sleep I experienced after George's visit Sunday.

Before he left that day, he said he hoped he would see us at some of the church and social events during the holidays. I know, from things he said, that he thinks everything will go on as it always has. But I know there will be change, and things will not be as they were. We will never be friends in the same way. I know this will happen. Yes, we will probably see him at social and holiday events, but he will be with someone else as a couple. That's as it should be. George needs to move on, even though I seem unable to do so. I can't plan to return to the schoolhouse or look to the future and envision a life as a teacher. As I fail to feel better, neither of those things seem remotely possible.

After lunch with Mother, I wrote some letters to friends, so Father can post them tomorrow. I also had Mother send a note to Dr. Kerrmann that I needed my medicine, even though it doesn't seem to help me feel better.

Later, Mrs. Hodge joined us for tea and brought me a cake which we all enjoyed.

After dinner, we spent a quiet evening reading the Bible and newspaper.

## Wednesday, December 8

There were snow squalls all day, and it was very cold. After breakfast, Father left early for work, wrapped up in his warm overcoat and scarf. I was glad I didn't have to go out and walk in the cold to the schoolhouse, though I have done it for several years, as a scholar and as Mrs. Baglin's helper. Feeling how I am now, it would be an ordeal.

As a scholar, I always looked forward to school. I loved to learn, and that was rewarded when Mrs. Baglin asked if I would help her after my years as a student were over. Then I walked to school in expectation of the day, anticipating what I would learn from her experience as a teacher. I have learned a great deal from her since and had hoped to continue to do so until I could become a teacher myself. Now I don't really believe that I will ever achieve what had been my goal almost all my life.

I didn't feel as well today and spent most of the day on the parlor sofa, reading. I also received a postal from Mary Greene, but no one came in the afternoon.

Mother, however, was busy all morning with household chores. She is also starting to plan for the Christmas holidays. I don't feel very enthusiastic about anything. What was once a time of great enjoyment has become a time of sadness. While I knew George would eventually move on with his life, I didn't believe it would come so soon. So much of what I enjoyed about the holidays was centered around my friends. With our friends and families, we went from one social or church event to another throughout December, with the highlight being Christmas Eve at our house.

I always enjoyed the parties on New Year's Eve, but they also have lost their appeal. I doubt if I will attend any. I dread what the year 1881 will bring. At best, it will be as this year has been for me, with pain, fatigue, and sadness.

### Thursday, December 9

It was a nice day and warmer than yesterday, so I felt considerably better. I helped Mother with some housework, something I had found difficult to do of late. It was almost enjoyable to dust the parlor and sweep up the kitchen as well as help with breakfast and lunch preparation. I wish every day could be like this.

I decided I felt well enough after lunch to take a short walk to enjoy the sunshine for a short time. About half way to the river, I began to feel tired and returned to the house for tea time and to visit with any callers who might have arrived.

By this time, I was quite ready to relax on the parlor sofa or visit with callers, but only Mr. Rorraback called. Shortly after, Father arrived home from work, and after some tea and cake with us, he and Mr. Rorraback went up town.

When it appeared no one else would call, Mother started

preparations for dinner, and I went back to the sofa, too tired by that time to be of much help to her.

Father returned about an hour later in time for dinner. When Mother finished cleaning up, she played the piano for a while, which Father and I both enjoyed. It is a very restful way to end the day Later, Father read the Bible and the newspaper while Mother knitted, and I read.

Since no one else called after dinner, we went early to bed.

## Friday, December 10

It was clear but very cold today. The mercury stood at 8 degrees above zero, the coldest day we have had so far. There has not been much snow, so traveling is not difficult by horse, carriage, or the cars. The snow squalls from the other day did not last.

Father left early this morning for work, and Mother and I had a quiet breakfast, after which she baked apple pies, so we would be prepared for any callers. It seems we don't have as much company as we once did. Of my friends, only Carrie seems to visit on a regular basis, despite her very busy social life. Holiday parties are beginning, but she never fails to stop by to tell me about who she saw and what happened at each social event. Other friends write to me occasionally, but I look forward to Carrie's visits. I think I miss the social events almost as much as I miss helping at the schoolhouse.

Dr. Kerrmann called this afternoon, bringing my medicine. He talked with Mother and me for a while and mentioned he would send another medicine in a few days. After we enjoyed tea and apple pie together, he and Mother went into the parlor to talk privately. I was anxious about what they discussed behind the closed door, but I was not included in the conversation.

I wish they would include me when he comes to see me. I am an adult, not a child to be shielded from bad news, if that is what it is. I need to know how I will be in the future, if I am going to get well. I am young and should be enjoying the holidays with my friends, but instead I am so often in pain I wouldn't enjoy the events if I could participate. The fatigue alone would keep me from active events, such as skating and sledding.

After Dr. Kerrmann left, Mr. Hodge called, and we spent some time talking with him until he left for home. Father arrived home in time for dinner, after which we played cards, but no one else called. Mother made no mention of her conversation with Dr. Kerrmann, but it seemed to me that she seemed overly subdued and distracted throughout the evening.

## Saturday, December 11

It was partly cloudy and not as cold as yesterday, so I felt somewhat better. Perhaps the medicine Dr. Kerrmann brought helped. I'm anxious to try the new medicine he promised to send me. Perhaps he has found something that would help this illness, whatever it is. No one seems to know, or, if they do, they are not telling me. They are treating me as if I was a child not capable of facing what is wrong with me.

After breakfast Uncle Henry came to help Father with butchering our pigs. Later, after lunch, Aunt Harriet arrived in time for tea and they stayed to supper before leaving for home.

I could not help worrying all day about what Dr. Kerrmann had said to Mother that caused her to be so quiet last night. Usually she enjoys playing cards with us, but she was certainly very distracted during our games. I want to say something to her, but I'm not sure how to bring up the subject without upsetting her.

Father did not appear to have noticed any difference in Mother last night, or if he did, he did not speak of it during our games. Later, when we went upstairs to bed, I did hear them talking for a while, but was unable to make out what or who they were talking about. My room is far enough away that it's impossible to eavesdrop, even if I was so tempted. I know Mother would not like that, nor Father, I would expect.

## Sunday, December 12

The day was dark, cloudy, and it did rain a little. Despite the sour weather, Mother and Father went to church while I spent time in the parlor reading the Bible. It's not the same as attending services, and I miss going, but on days like this, my pains seem more intense than when it is sunny and warm. I much prefer to stay near the fire where I can feel warm, though I still miss seeing my friends after the service. We always gathered together to talk while the adults had coffee and planned future church events.

When Mother and Father returned home, they had a surprise for me. Sarah, Frank, and Normie had met them at the church, and came for lunch.

It was a lovely surprise. I miss Sarah when she is unable to come to visit because of her many responsibilities to her family and her church in New Milford. She has come more recently since I have been unable to help Mother as much. She has been a great help to Mother, but her helping take over some of my chores does not give her much time to visit with me.

A Sunday visit from Sarah and her family, without chores for her to do, was just what I needed to lift my spirits on such a gloomy day. She did help Mother with lunch and cleaning up after, but during the afternoon we spent time together, talking, playing cards and board games, and enjoying Normie's antics. He is getting so big and jabbers away all the time. We read him some books he had brought with him, and Frank and Father took him outside for a while to play so he would go down for a nap later.

I don't know what Mother and Sarah talked about while alone in the kitchen after lunch, but Sarah did seem a little distracted during some of our games. When she saw me watching her, she would give me a big smile and set about winning the game. She's a great competitor, and always has been, whether it's cards or games. .

Dwight Evans was also here to supper, and Mrs. Divine and Mrs. Baglin called in the evening after Sarah and her family left for home.

### Monday, December 13

It was cloudy and snowed in the forenoon. It was also very cold. Winter-like temperatures are beginning to be the norm now, and I was glad to stay inside all day. I have given up trying to walk outside on these cold days. I want to exercise more, but I just feel so chilled when I come back inside that it takes me a long time to warm up. I'm very content to stay by the fireplace in the parlor.

Sarah, however, has no problem coming out in the cold. Frank was not working today so he stayed home with Normie so Sarah could come here in the morning to help Mother with plans for Christmas. She and Mother spent some time hanging a wreath on the front door that Sarah had purchased at the church fair.

It was a plain wreath when it arrived but by the time they had decorated it with pine cones and a beautiful red bow, it looked quite splendid.

They have sent off letters to family members to see who will be with us for Christmas Eve and Christmas Day so they can know how many there will be. Those replies are beginning to come in the mail. Everyone always brings something to add to the feast for both days. I know Aunt Fannie and her family will probably be here overnight as always which adds to the festivities, especially Christmas Eve and morning.

It's difficult to believe that things have changed so much for me since last Christmas. Last year I was helping Mrs. Baglin, helping Mother with baking and decorating, going to parties with my friends, and enjoying all the outdoor fun of sleighing and skating. My favorite has always been hitching Bessie up to the sleigh and riding around town wrapped up in blankets against the cold to see all the Christmas trees in the windows and colorful wreaths on the doors.

Now it seems all I do is sit around and watch everything happening without me. I know I shouldn't feel that way because everyone tries to include me as much as I am able, but I tire so quickly. Christmas Eve is always fun, with family and friends together, singing carols, playing parlor games. I'm sad, too, because this year there will be no George to partner with for charades. He is moving on with his life, which I knew would happen, but it still changes the way I remember the holiday.

I want to go to church on Christmas Day because it has always been tradition for all our family members to attend together after breakfast, but I won't know until that morning whether it is possible.

When Father came home from work, he went up town. I imagine he is beginning to think about Christmas shopping.

My new medicine came today, and I feel better since I have taken it.

## Tuesday, December 14

It was a nice day and not very cold so I went down to Mrs. Hodge's for a visit. I wanted Mother to go with me, but she said she had too much to do to go calling today.

I enjoyed the visit with Mrs. Hodge, but she seemed most concerned about my health. Because she said I was looking thinner than ever, she insisted that I be weighed. I weighed 93 ½ pounds, so I have lost more weight. I'm beginning to be very concerned that I will never be able to return to the schoolhouse to help Mrs. Baglin. I don't feel that I am getting better, no matter how much I rest and eat well.

While I was visiting with Mrs. Hodge, Ella Pierce stopped in. She had come up to see me and stopped at Mrs. Hodge's when she saw Bessie tied up outside.

We had a nice visit though I left dispirited because of my new weight loss. At dinner, I could not help feeling low, and Mother asked what was wrong. I told her about Mrs. Hodge weighing me and that I had again lost more weight. I feel as if I eat a great deal, but it isn't making me gain weight. Whatever can be wrong with me.

As I sit writing this before going to sleep, Diary, I keep wondering about the wasting diseases I hear about. Many people do not survive their effects. It is said that one of them is termed consumption because it consumes a person.

I keep telling myself I must keep up my efforts to get better. I cannot allow myself to think I may have such an illness. I am too young and have not begun to live my life.

### Wednesday, December 15

It was partly cloudy today, but somehow it seemed brighter because Father didn't have to work and had gone to New Milford and brought home Sarah and Normie. I always seem to feel better when Sarah is around, and Normie is such a delight. He makes me smile and laugh with his antics. He is getting so big and becoming very social.

Of course, Sarah is here to help Mother with preparations for Christmas. She brought with her some of the mail from members of the family who intend to spend the holidays with us. They spent part of the afternoon going through the promises of food for either Christmas Eve and Christmas Day. They then set about determining what else would be needed to round out the offerings for the two parties.

While Mother and Sarah were busy with their planning, I kept

Normie busy with his toys and read him some of his Christmas books. He, of course, is looking forward to all the festivities and is much more excited about Santa Claus than he was last year. I wish I could feel more excited.

Father said he would be going down in the woods to pick out our Christmas Tree on Saturday, so Sarah and I can decorate it on the weekend. While I can't seem to feel too excited this year, having Sarah here does help cheer me up. I'm sad, though, when I think that this will be the first Christmas without Grandfather. I miss him every time I look at the ferrule he carved for me when I would become a teacher. It was sweet of him, even though I would never use it to discipline girls.

After dinner Mother played some carols on the piano with Normie perched on the bench beside her. He loves it when she plays, and it was fun to hear him try to sing along though his words were quite different from the ones she sang.

While Father was out today, he saw Dr. Kerrmann, and I am to commence taking a new medicine tonight. It seems as if I am trying a new medicine every week. Certainly, one of them should be able to help me.

**Thursday, December 16**

The day was blustery and cloudy part of the time. Sarah and I made some decorations for the house with greenery, red berries, and pine cones she had gathered in the woods. She also had brought some ribbon to make bows for the tree and some red and dark green ones for the decorations. They look very festive placed about the house and on the front porch.

Later, after he came home from work, Father carried Sarah and Normie home. They will come back Saturday afternoon with Frank, so we can decorate the tree. They are to stay overnight and return home on Sunday afternoon.

Aunt Harriet and Uncle Henry joined us in time for tea and brought me a pie, then stayed with us for dinner. I was tired after all our decorating today, so I went early to bed, leaving them playing cards in the dining room.

## Friday, December 17

It was a pleasant day but windy. It was quiet without Sarah and Normie here, but they will be back tomorrow when we will decorate the tree together.

Mother has been busy making popcorn for us to string for the tree. After lunch, she went out to make calls and do some shopping.

I spent the afternoon getting out our decorations so they will be ready to go on the tree. I keep thinking about how excited I was last year and how different my feelings are this year. It's only seven days to Christmas Eve and members of the family will be arriving that day. Several will be staying overnight, as always. Our house will be filled with all ages looking forward to Christmas.

I did not feel very well today. My side ached worse. I wish I could see ahead to what my future would be, then perhaps I could be more cheerful.

No one came to call. Everyone is probably preparing for their own holiday celebrations or out shopping. When Mother returned, I spent a quiet afternoon while she wrapped presents and did some cleaning. After dinner, we played cards for a while before going early to bed.

## Saturday, December 18

It was a nice winter's day, sunny and bright but cool.

Father went up town and took the train to New Milford early so he could get his shopping done before stopping at Sarah's for lunch. Then they all came home here together.

I got some letters from friends yesterday and spent some time in the morning re-reading them and writing replies so they can be posted in time for them to arrive before Christmas.

I felt better today and sewed more than I have in a long time. When Sarah arrived, she brought some lace doilies that we folded in half and decorated with fabric roses, bits of holly, ribbons and bows to hang on the tree. She had made some for her church fair and thought they would be a nice addition to our other decorations. Sarah pestered Father and Frank until they gave in and began stringing the popcorn to add to the strands Sarah and I had prepared earlier.

Before Mother began preparing dinner, we all enjoyed some

eggnog while decorating the tree. After dinner, we finished the final touches on the tree, with Sarah placing our Christmas angel on the top. It does look beautiful, and the pretty lace ornaments are just what it needed.

Mother played some carols, and we all sang, even Normie, although sometimes the words were not quite the same. He was ever so excited with Santa coming soon and was quite unhappy when it was time for him to go to bed. I read him a story, and then Frank carried him upstairs to his bed.

When Frank returned, we had some more eggnog and cookies while enjoying the tree.

I even felt better at night. I think having everyone here makes me forget my troubles, and everyone else seemed in more cheerful moods than usual.

### Sunday, December 19

It was clear but windy today. Sarah, Frank, and Normie went home in the early afternoon. The house was very quiet without them, but they will be back on Christmas Eve, along with Aunt Fannie and her family and others who will be staying the night.

No one called until Frank Harmon and his brother, Ed came over in the afternoon and visited with Mother and Father for a while. Mr. Hodge came up later and stayed for dinner. He always enlivens the conversation with stories about activities and socials going on in town and at the churches. I couldn't help thinking that last year I was a participant at some of those gatherings.

During the afternoon, I spent time in the parlor admiring our tree and reading some of Mother's magazines. I am beginning to be more excited about the holidays. It's probably because I'm looking forward to seeing everyone, and particularly will enjoy all the cousins. Willie will be here, and he is always fun. It will also be more fun this year because Normie is older and beginning to understand what the holiday is all about.

Sarah's church in New Milford has an adult watch the small children while their parents attend services. They play games and read stories about Jesus with the older children, but Normie isn't quite ready for that. Instead, he enjoys the games and just running around. Sarah said he keeps the teenage helper busy during that hour.

## Monday, December 20

It was a cloudy day and looked like snow, but it didn't.

Mother washed as she usually does on Monday. I did not feel very well so I spent most of the day on the parlor sofa reading and just enjoying our beautiful tree. Mother put a yule log* that Father had made next to the hearth and decorated it with greenery and red candles. It was very festive looking.

*Yule log: a large log traditionally burned in the fireplace at Christmas, or, in this instance, a small white birch log decorated with candles and greenery.

In the afternoon, Mr. Hodge came up in time for tea and visited with us for a while. He and Mrs. Hodge will be with us for our Christmas Eve party. As I had hoped, he said Mrs. Hodge is going to bring a pumpkin pie to add to the desserts. She makes pies almost as good as Mother's, and I look forward to them every year. Pumpkin pie is my favorite part of Thanksgiving and Christmas, just as strawberry shortcake is my summer favorite.

I keep thinking that whatever is wrong with my health has not diminished my love for food. I just can't eat as much as I once did, but that's probably because I am not as active as I once was. It seems like I don't do much at all when I compare what I did last year. I was helping Mrs. Baglin as well as going to parties and church activities and making calls with Mother. Somehow it seems like much longer than a year.

## Tuesday, December 21

It was clear and not very cold. I felt better so I sewed considerable today and finished a skirt and shirtwaist that I plan to wear on Christmas Eve. I'm not as good a seamstress as Sarah, but I manage with help from Mother. The new sewing machine helps a great deal because not so much has to be done by hand any more.

Only three more days before Christmas Eve. I'm sure we will be very busy that day with all those who are staying the night arriving on the cars or by carriage. Father has been busy preparing the barn for the extra horses and clearing areas for storage of the carriages and buggies.

Mother has started baking bread, rolls, and pastries, and has been going through the offers of food to see if anything else is needed. We always have extra just in case someone doesn't come because they were ill or had unexpected company arrive at their home. Usually Mother's and the aunts planning is very good, and there is always a great deal of food for both Christmas Eve and Christmas Day. There is always plenty left over for snacking Christmas Day evening and the following day, even if Aunt Fannie and her family stay longer.

While I enjoy the two days, I have always loved Christmas Eve because of the caroling and games, and Christmas morning breakfast when everyone who stayed the night join us around the dining room table. Aunt Fannie and Sarah are usually helping Mother in the kitchen, so I have never had to be of too much assistance at those times. My feelings about Christmas Eve are different this year, though, because I will not have George as a partner for charades. It would not be seemly if he is calling upon someone. George and I always won most of the games, but this year Sarah and Frank will no doubt excel.

### Wednesday, December 22

The weather was the same as yesterday, so it was mostly cloudy all day and though it still looked like it might snow, it didn't. Hopefully the weather will hold through the holiday, so everyone will be able to get to us without any difficulty.

Mother was busy baking and cleaning in preparation for Christmas Eve. I felt better today so I helped with some of the cleaning and prepared the pie shells for the apple and pumpkin pies she would bake later. They are easy to do while sitting, but just rolling out the pastry made me feel tired and my arms ached from the repetitive movements.

Sarah and Normie stopped in for a short time in the afternoon to bring in presents for under the tree. They couldn't stay very long because Sarah needed to get home to finish preparations for Christmas Eve. Since they will be staying with us that night, she was careful to bring in presents for Normie that are from Santa. Mother hid them in a closet until late Christmas Eve when they will be placed under the tree. Normie isn't old enough to question how Santa will know he is here rather than at home in New Milford. Hopefully that is many years away.

Ella Lattin and her husband, John, came to dinner and stayed all night. Afterwards we played cards for a while, then Mother played the piano, and we sang carols until it was time to go to bed.

## Thursday, December 23

It was a nice day. Ella and John went away about 11, then Mother and I went to Sarah's for lunch. I stayed with Normie while Sarah and Mother went down on the Green to do some shopping for Christmas Eve. We played with his trucks and soldiers, and I read to him from one of his books.

Later when we came home, I sewed some more, making the finishing touches on the dress I will wear tomorrow night. It is a soft rose color and has lace on the collar and cuffs of the sleeves. I finished just in time to show the dress to Carrie, who stopped by for a short time. She loved my dress and said it would be wonderful for Christmas Eve.

While she was her usual talkative self, telling about all the parties and socials she had attended recently, she did seem secretive about something. I wonder if she has met someone at one of the socials who she thinks may ask to call on her?

Carrie and I are the same age so I would not be surprised if she is beginning to think of getting married one day. I think it's what most young women believe. I always seemed to be different because all I wanted was to be a teacher, and I knew if I married I might have to give up teaching to take care of my home and children. I knew I was not ready for that.

If Carrie has met someone, if that is why she was somewhat secretive when I asked her who was at the parties, would I be envious? Dear Diary, I would not. I would be happy for her if it was what she really wanted. She is my best friend, and I want the best for her. I would never want her to be unhappy. The wonderful thing would be that because we are women, our friendship could continue, unlike that with George. I could be "Aunt Eunice" to her future children. It would not be unseemly for us to remain friends and visit back and forth.

Carrie did have some sad news, and perhaps that was the reason for how much she said. Alice Ward, who died recently after being ill for some time, was buried today. Carrie's mother and father attended the funeral.

After Carrie left for other calls, Father came home from work early, bringing me an orange, which I enjoyed. He knows how much I love them, and always thinks of me when he is in a market and sees them.

## Friday, December 24

It was a cloudy day, but there was no snow, so everyone had no problems getting here for the party.

No one called during the morning. Most of our friends and neighbors came later, some following evening church services. Mother was busy all morning, making desserts, and ensuring everything was ready for tonight. Some of the food for the buffet was brought by our guests so there was enough food for dinner.

Sarah, Frank, and Normie arrived early in the afternoon, followed by Aunt Fannie, Uncle Philip, Willie, Nellie, and Winston. After getting their baggage put away in the spare bedrooms, Aunt Fannie and Sarah set about helping Mother in the kitchen, while Uncle Phil and Frank kept Normie busy prior to his nap.

There was nothing I needed to do so I spent some time with Willie, Nellie, and Winston in the parlor, playing cards and talking. It was so nice to have them here, and even better that they will be staying through Sunday. I have noticed that I feel better when people are around. It takes my mind off my aches and pains and worries.

Around 6 p.m., guests began to arrive. Bertie Hodge and Albert Barnes were among the first to arrive, followed by Carrie and her parents. Carrie helped with their coats and hung them in the hall closet before joining me at the front door where I had been watching as other buggies and wagons came down the road. Father was outside to help with unhitching horses and taking them to the barn. Uncle Phil had gone out to help.

I had taken some food into the kitchen when Carrie came and told me her news. It was not what I expected. It was about George. I could not have been more surprised. She had seen him at several parties and found out through her friends that he is not calling on anyone. I wondered what had happened to the daughter of his parents' friends, but she didn't know and hadn't thought to ask.

She hinted that perhaps George was waiting to see how my health would be in the future and if I would change my mind. She is such a romantic. George understood my reasons for not accepting his request to call on me. If I am better in the new year, I want to go back to the schoolhouse with Mrs. Baglin and continue with teaching.

When George and his parents arrived before dinner, a game of charades was beginning. Just as in the past, we partnered in the games. As Carrie said later, it was like old times. But I know changes will certainly come, and tonight was just a moment in time that would eventually change.

### Saturday, December 25

It was a cloudy Christmas Day, but still no snow. Carrie had stayed the night, and we spent most of the time talking about the party and who was there, though we agreed there seemed to be mostly family and fewer friends than other years. Perhaps they also were having parties.

Carrie had not given up on her romantic idea that George is waiting for me to change my mind about calling on me as a suitor. I could not convince her otherwise, but I know with certainty that George understood and that he will eventually move on with his life. That change is inevitable.

Normie had knocked on my door very early. Little could he know that we had barely gotten to sleep, but Sarah realized at once when she saw our sleepy faces, probably remembering when she and I had done the same thing.

Carrie stayed for breakfast, after which we all grouped around the Christmas tree to exchange our presents. I had saved Carrie's gifts for her, knowing she would be here to open them.

Normie, of course, was so excited he could barely keep still. It had been all Sarah and Frank could do to get him to eat his breakfast. Aunt Fannie finally took Normie into the parlor to see the gifts and convinced him they would still be there after breakfast.

As usual, gift exchanging was noisy and fun with Willie and Nellie helping Normie with opening his gifts. His squeals and giggles had us all in good humor. Afterwards everyone went to services to meet the rest of the aunts, uncles, and cousins who would be coming for dinner later. I'm sure our family helped fill the church to capacity.

Since it was so cold, Mother did not think I should go so I stayed home with Normie. Since he was busy playing with all his new toys, I set the table for dinner. Unlike the buffet last night, with everyone taking their plates and sitting wherever they wished, Christmas dinner is more formal, with Mother using the good china and glassware. Sarah had made a pretty centerpiece from greens, berries, and holly, and I placed red candles on each side of it.

I checked on the turkey and ham that were baking, and when Mother, Sarah, and Aunt Fannie returned, we prepared vegetables. We had desserts left over from last night so there was nothing to prepare except some dinner rolls. Soon the rest of the family arrived, and the house was filled with laughter and stories. I love to hear Mother and her siblings talk about the past, and their lives as children. Grandfather, bless his soul, raised them by himself. Mother always says he had no problem being both mother and father and could be comforting as well as a disciplinarian when required. As with all large families, the older children helped with their younger siblings.

After dinner, which proved as story filled as ever, we took our desserts and coffee into the parlor, so we could enjoy the tree and decorations. While Mother and the aunts cleaned up the kitchen and dining room, the rest of us played cards and board games, depending on the age of the players.

During this time, Mrs. Baglin came and brought me my presents that were on the tree. I was touched that the scholars remembered me, and each had sent a note hoping I would soon be back in school. I admit to some tears when I read them later, not knowing whether I would ever be able to be there again.

Mrs. Baglin said she had heard, sadly, that British novelist Mary Ann Evans, who wrote as George Eliot, has died. I have read her books and will dearly miss her writings.

Later in the afternoon, most of the relatives departed for their own homes, except for Aunt Fannie and her family. They are to leave tomorrow for New York. Carrie had also gone home for her family's Christmas dinner.

## Sunday, December 26

It was a cold, cloudy day. It snowed some but didn't amount to much. We were going to Sarah's but it was a bad day, so we decided to stay home.

No one even went to church. I suppose it doesn't matter since they were just there on Christmas Eve, although I would imagine the church was not as full today as it had been. So many people don't come if Christmas services fall close to Sunday services.

Aunt Fannie and Mother made a nice breakfast for all of us. I was sad that Aunt Fannie and her family would be leaving after lunch, but Uncle Phillip has work tomorrow, and there is school, of course. If I was still helping Mrs. Baglin, I, too, would be preparing for tomorrow. I miss that and hope I will be able to continue with her soon, but I often wonder if I will.

I always find it strange the day after Christmas. During Christmas Eve and Christmas day, it seems the house is just filled with family and friends, and then, the next day, everyone is gone. It is always so quiet as it was today in the afternoon. Aunt Fannie always hates to leave, but she has volunteer activities to tend and a home to run.

I suppose other people were enjoying a peaceful day at home because no one called, and Mother and Father also did not make any calls. I think they were thankful to have a day of rest before returning to chores and work. Of course, Mother cooked dinner. We're still eating leftovers, so it was just a case of warming them up. Father, of course, had to take care of the animals and clean the barn. There is no day of rest for farmers.

I felt better today. I think it's because we had so much company that I just didn't think of my usual aches and pains and just enjoyed the family.

### Monday, December 27

It was a cloudy, dark day with snow squalls. I felt so much better that I cut out my apron and sewed some on the machine. Mother was busy doing the washing, and then hanging it on lines near the kitchen stove to dry. It was just not a good day for drying outside.

Father, of course, had gone to work so Mother fixed us a nice lunch of leftovers. I was particularly pleased that there were several desserts left over from Christmas.

Of course, it's good to have the extra desserts in case we had callers, but because the day was so sour, no one came in the afternoon or evening. They were probably happy to stay home rather than brave the cold. Even Carrie, who usually doesn't mind the cold, did not call. She's probably enjoying being at home after all the holiday events and parties. I wish I could have accompanied her to them, but it was not to be. I am just not strong enough to do much these days.

As I sewed, I found myself thinking about our Christmas Eve party. Aside from family members, who always come, there seemed to be fewer neighbors and friends. I wonder why. Perhaps they had other invitations or were giving parties themselves. We usually receive some invitations to other parties on Christmas Eve, but always send our regrets as we would be entertaining ourselves. I sometimes wonder if it is because I have been sick for so long.

I miss Aunt Fanny, Uncle Philip, and the cousins. It will probably be some time before we see them again, now that the holidays are almost over. Of course, there is New Year's to look forward to, but I find it difficult to face, knowing I most likely will not be going to the schoolhouse at that time, if ever.

We will probably go to Sarah's on New Year's Day, now that she is in her new home and able to entertain more often. It will give Mother a rest. Perhaps some of Mother's sisters and brothers will also go. That would be nice, especially if Aunt Fanny came. I suppose it would depend on whether Uncle Philip will have work the day after New Year's.

## Tuesday, December 28

It was clear today but cold. Father did not have work, except here at home, so he went up town to do some shopping. Mother did some more wash, and I sewed a little and washed the lunch dishes.

When Father returned, he brought me three oranges., which he knows I love. Ella Lattin and Lena as well as Dwight Evans called in time to enjoy tea and cake with us. It was good to see them, and we had an enjoyable time.

Before dinner, I wrote Willie a letter, which Father will post for me tomorrow. Willie was just here for Christmas, but I wanted to ask him if he knows whether they would be going to Sarah's on New Year's Day. If they decide not to come, it will probably be a while before we see them again, what with Uncle Philip's work, school, and Aunt Fannie's many activities.

It will be a long winter, especially since I have reconciled myself that I won't be going back to the schoolhouse to help Mrs.

Baglin, who said nothing about it when she brought my presents on Christmas. I wanted to ask, but, in my heart, I knew Dr. Kerrmann would not approve.

I was in bad humor today, knowing that, if I was to go back, someone would have told me by now. Mother and Father have not mentioned it, nor has Dr. Kerrmann come to see me recently. He sees that my medicines come as I need them, but I don't think he even believes that they help me. I think everyone knows what I myself have had to admit, my dream of becoming a teacher is gone forever. I often look at Grandfather's gift of the ferule, and I feel so sad. He was so proud of me wanting to be a teacher.

Whatever wasting disease is causing my health to fail and my weight loss is winning the battle against my body. Is it consumption? I know people who have suffered some of the same symptoms I have, and their illnesses were called consumption, because the disease consumes the body. The last time I was weighed, I was 89 and a half pounds. I haven't weighed so little since I was a child.

What will I do in the future? Will I live with Mother and Father and become a burden to them? Already I'm not able to do many of the things to help that I once did. Will I die, just as so many others have from consumption? Some people believe moving to a different climate might help, but I could never do that, and Mother and Father would not be able to go with me, even if we could afford it. And in the end, would it help? Perhaps not. There is just no medicine that seems to help.

### Wednesday, December 29

It was a hard, snowy day, and quite a lot of snow fell. I was feeling poorly again today and dispirited from all my thoughts about what my future might be. Every night Father reads from the Bible, and Mother and Father go to church every Sunday, unless the weather is too sour, and take part in church activities.

I listen as he reads the familiar passages I have heard since I was a child, but, in my mind, I wonder if you die, do you just go into nothingness or is there life after death? I would like to believe that I will see Grandfather again, and that he is waiting to welcome me there. I want to believe that he is again with Grandmother Laura, who died so many years before him.

I remember the Bible verses that speak of Heaven, such as John 11:28-29, "He who believes in me will live, even though he dies" and Psalm 23:6," I will dwell in the house of the Lord forever." Why do I find it so difficult to believe what is written in the Bible? Why do I have so many doubts?

I have gone through these doubts before, and still have no answers to so many questions. I do know I'm taking each day as it comes, enjoying my family and friends, and the beauty of our world. It is impossible to know what lies ahead, and I must stop worrying about what I cannot control. Everyone is doing everything they can to help me. If I am not getting better, it is because it is not meant to be.

## Thursday, December 30

It was a very cold day, the coldest we have had this winter, and you could feel the cold through the walls of the house. The wind whistled, and windows rattled. Father left for work bundled up in his overcoat, hat, scarf, and boots. I was almost glad I did not have to go out but thought of the scholars who would soon be heading for school in this cold and how much I miss them.

I didn't feel quite as well today. The cold seems to go right through to my bones. Everything hurts, my arms, legs, back, and chest. The cough has returned and is unrelenting despite all the potions and syrups I have been given.

For breakfast, I had enjoyed one of the oranges Father had brought me. It was very good, and surprisingly, the juice seemed to calm my sore throat, at least for a while. All day though, I felt the fatigue that often accompanies my aches and pains.

In the afternoon, Dwight Evans came, and Mother and I enjoyed tea and pie with him. I was so tired by that time, I could barely keep my eyes open and my mind on conversation about the upcoming holiday. Everyone but me seems to be happy about the new year, but I can't get excited about spending more time at home instead of going to the schoolhouse.

On days like this, when I am so tired and filled with pain, I find it difficult to find anything of interest to do. Even reading becomes a chore and crocheting and knitting take too much concentration when I am in pain.

### Friday, December 31

It is New Year's Eve, and it is clear but cold. Tomorrow is the new year, and I can't help but wonder what it will hold for me.

We did have some callers during the day. Eliza called, and Mrs. Veilly was here and spent the early part of the afternoon with us. Later Carrie came, and I went to the Hollow with her., thinking it would make me feel better to get out in the fresh air. When we returned, we had tea and cake with Mother and Father, and then Carrie went home, and I came to my room to rest for a while.

### Saturday, January 1, 1881

This is my final entry, and I must write on the blank pages at the back of the book because there is no other space. This journal is filled with my hopes and dreams as well as concerns for my future.

We did go to Sarah's today, but no one else came. It was very cold, and everyone must be staying in their warm homes. I think Sarah was disappointed, but we had a good visit with her, Frank, and Normie.

Sarah gave me a cup and saucer for my collection and some candy, and Father gave me an orange and some candy. My sweet tooth will be very satisfied.

We did not stay too long after lunch because Mother and Father were concerned about how cold it would be for the ride home later in the day. I must admit I was glad to return home. I just could not get warm today. My whole body seems to ache, and the cough is unrelenting. I feel so low in spirit, wondering what the new year will hold for me.

Though at times my spirit fails me and the bitter tear drops fall
Though my lot is hard and lonely
Yet I hope…I hope through all.

Oh, too soon to be at home over there by the side of the river of light
Where saints all immortal are echoed in the garlands of white.
When this you discover, remember your lover Sorrow, which drinks the blood, turns youth to age and leaves the heart a desert.

The heart that has truly loved never forgets but as truly loves on to the close.

As the sunflower turns to its God when it sets the same look that it turned when it rose.

When the golden sun is setting and from care your heart is free and of absent friends are thinking, please reserve some thoughts for me.

## Epilogue

Eunice was remembered. Her sister, Sarah, kept Eunice's ferule and diary in memory of her, and later passed them down to her daughter Eunice, her sister's namesake, who was this writer's grandmother. Through her, the ferule and diary came to me, and I was moved, after reading the diary of her aunt, to write a fictional story based on her life in 1880. She has not been forgotten.

Eunice Nicholson died August 15, 1882 at the age of 22 from what then was called consumption because it was said to consume a person—it is now known as tuberculosis.

The script on her tombstone in Old South Cemetery on Squire Road, Roxbury, Connecticut, reads:

"Our daughter dear we loved so well, Has left us here alone to dwell, With prospects bright to meet above, Where all is happiness and love."

No further diaries seem to have been kept by Eunice or, if they did exist, we have not been fortunate enough to have them pass down to us. By 1881 she may have been too ill to keep one so there is no way to know how she spent the last years of her all too short life.

But in 1880, she was already beginning to experience many of the symptoms that were also typical of other "wasting" diseases as they were called, such as coughing, sore throat, pain, fast pulse, weight loss, fevers, difficulty in breathing, night sweats, exhaustion, and swollen joints.

The once very active Eunice may have spent her last years as an invalid. While some patients did experience remission, it was usually followed by a relapse.

Doctors would most likely have treated Eunice at home. Unfortunately, their ability to provide care was limited. Since consumption was thought at that time to be caused by hereditary susceptibility and "bad air" in the environment, doctors could only recommend exercise, diet, and moving to a better climate, such as the Adirondacks in New York or out west to Colorado, New Mexico, Arizona, and California, where it was believed the air had curative properties. Most people were not wealthy enough to move.

Tuberculosis was not known to be communicable from an infected person to one who was healthy until 1882 when Robert Koch, a physician and scientist., discovered and isolated the bacterium that causes the disease. His discovery helped germ theory gain more legitimacy and convinced physicians and public health experts that TB was contagious. In 1905, in a lecture, Dr, Koch said "one in seven of all human beings die from tuberculosis."

After Eunice died, her parents continued to live for several years in their home in Roxbury near the Shepaug River. Her mother, Aura Nicholson died on May 18, 1900, several months after suffering a stroke that left her bedridden. At that time, Eunice's father, Cyrus, according to stories in "The Newtown Bee", gave up activities, such as hunting and fishing with his friends, to care for his wife Aura.

A story in The Newtown Bee about Aura Nicholson's illness noted "She is ready and willing to go and tells her many friends that she is soon to meet her daughter who has proceeded her to that happy home. The thought makes her happy and she looks forward to that meeting with joy."

Following his wife's death, Cyrus remained in the family home until 1901, when he left Roxbury to live with daughter Sarah's family in New Milford. On February 17, 1904, he died there suddenly of a heart attack.

Both are buried, one on each side of Eunice, in Old South Cemetery in Roxbury.

Sarah Nicholson Pelton and her husband, Frank, had three daughters in addition to Norman (Normie). They were Lulu, born October 22, 1881, who would have been ten months old when Eunice died; Eunice, my grandmother, who was born September 15, 1887, the only one of Sarah's daughters to have children; and Verona, born January 31, 1892.

Sarah died May 17, 1925 in Danbury at the home of her daughter, Eunice Pelton Rydell. She was predeceased by Frank in 1911.

Norman followed his father's trade as a plumber. He and his wife Kathryn had one child, a daughter, Norma. He died August 6, 1964 in Danbury and is buried near his parents and two of his sisters and other family members in Center Cemetery in New Milford.